BAD KITTY

Takes the Test

NICK BRUEL

SQUARE
FISH

A NEAL PORTER BOOK
ROARING BROOK PRESS
NEW YORK

To Aurora

An imprint of Macmillan Publishing Group, LLC
175 Fifth Avenue, New York, NY 10010
mackids.com

Our books may be purchased in bulk for promotional, educational, or business use. Please
contact your local bookseller or the Macmillan Corporate and Premium Sales Department at
(800) 221-7945 ext. 5442 or by e-mail at MacmillanSpecialMarkets@macmillan.com.

Library of Congress Cataloging-in-Publication Data

Names: Bruel, Nick, author, illustrator.
Title: Bad Kitty takes the test / Nick Bruel.
Description: New York : Roaring Brook Press, 2017. | Series: Bad Kitty |
    "A Neal Porter Book" | Summary: Because of a recent string of
    embarrassing behavior, Kitty's cat license has been revoked and she must
    take a test to get it back so she can still be a cat.
Identifiers: LCCN 2016027113 | ISBN 978-1-250-14354-9 (Square Fish paperback)
Subjects: | CYAC: Cats–Fiction. | Behavior–Fiction. | Test
    anxiety–Fiction. | Humorous stories. | BISAC: JUVENILE FICTION / Animals
    / Cats. | JUVENILE FICTION / Humorous Stories.
Classification: LCC PZ7.B82832 Baok 2017 | DDC [E]–dc23
LC record available at https://lccn.loc.gov/2016027113

Special Book Fair Edition ISBN 978-1-250-19597-5
Originally published in the United States by Neal Porter Books/Roaring Brook Press
First Square Fish edition, 2018
Square Fish logo designed by Filomena Tuosto

5 7 9 10 8 6

AR: 3.4 / LEXILE: 650L

• CONTENTS •

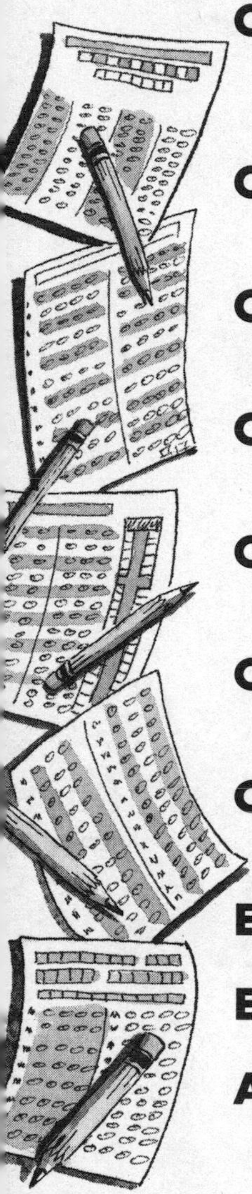

•CHAPTER ONE•

BAD KITTY DOES NOT LIKE BIRDS

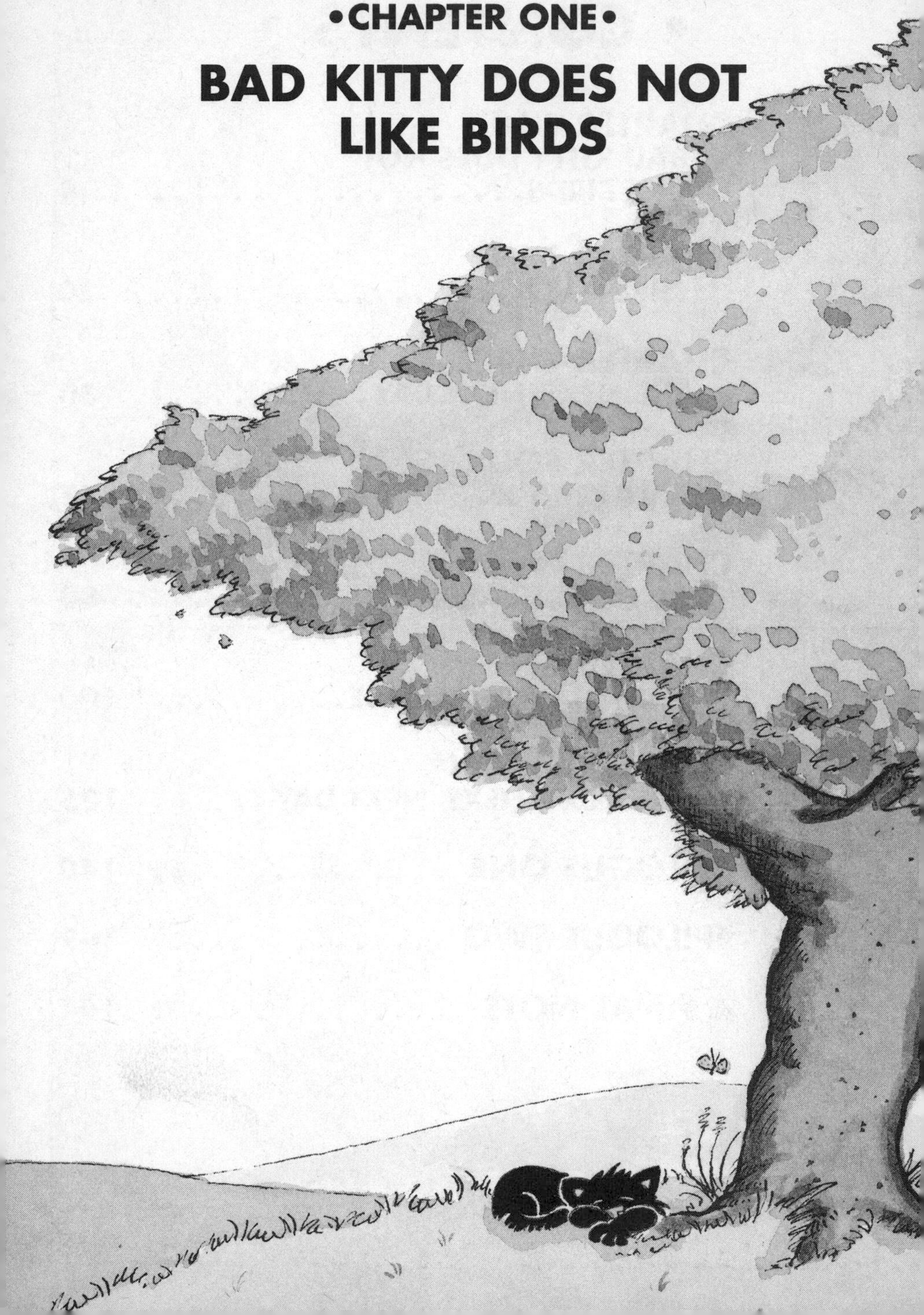

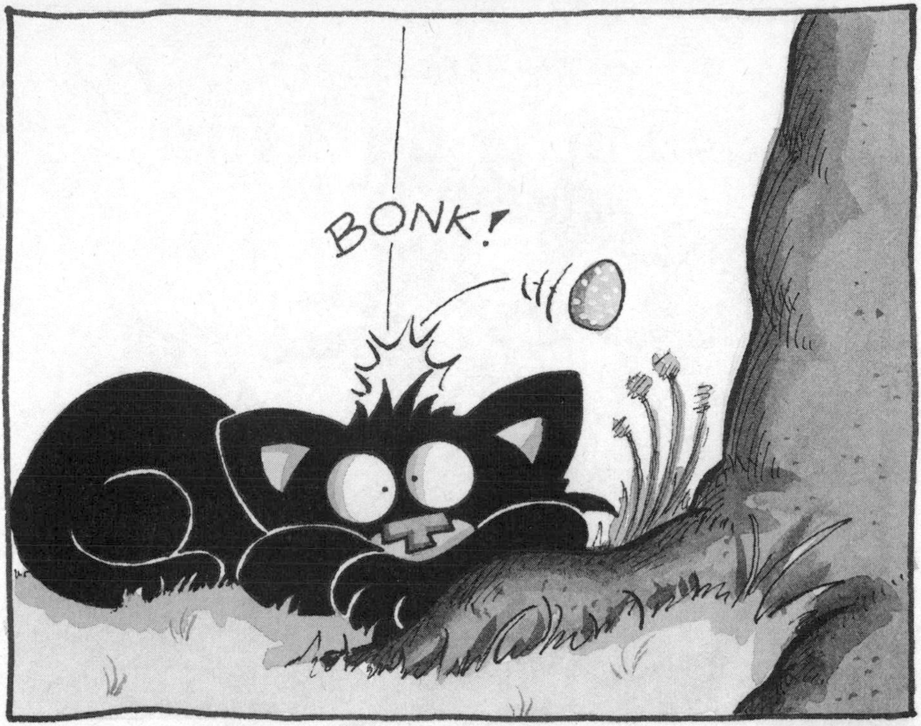
BONK!

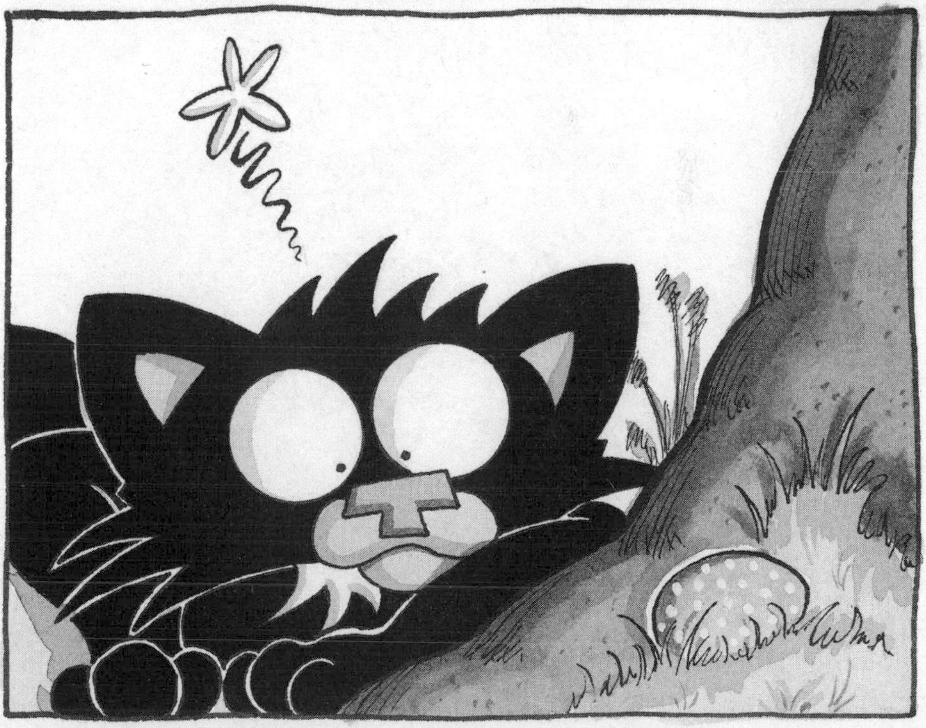

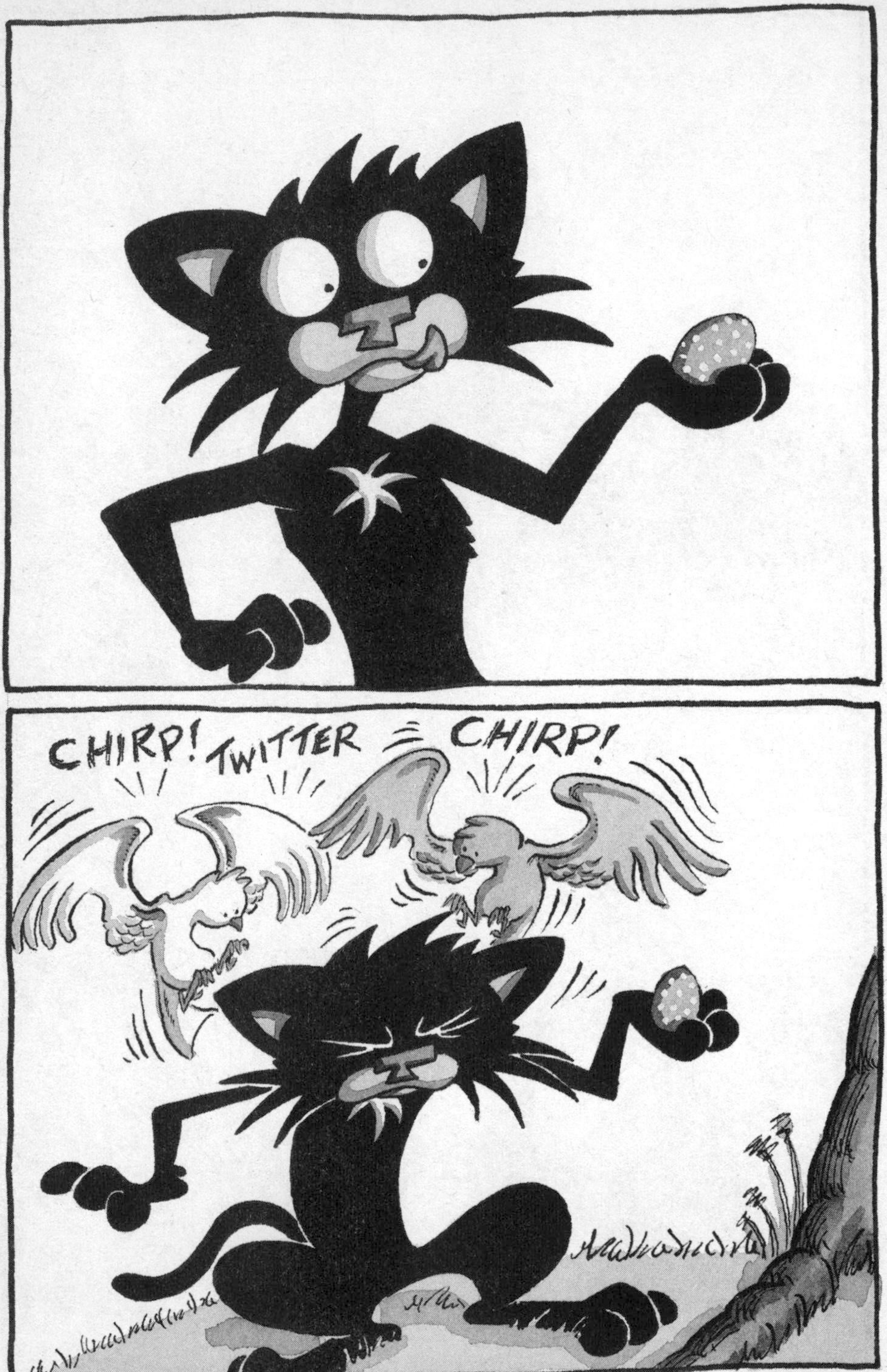
CHIRP!
TWITTER
CHIRP!

Kitty loves birds.

She loves how they flit.
She loves how they flap.
She loves how they flutter.

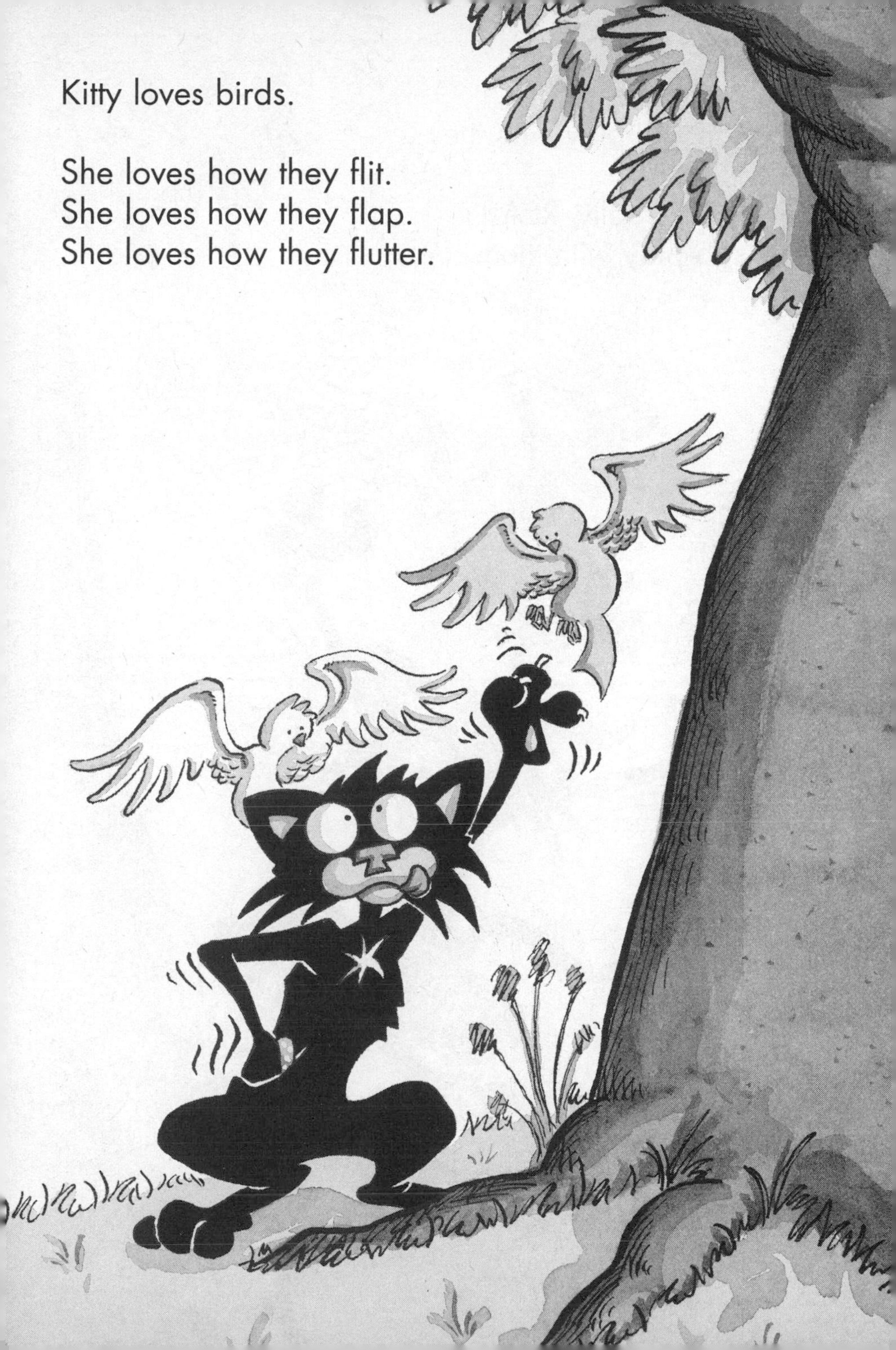

When Kitty sees birds,
she wants to play with them.

She really, really, REALLY
wants to play with them.

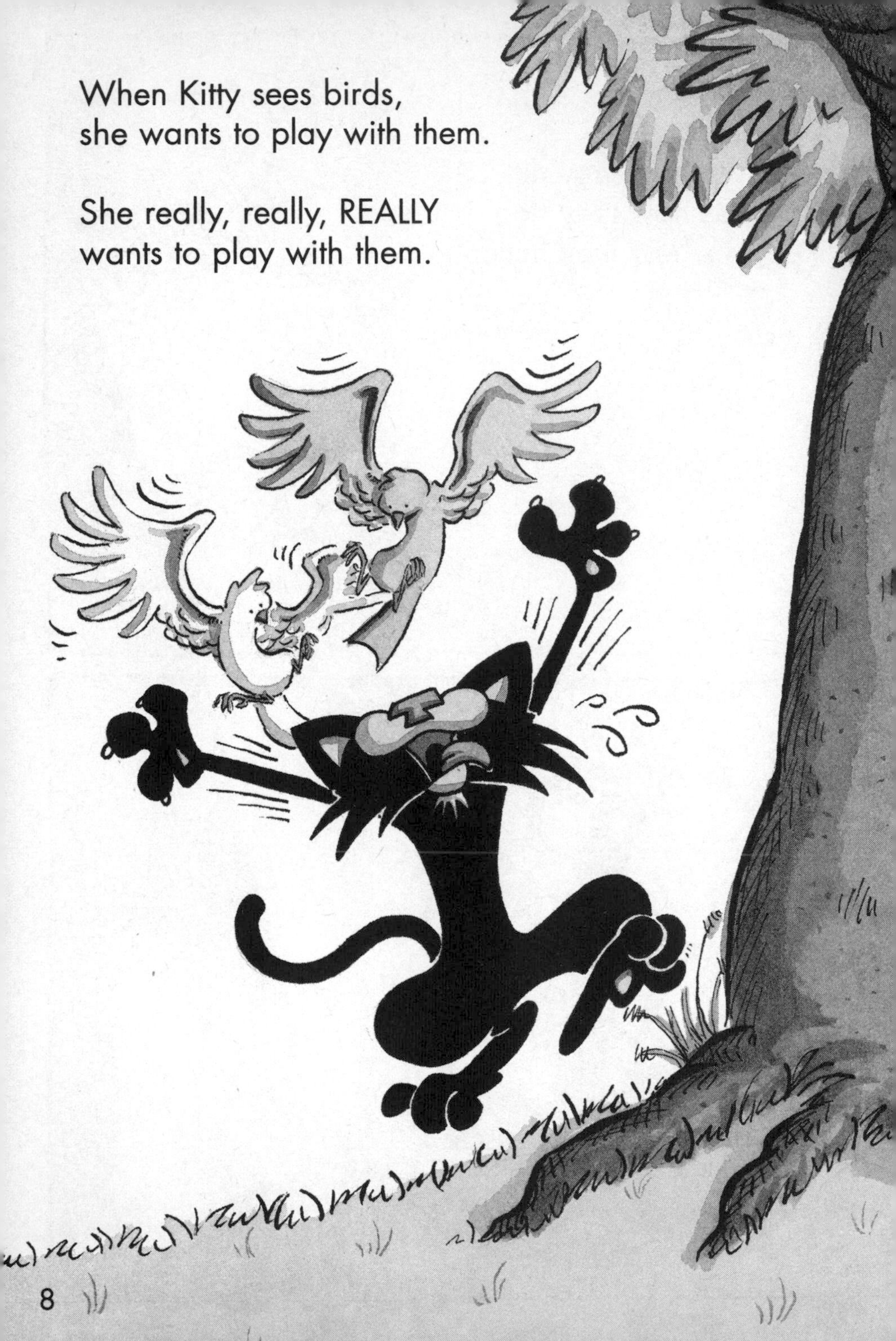

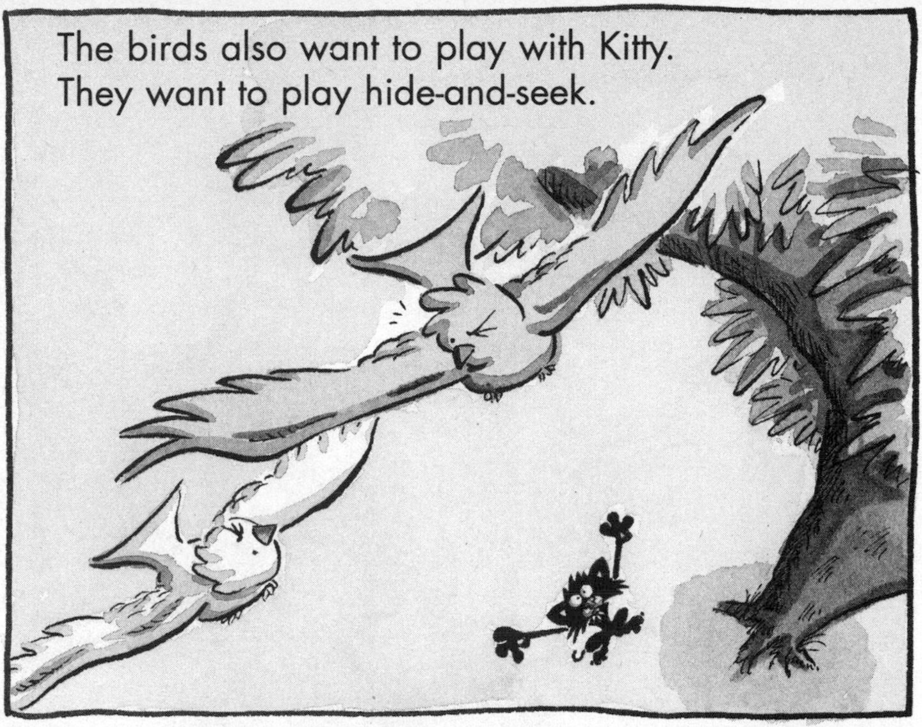
The birds also want to play with Kitty.
They want to play hide-and-seek.

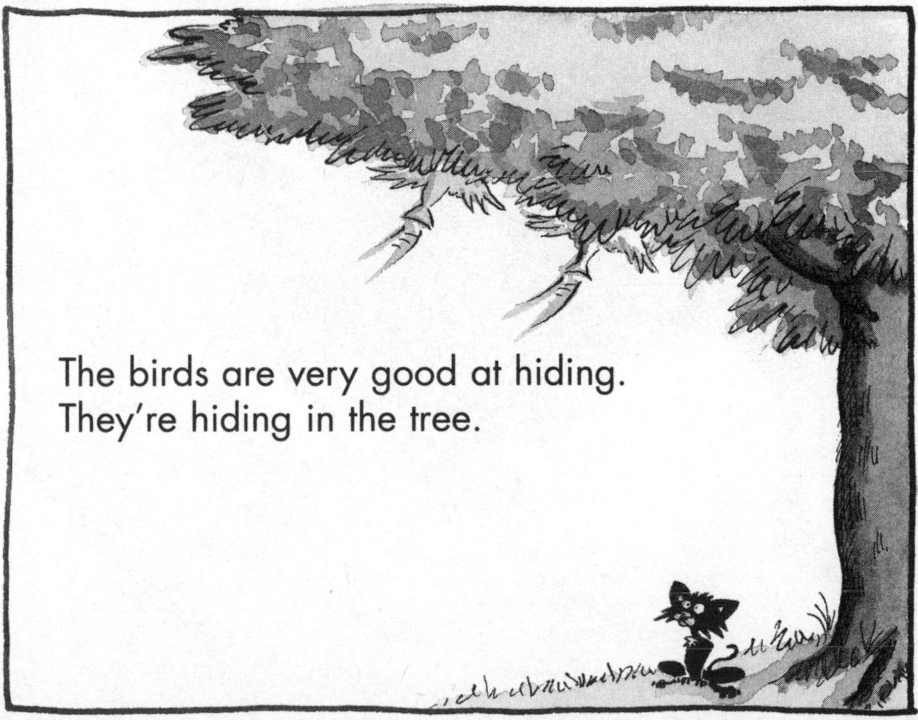
The birds are very good at hiding.
They're hiding in the tree.

But Kitty sees them!

Kitty is very good at seeking.
And she's very good at climbing.

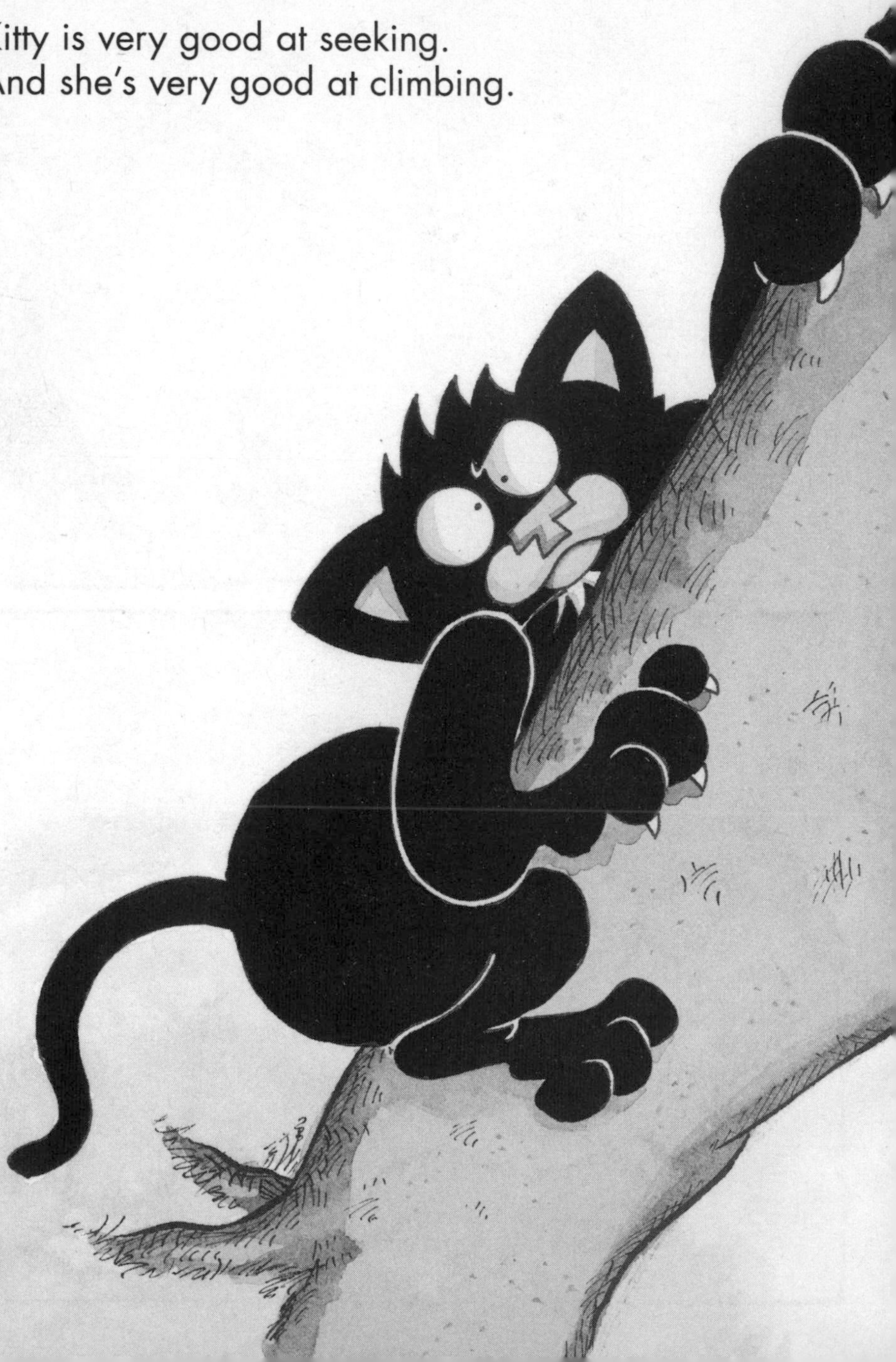

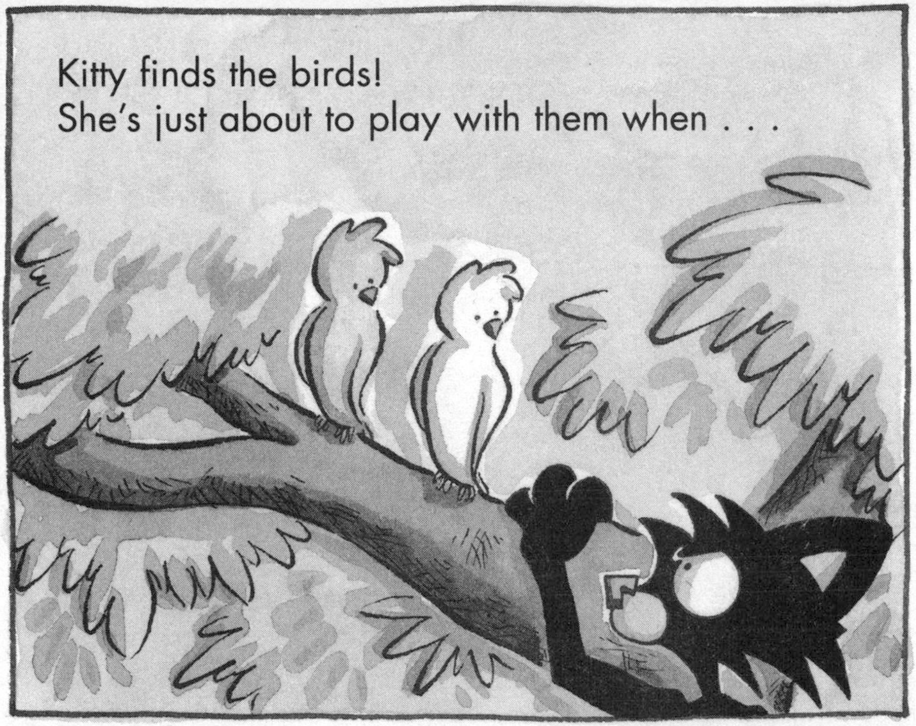
Kitty finds the birds!
She's just about to play with them when . . .

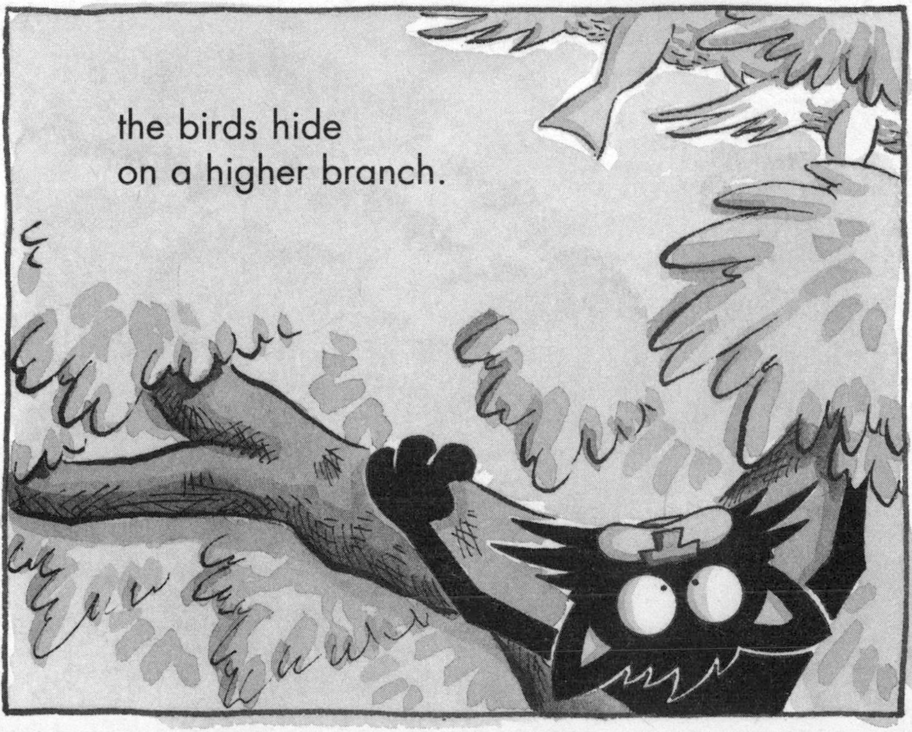
the birds hide
on a higher branch.

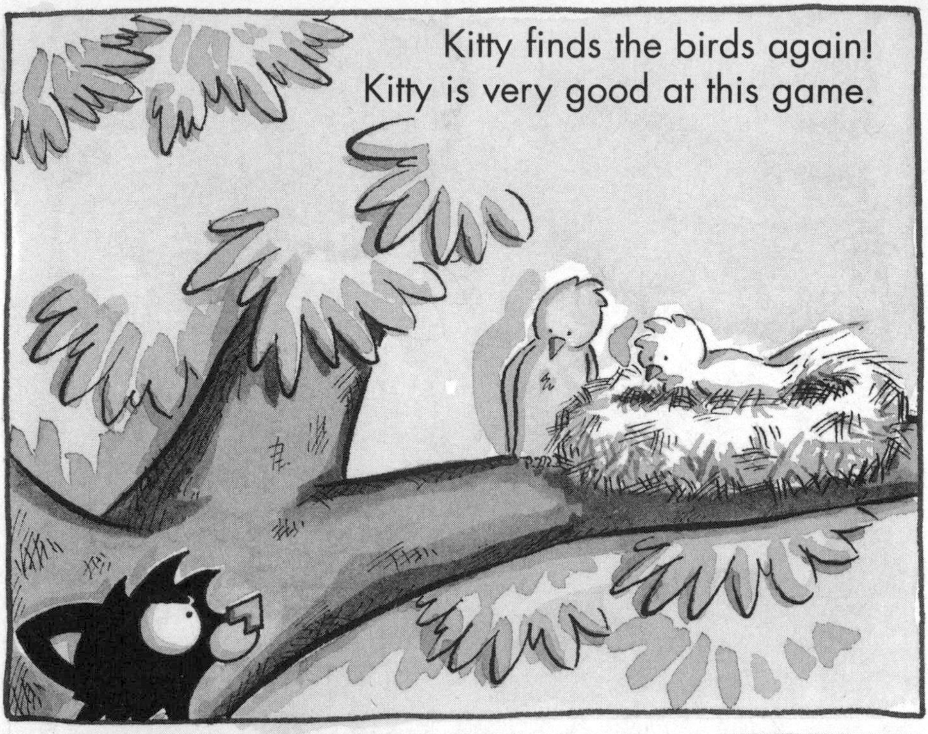
Kitty finds the birds again!
Kitty is very good at this game.

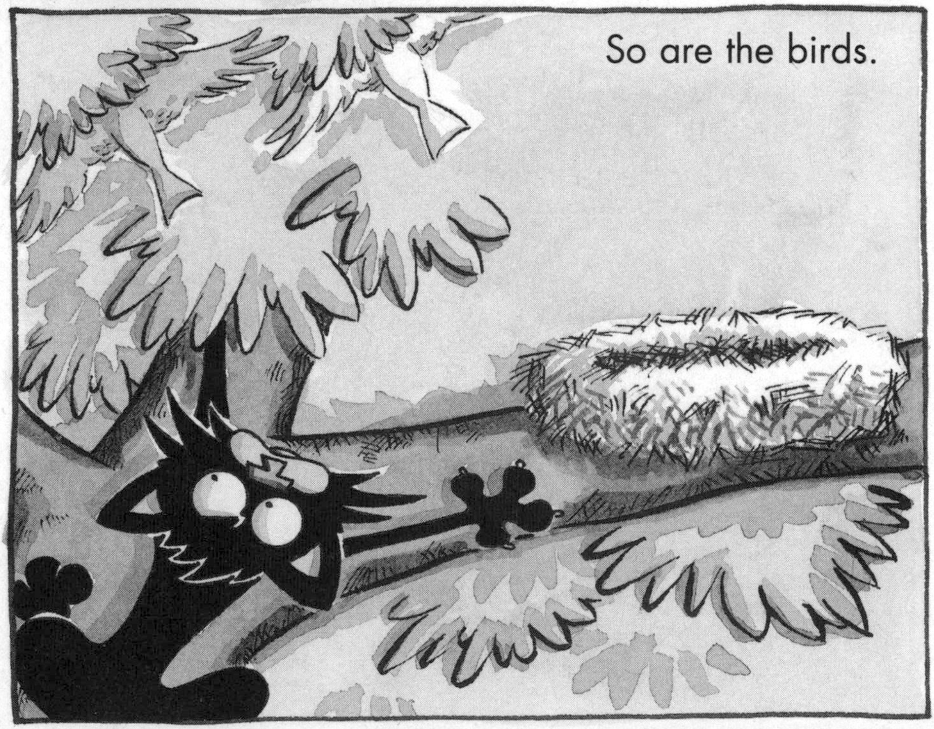
So are the birds.

The birds keep hiding higher and higher.

Kitty keeps climbing higher and higher.

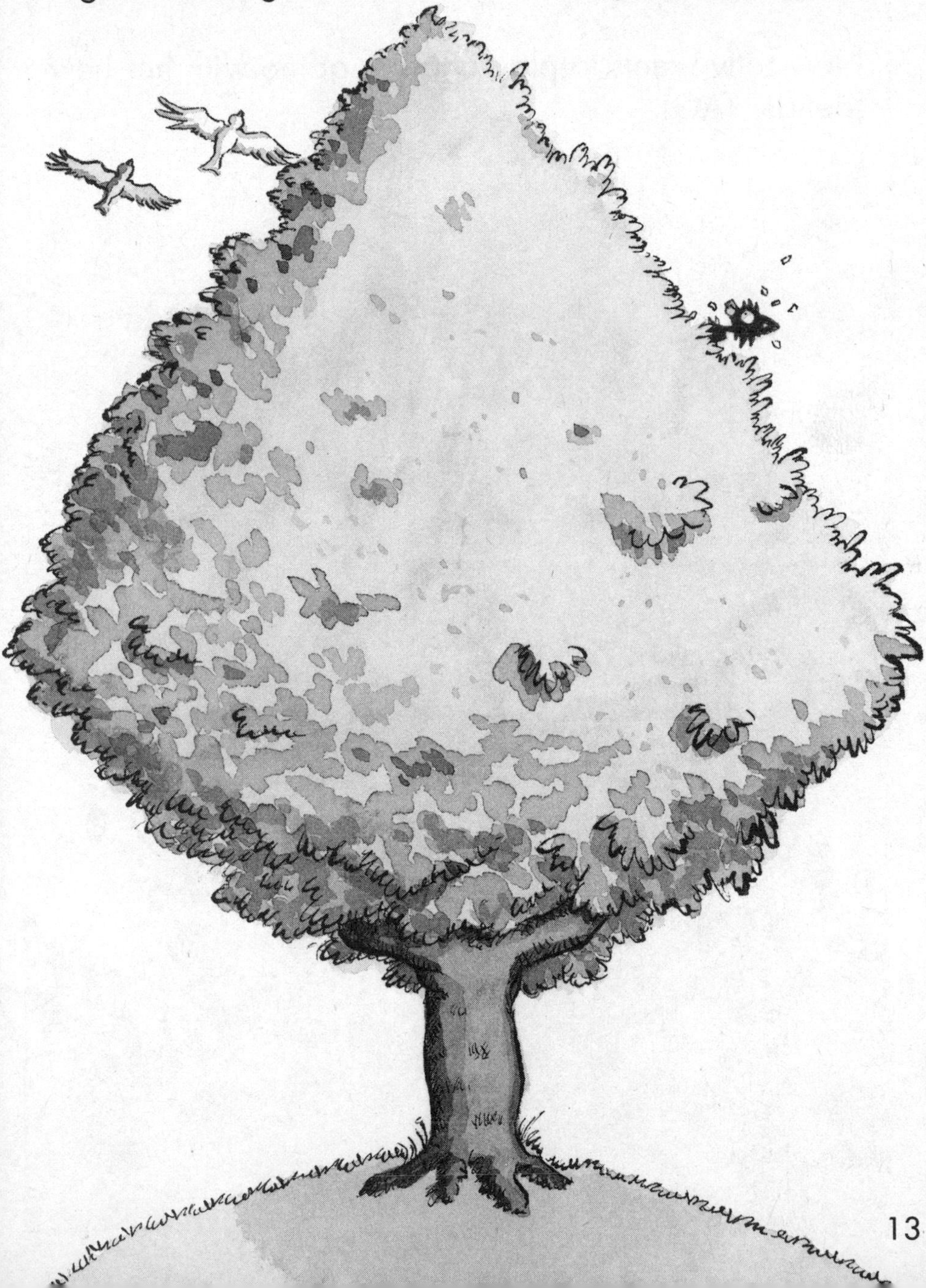

Soon, the birds are at the top of the tree. There is no tree left.

Now Kitty wants to play another game with her new friends: TAG!

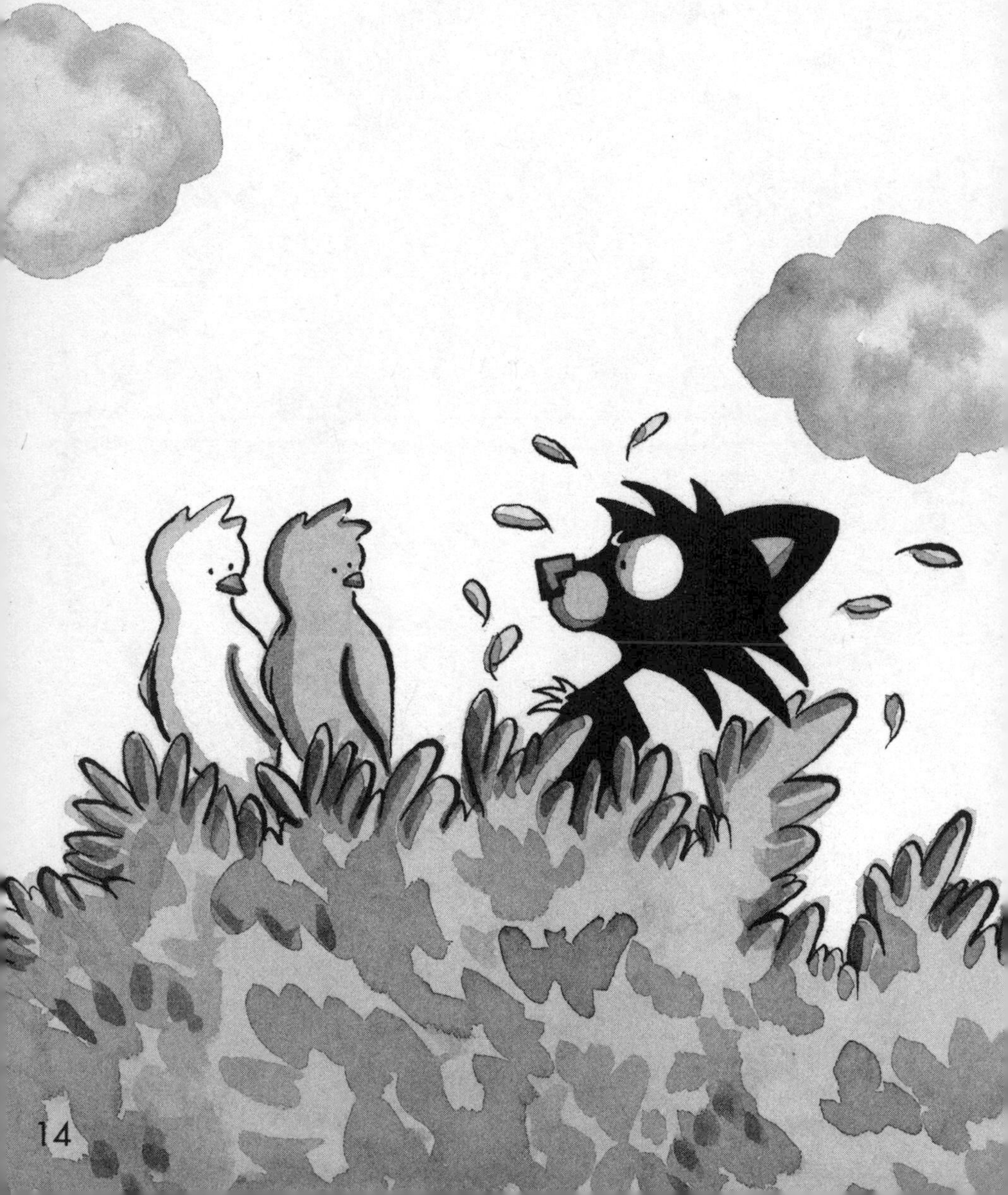

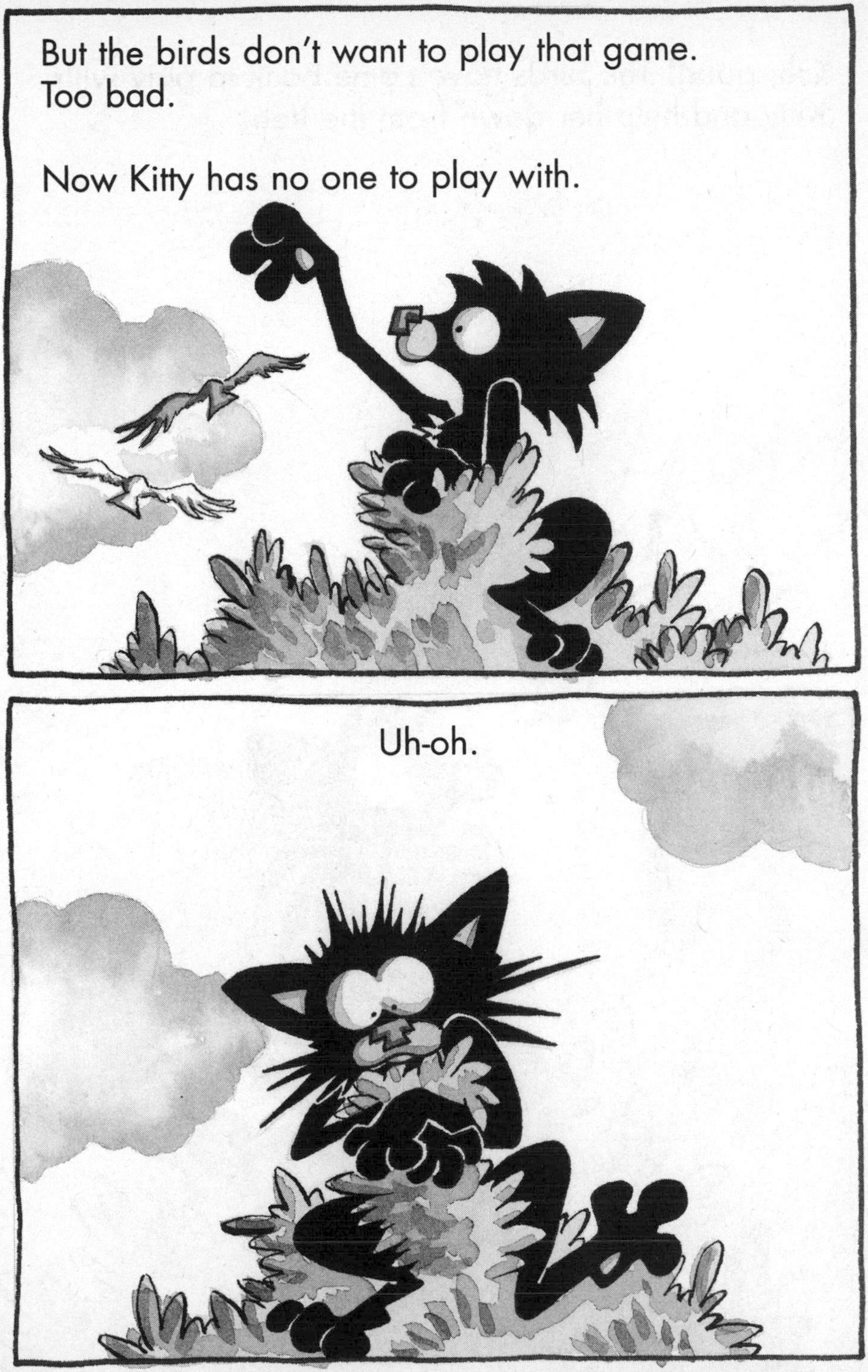
But the birds don't want to play that game.
Too bad.
Now Kitty has no one to play with.
Uh-oh.

Oh, good! The birds have come back to play with Kitty and help her down from the tree.

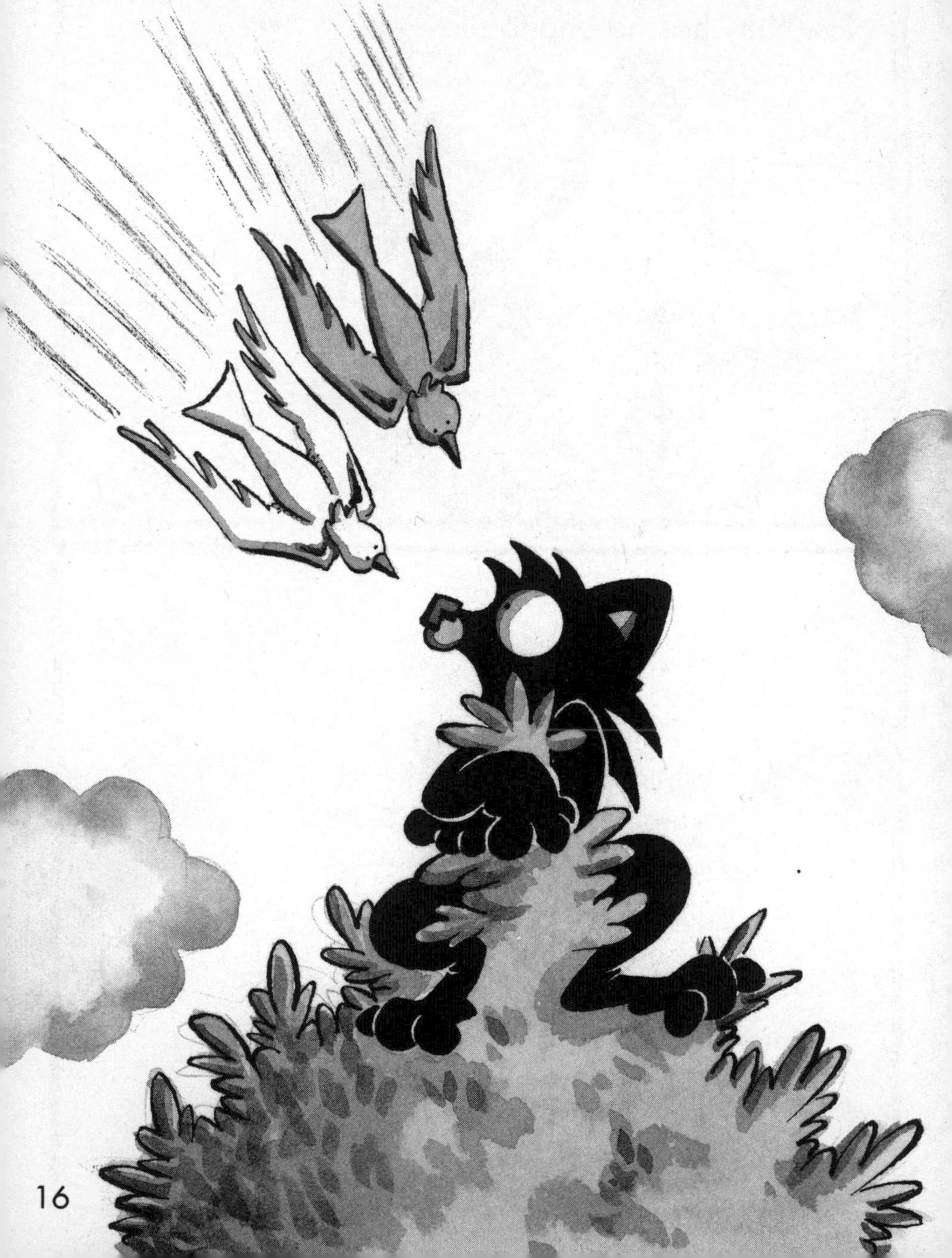

But Kitty does not want their help. She just wants to go home.

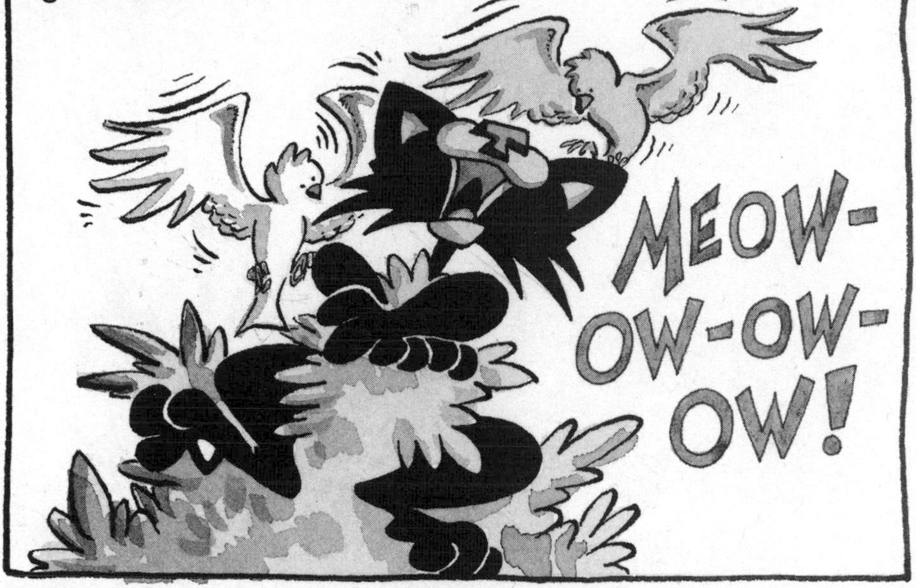
MEOW-
OW-OW-
OW!

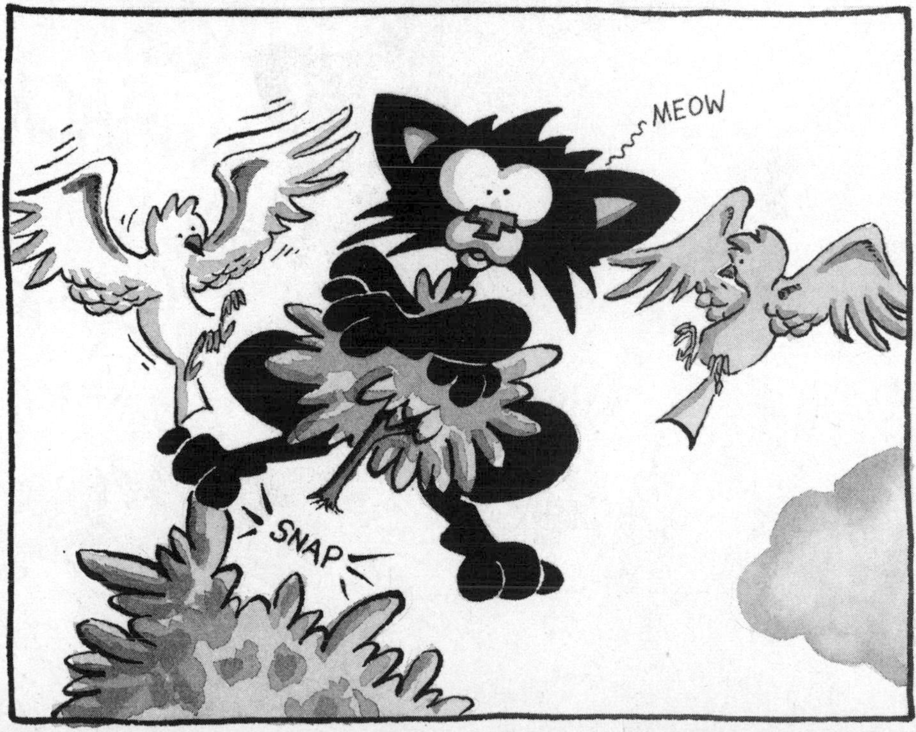
MEOW
SNAP

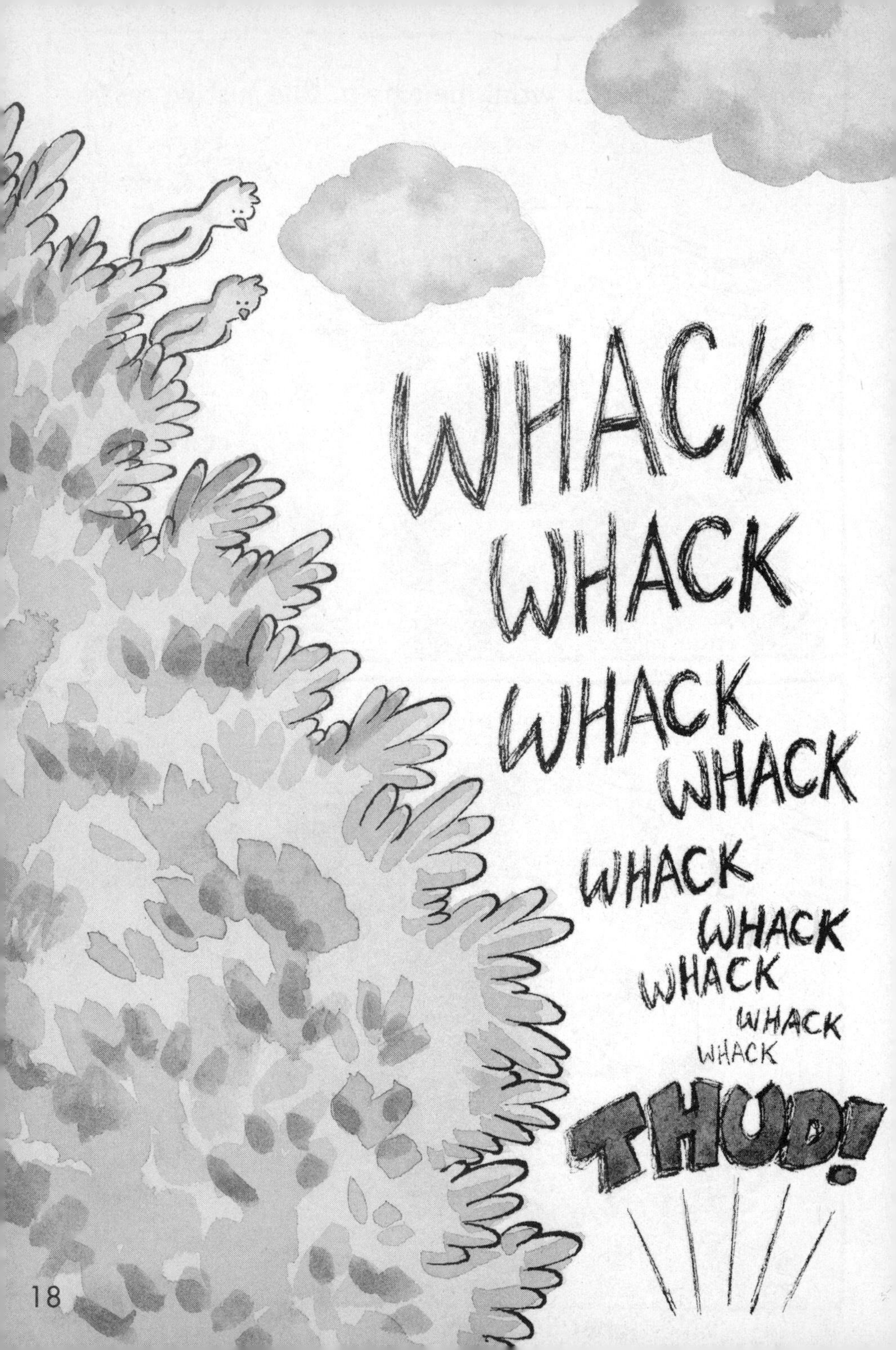
WHACK
WHACK
WHACK
WHACK
WHACK
WHACK
WHACK
WHACK
WHACK
THUD!

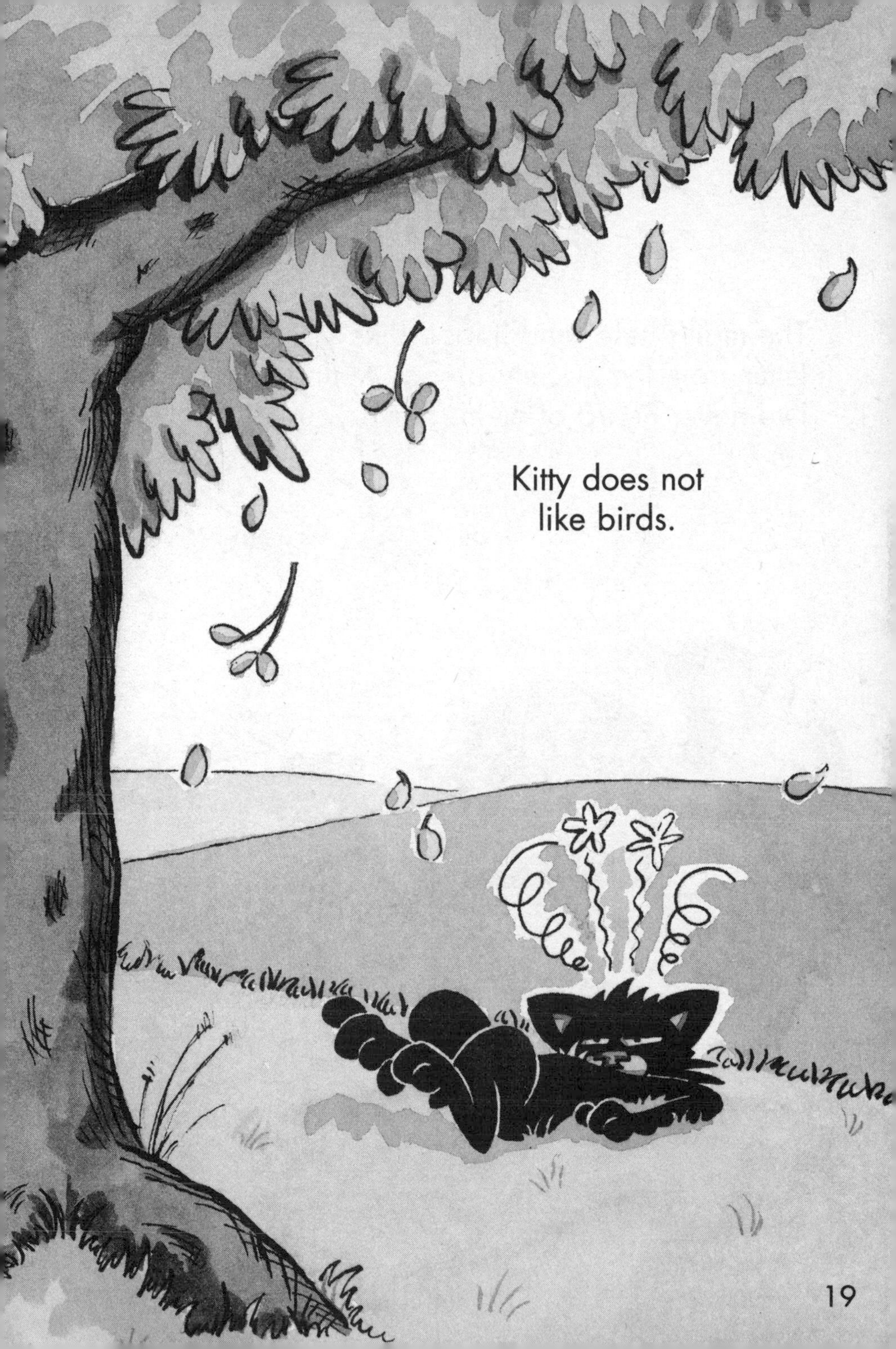

Kitty does not
like birds.

•CHAPTER TWO•

THE NEXT DAY

Good morning, Kitty.

The mail's here, and it looks like you have a certified letter from the Society of Cat Aptitude Management. I've never heard of them. Have you?

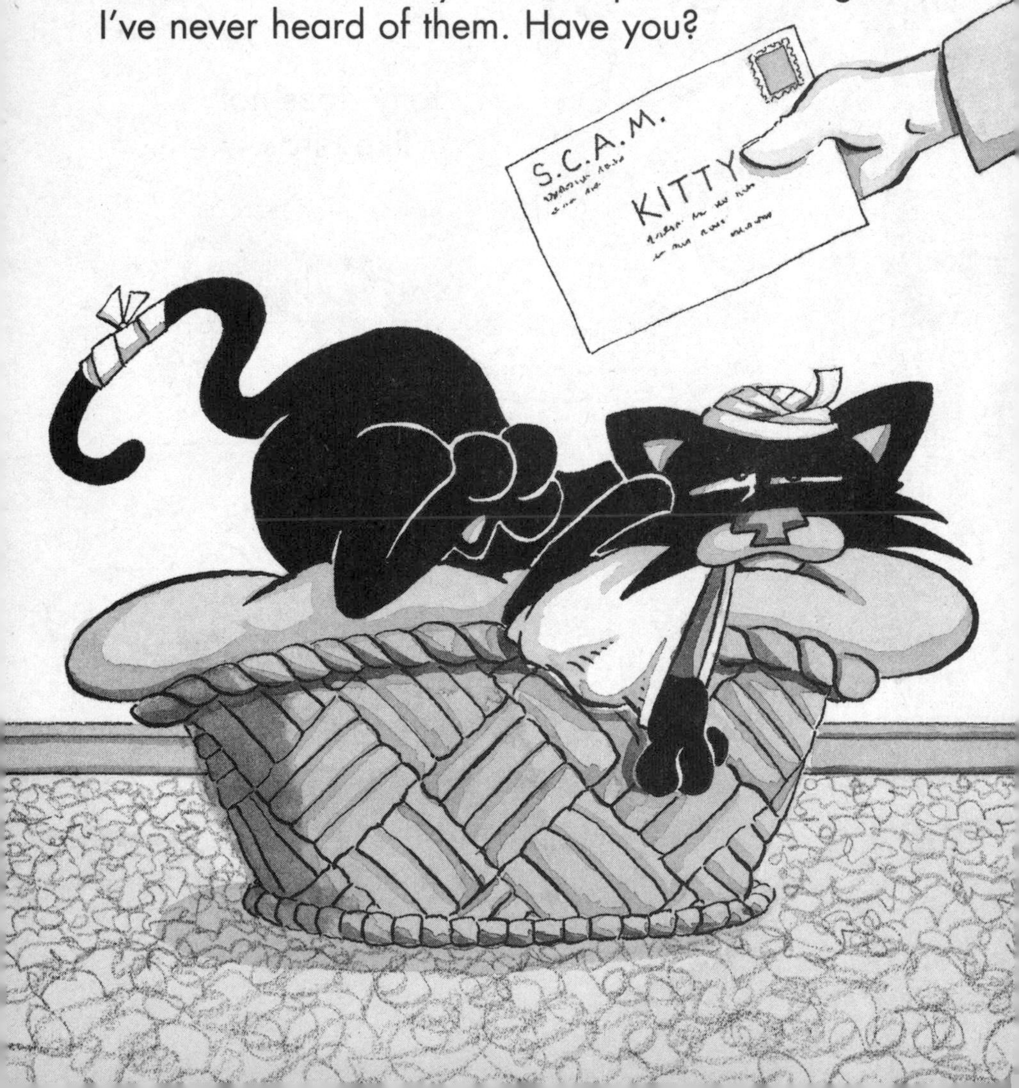
S.C.A.M.
KITTY

Uh-oh. This doesn't look good.

It looks like they know about your run-in with those birds yesterday. Apparently it's considered the most recent instance in a long line of "shameful un-catlike embarrassments." Others include the time you . . .

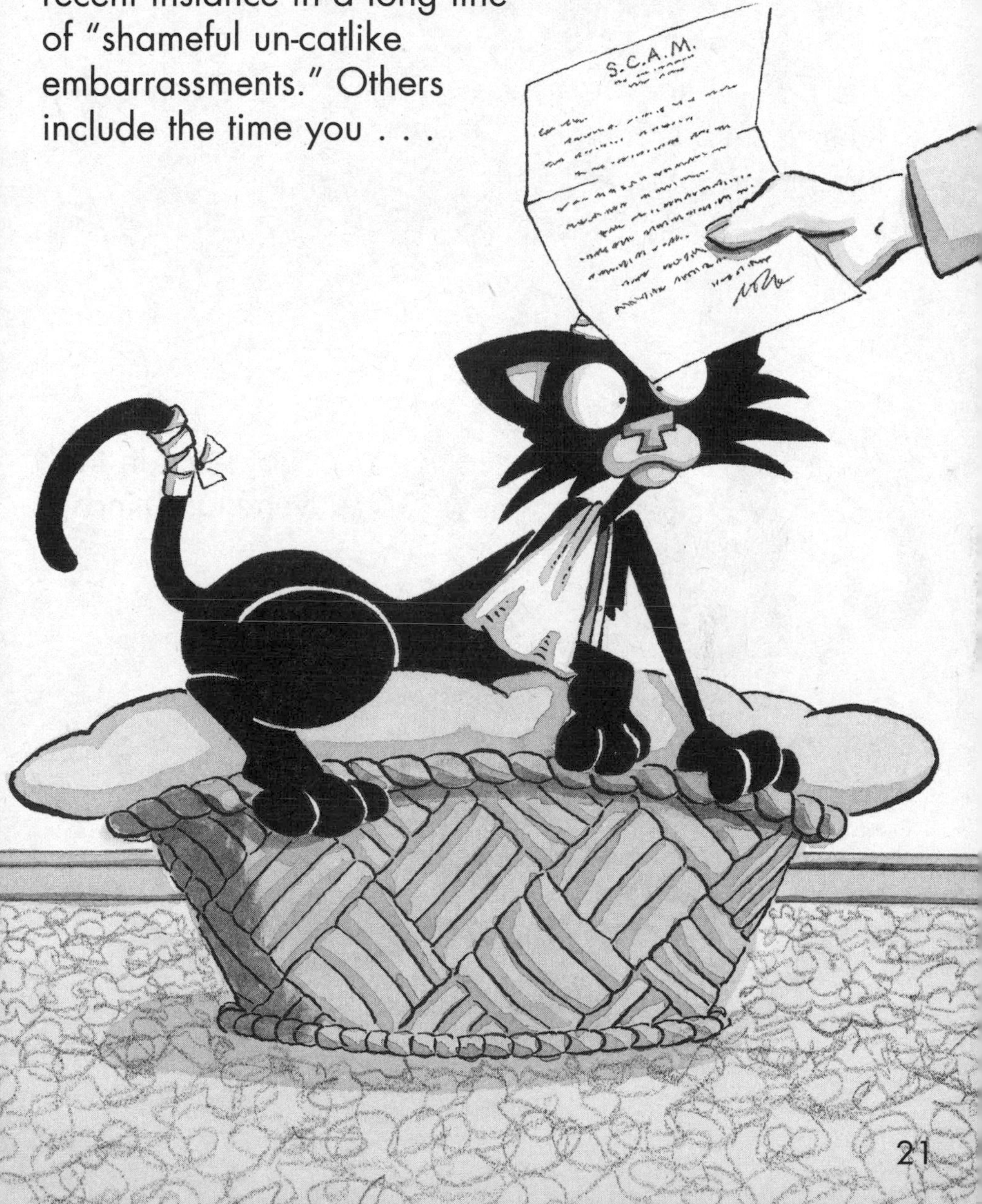
S.C.A.M.

woke up suddenly and
fell behind the
sofa,

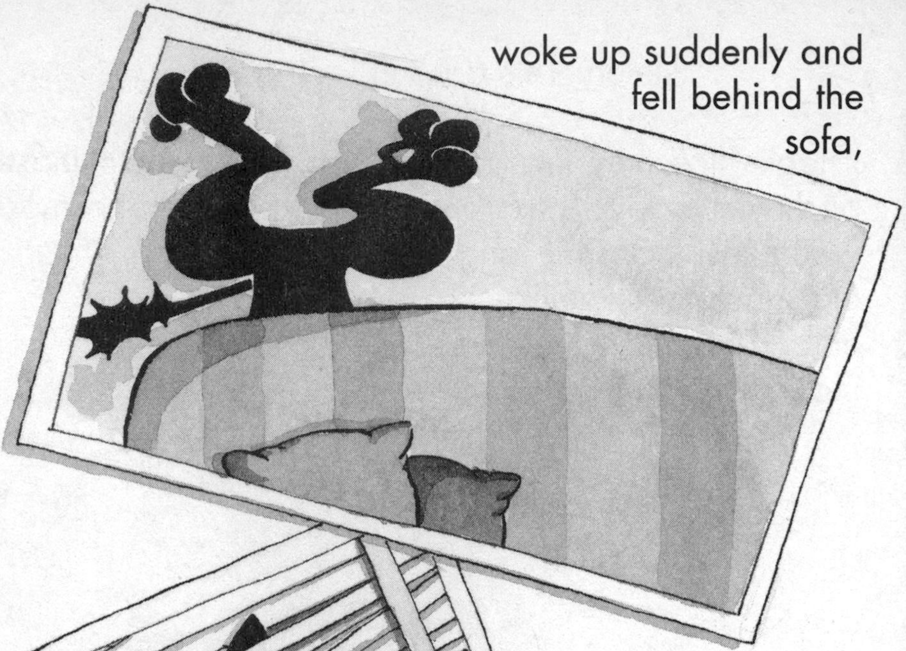

got stuck in the
venetian blinds,

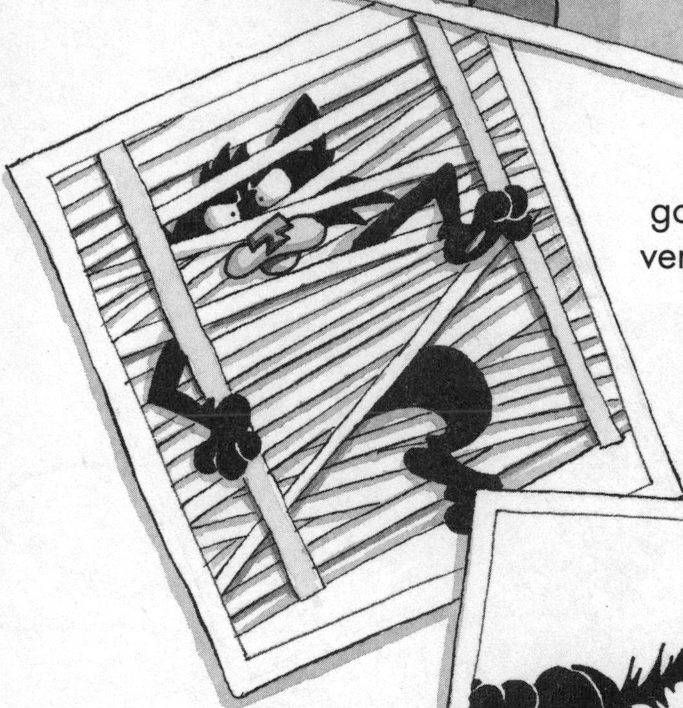

were frightened by
a spider, which
turned out to be
a ball of lint,

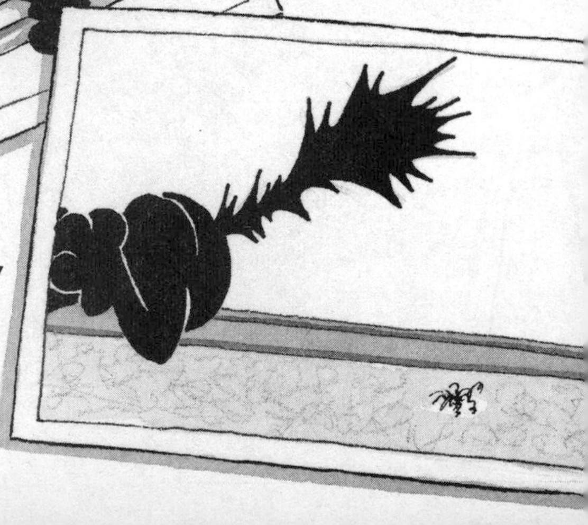

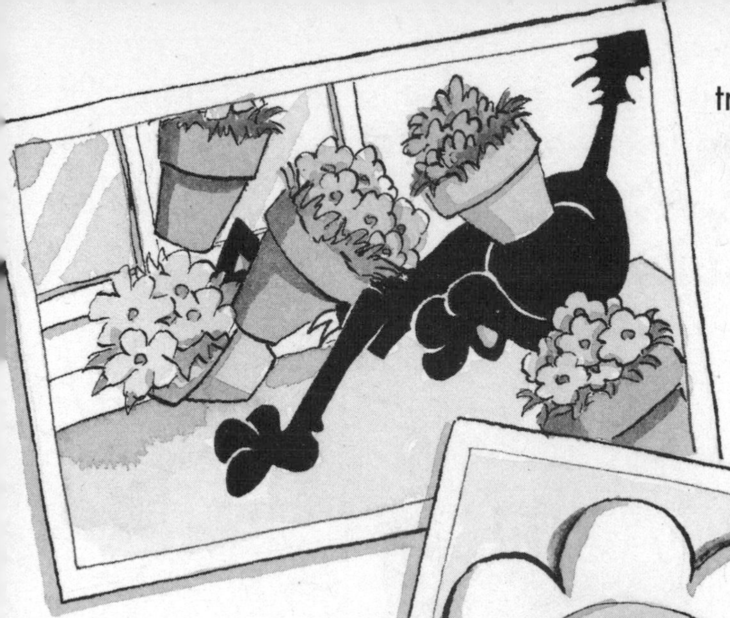

tried to jump
on the desk
but landed
in the
plants,

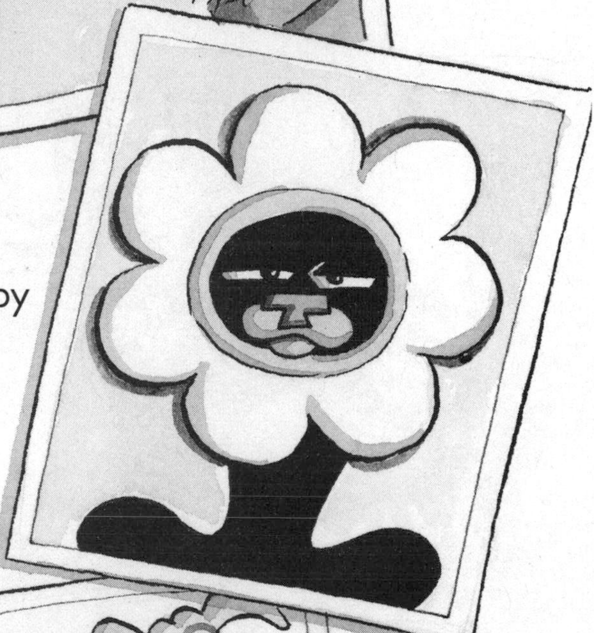

allowed the baby
to dress you up
for Halloween,

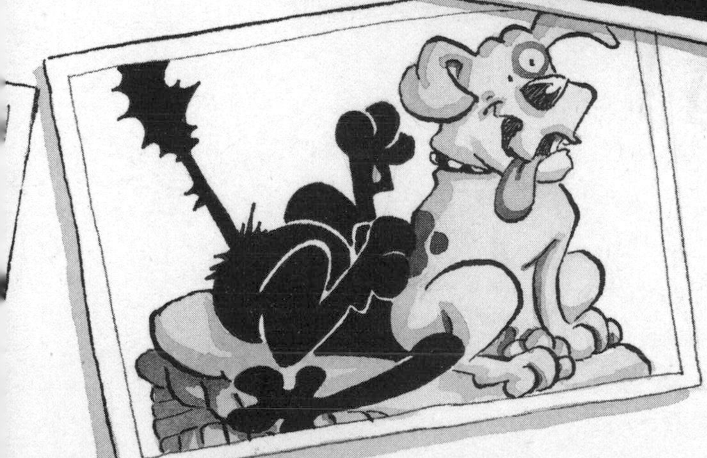

and let the
dog sit on
you while
you were
sleeping.

So apparently because of this recent string of embarrassing behavior, your cat license has been REVOKED.

I didn't even know there was such a thing.

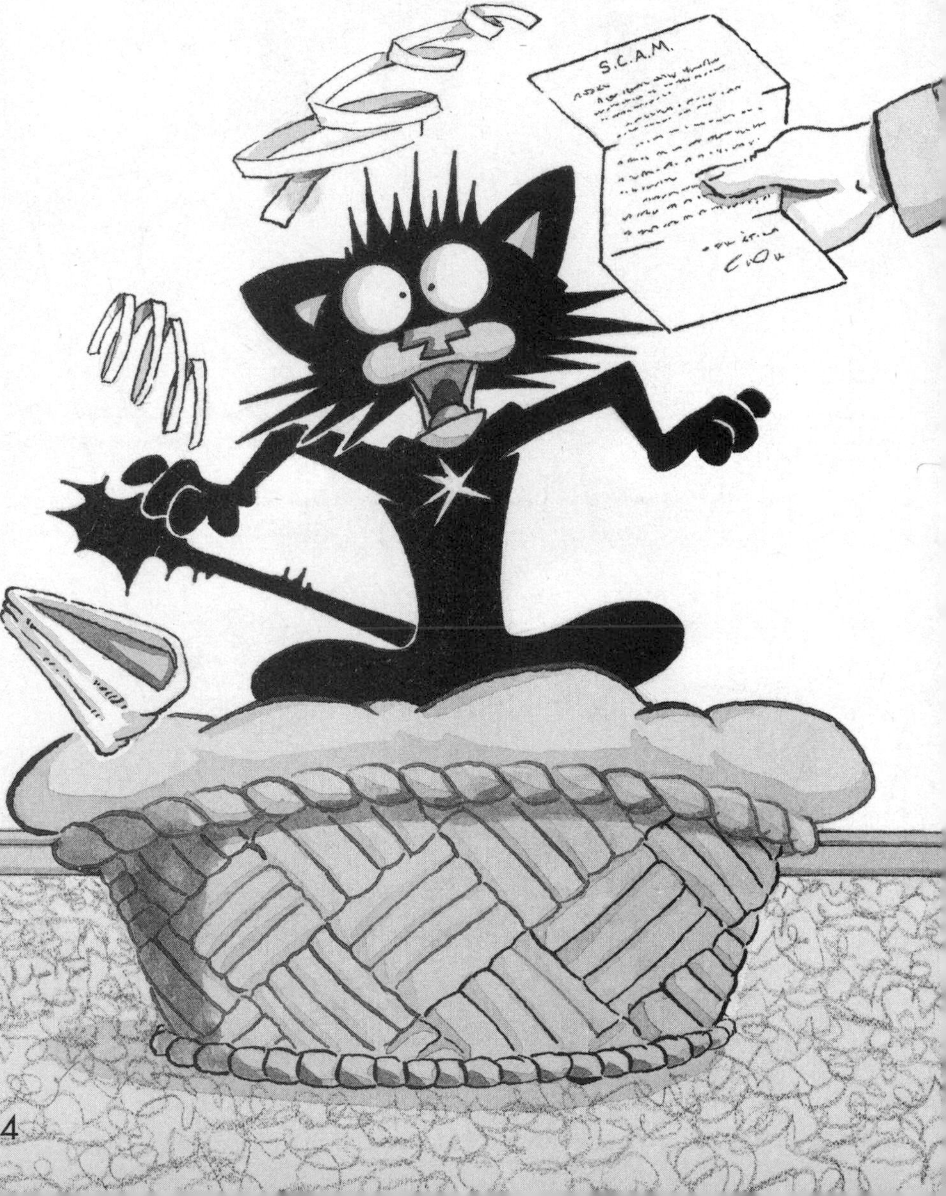
S.C.A.M.

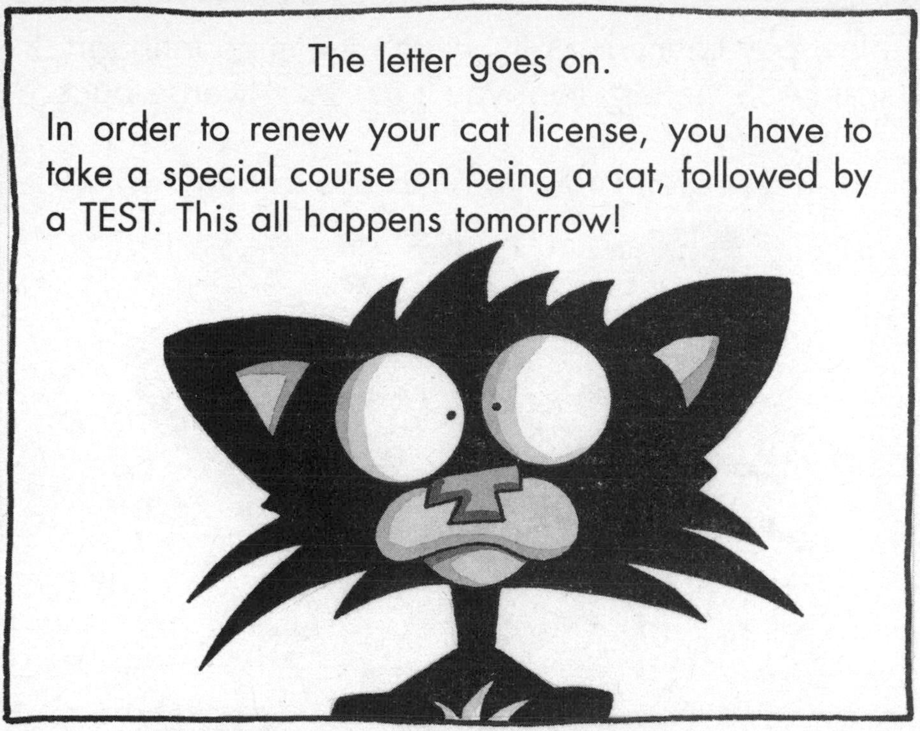
The letter goes on.
In order to renew your cat license, you have to take a special course on being a cat, followed by a TEST. This all happens tomorrow!

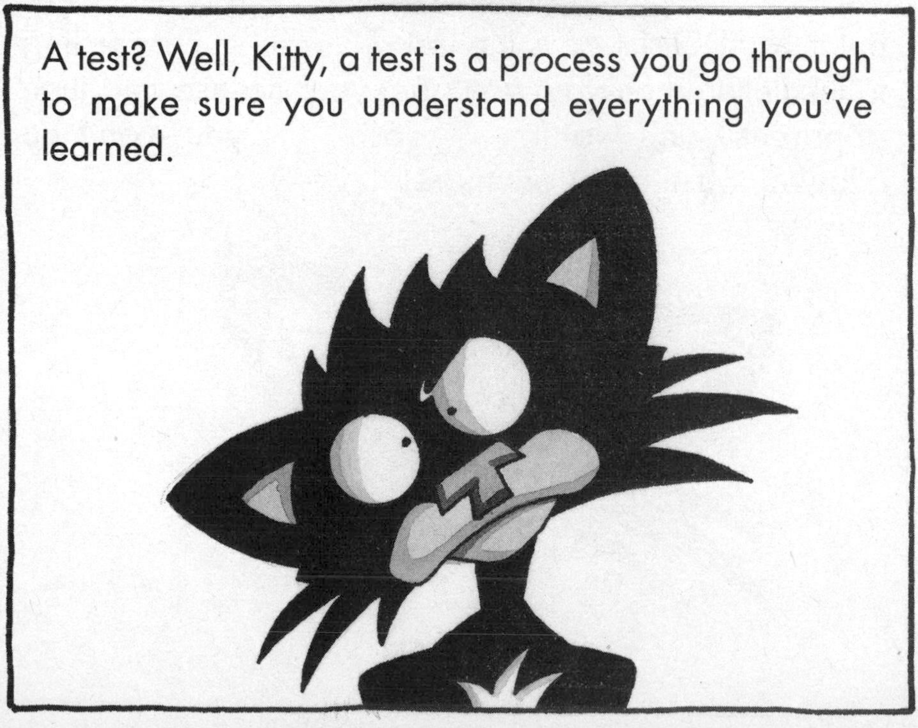
A test? Well, Kitty, a test is a process you go through to make sure you understand everything you've learned.

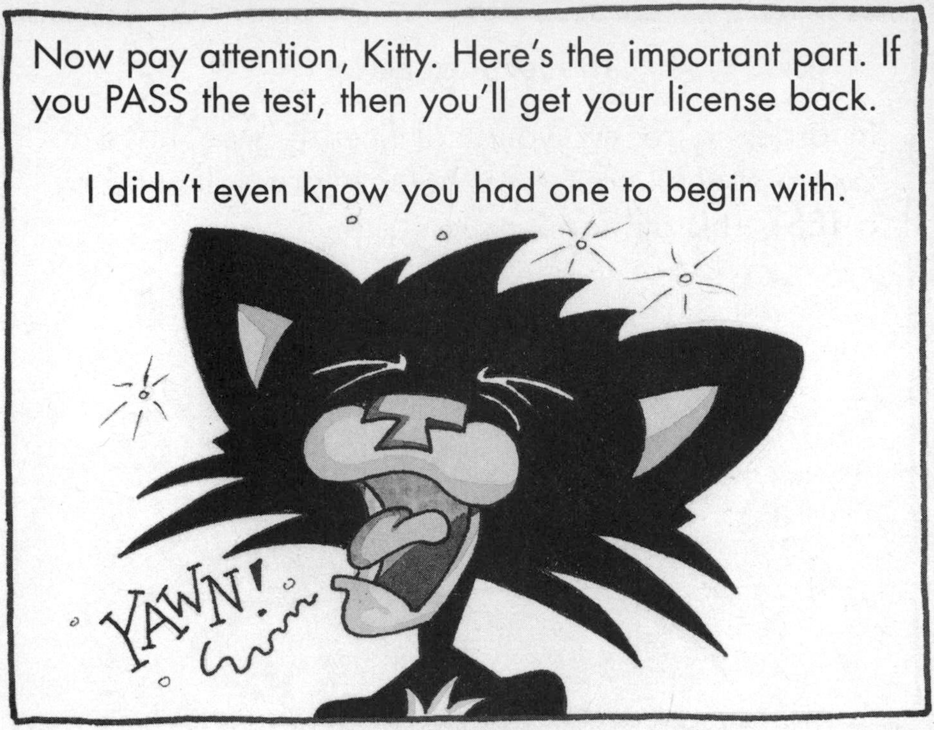
Now pay attention, Kitty. Here's the important part. If you PASS the test, then you'll get your license back.
I didn't even know you had one to begin with.
YAWN!

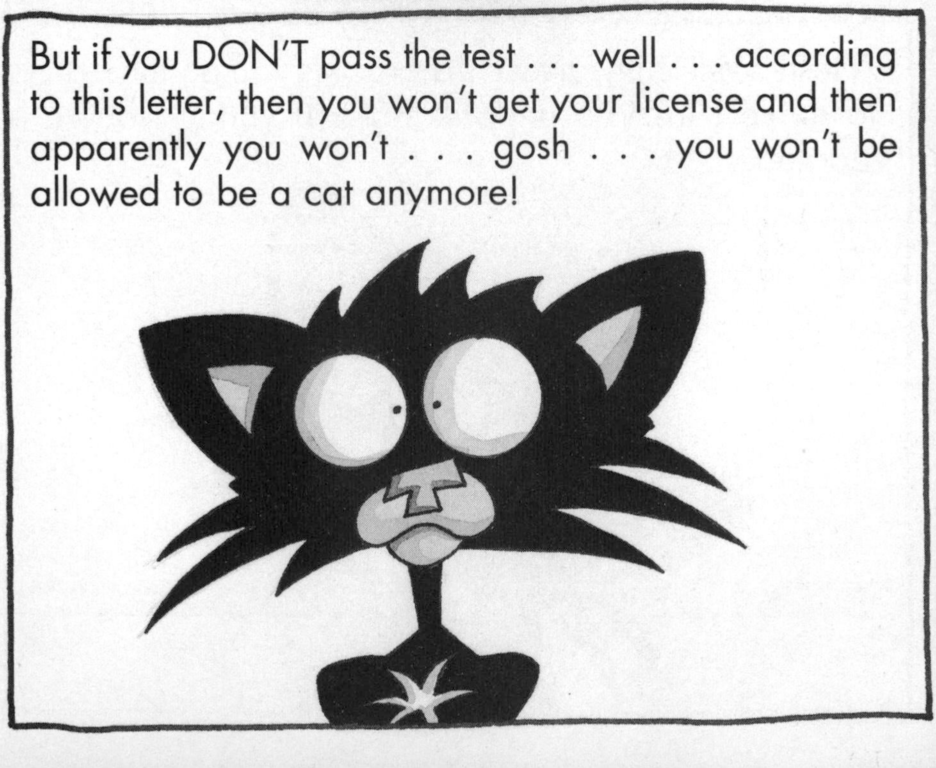
But if you DON'T pass the test . . . well . . . according to this letter, then you won't get your license and then apparently you won't . . . gosh . . . you won't be allowed to be a cat anymore!

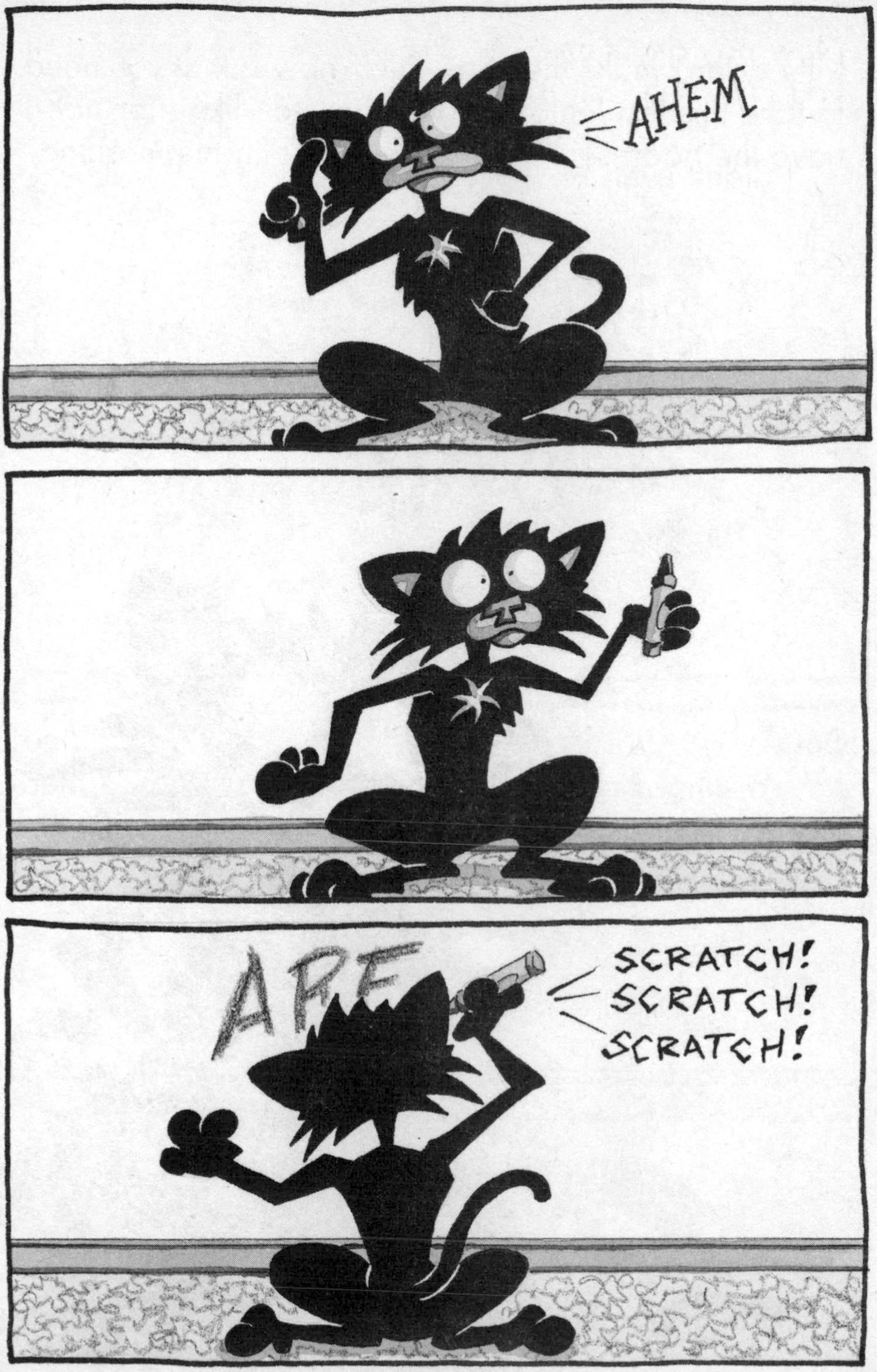
AHEM
ARE
SCRATCH!
SCRATCH!
SCRATCH!

Kitty, I don't make the rules. All I know is that you need to take this test tomorrow whether you like it or not. I have the address. I'll bring you there in the morning.

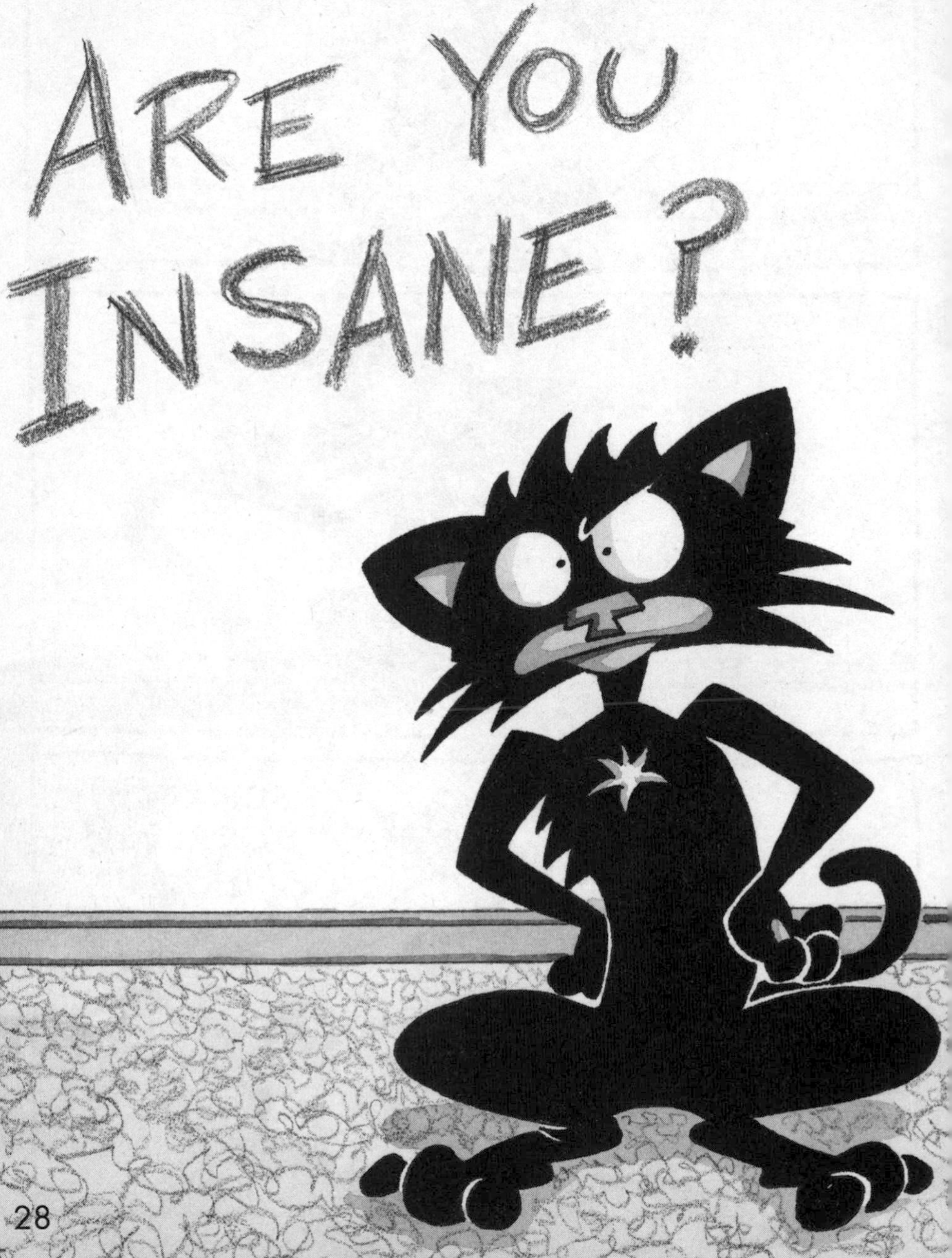
ARE YOU INSANE?

And will you please stop writing on the walls?! I've had to call the painters 14 times this month.

Kitty?! **KITTY!!!**
Sigh.

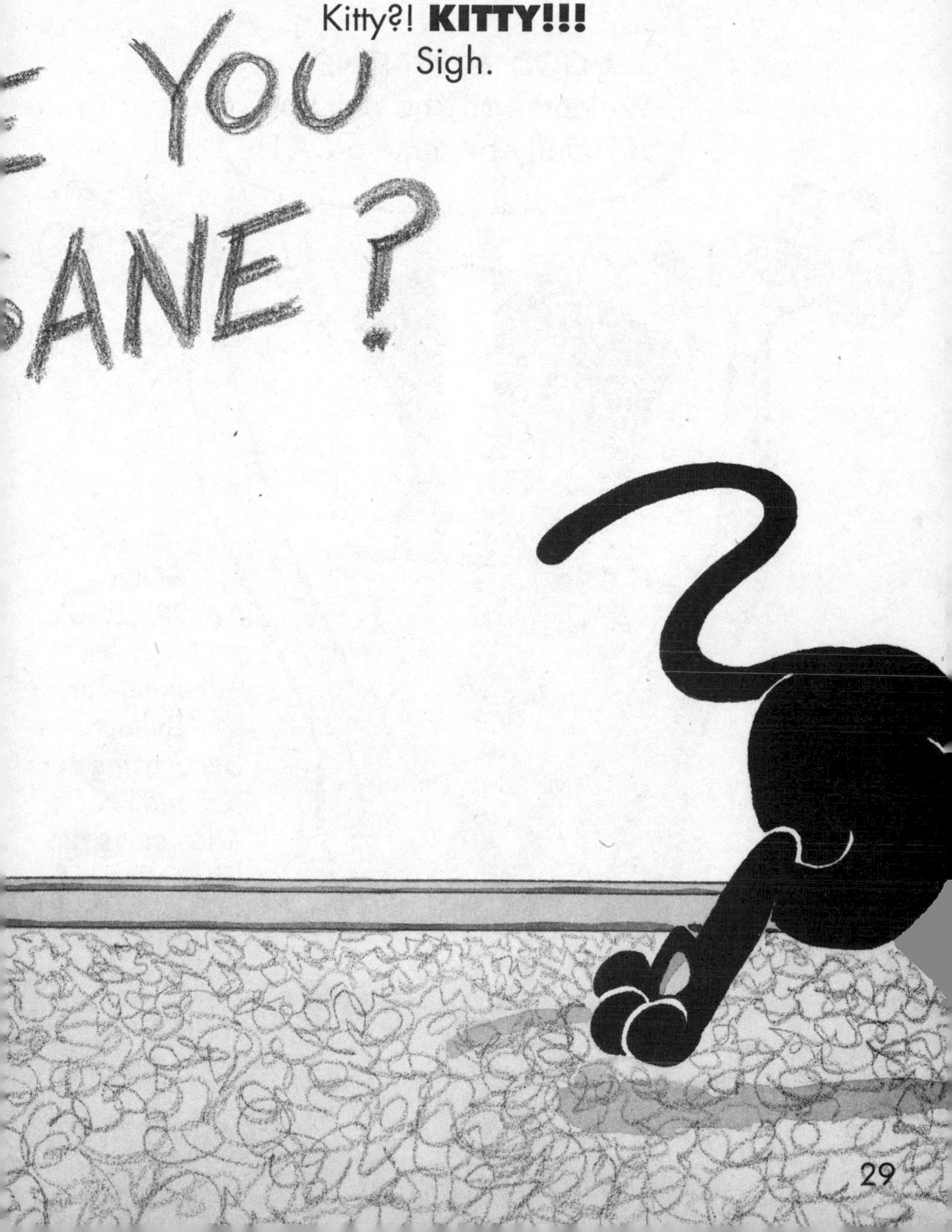
YOU
ANE?

•CHAPTER THREE•

THE NEXT, NEXT DAY

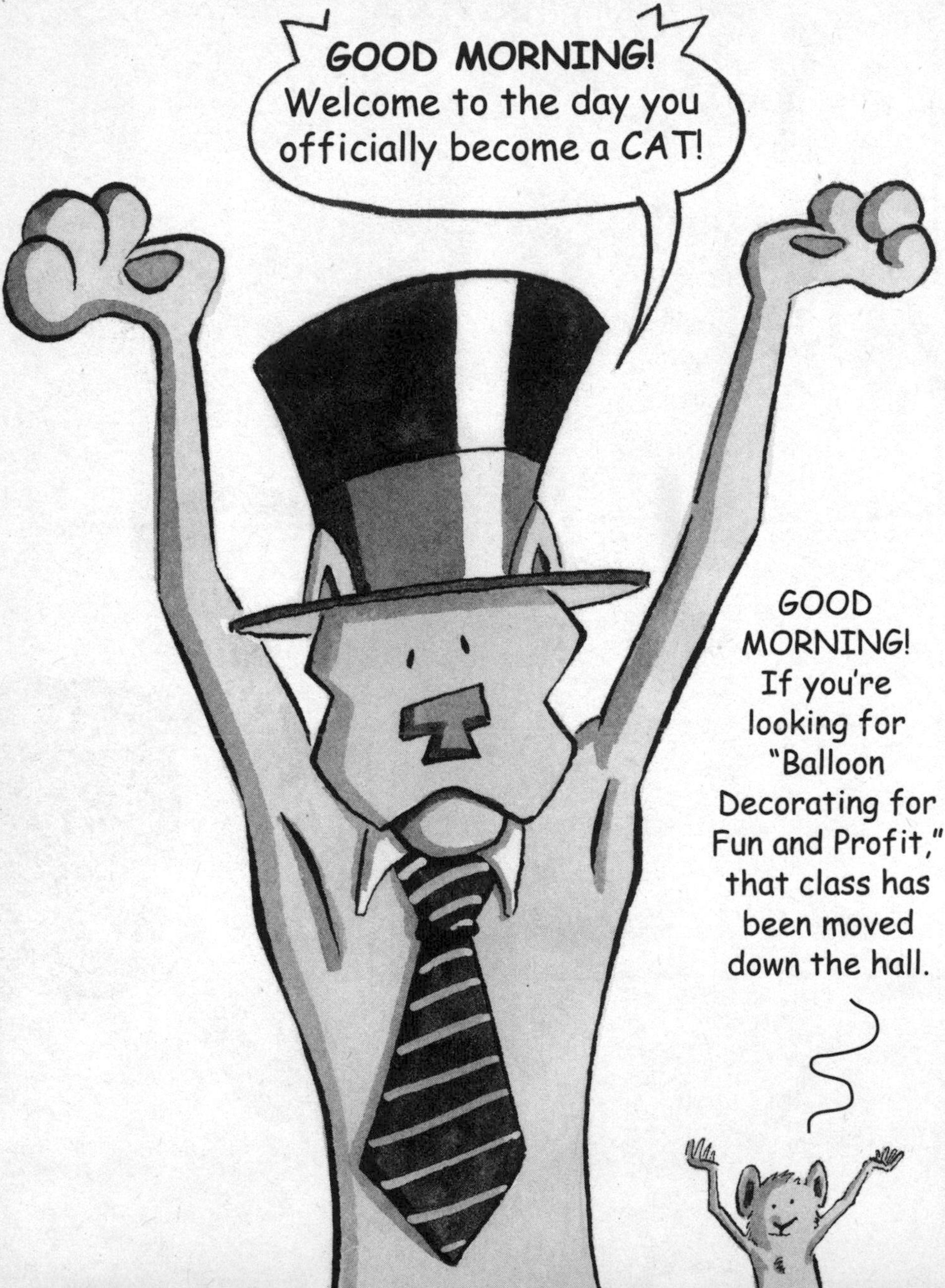

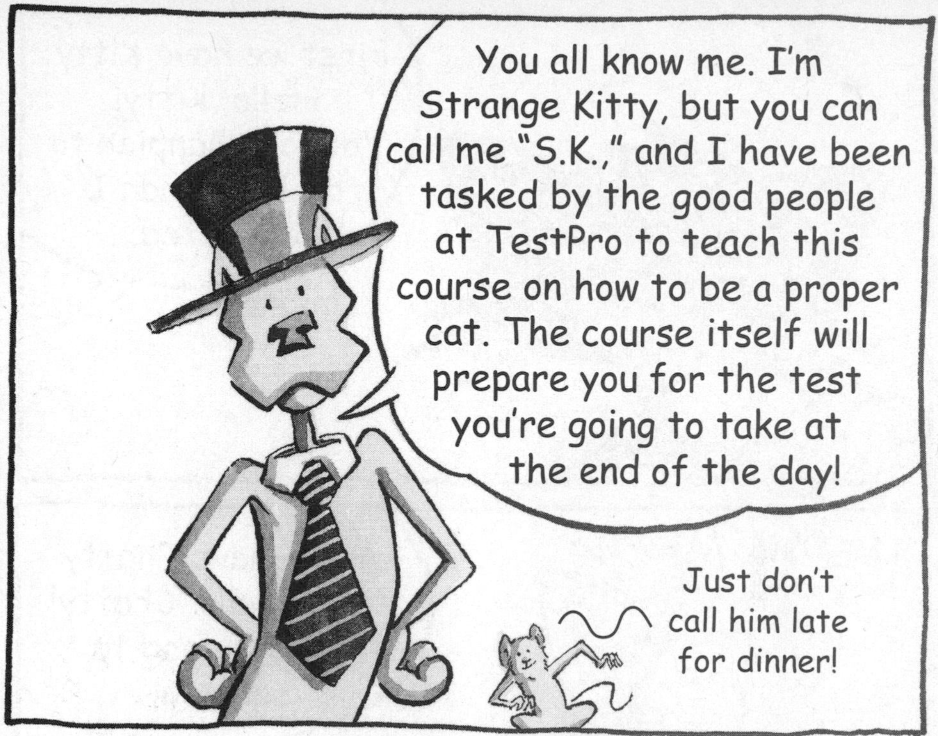
You all know me. I'm Strange Kitty, but you can call me "S.K.," and I have been tasked by the good people at TestPro to teach this course on how to be a proper cat. The course itself will prepare you for the test you're going to take at the end of the day!
Just don't call him late for dinner!

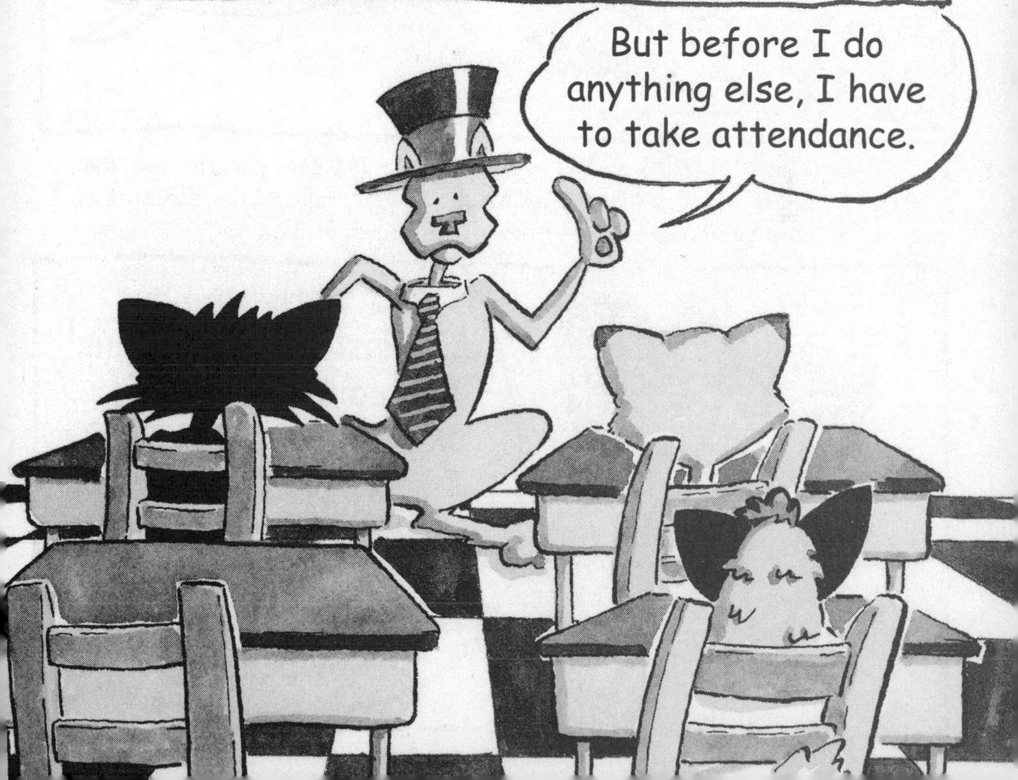
But before I do anything else, I have to take attendance.

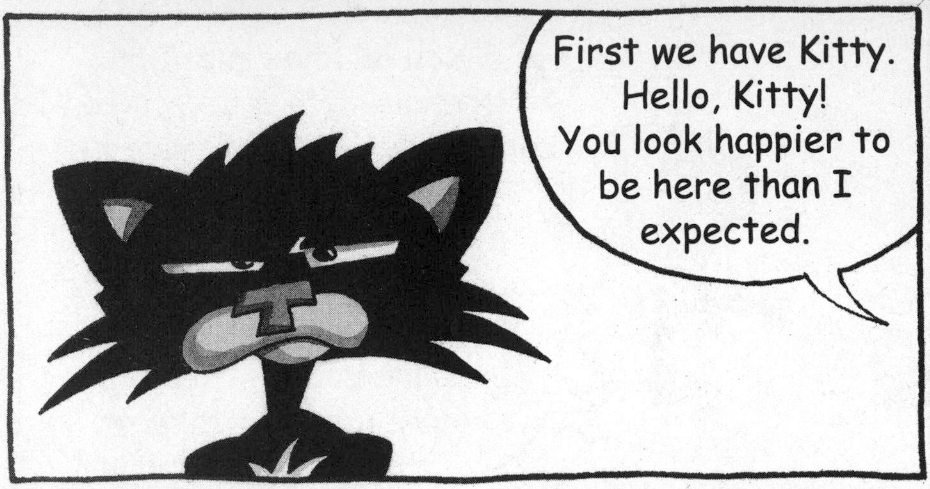
First we have Kitty. Hello, Kitty! You look happier to be here than I expected.

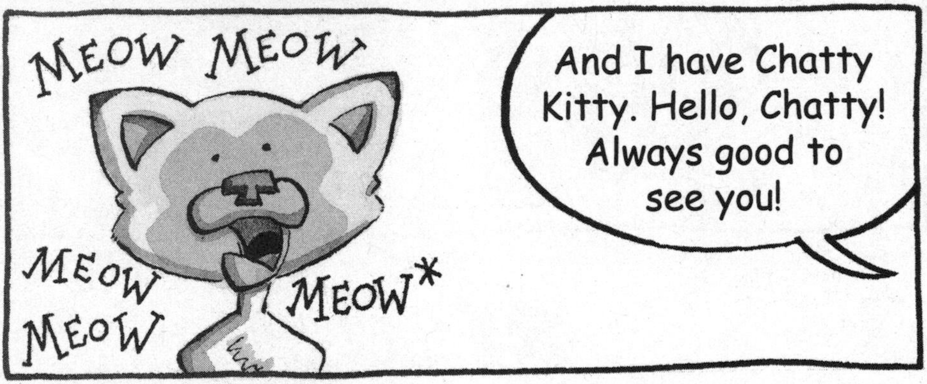
MEOW MEOW
MEOW MEOW
MEOW*
And I have Chatty Kitty. Hello, Chatty! Always good to see you!

* I HAVE to pass this test! I NEED to pass this test. If I don't pass this test, then I won't be a cat. I don't know what I'd be. Maybe I'd be a walrus. I don't want to be a walrus. I'm sensitive to cold weather. I haven't slept in three days.

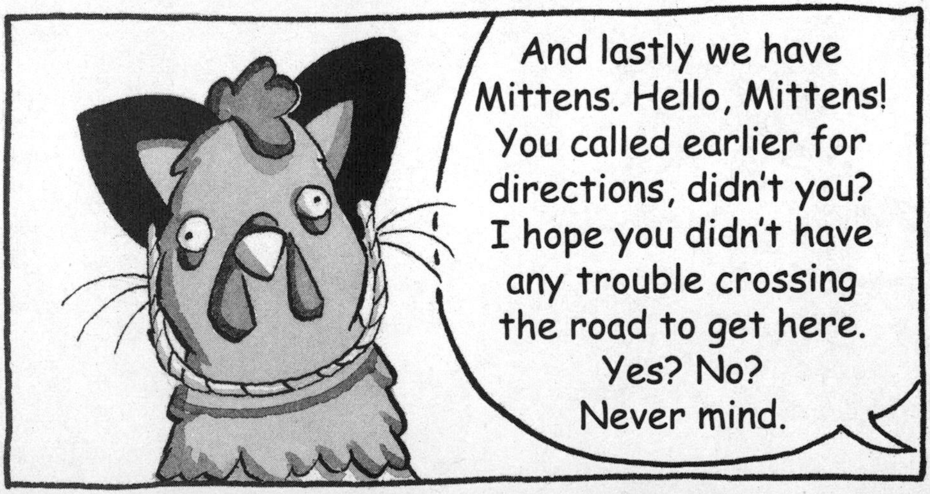
And lastly we have Mittens. Hello, Mittens! You called earlier for directions, didn't you? I hope you didn't have any trouble crossing the road to get here. Yes? No? Never mind.

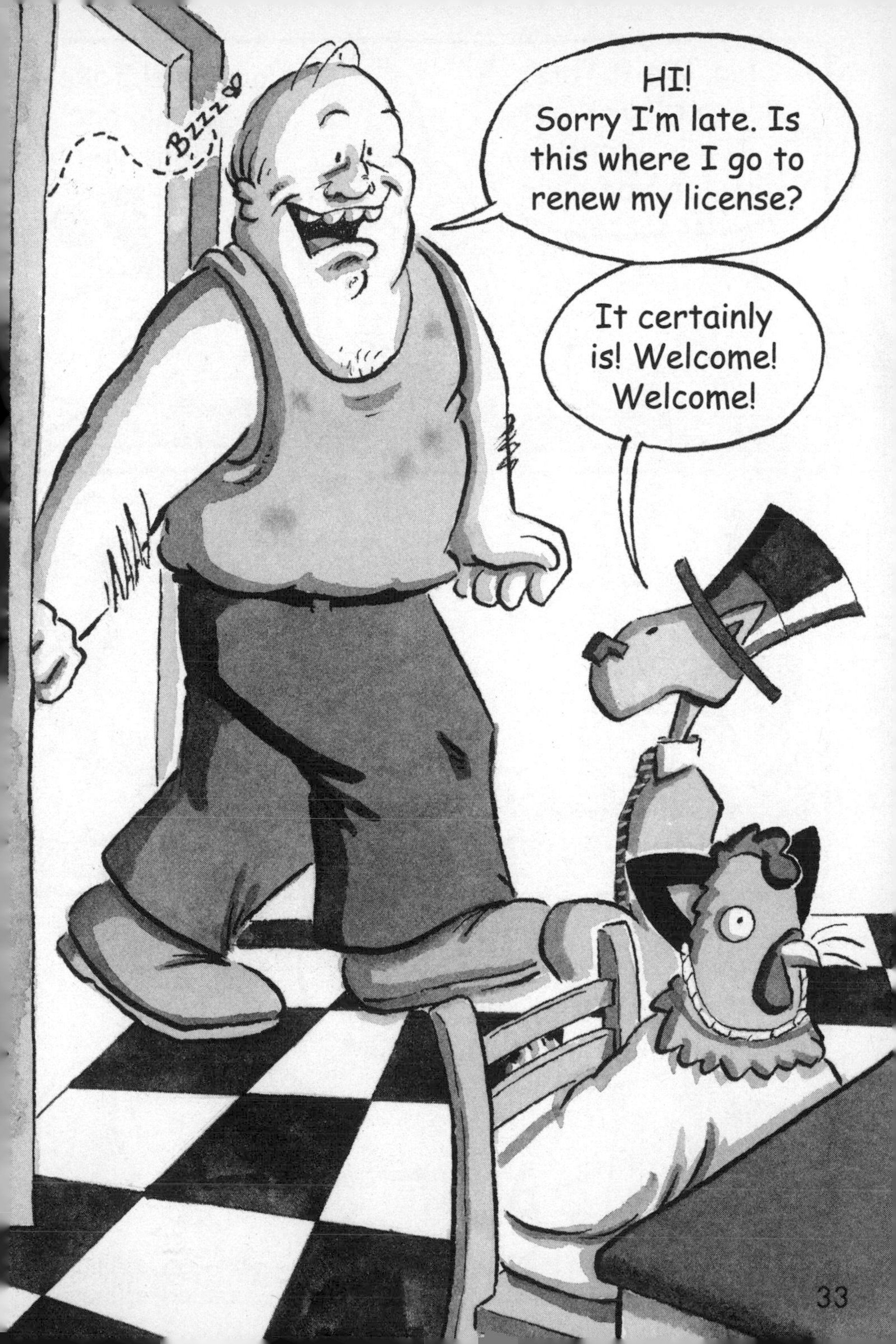

Bzzz
HI! Sorry I'm late. Is this where I go to renew my license?
It certainly is! Welcome! Welcome!

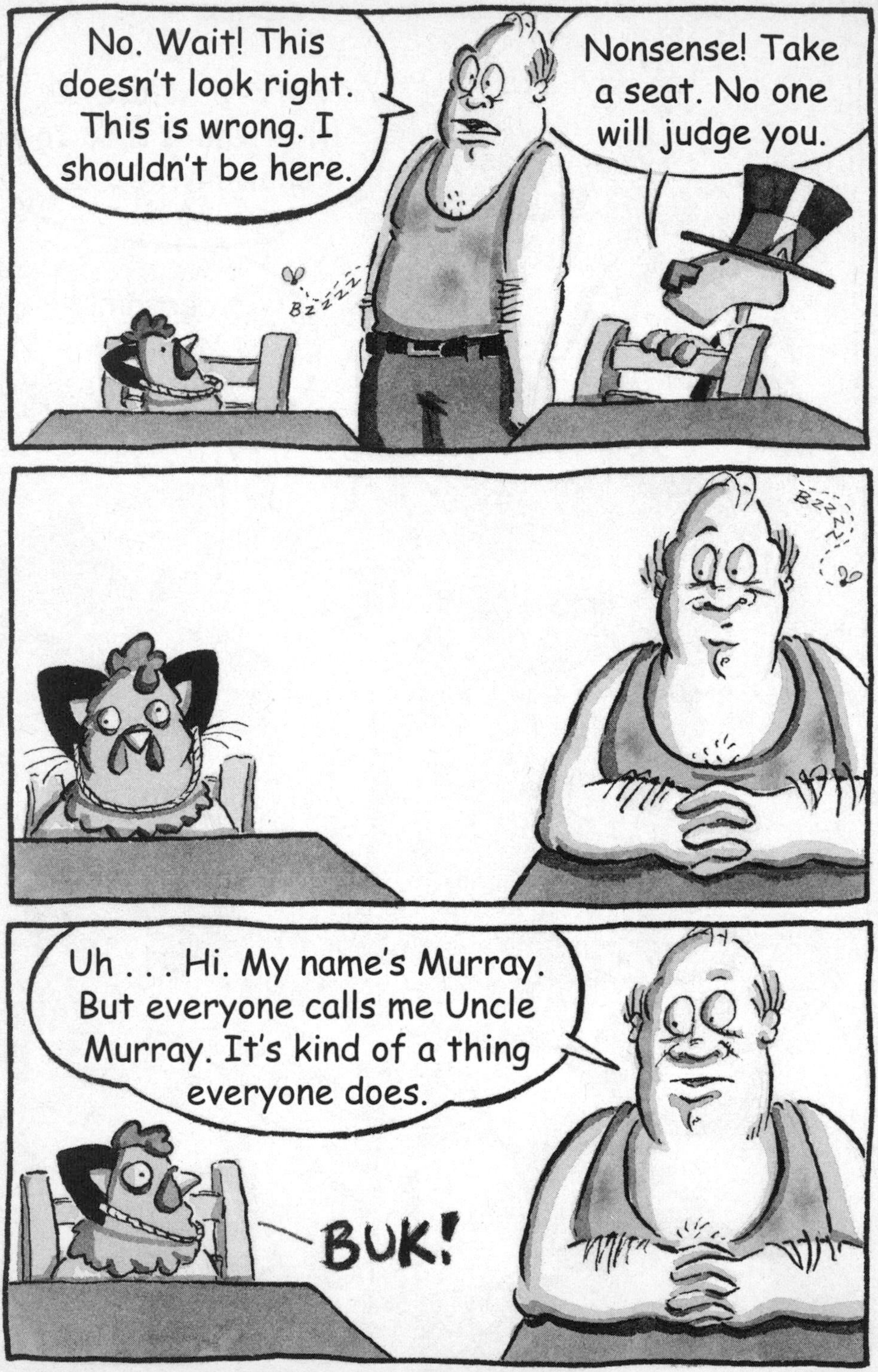
No. Wait! This doesn't look right. This is wrong. I shouldn't be here.
Nonsense! Take a seat. No one will judge you.
Bzzzz
Bzzzz
Uh . . . Hi. My name's Murray. But everyone calls me Uncle Murray. It's kind of a thing everyone does.
BUK!

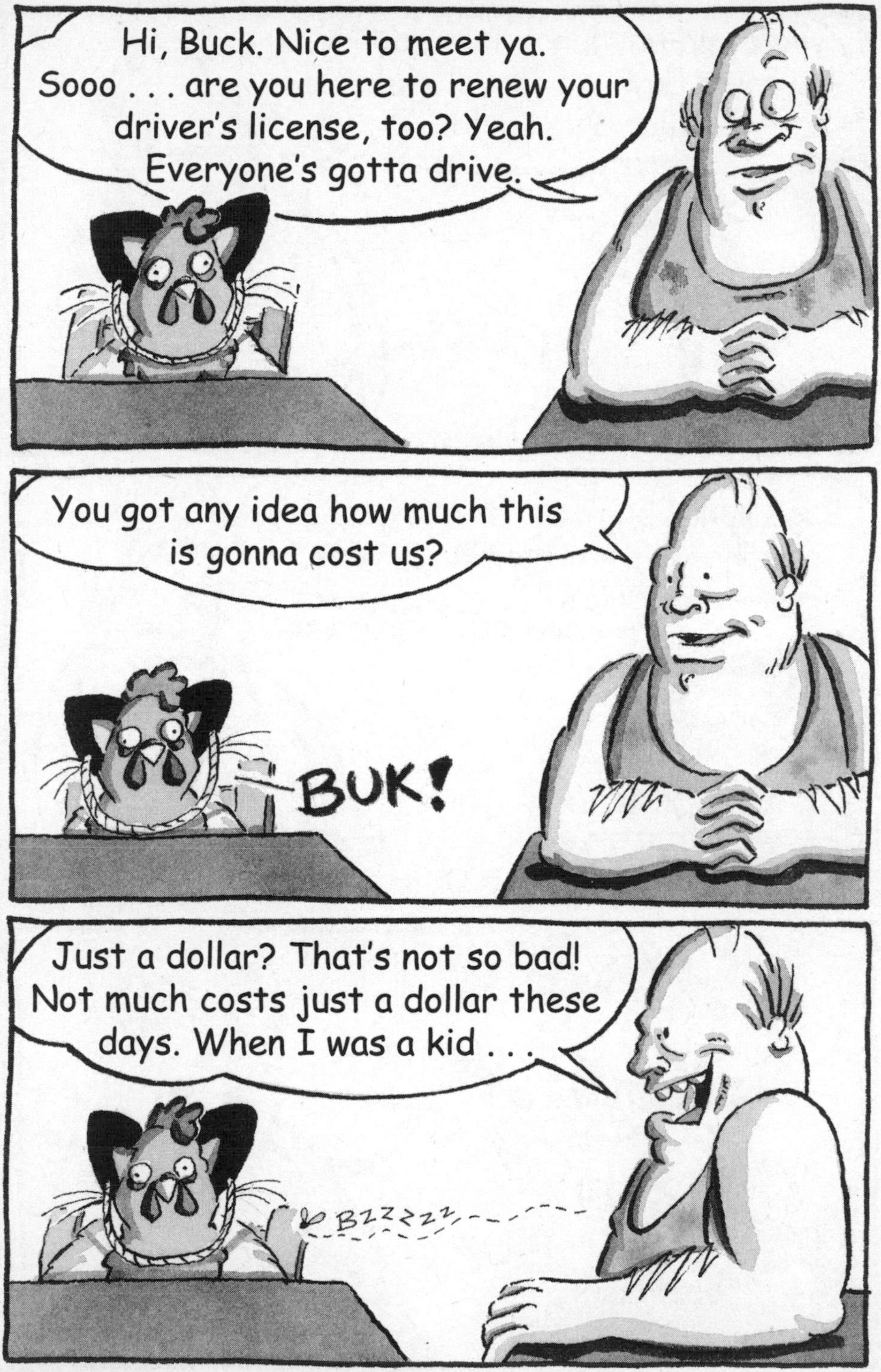
Hi, Buck. Nice to meet ya. Sooo . . . are you here to renew your driver's license, too? Yeah. Everyone's gotta drive.
You got any idea how much this is gonna cost us?
BUK!
Just a dollar? That's not so bad! Not much costs just a dollar these days. When I was a kid . . .
BZZZZZ

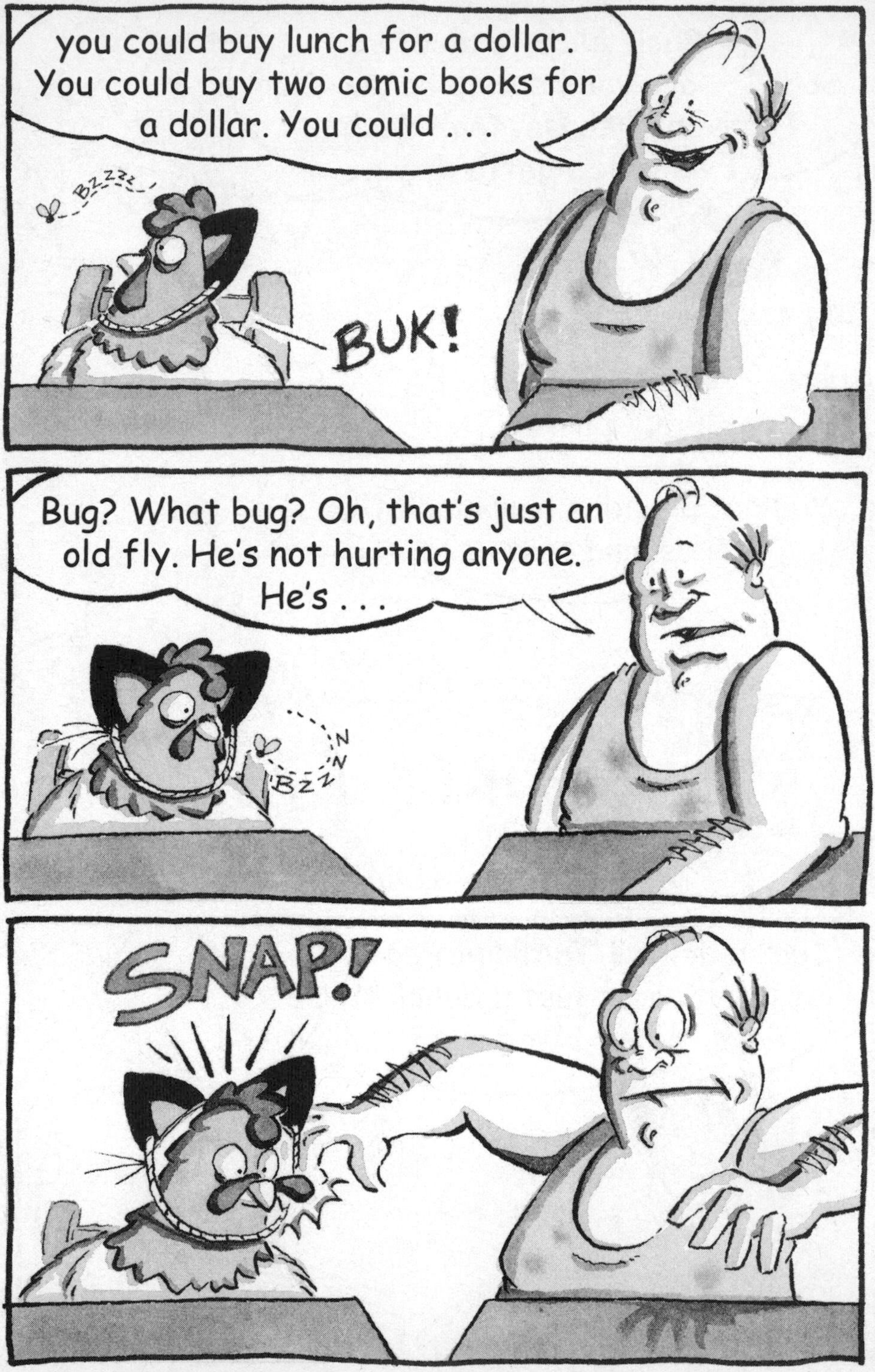
you could buy lunch for a dollar. You could buy two comic books for a dollar. You could . . .
BZZZZ
BUK!
Bug? What bug? Oh, that's just an old fly. He's not hurting anyone. He's . . .
BZZZ
SNAP!

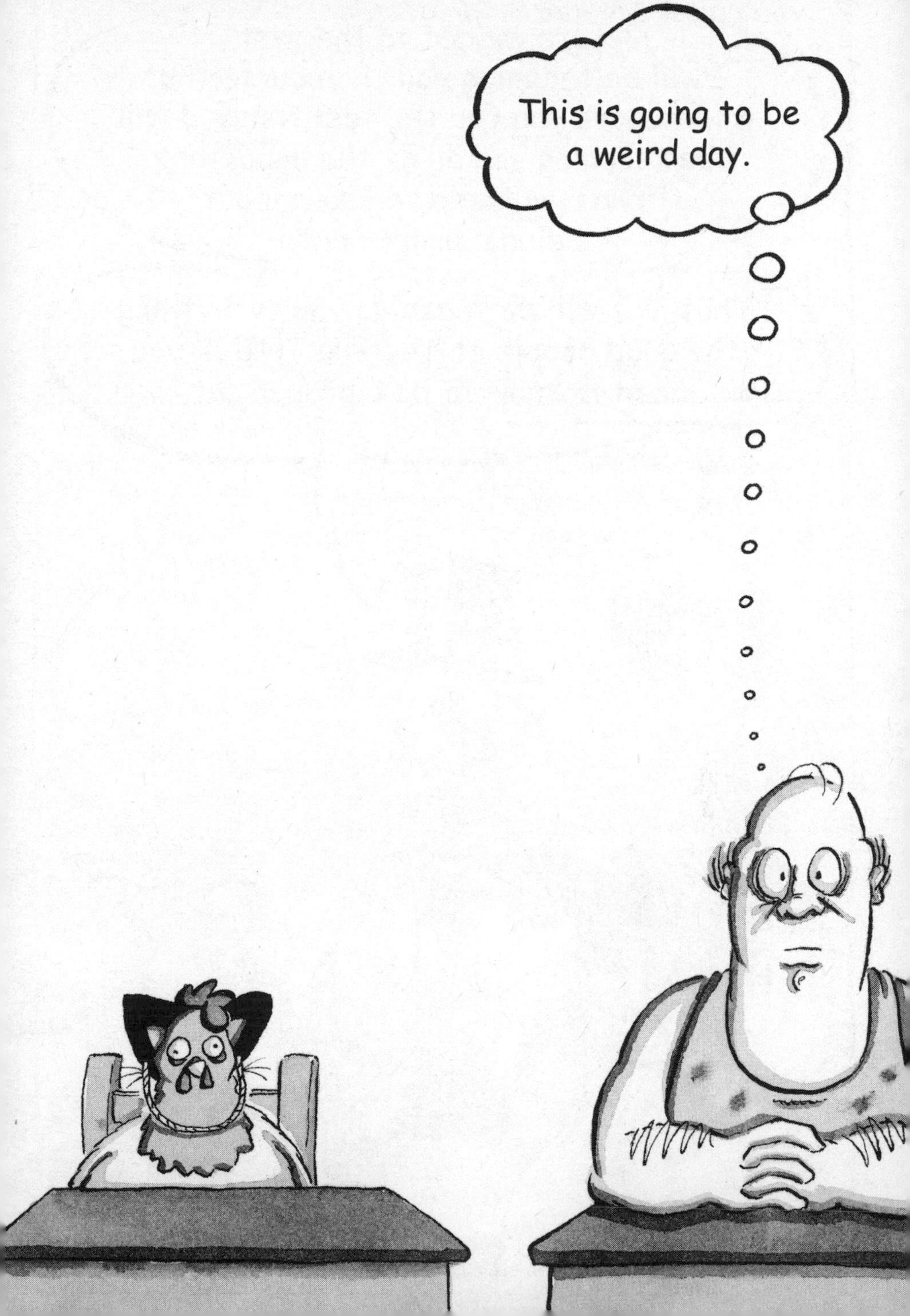
This is going to be a weird day.

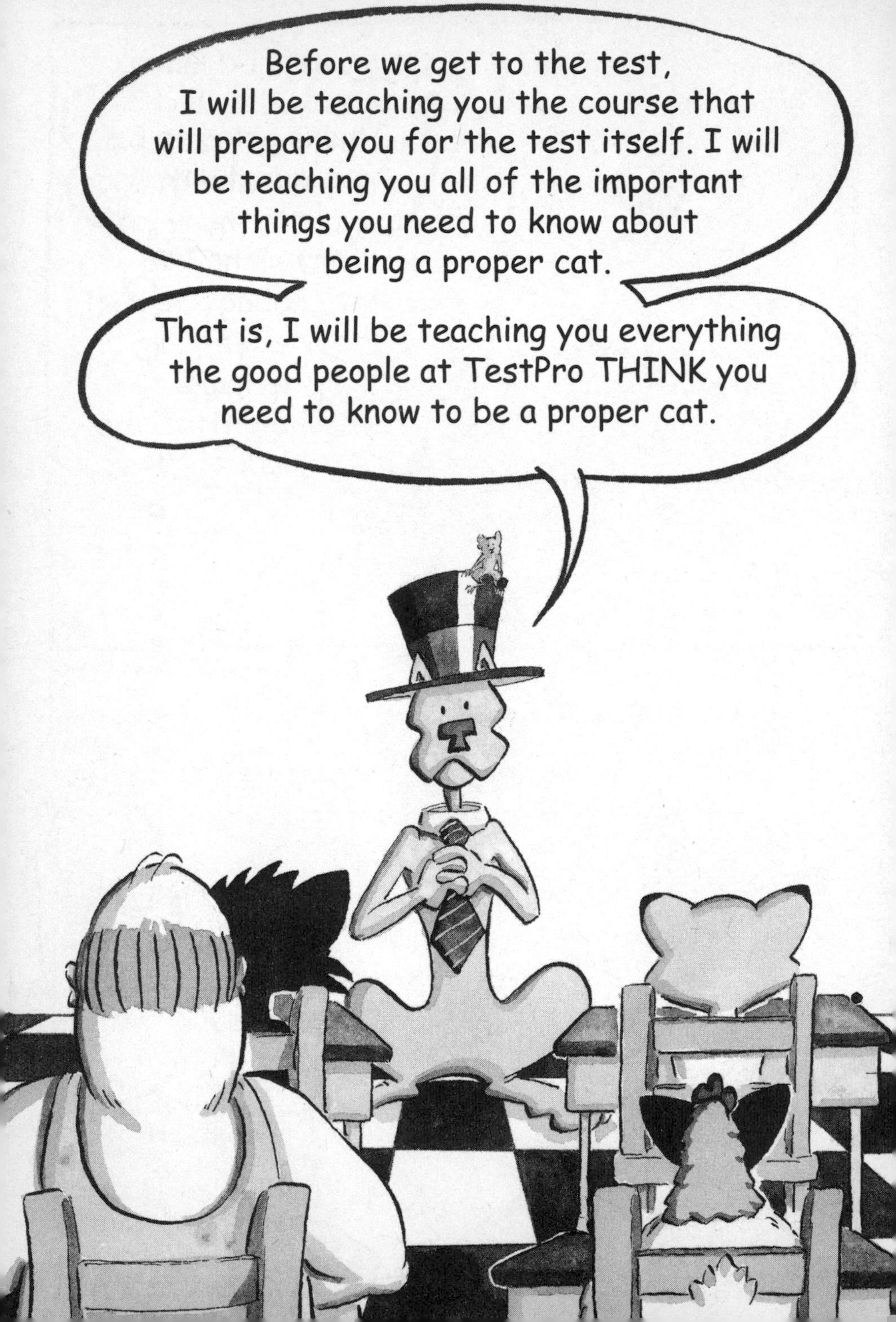
Before we get to the test, I will be teaching you the course that will prepare you for the test itself. I will be teaching you all of the important things you need to know about being a proper cat.
That is, I will be teaching you everything the good people at TestPro THINK you need to know to be a proper cat.

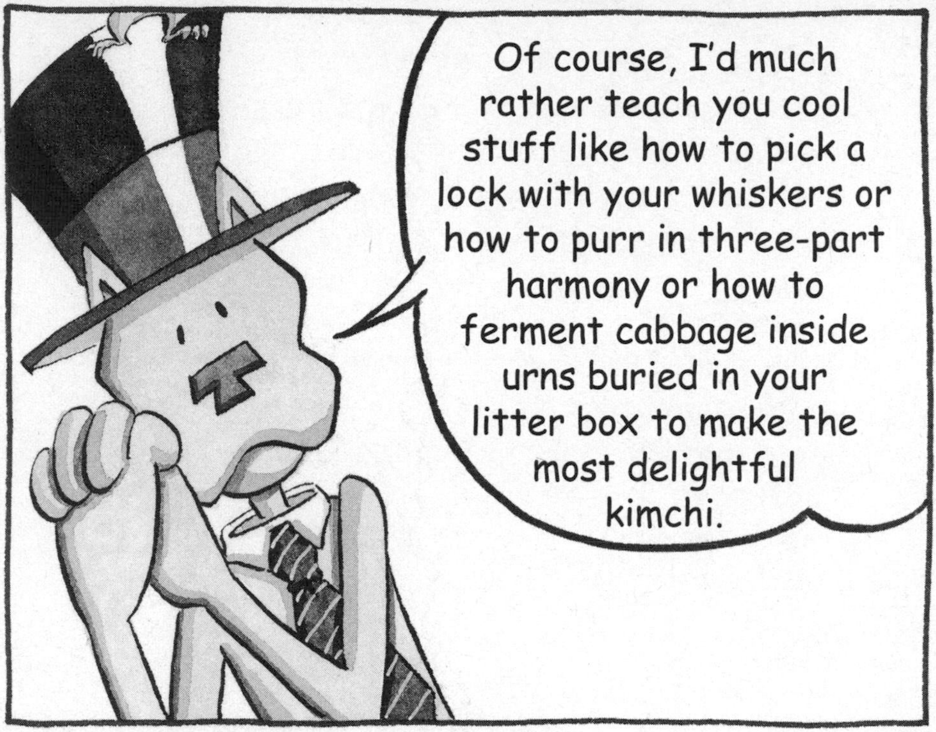
Of course, I'd much rather teach you cool stuff like how to pick a lock with your whiskers or how to purr in three-part harmony or how to ferment cabbage inside urns buried in your litter box to make the most delightful kimchi.

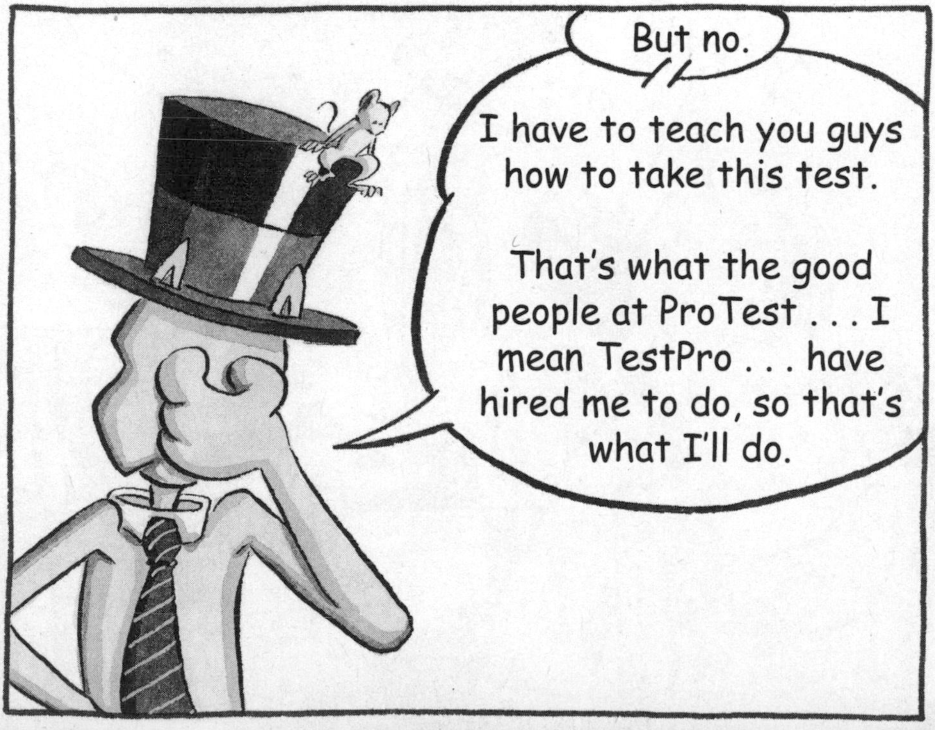
But no.
I have to teach you guys how to take this test.
That's what the good people at ProTest . . . I mean TestPro . . . have hired me to do, so that's what I'll do.

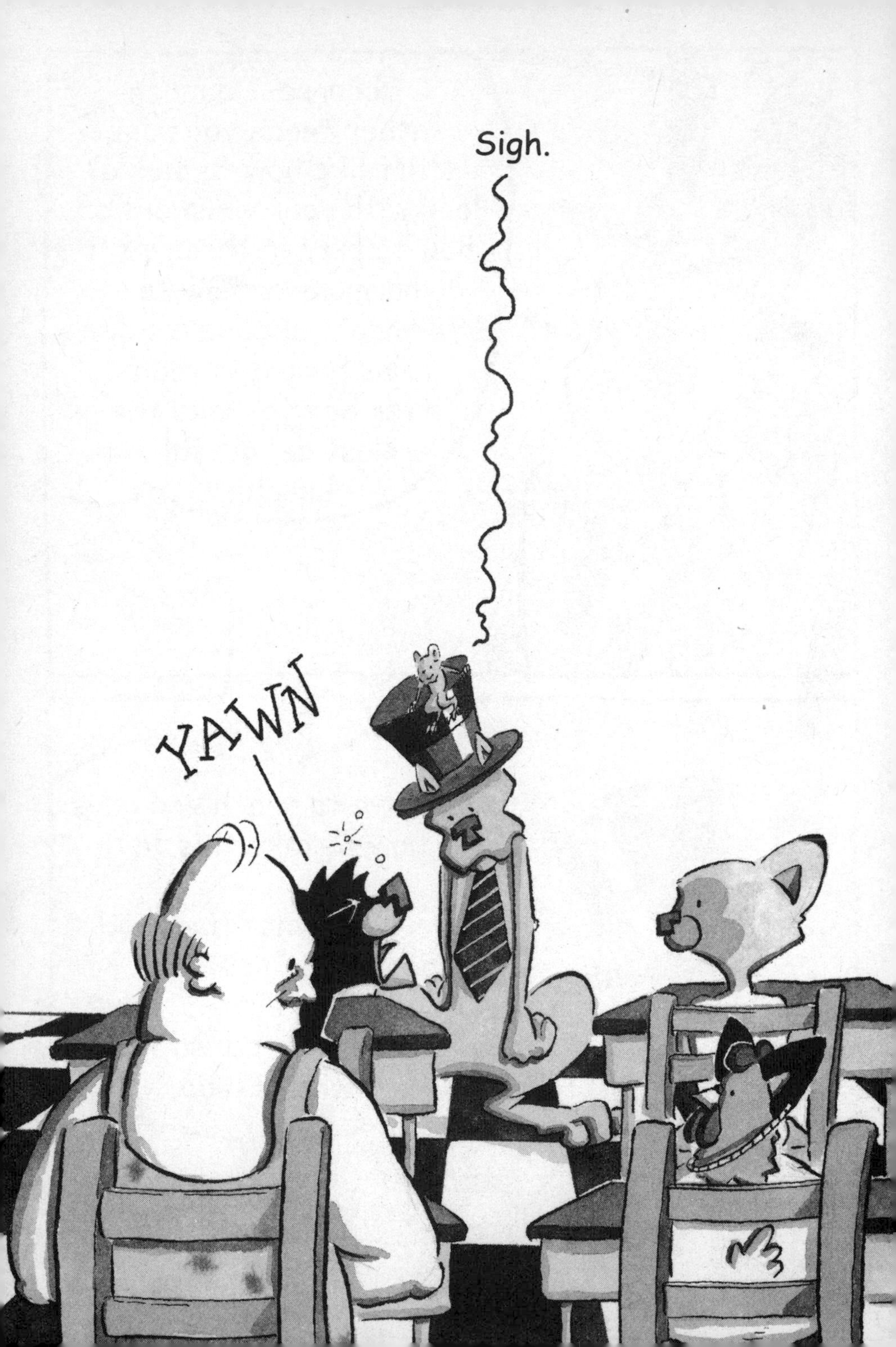
Sigh.
YAWN

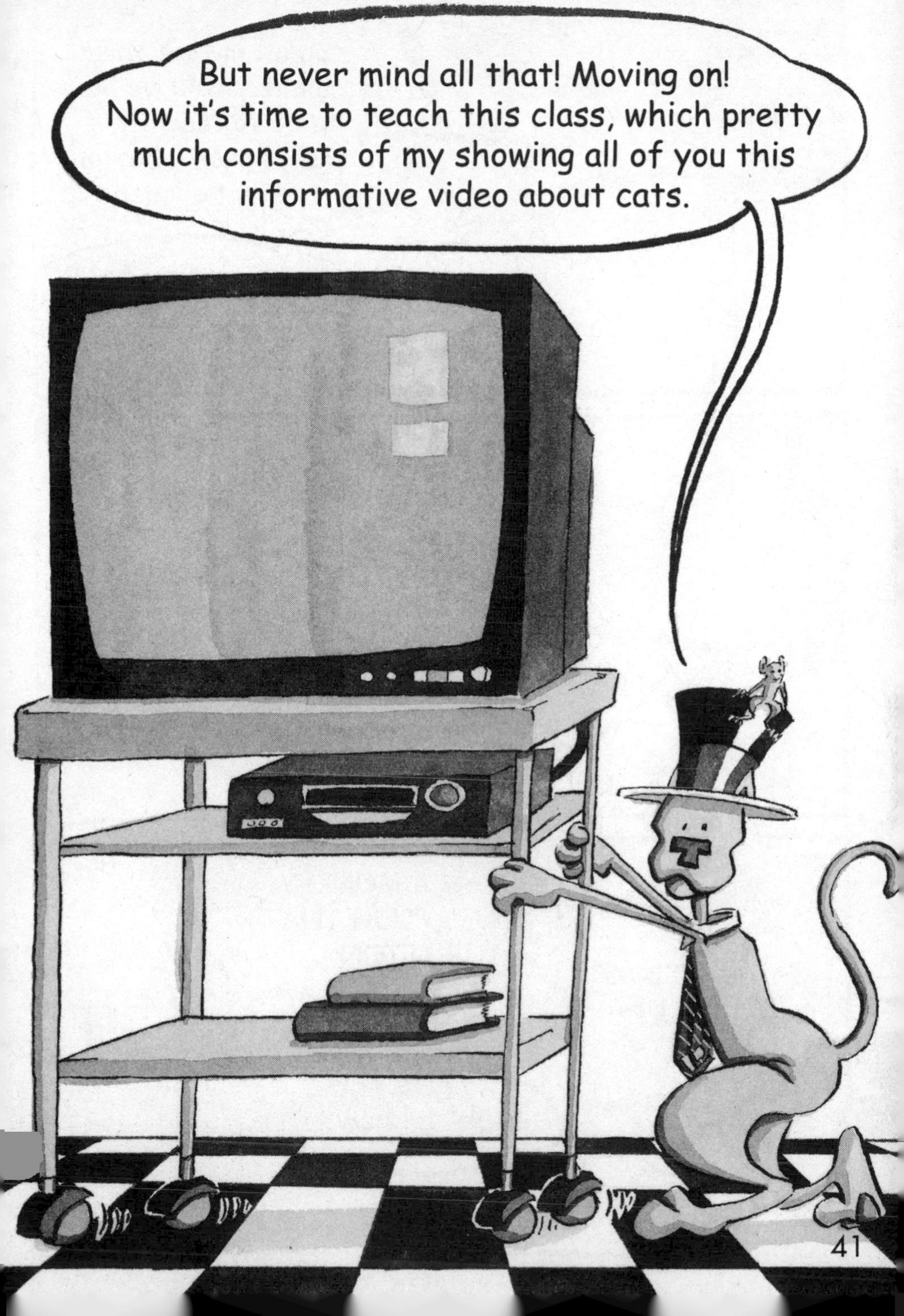
But never mind all that! Moving on! Now it's time to teach this class, which pretty much consists of my showing all of you this informative video about cats.

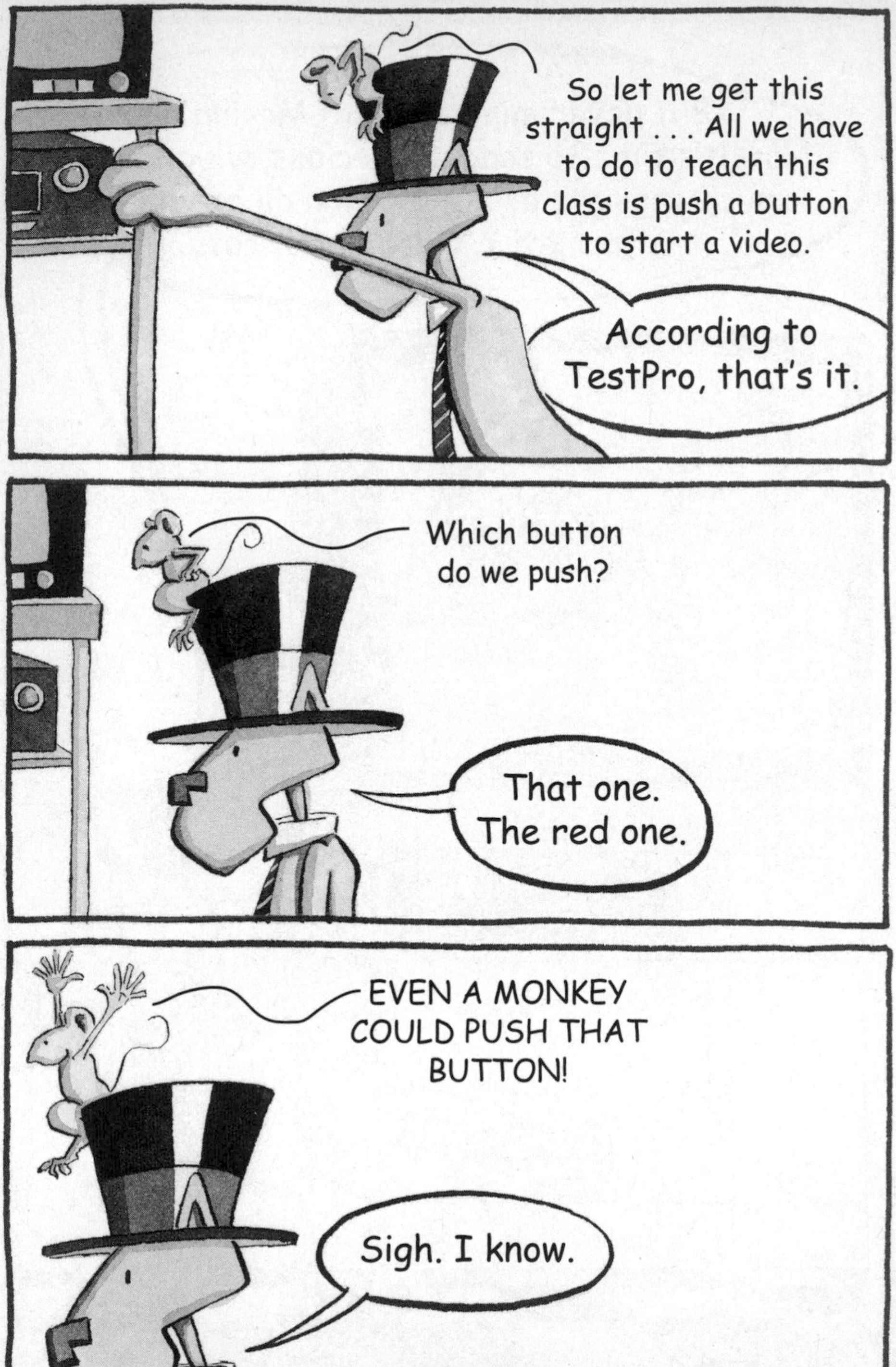
So let me get this straight . . . All we have to do to teach this class is push a button to start a video.
According to TestPro, that's it.
Which button do we push?
That one. The red one.
EVEN A MONKEY COULD PUSH THAT BUTTON!
Sigh. I know.

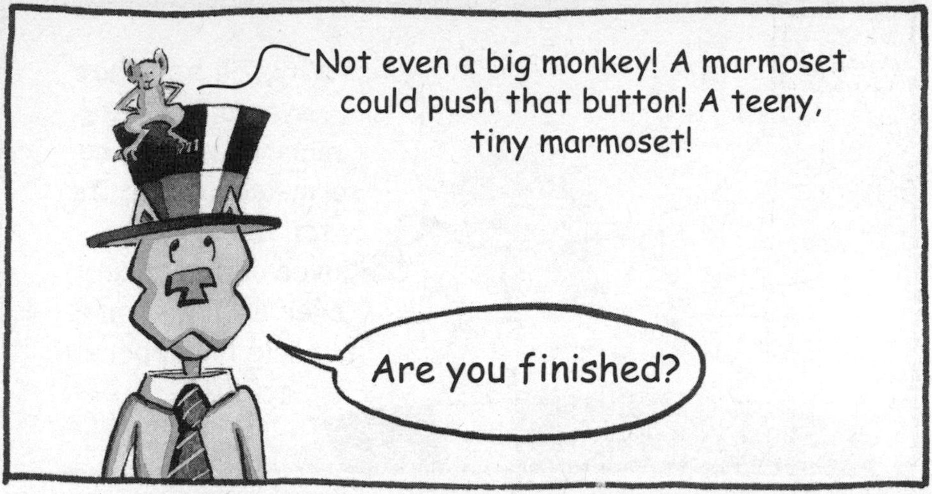
Not even a big monkey! A marmoset could push that button! A teeny, tiny marmoset!
Are you finished?

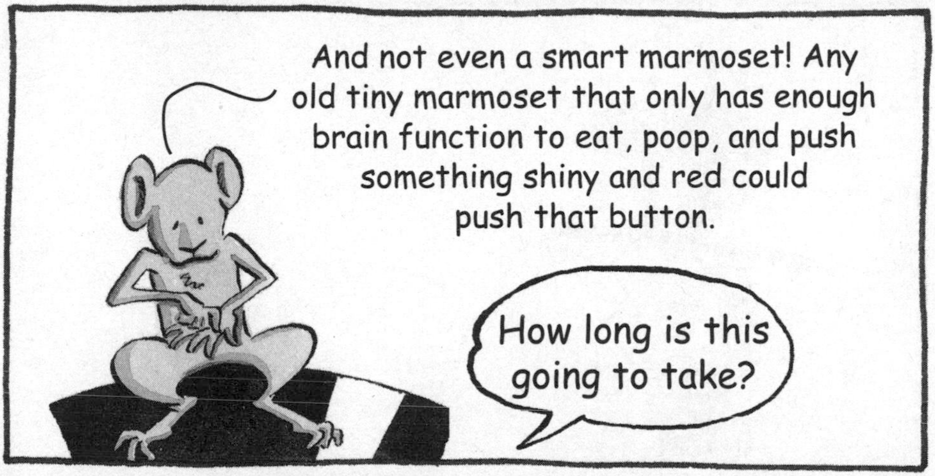
And not even a smart marmoset! Any old tiny marmoset that only has enough brain function to eat, poop, and push something shiny and red could push that button.
How long is this going to take?

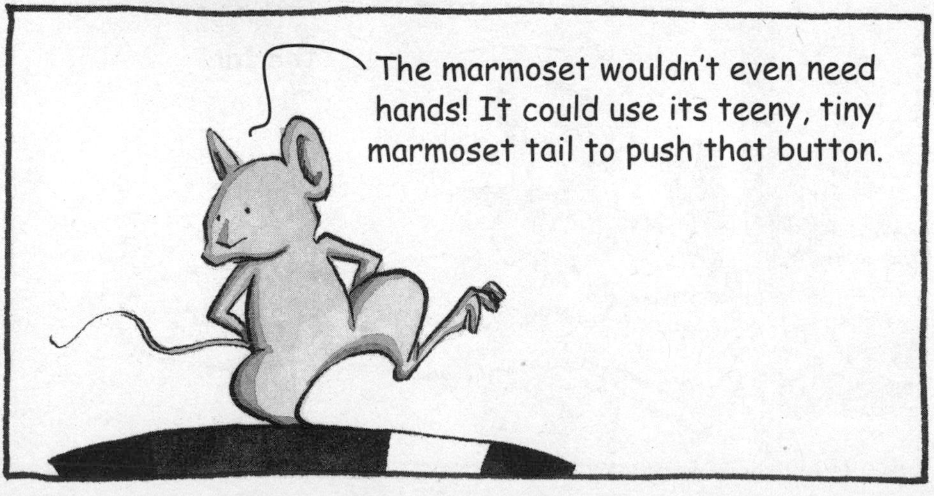
The marmoset wouldn't even need hands! It could use its teeny, tiny marmoset tail to push that button.

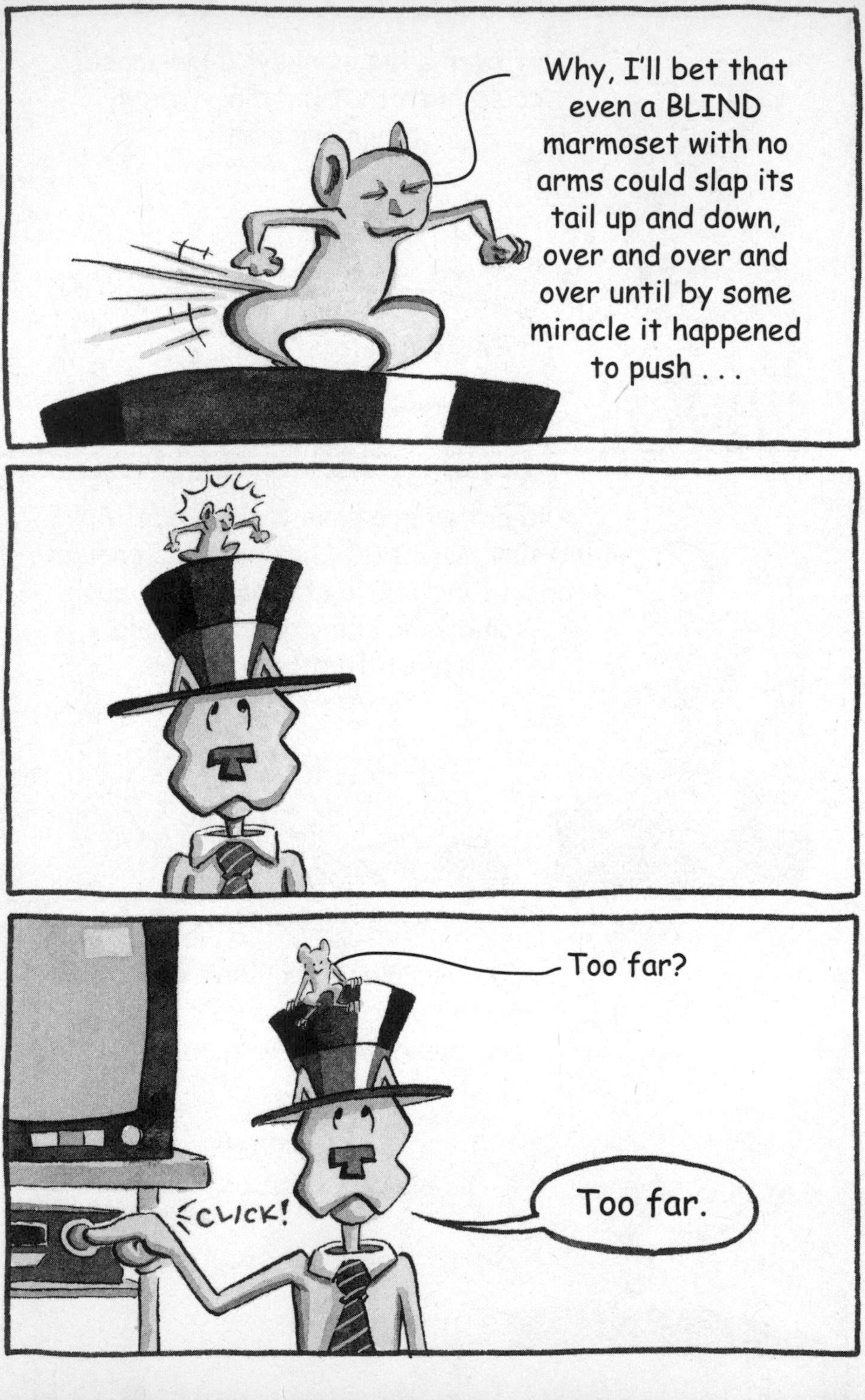
Why, I'll bet that even a BLIND marmoset with no arms could slap its tail up and down, over and over and over until by some miracle it happened to push . . .
Too far?
CLICK!
Too far.

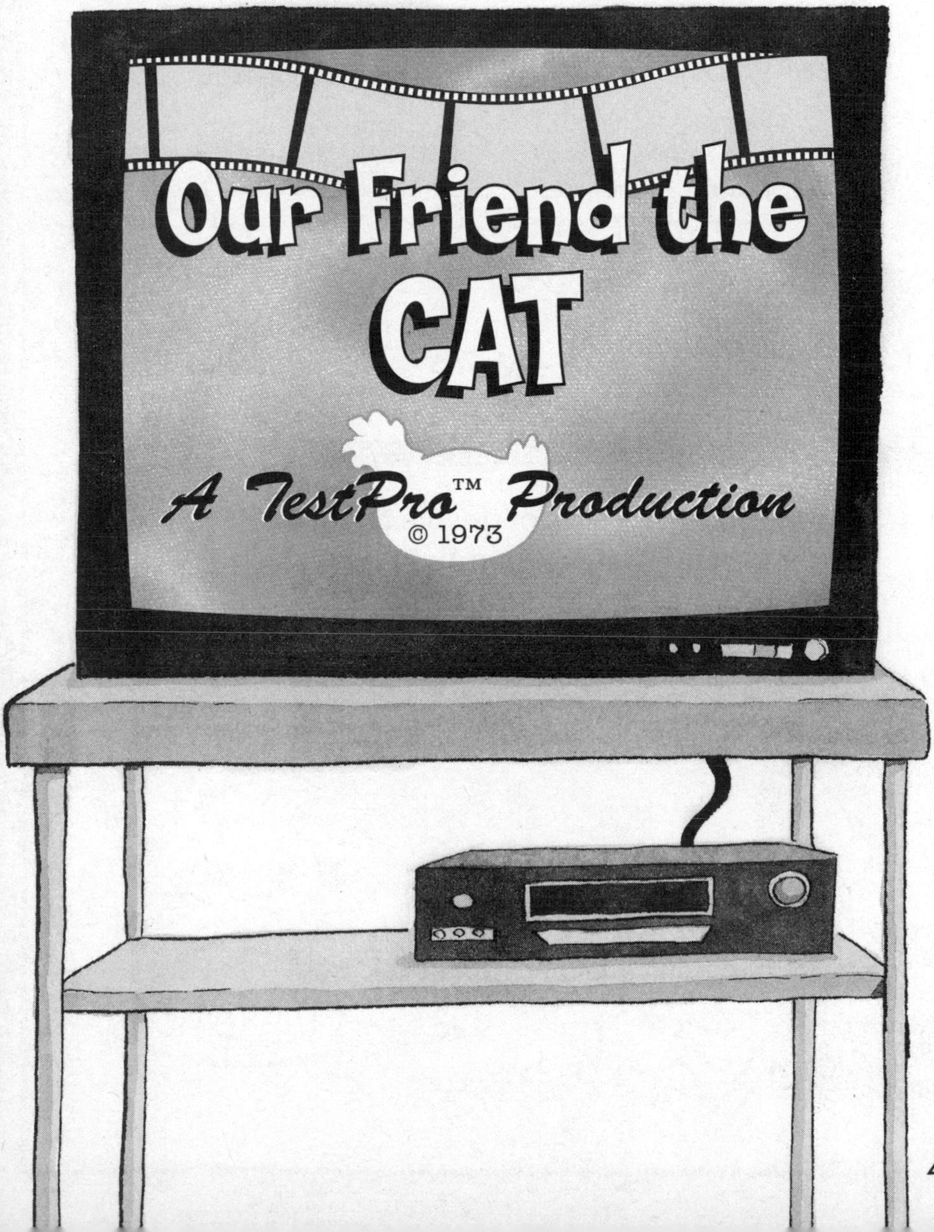
Our Friend the
CAT
A TestPro™ Production
© 1973

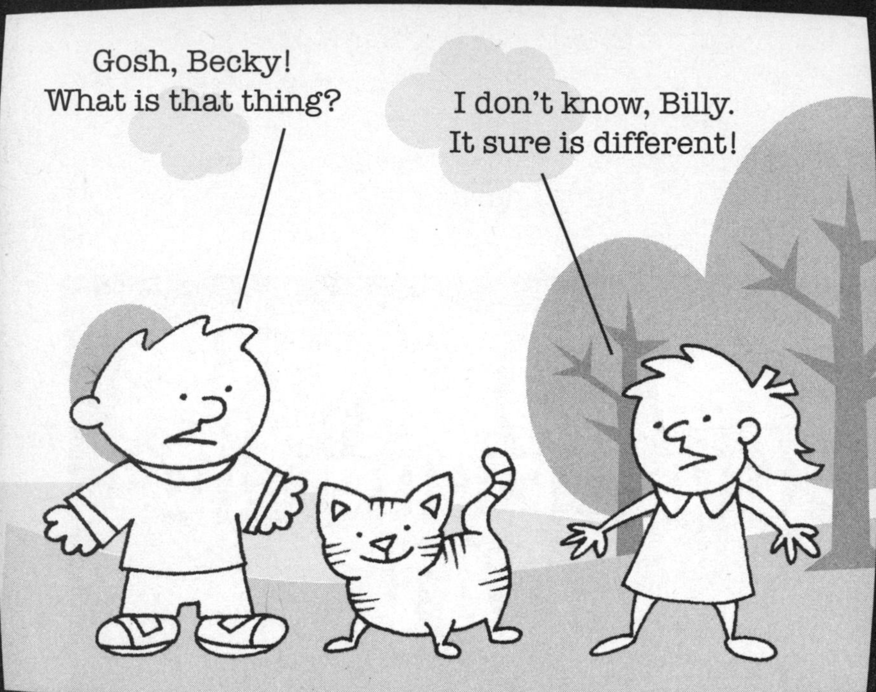
Gosh, Becky!
What is that thing?
I don't know, Billy.
It sure is different!

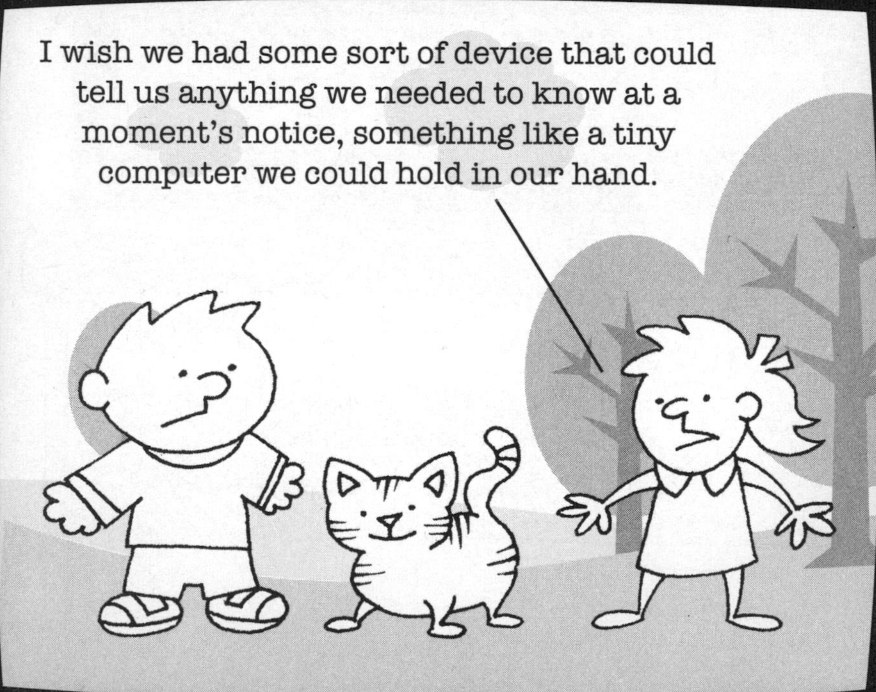
I wish we had some sort of device that could tell us anything we needed to know at a moment's notice, something like a tiny computer we could hold in our hand.

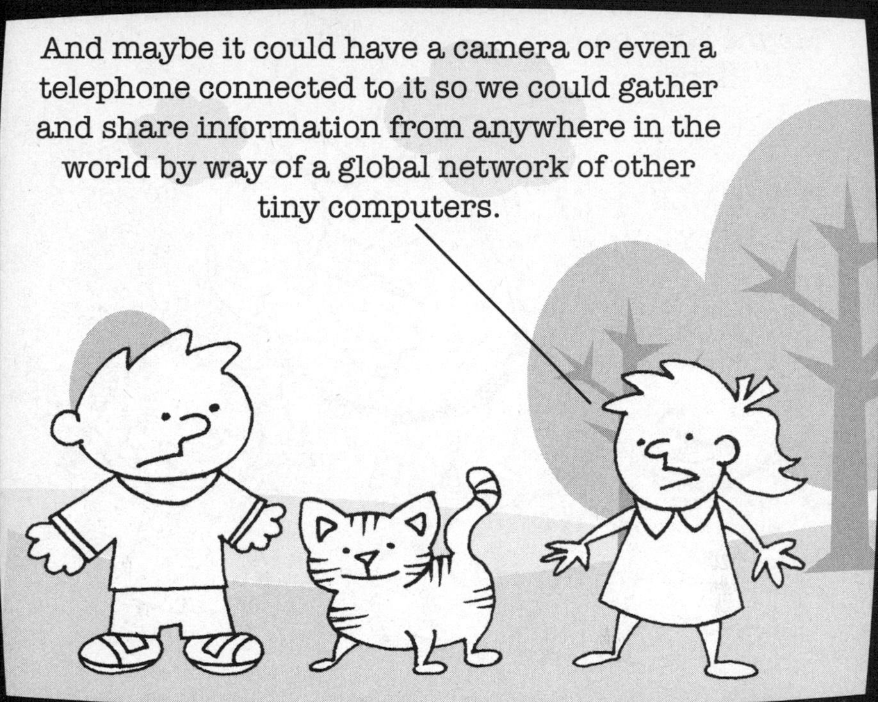
And maybe it could have a camera or even a telephone connected to it so we could gather and share information from anywhere in the world by way of a global network of other tiny computers.

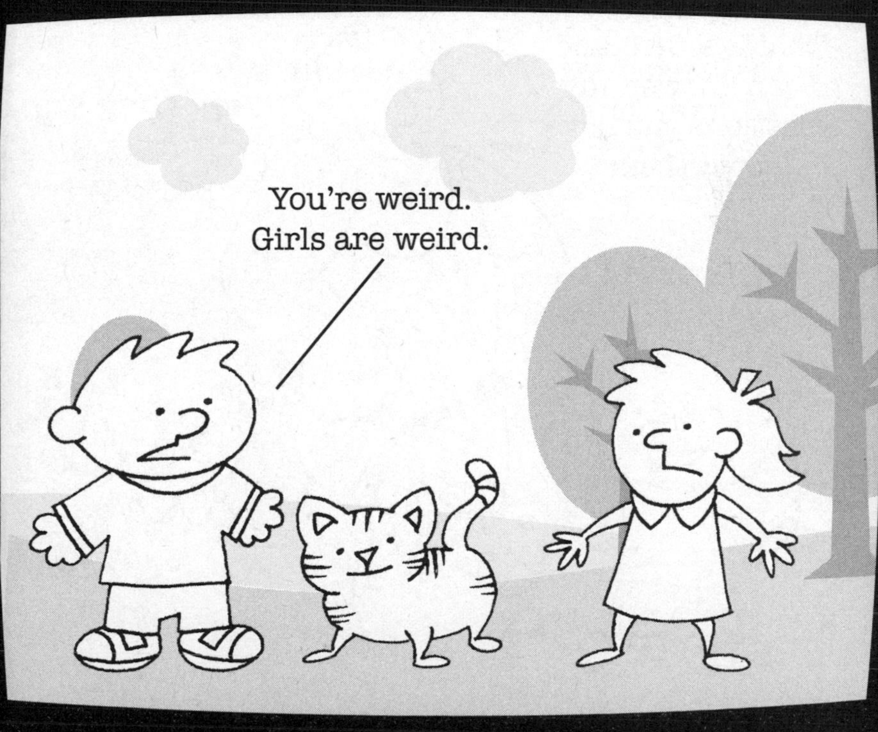
You're weird.
Girls are weird.

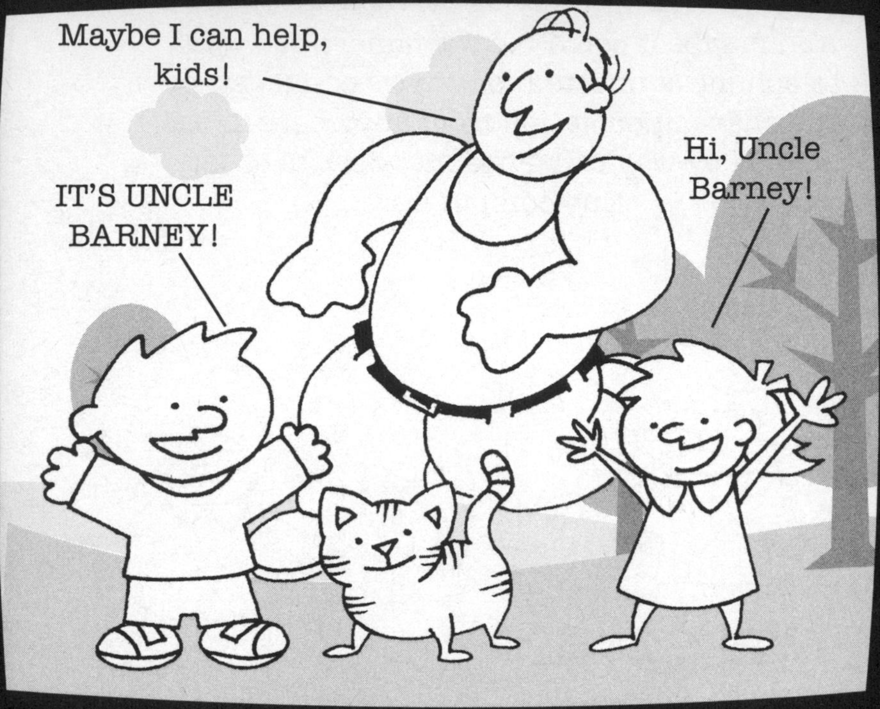
Maybe I can help, kids!
IT'S UNCLE BARNEY!
Hi, Uncle Barney!

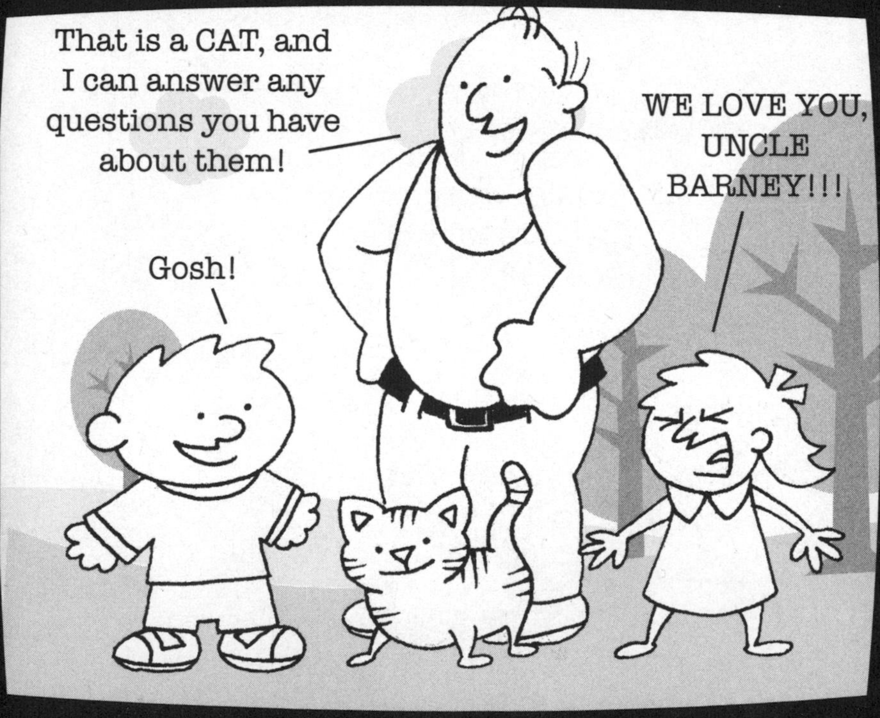
That is a CAT, and I can answer any questions you have about them!
WE LOVE YOU, UNCLE BARNEY!!!
Gosh!

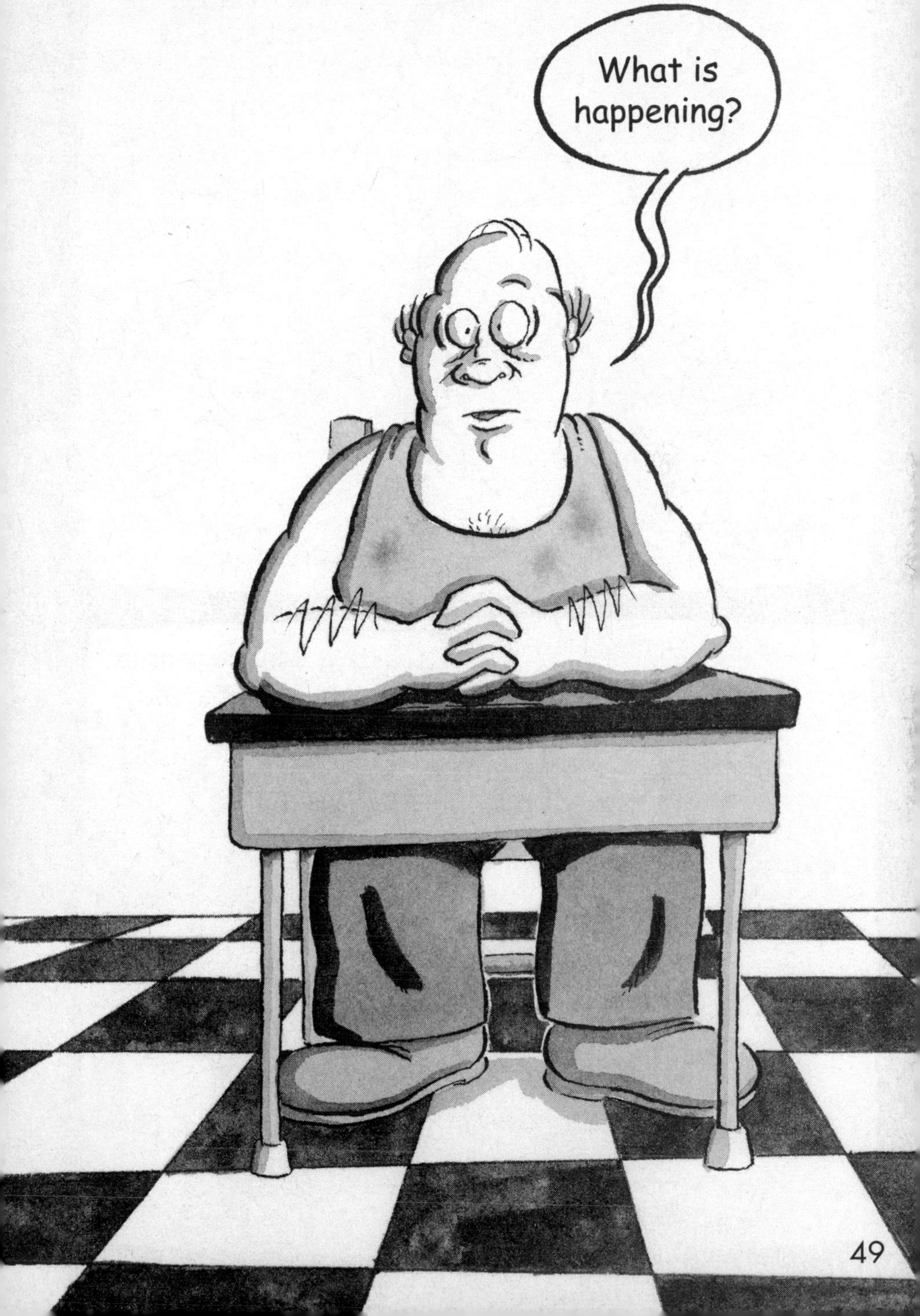
What is happening?

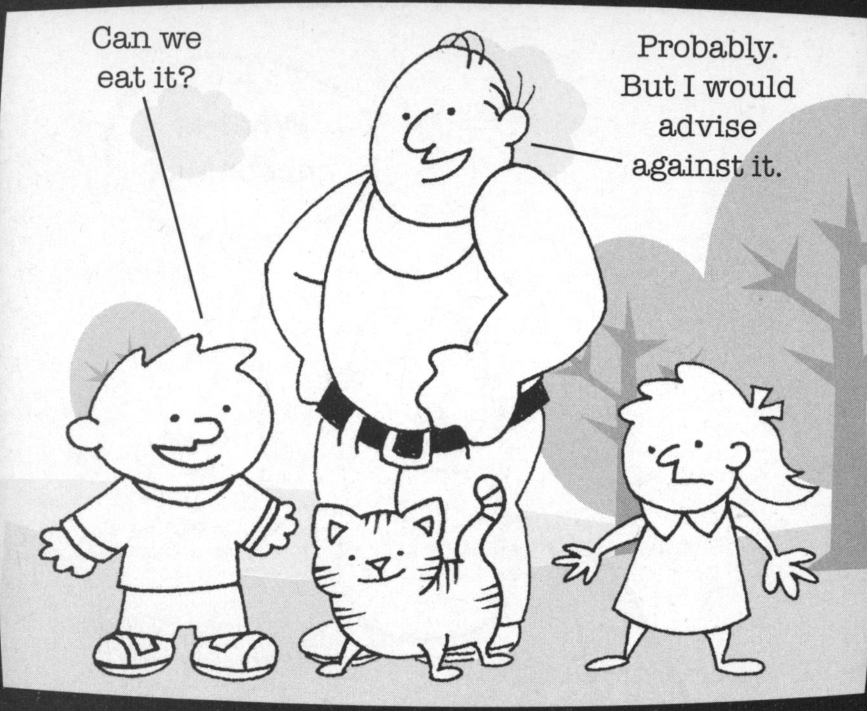
Can we eat it?
Probably. But I would advise against it.

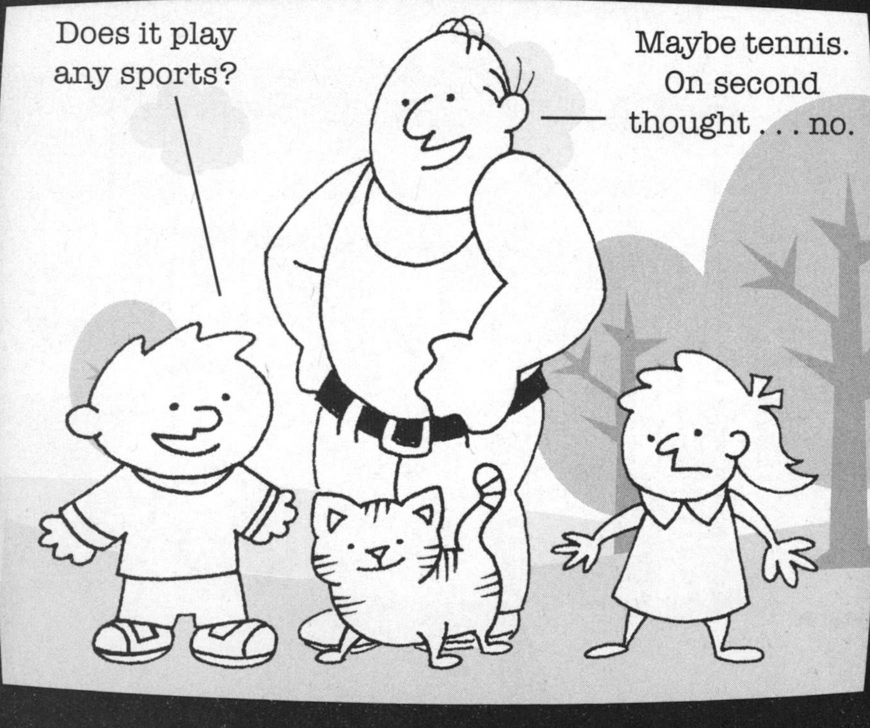
Does it play any sports?
Maybe tennis. On second thought . . . no.

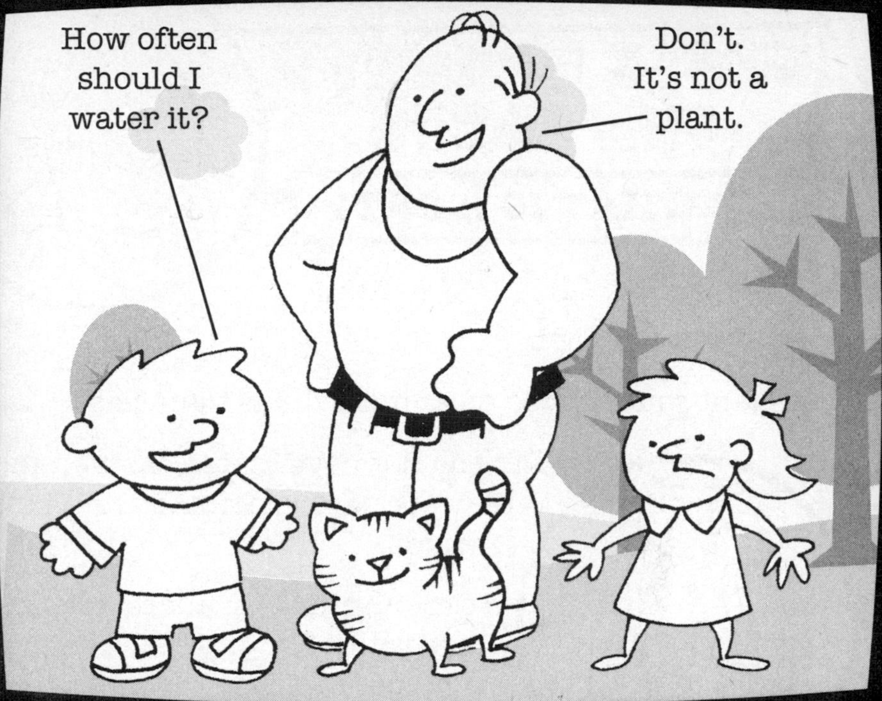
How often should I water it?
Don't. It's not a plant.

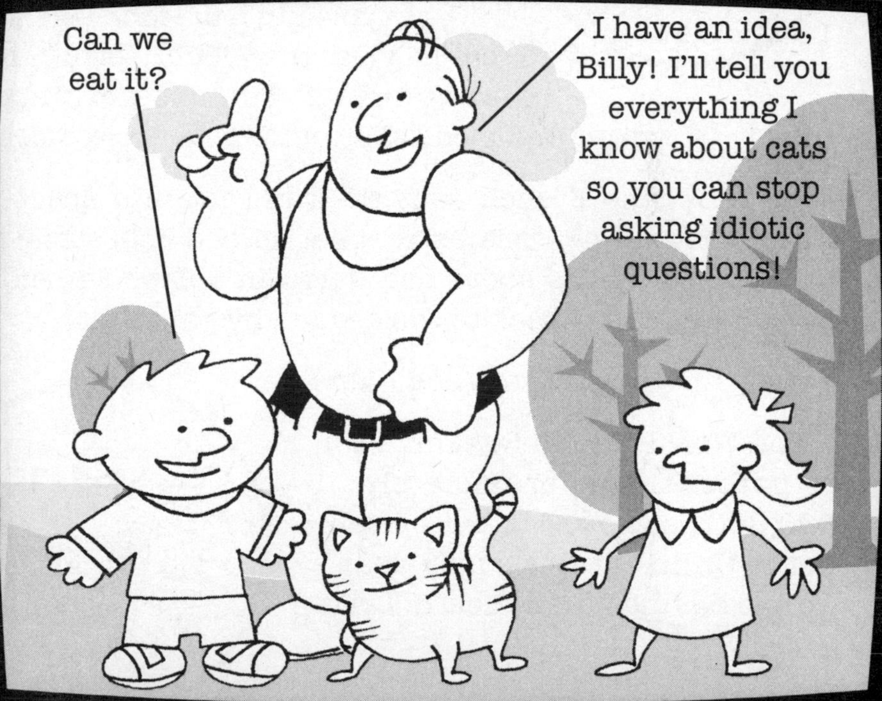
Can we eat it?
I have an idea, Billy! I'll tell you everything I know about cats so you can stop asking idiotic questions!

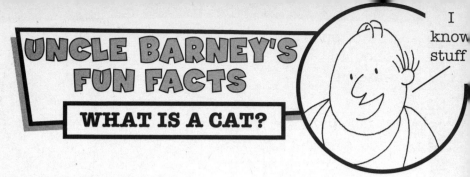

UNCLE BARNEY'S FUN FACTS

WHAT IS A CAT?

I know stuff

- A cat is an animal.

- A giant squid is also an animal. It has tentacles.

NOT A CAT

- Cats do not have tentacles, therefore they are rarely mistaken for giant squids.

- Other animals that are not cats are squirrels, giraffes, lobsters, and porcupines.

- Cats typically have four legs. If a cat has less than four legs or more than four legs, then something is wrong and medical attention may be required.

- In 1963, the French sent the first cat into space, a black-and-white Parisian street cat named Félicette who traveled 100 miles above the Earth in a capsule before descending safely back to the ground by parachute.

- "Cat" in Vietnamese is *con mèo*.

- The World Health Organization estimates that approximately 400,000 people are bitten by cats in the United States every year. No one has died from their injuries.

- "Cat" in Swahili is *paka*.

• Legend has it that Sir Isaac Newton, the scientist and mathematician who discovered gravitational mechanics and created calculus, also invented the cat flap on doors because he was tired of constantly getting up from his experiments to let his cat, Spithead, in and out of his study.

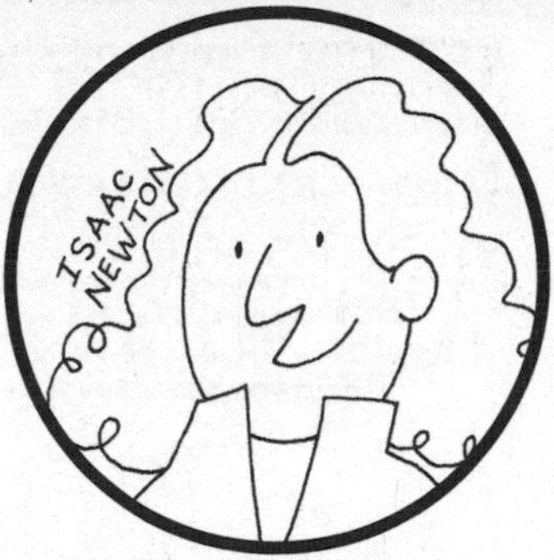
ISAAC NEWTON

• That's right . . . Sir Isaac Newton named his cat Spithead.

• "Cat" in Icelandic is *köttur*.

• "Cat" spelled backward is "tac," which are the first three letters in the word "taco," which is a delicious food that cats will sometimes eat when dropped on the floor.

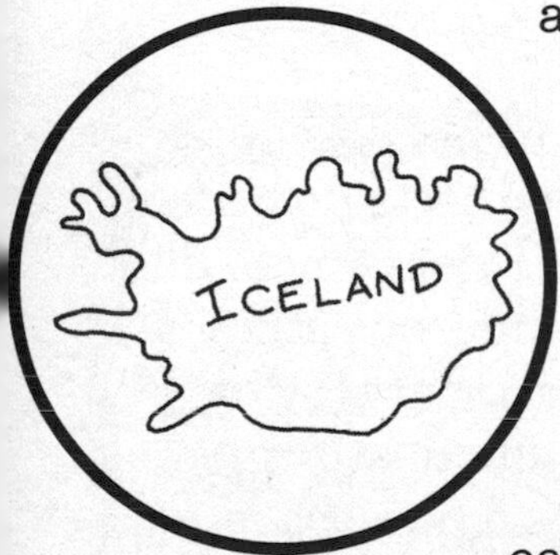
ICELAND

• In the early 1960s, the CIA launched Operation Acoustic Kitty, an actual plan to use cats as spies. Cats would be trained to eavesdrop on Russian conversations. They would be released nearby with microphones implanted in their ears, transmitters attached to their collars, and antennae tied to their tails. The first cat agent was deployed and then run over by a taxi moments later. Twenty million dollars was spent on the program that was terminated shortly thereafter.

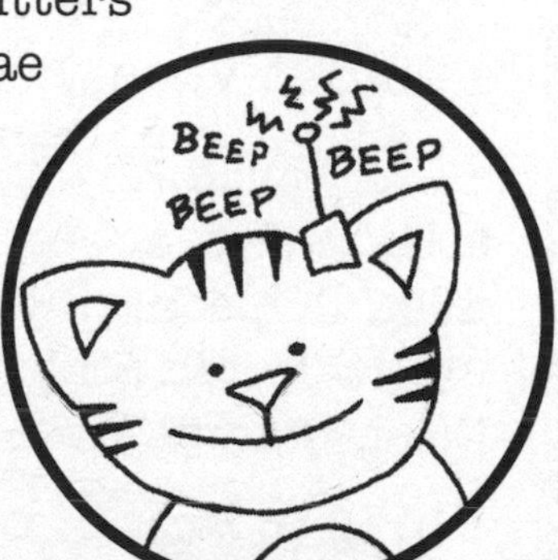
BEEP
BEEP
BEEP

• Spithead.

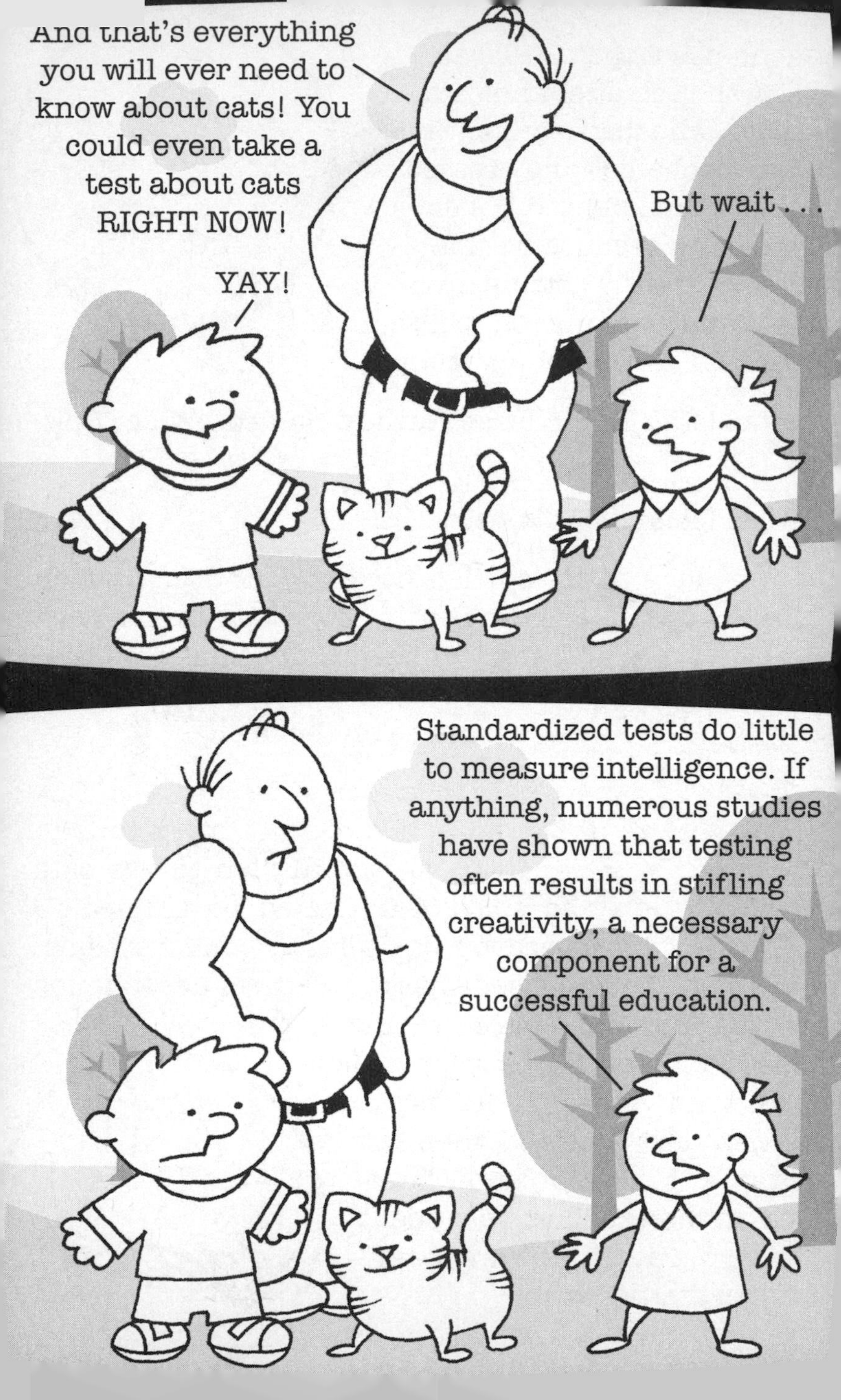
And that's everything you will ever need to know about cats! You could even take a test about cats RIGHT NOW!
YAY!
But wait . . .
Standardized tests do little to measure intelligence. If anything, numerous studies have shown that testing often results in stifling creativity, a necessary component for a successful education.

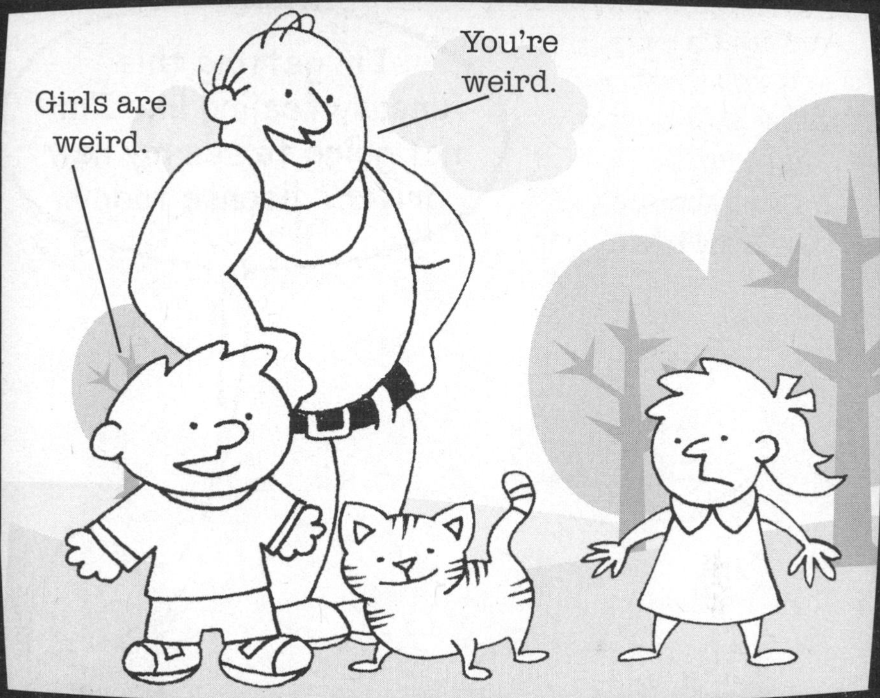
Girls are weird.
You're weird.

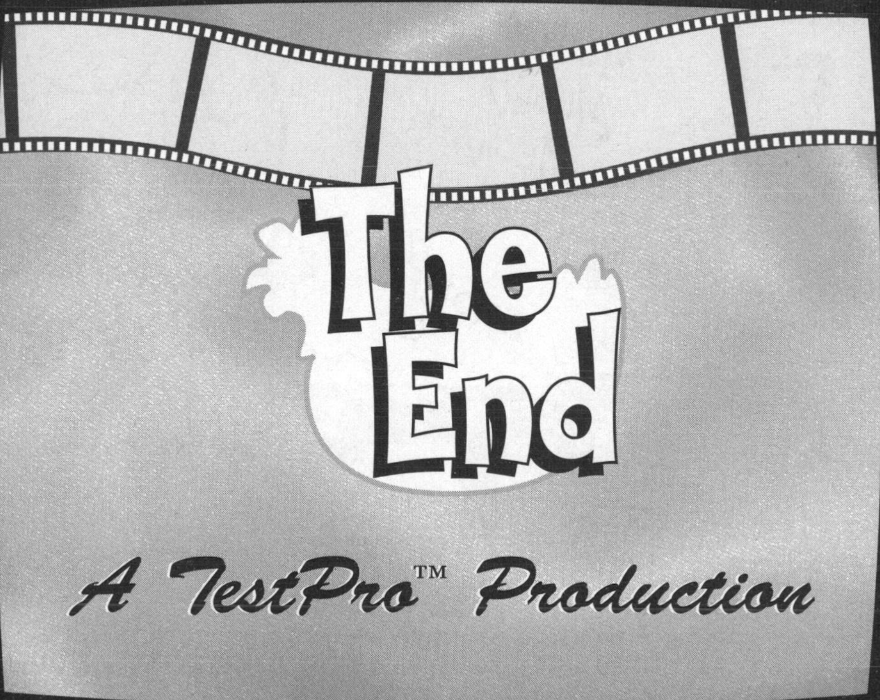
The End
A TestPro™ Production

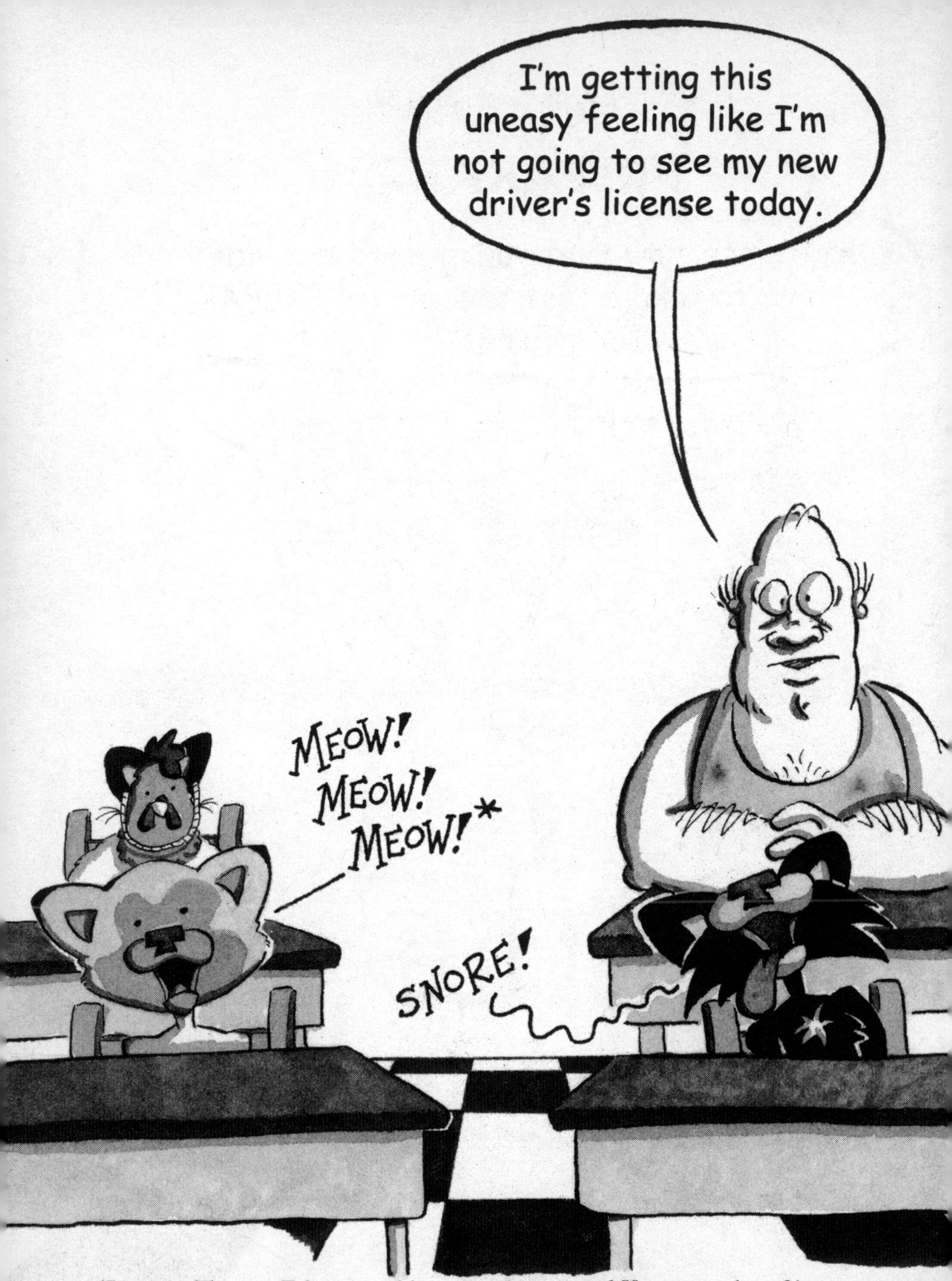
I'm getting this uneasy feeling like I'm not going to see my new driver's license today.
MEOW! MEOW! MEOW!*
SNORE!

*In 1894, Thomas Edison used his recently invented Kinetograph to film two cats boxing. It is considered to be the very first cat video. I hope THAT'S on the test!

•CHAPTER FOUR•

PREPARATION

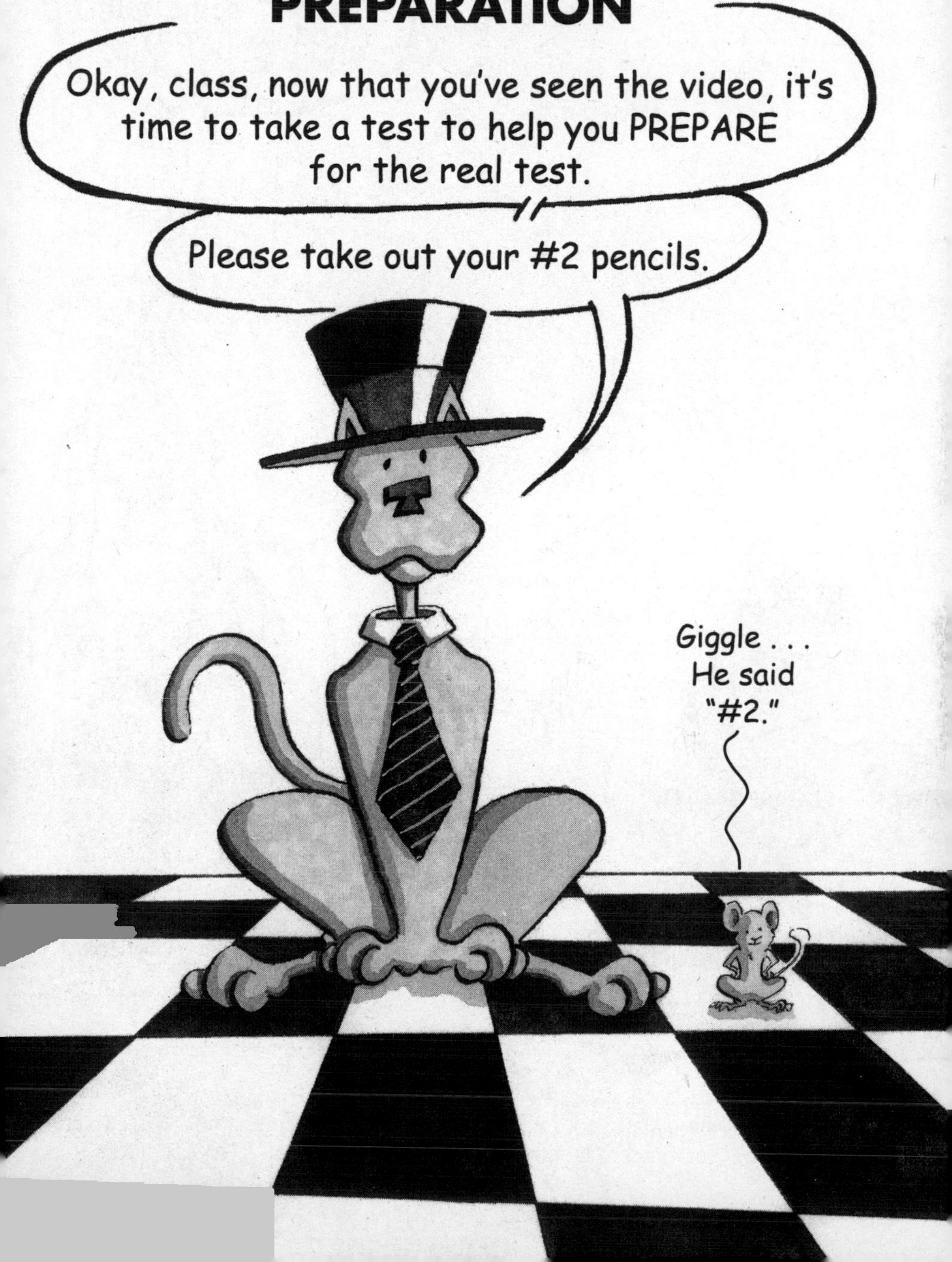
Okay, class, now that you've seen the video, it's time to take a test to help you PREPARE for the real test.
Please take out your #2 pencils.
Giggle . . . He said "#2."

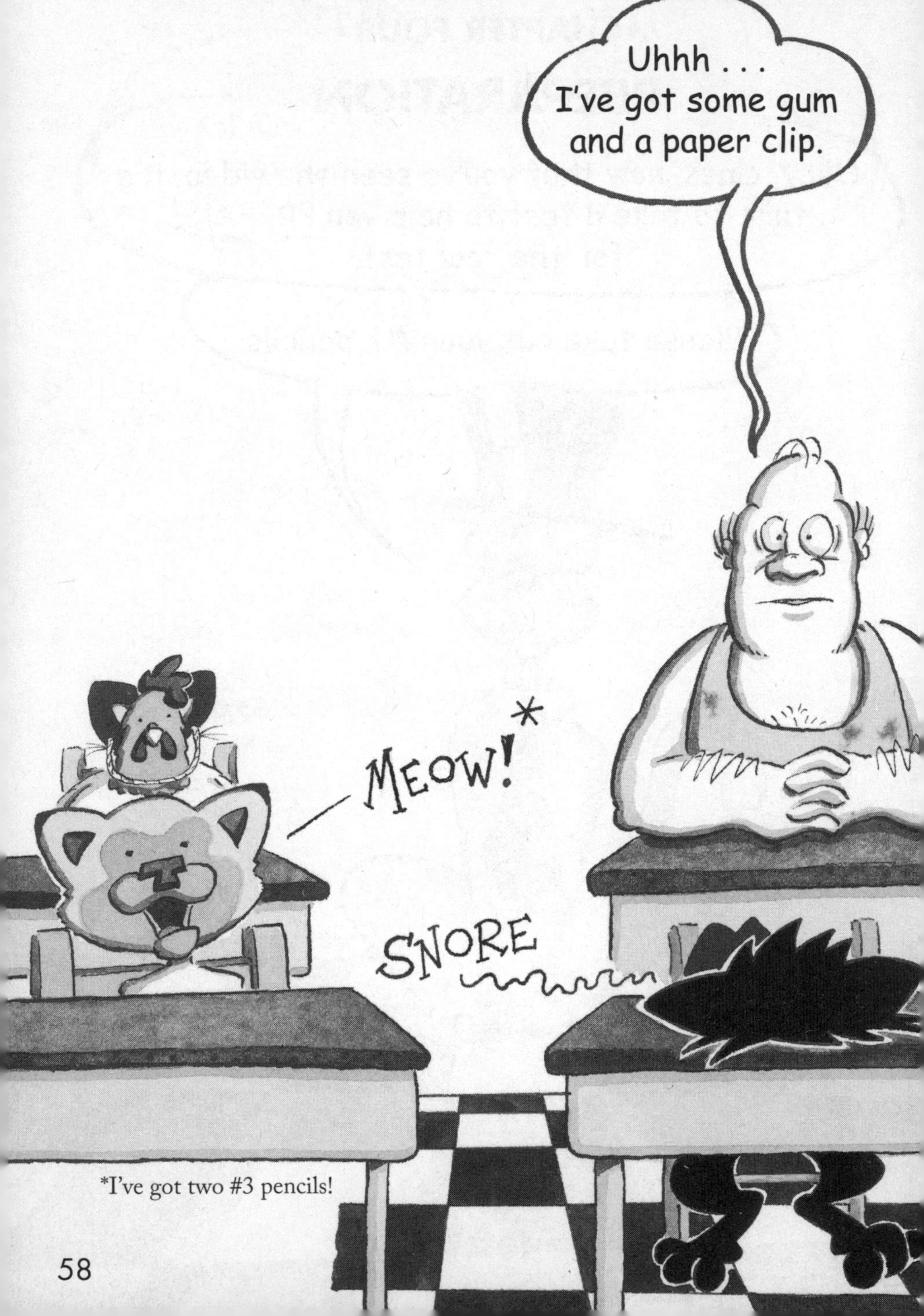
Uhhh . . .
I've got some gum and a paper clip.
MEOW!*
SNORE

*I've got two #3 pencils!

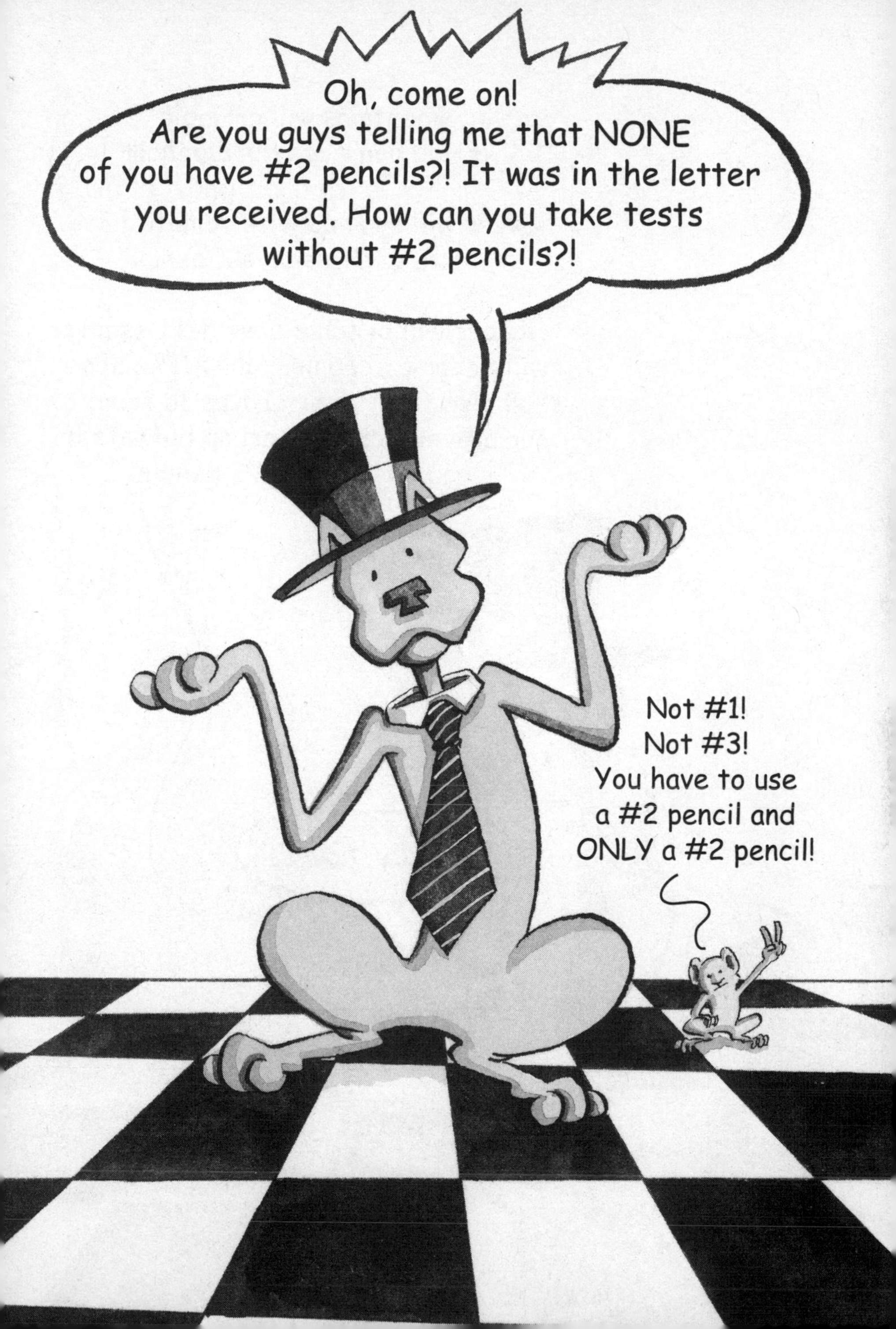
Oh, come on! Are you guys telling me that NONE of you have #2 pencils?! It was in the letter you received. How can you take tests without #2 pencils?!
Not #1! Not #3! You have to use a #2 pencil and ONLY a #2 pencil!

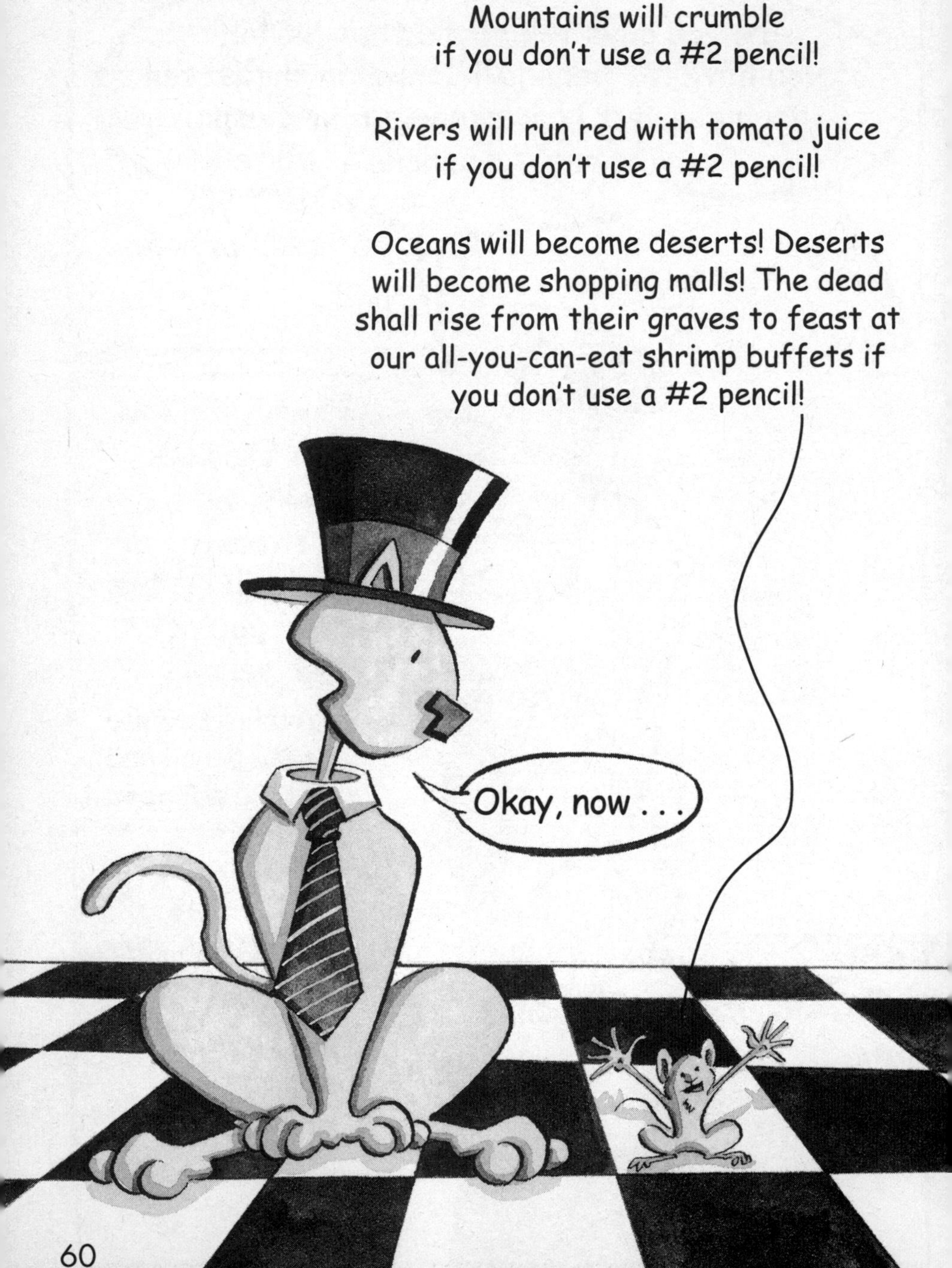
Mountains will crumble if you don't use a #2 pencil!
Rivers will run red with tomato juice if you don't use a #2 pencil!
Oceans will become deserts! Deserts will become shopping malls! The dead shall rise from their graves to feast at our all-you-can-eat shrimp buffets if you don't use a #2 pencil!
Okay, now . . .

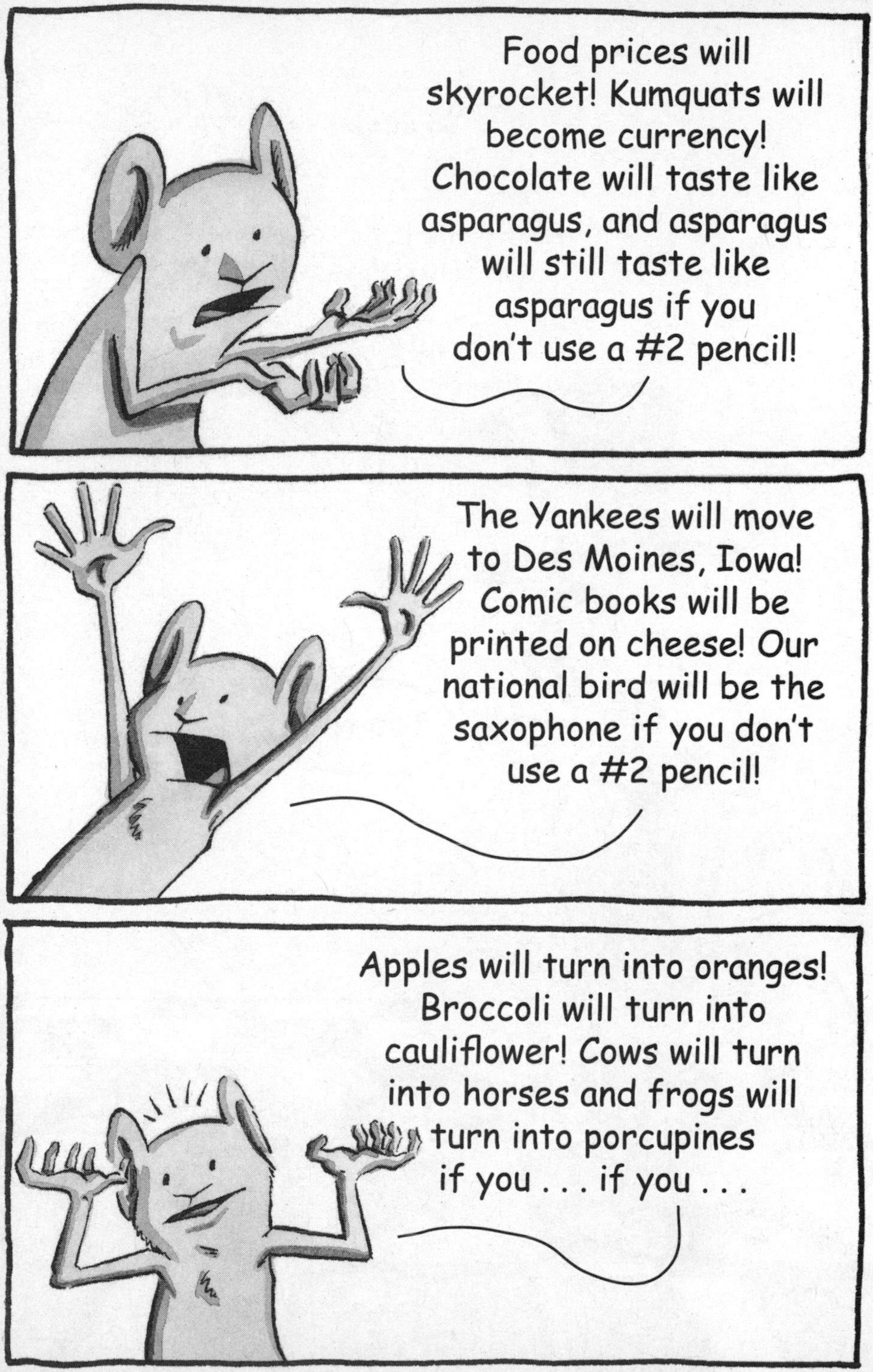
Food prices will skyrocket! Kumquats will become currency! Chocolate will taste like asparagus, and asparagus will still taste like asparagus if you don't use a #2 pencil!
The Yankees will move to Des Moines, Iowa! Comic books will be printed on cheese! Our national bird will be the saxophone if you don't use a #2 pencil!
Apples will turn into oranges! Broccoli will turn into cauliflower! Cows will turn into horses and frogs will turn into porcupines if you . . . if you . . .

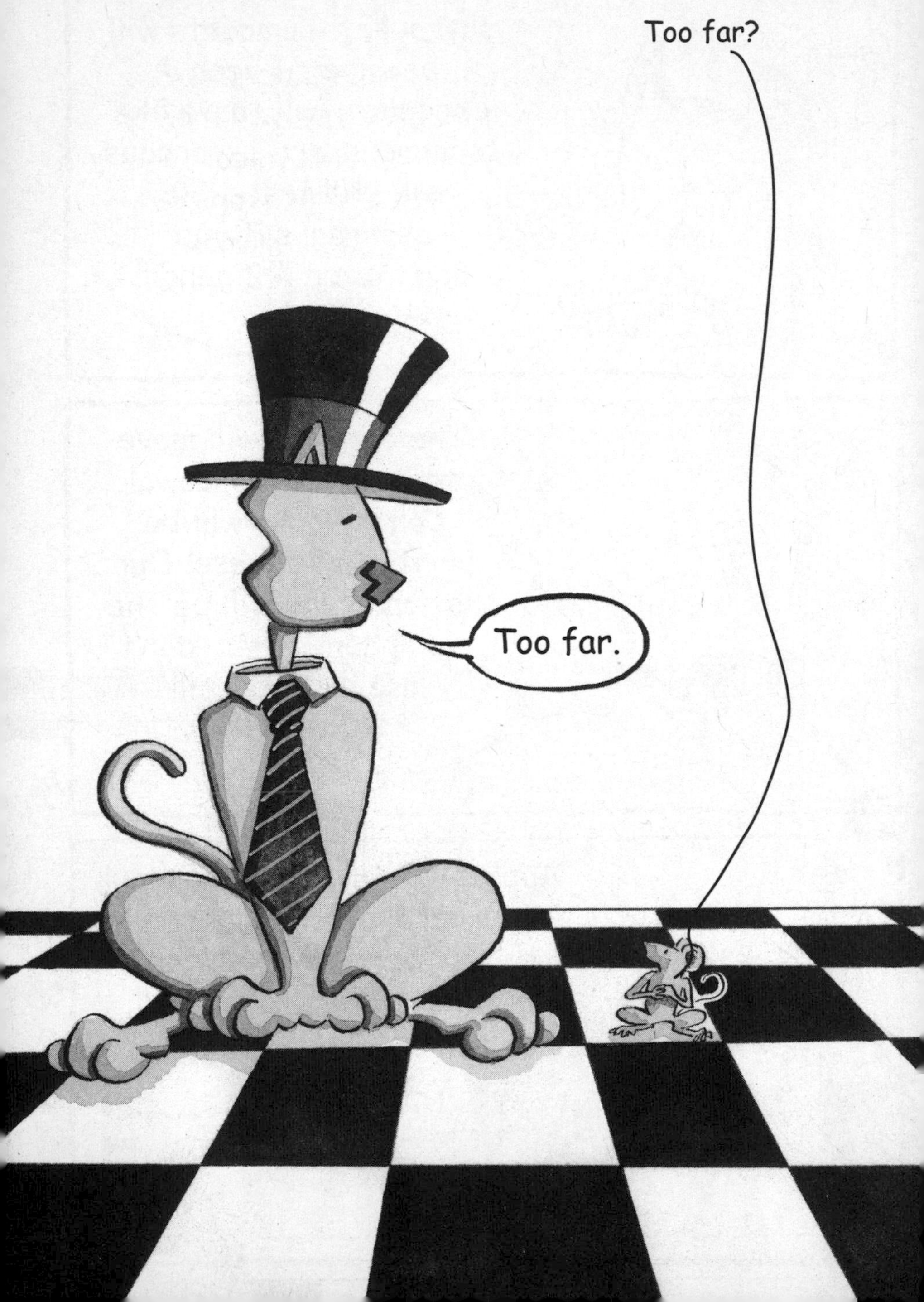
Too far?
Too far.

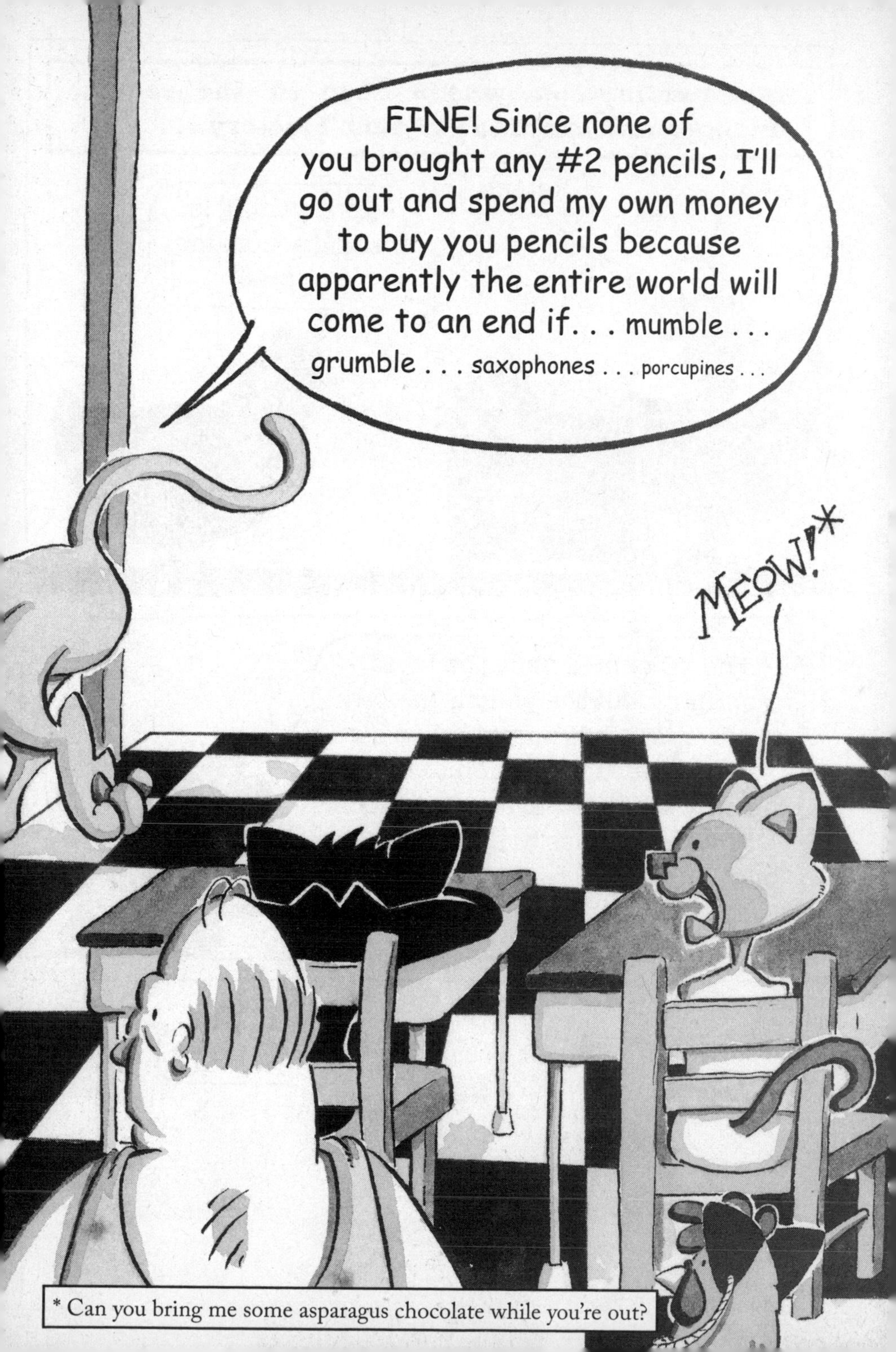
FINE! Since none of you brought any #2 pencils, I'll go out and spend my own money to buy you pencils because apparently the entire world will come to an end if. . . mumble . . . grumble . . . saxophones . . . porcupines . . .
MEOW!*

* Can you bring me some asparagus chocolate while you're out?

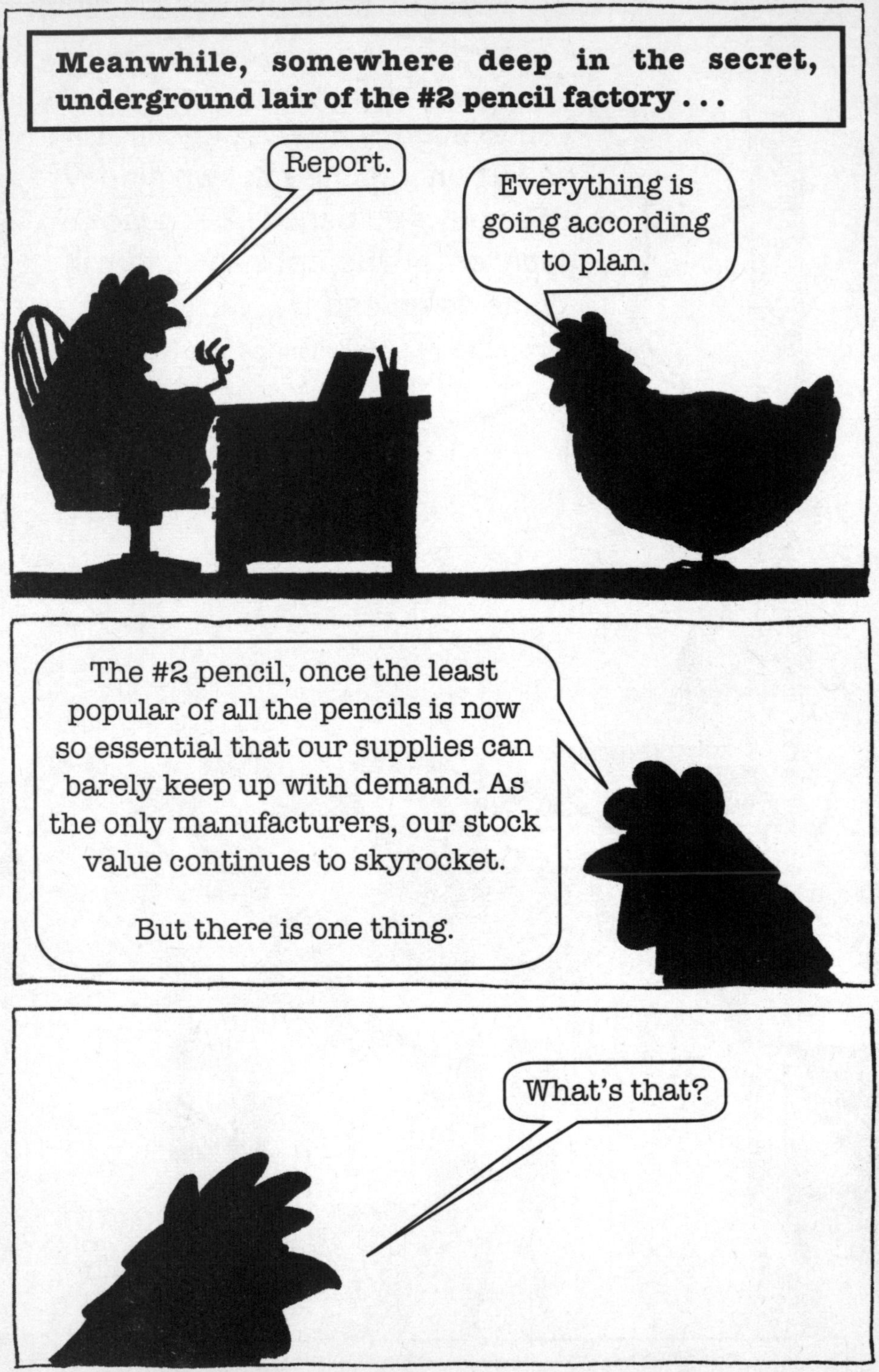

Meanwhile, somewhere deep in the secret, underground lair of the #2 pencil factory . . .
Report.
Everything is going according to plan.
The #2 pencil, once the least popular of all the pencils is now so essential that our supplies can barely keep up with demand. As the only manufacturers, our stock value continues to skyrocket.
But there is one thing.
What's that?

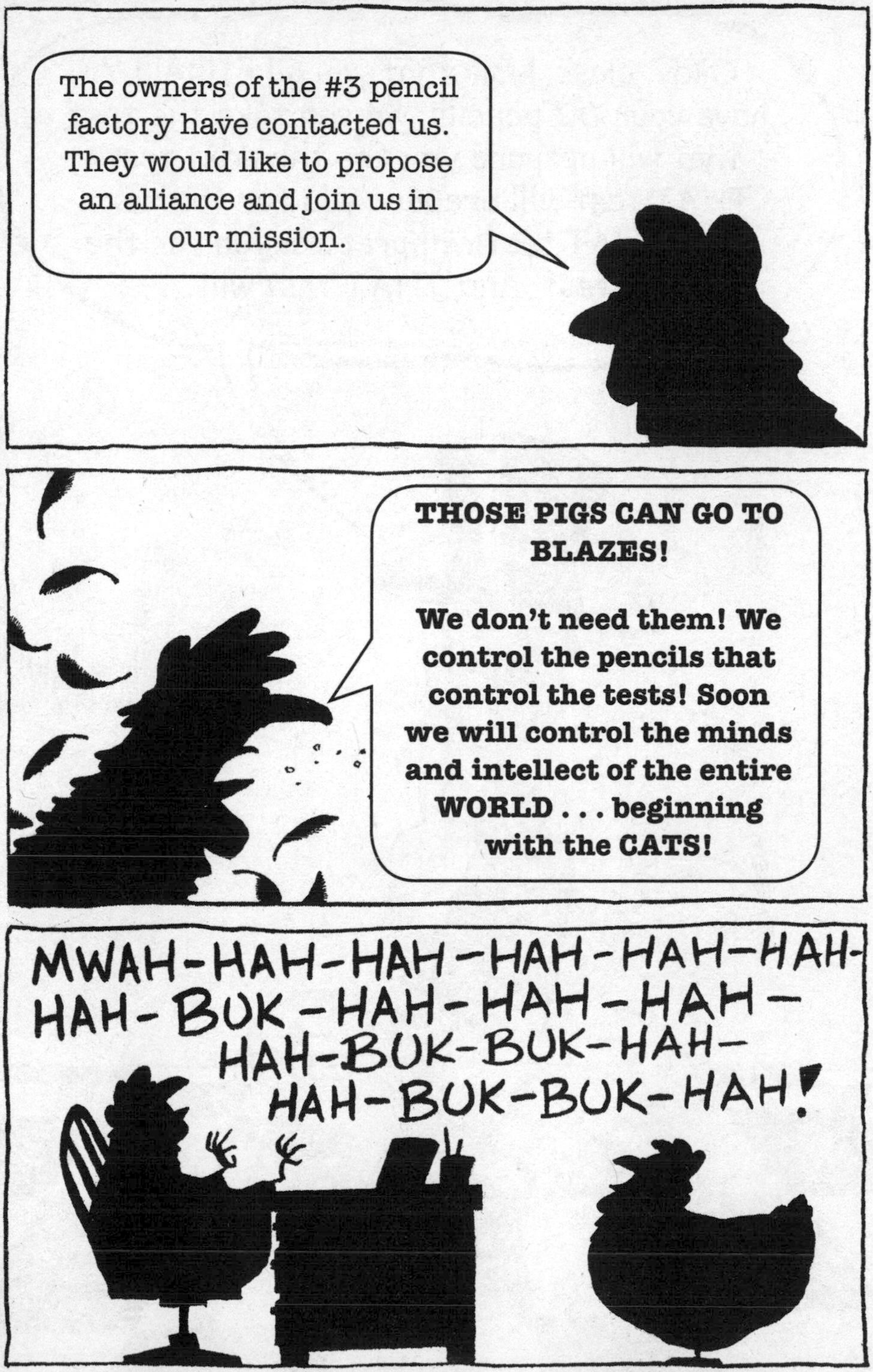

The owners of the #3 pencil factory have contacted us. They would like to propose an alliance and join us in our mission.
THOSE PIGS CAN GO TO BLAZES!
We don't need them! We control the pencils that control the tests! Soon we will control the minds and intellect of the entire WORLD . . . beginning with the CATS!
MWAH-HAH-HAH-HAH-HAH-HAH-HAH-HAH-BUK-HAH-HAH-HAH-HAH-BUK-BUK-HAH-HAH-BUK-BUK-HAH!

Okay, class. Now that you all FINALLY have your #2 pencils, we can take the test that will prepare you for the next test. THAT test will prepare you for the next test. THAT test will prepare you for the next test. And THAT test will . . .

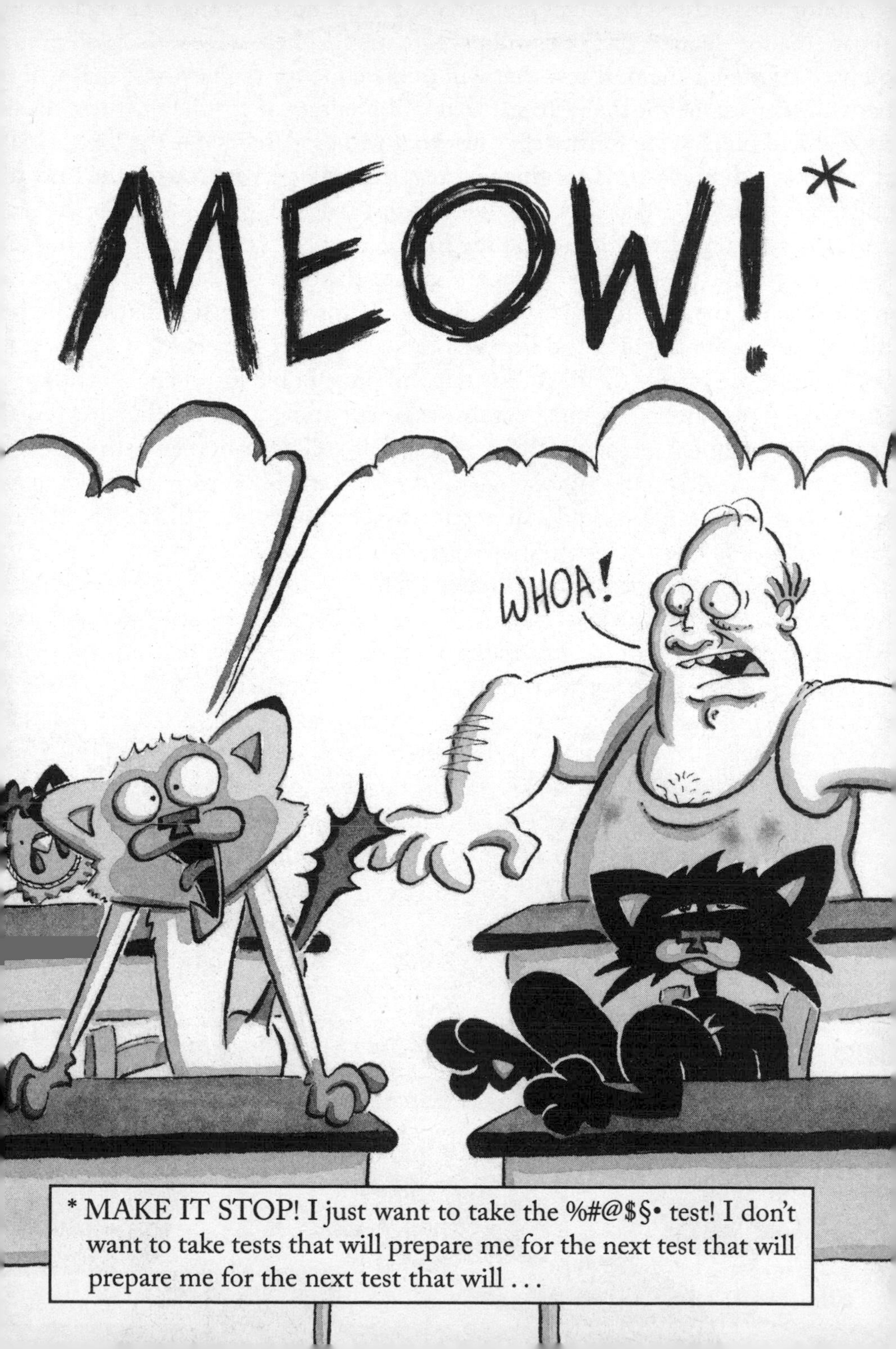
MEOW!*
WHOA!
* MAKE IT STOP! I just want to take the %#@$§• test! I don't want to take tests that will prepare me for the next test that will prepare me for the next test that will . . .

the next test that will prepare me for the next test that will prepare me for the n
for the next test that will prepare me for the next test that will prepare me for
me for the next test that will prepare me for the next test that will prepare me
epare me for the next test that will prepare me for the next test that will prepar
l prepare me for the next test that will prepare me for the next test that will pr
will prepare me for the next test that will prepare me for the next test that will
that will prepare me for the next test that will prepare me for the next test that
ext test that will prepare me for the next test that will prepare me for the next
he next test that will prepare me for the next test that will prepare me for the n
for the next test that will prepare me for the next test that will prepare me for
me for the next test that will prepare me for the next test that will prepare me
epare me for the next test that will prepare me for the next test that will prepar
l prepare me for the next test that will prepare me for the next test that will pr
will prepare me for the next test that will prepare me for the next test that will
that will prepare me for the next test that will prepare me for the next test that
ext test that will prepare me for the next test that will prepare me for the next
he next test that will prepare me for the next test that will prepare me for the n
for the next test that will prepare me for the next test that will prepare me for
me for the next test that will prepare me for the next test that will prepare me
epare me for the next test that will prepare me for the next test that will prepar
l prepare me for the next test that will prepare me for the next test that will pr
prepare me for the next test that will prepare me for the next test that will
that will prepare me for the next test that will prepare me for the next test that
ext test that will prepare me for the next test that will prepare me for the next
he next test that will prepare me for the next test that will prepare me for the n
for the next test that will prepare me for the next test that will prepare me for
me for the next test that will prepare me for the next test that will prepare me
epare me for the next test that will prepare me for the next test that will prepar
prepare me for the next test that will prepare me for the next test that will pr
will prepare me for the next test that

MEOW! MEOW!
MEOW!
MEOW!
EOW! MEOW!
MEOW! *

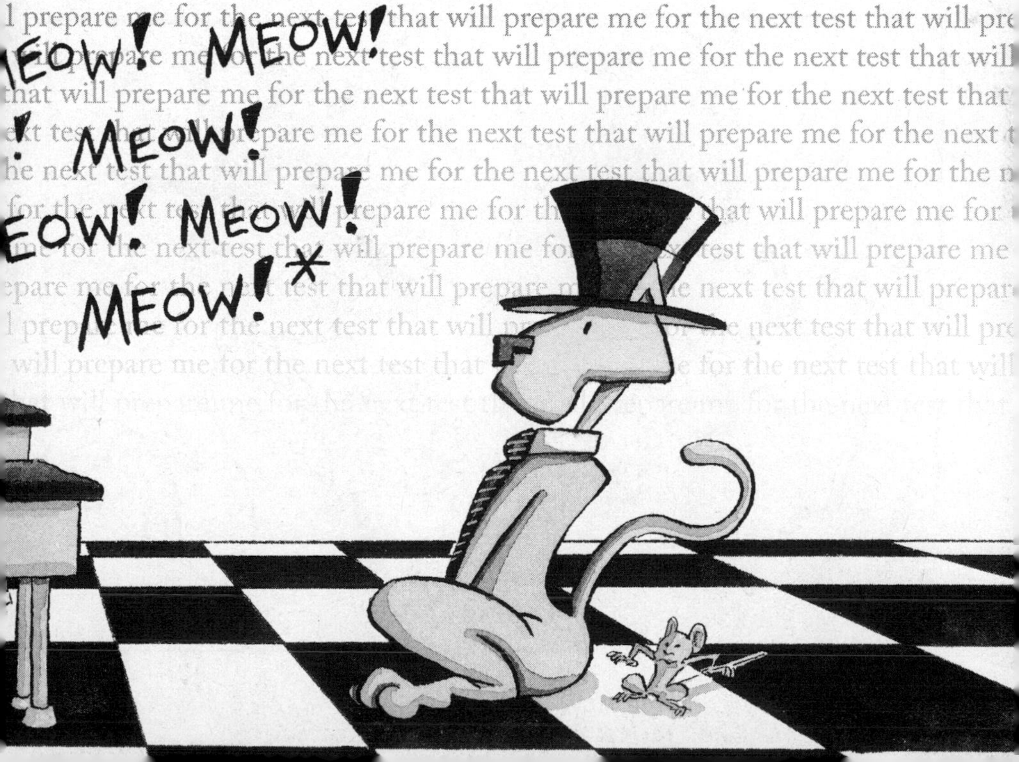

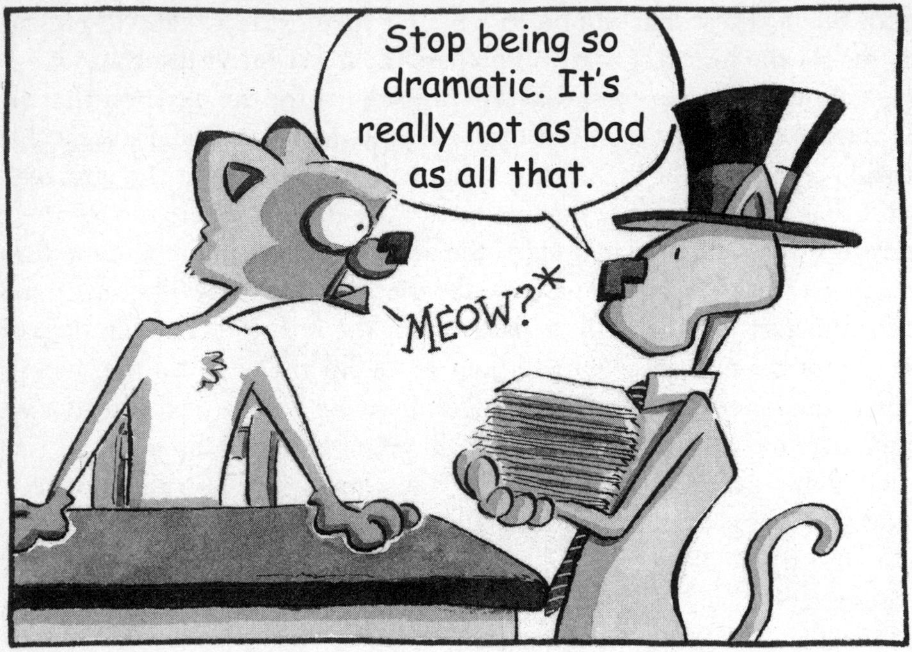
Stop being so dramatic. It's really not as bad as all that.
MEOW?*

* How many tests is it really?

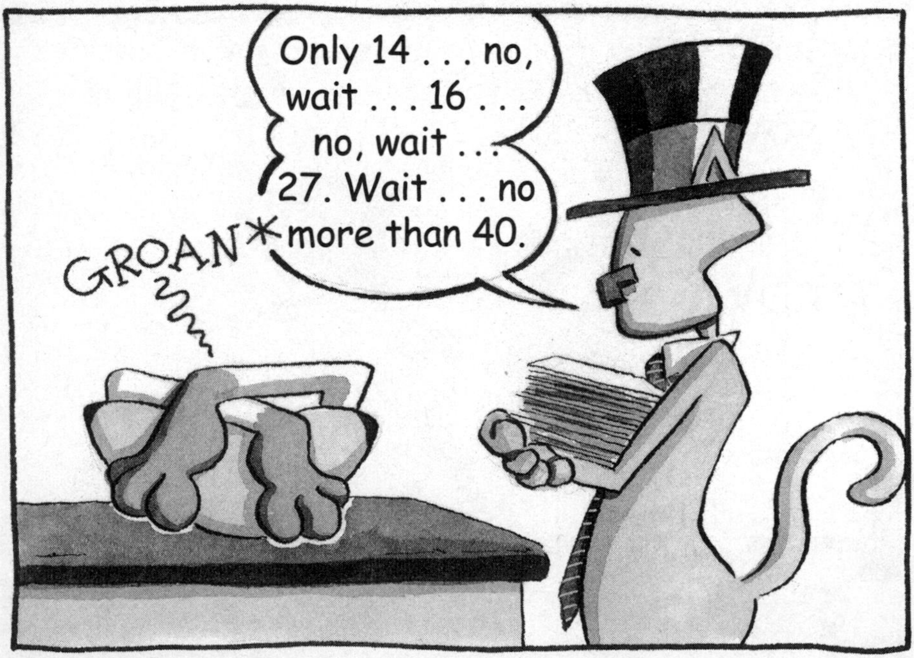
Only 14 . . . no, wait . . . 16 . . . no, wait . . . 27. Wait . . . no more than 40.
GROAN*

* Groan

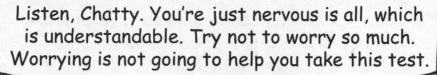

Listen, Chatty. You're just nervous is all, which is understandable. Try not to worry so much. Worrying is not going to help you take this test.

I'll make a deal with you. If you pass the final test, I'll buy you a chocolate tuna milkshake in celebration. And if you don't pass, I'll still buy you one to make you feel better. Deal?

MEOW*

* That sounds simultaneously disgusting and exquisite.

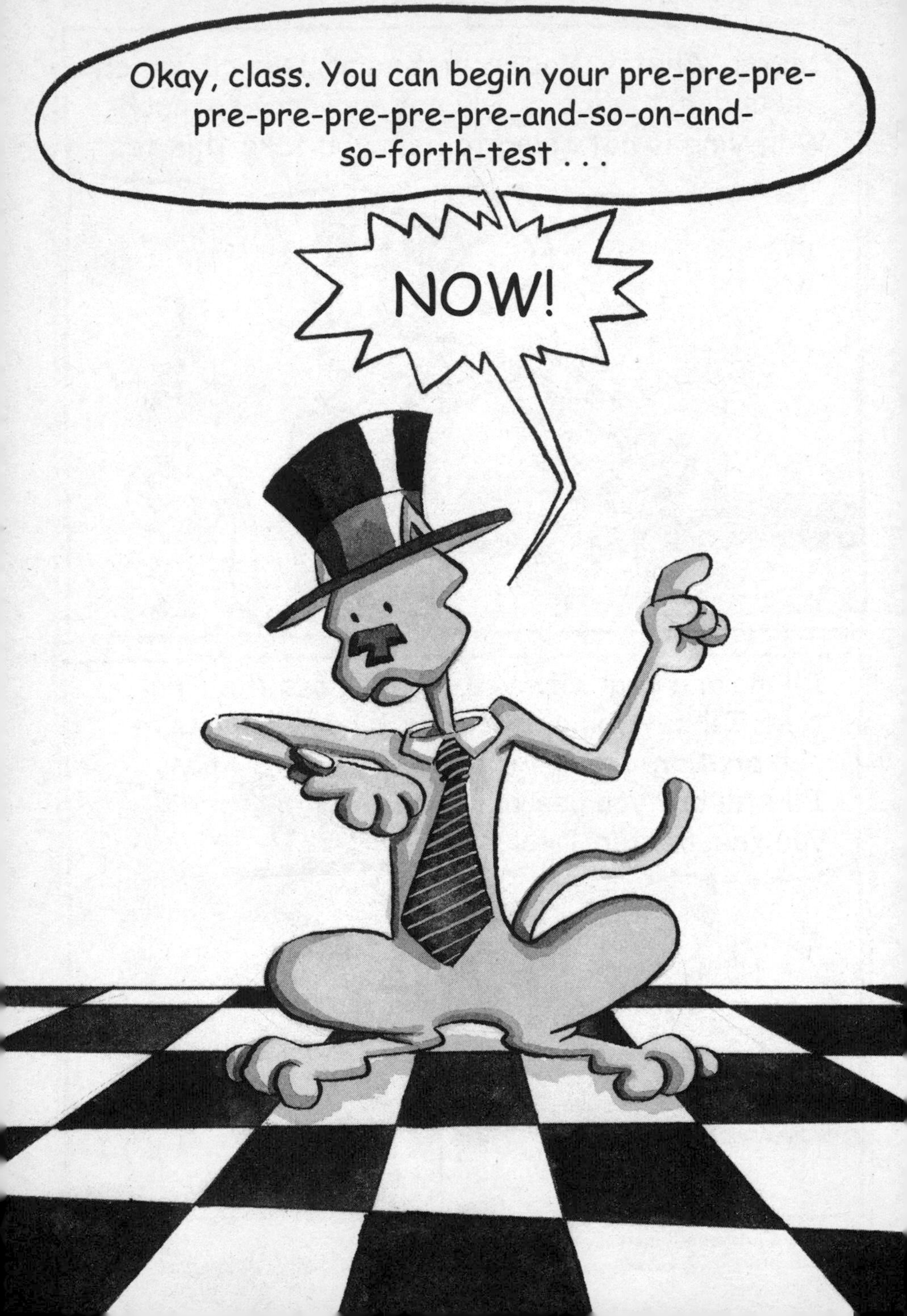
Okay, class. You can begin your pre-pre-pre-pre-pre-pre-pre-pre-pre-and-so-on-and-so-forth-test . . .
NOW!

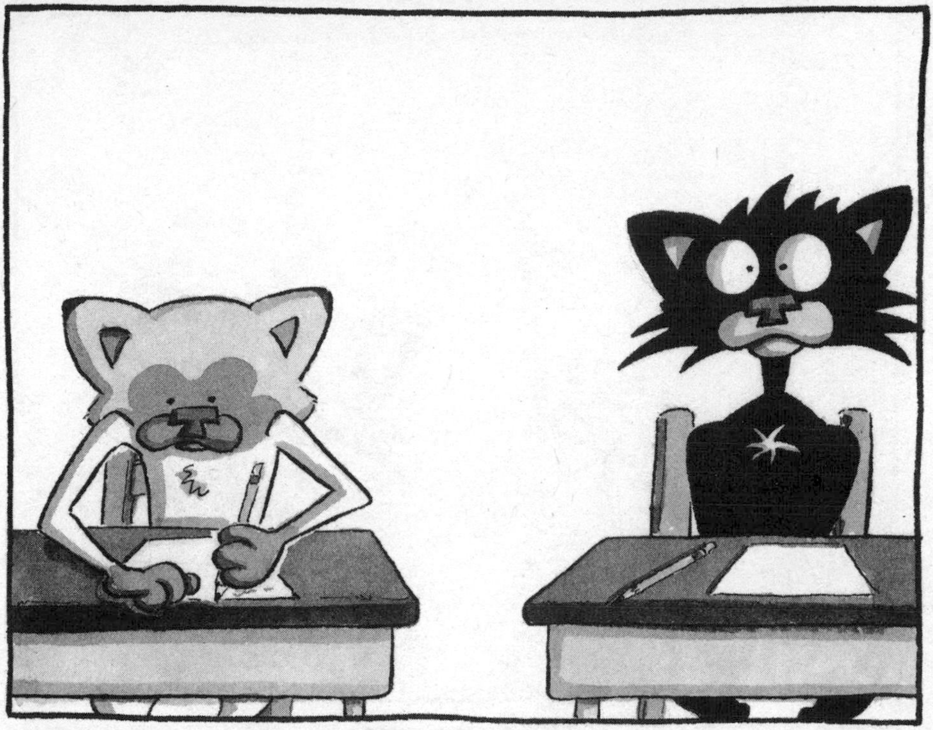
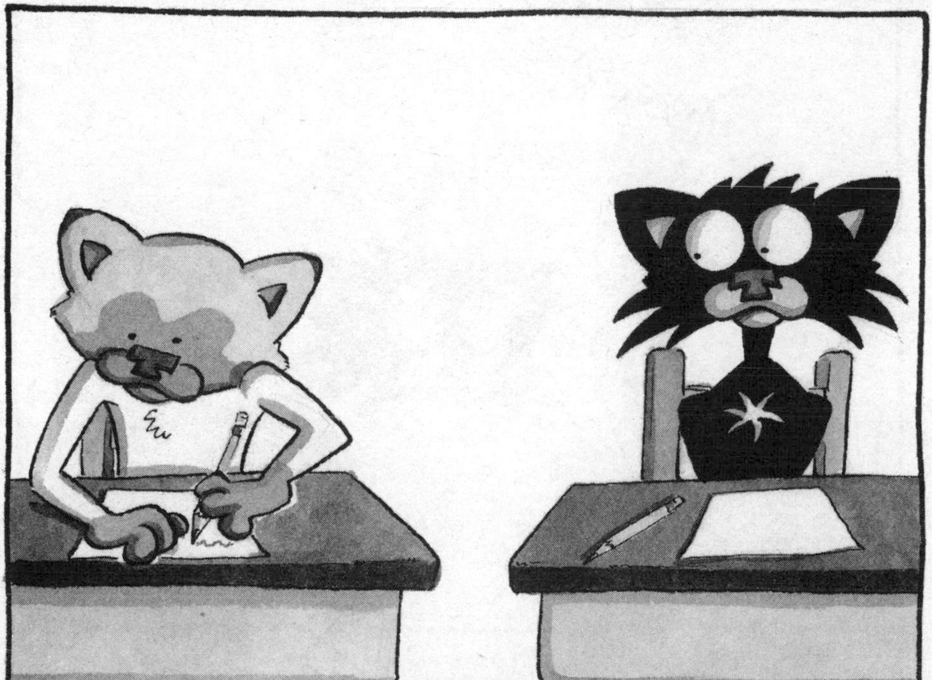

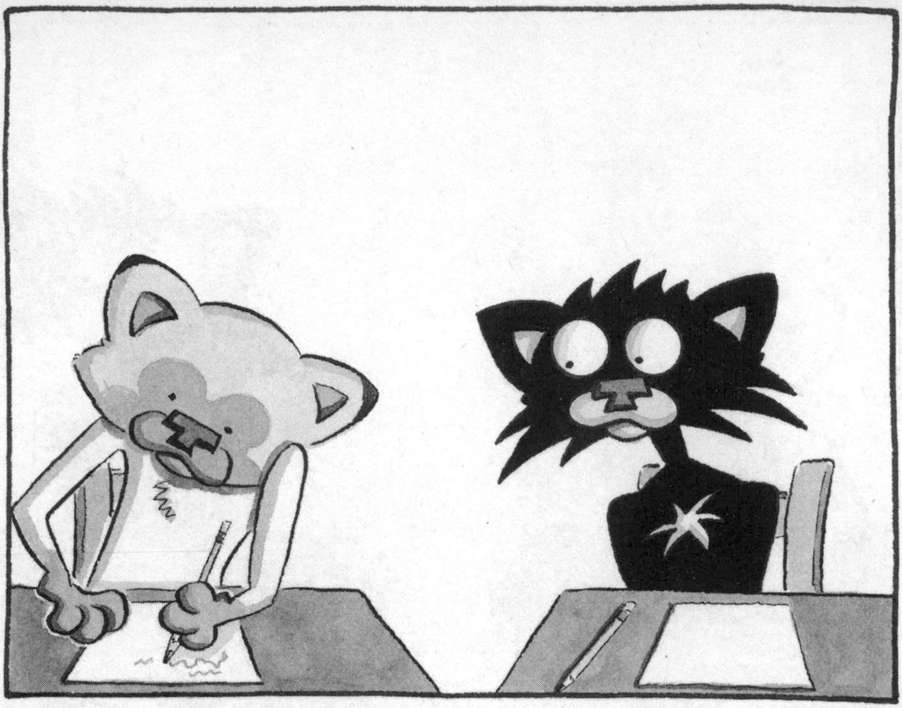

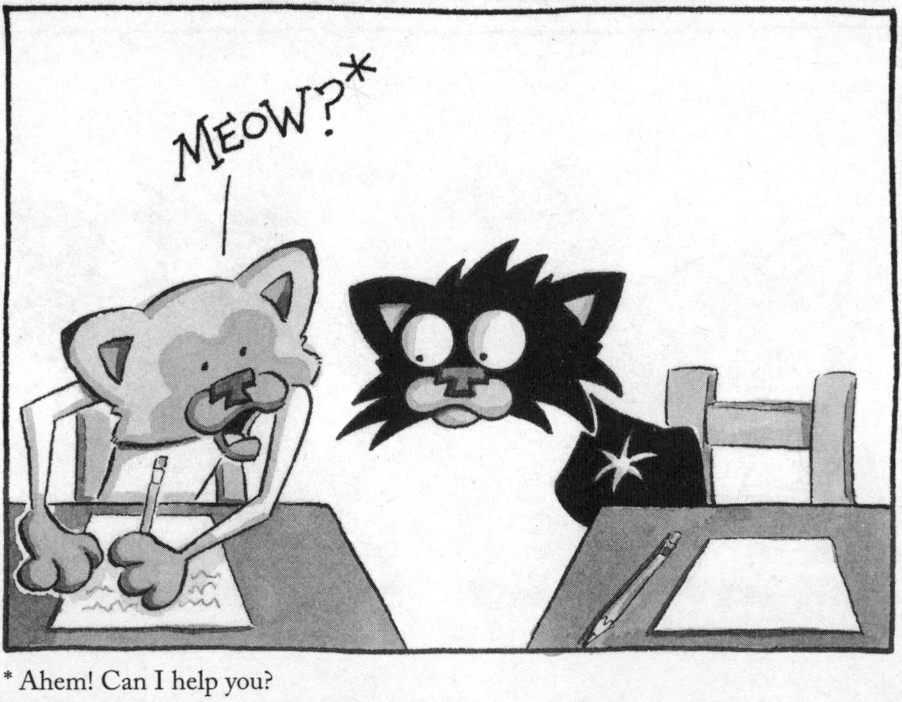
MEOW?*

* Ahem! Can I help you?

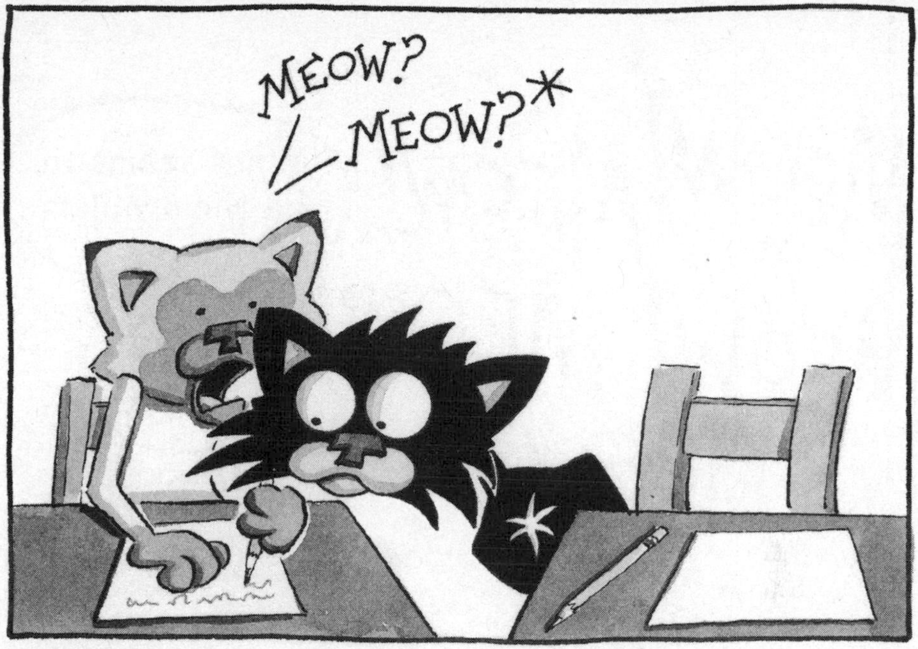
MEOW?
MEOW?*

*Are you looking for something? Did you lose your pencil? Do you need more paper?

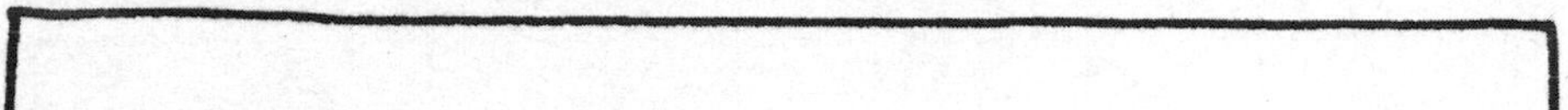
MEOW
MEOW
MEOW!*

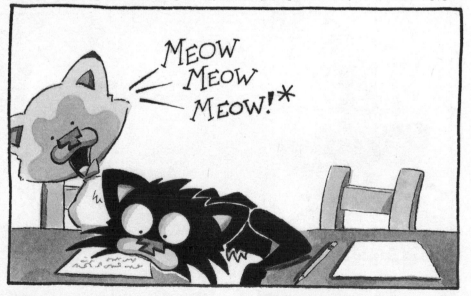

* Are you aware that psychologists recommend clear personal boundaries be set between two individuals in order to ensure an environment wherein their relationship can remain mutually respectful and supportive? And I can smell what you had for lunch.

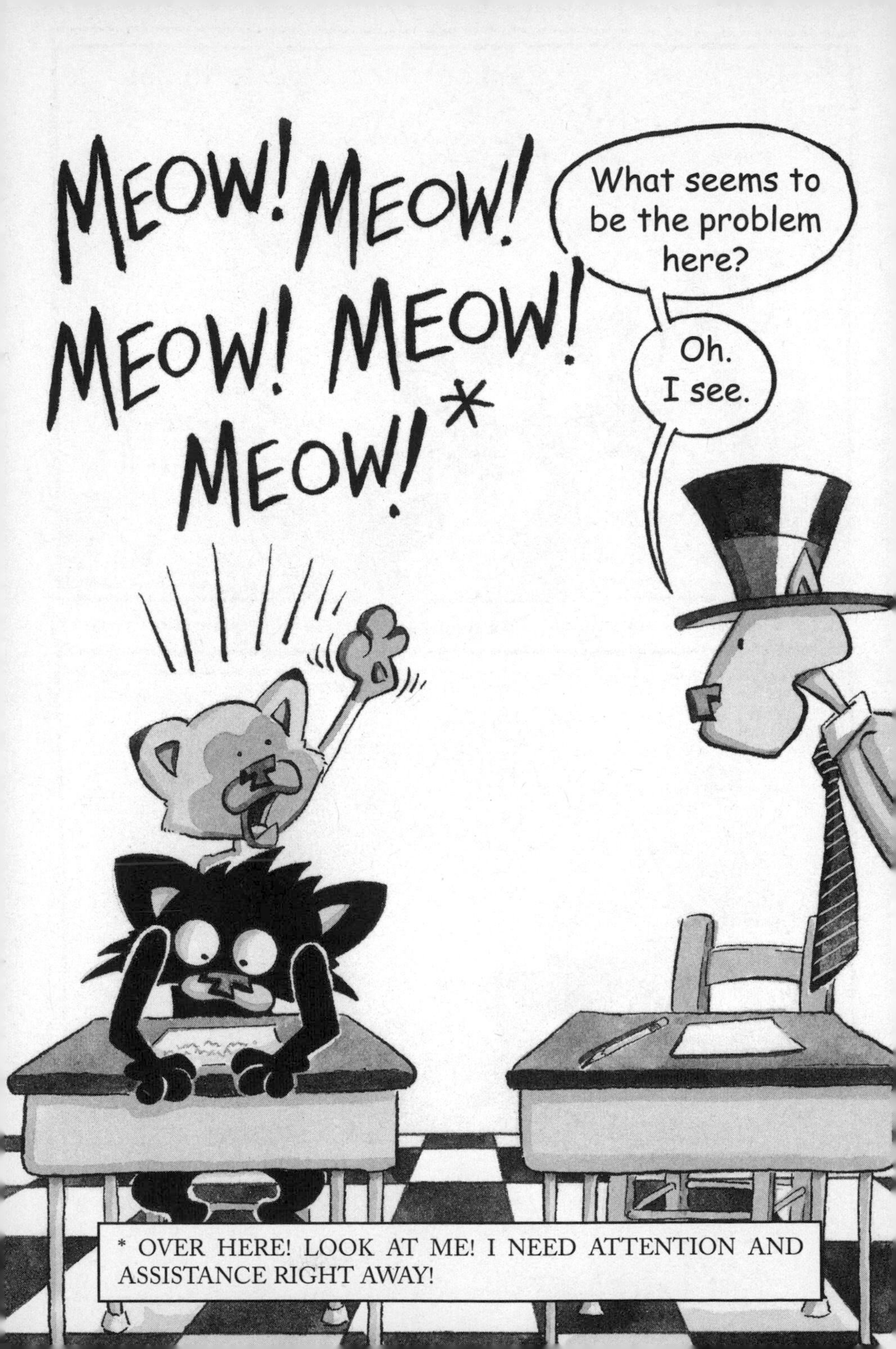

MEOW! MEOW! MEOW! MEOW! MEOW!*
What seems to be the problem here?
Oh. I see.
* OVER HERE! LOOK AT ME! I NEED ATTENTION AND ASSISTANCE RIGHT AWAY!

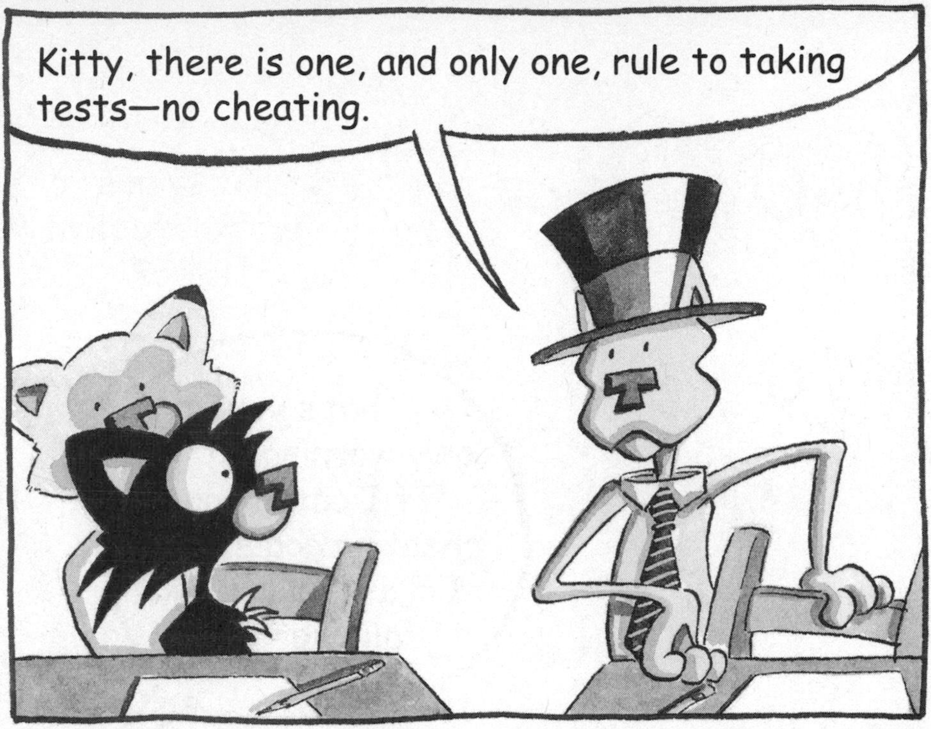
Kitty, there is one, and only one, rule to taking tests—no cheating.

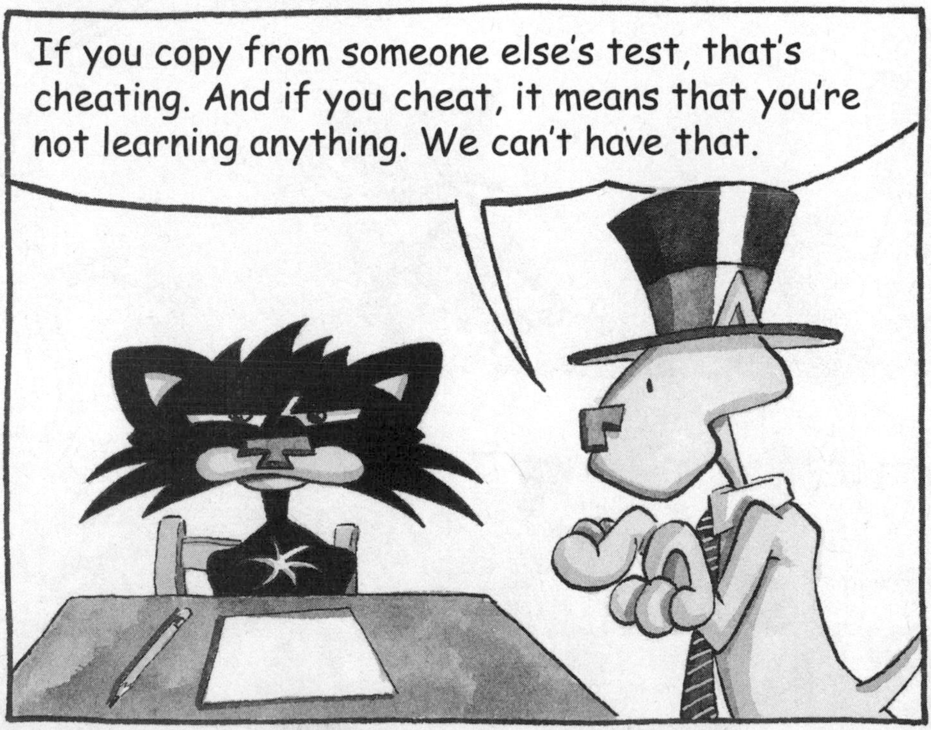
If you copy from someone else's test, that's cheating. And if you cheat, it means that you're not learning anything. We can't have that.

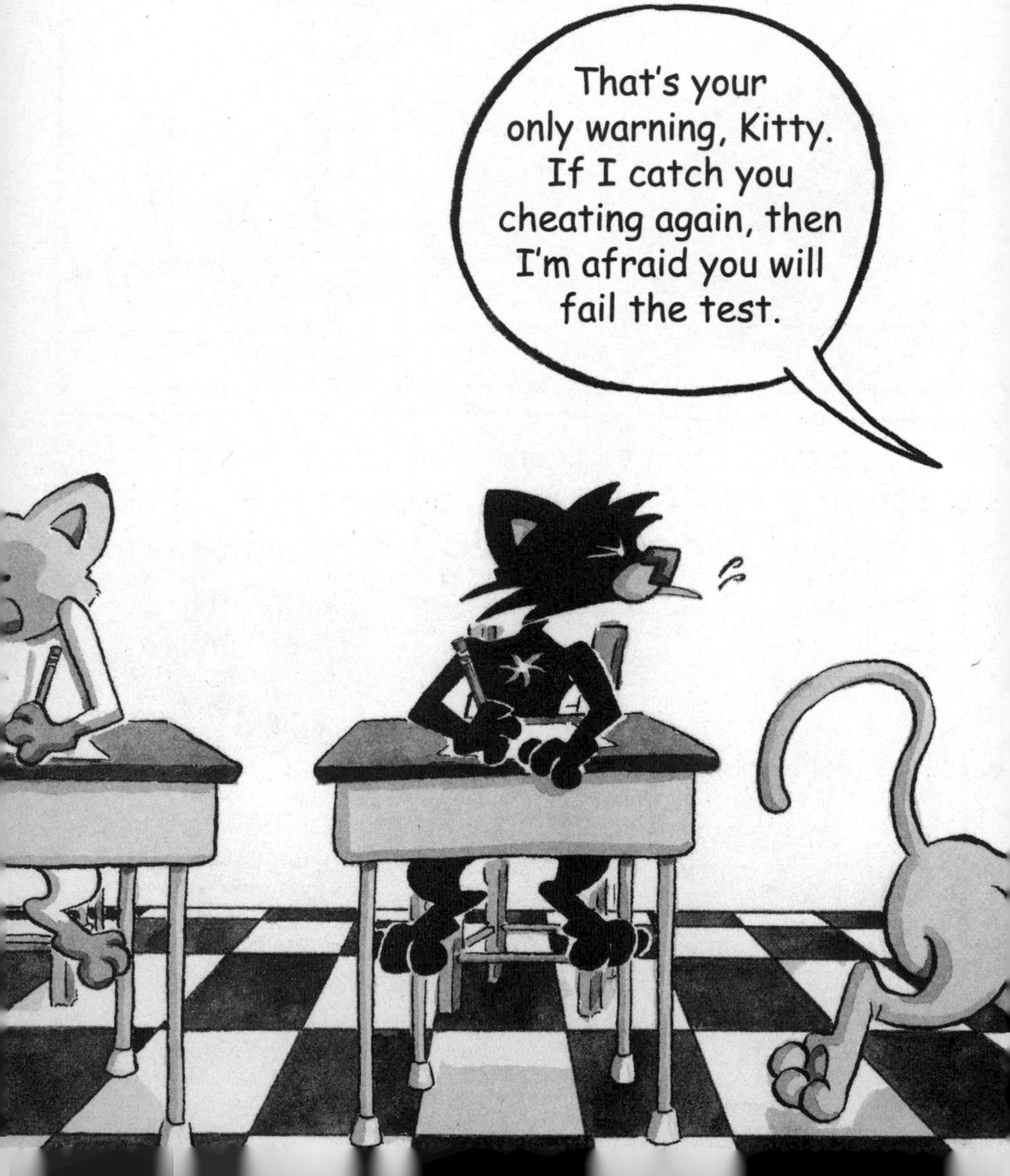
That's your only warning, Kitty. If I catch you cheating again, then I'm afraid you will fail the test.

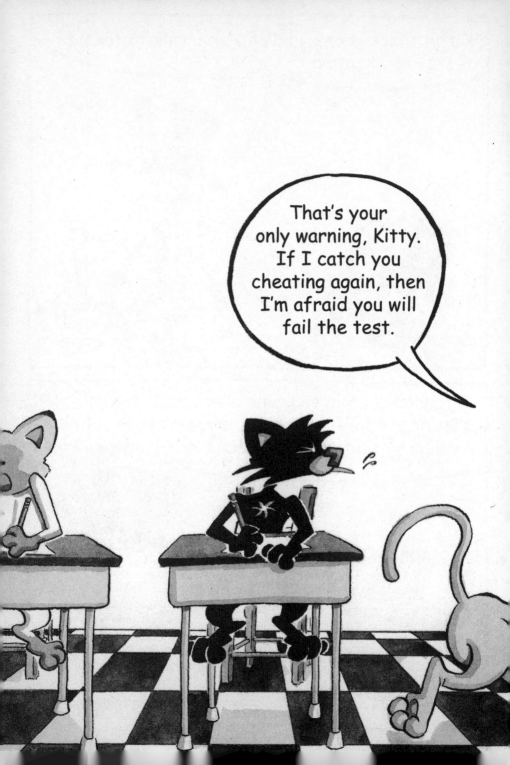

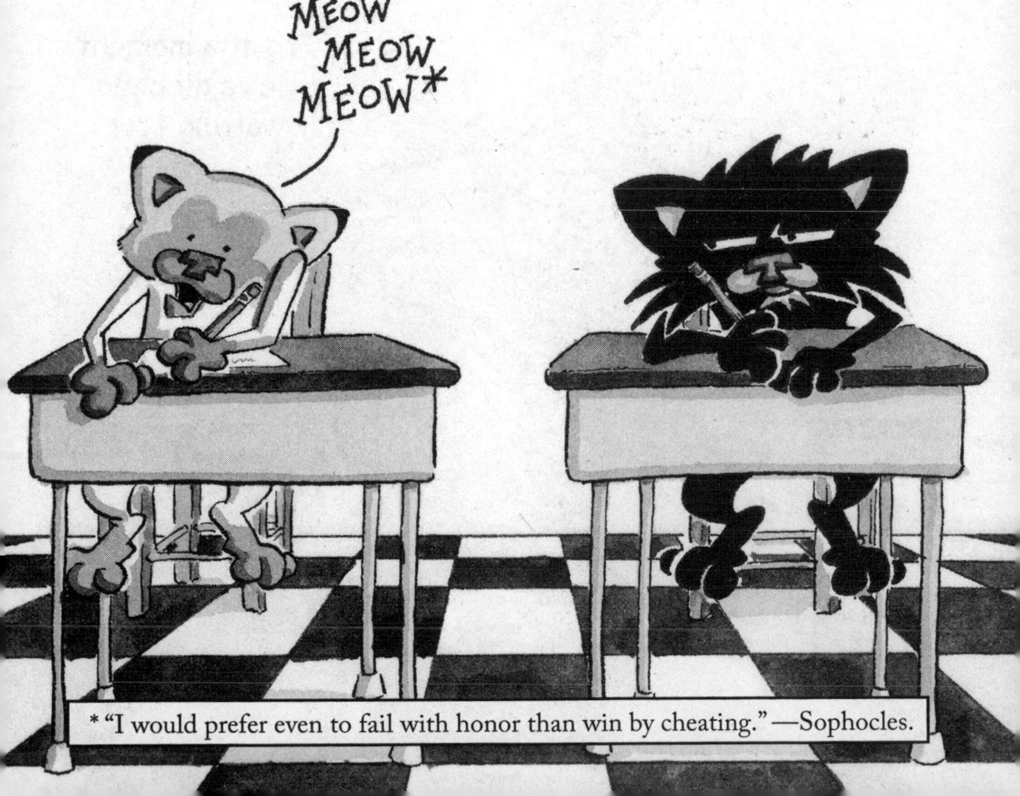
MEOW
MEOW
MEOW*

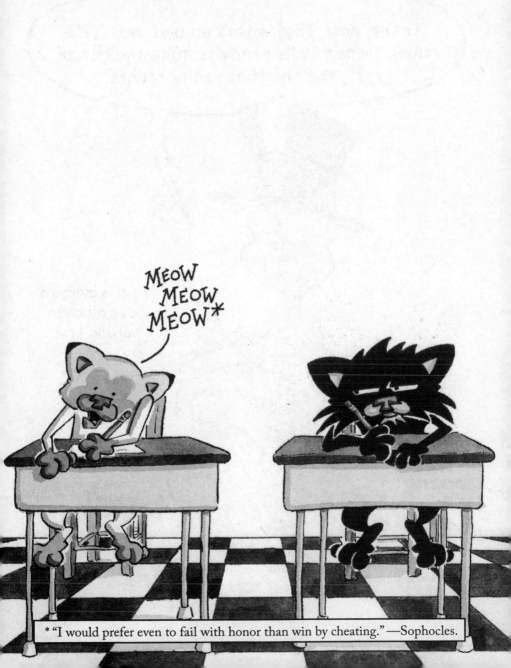

* "I would prefer even to fail with honor than win by cheating." —Sophocles.

•CHAPTER FIVE•

14 HOURS LATER

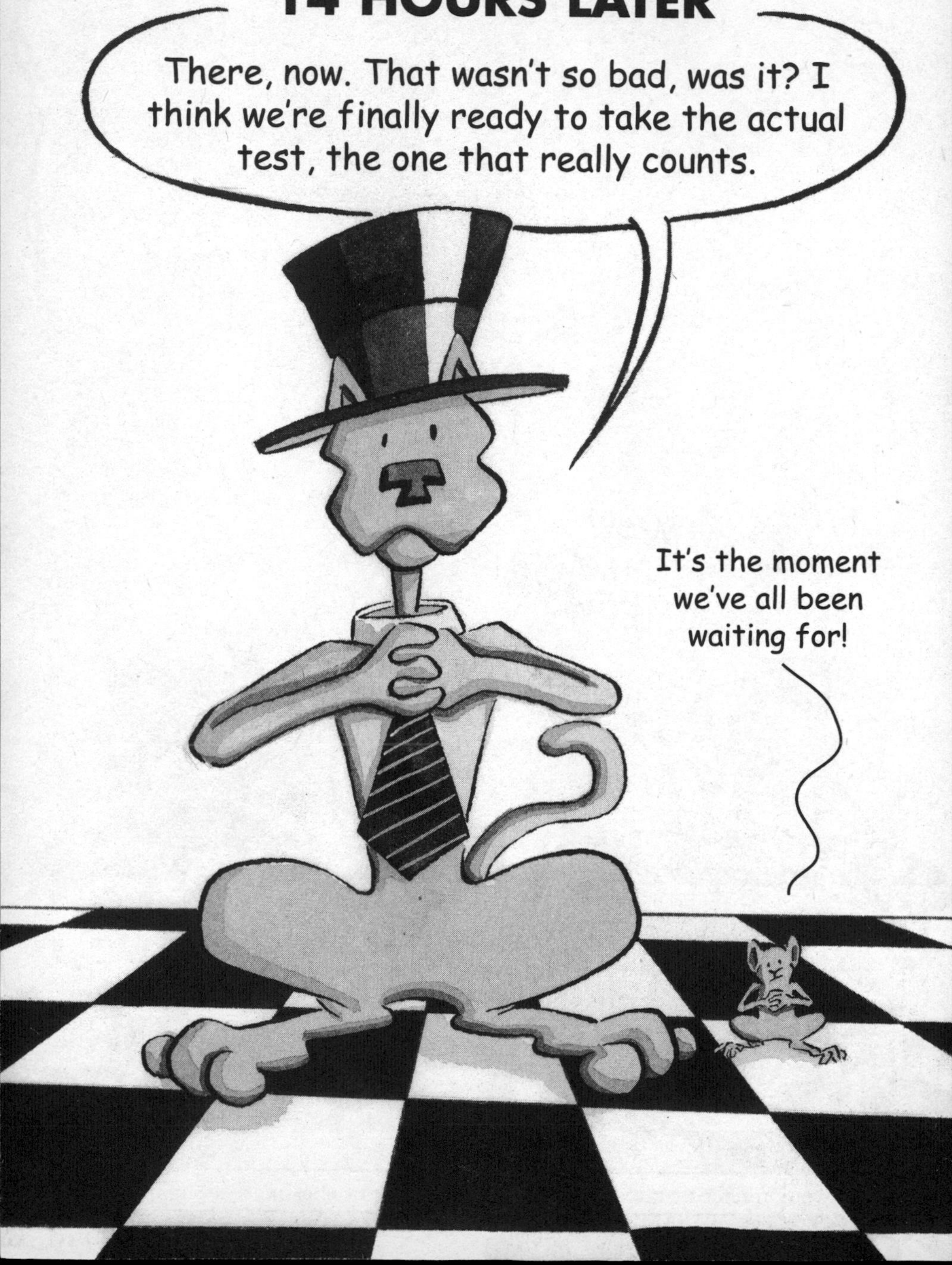

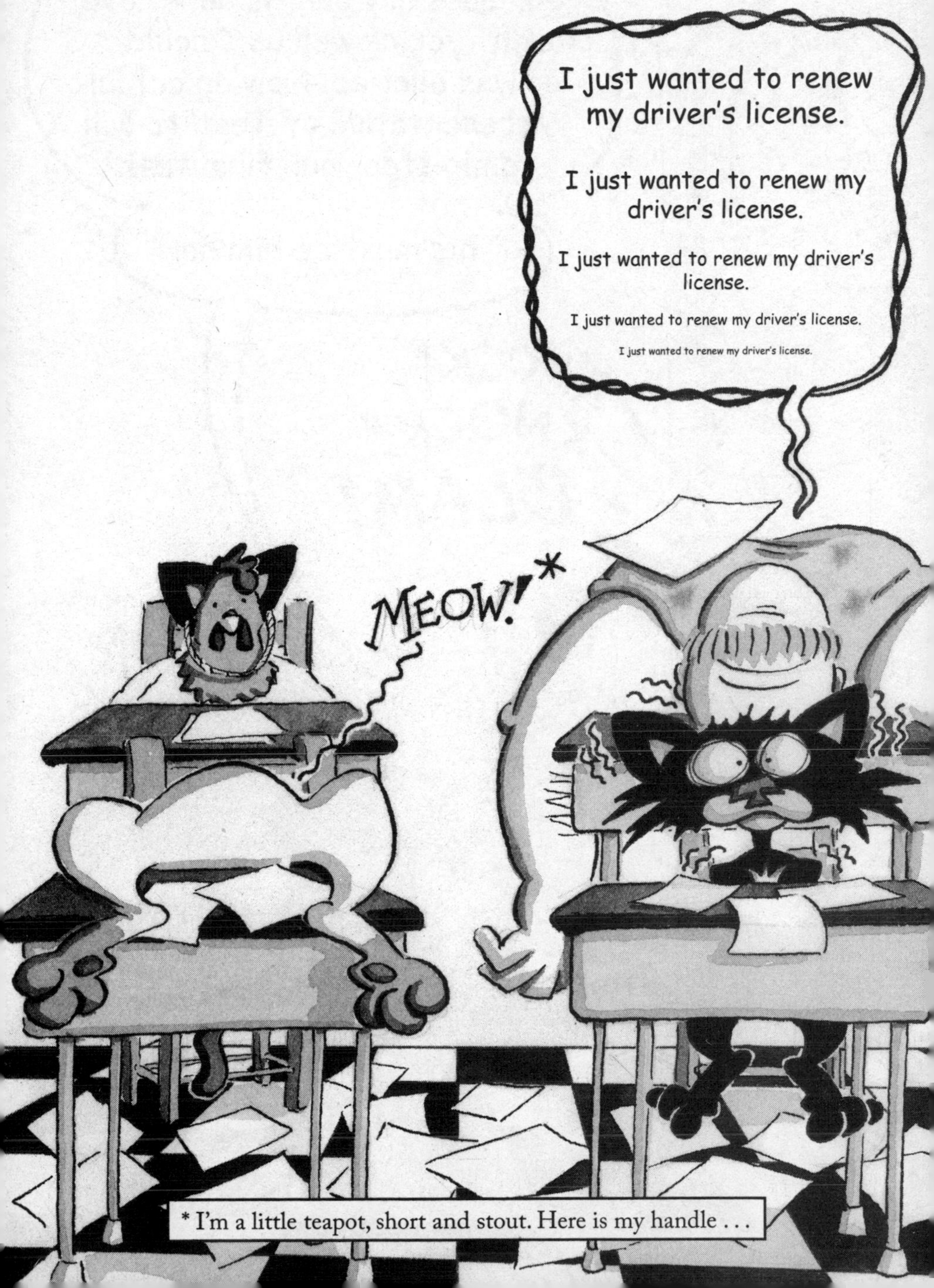
I just wanted to renew my driver's license.
I just wanted to renew my driver's license.
I just wanted to renew my driver's license.
I just wanted to renew my driver's license.
I just wanted to renew my driver's license.
MEOW!*
* I'm a little teapot, short and stout. Here is my handle . . .

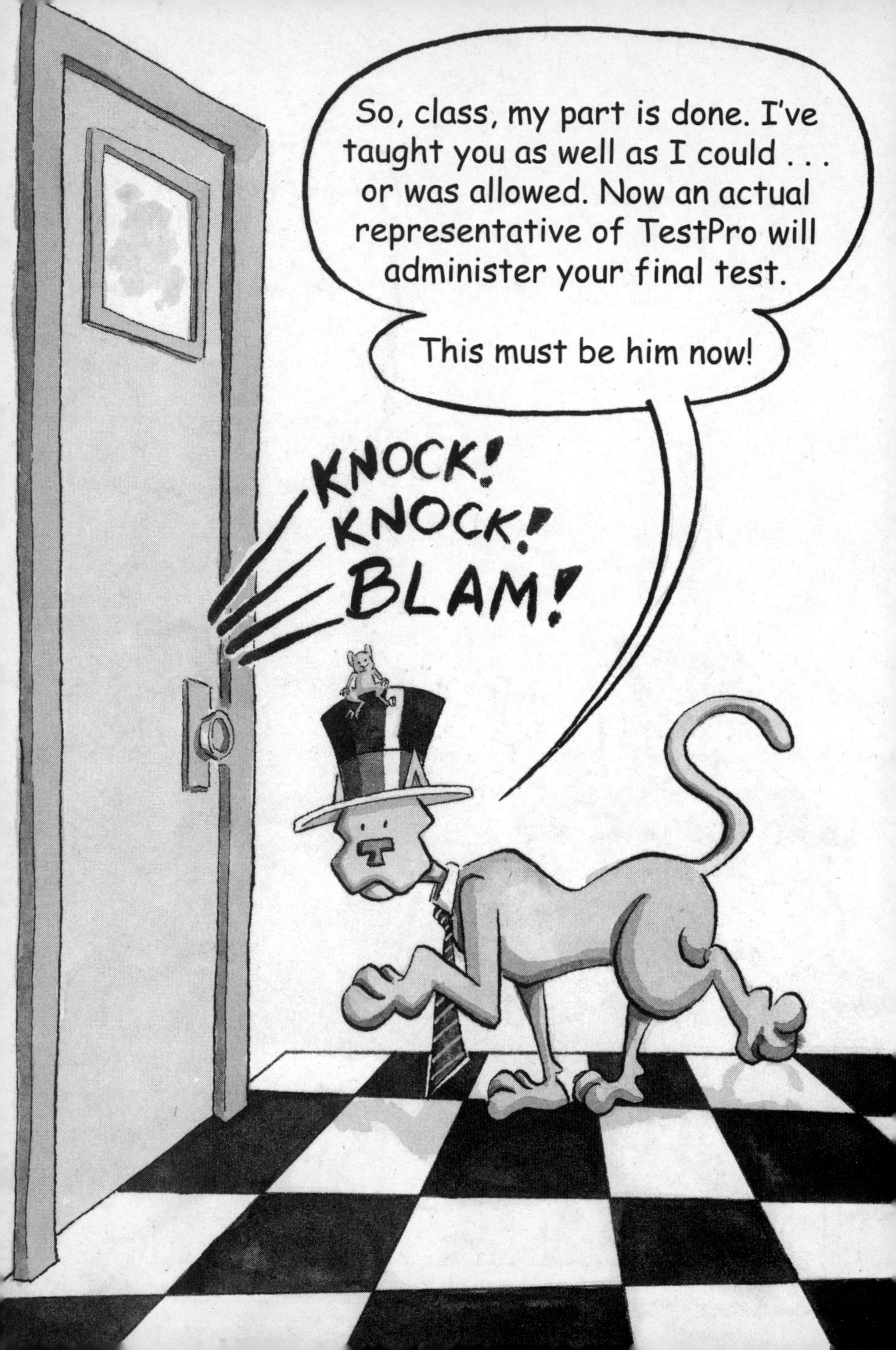
So, class, my part is done. I've taught you as well as I could . . . or was allowed. Now an actual representative of TestPro will administer your final test.
This must be him now!
KNOCK! KNOCK! BLAM!

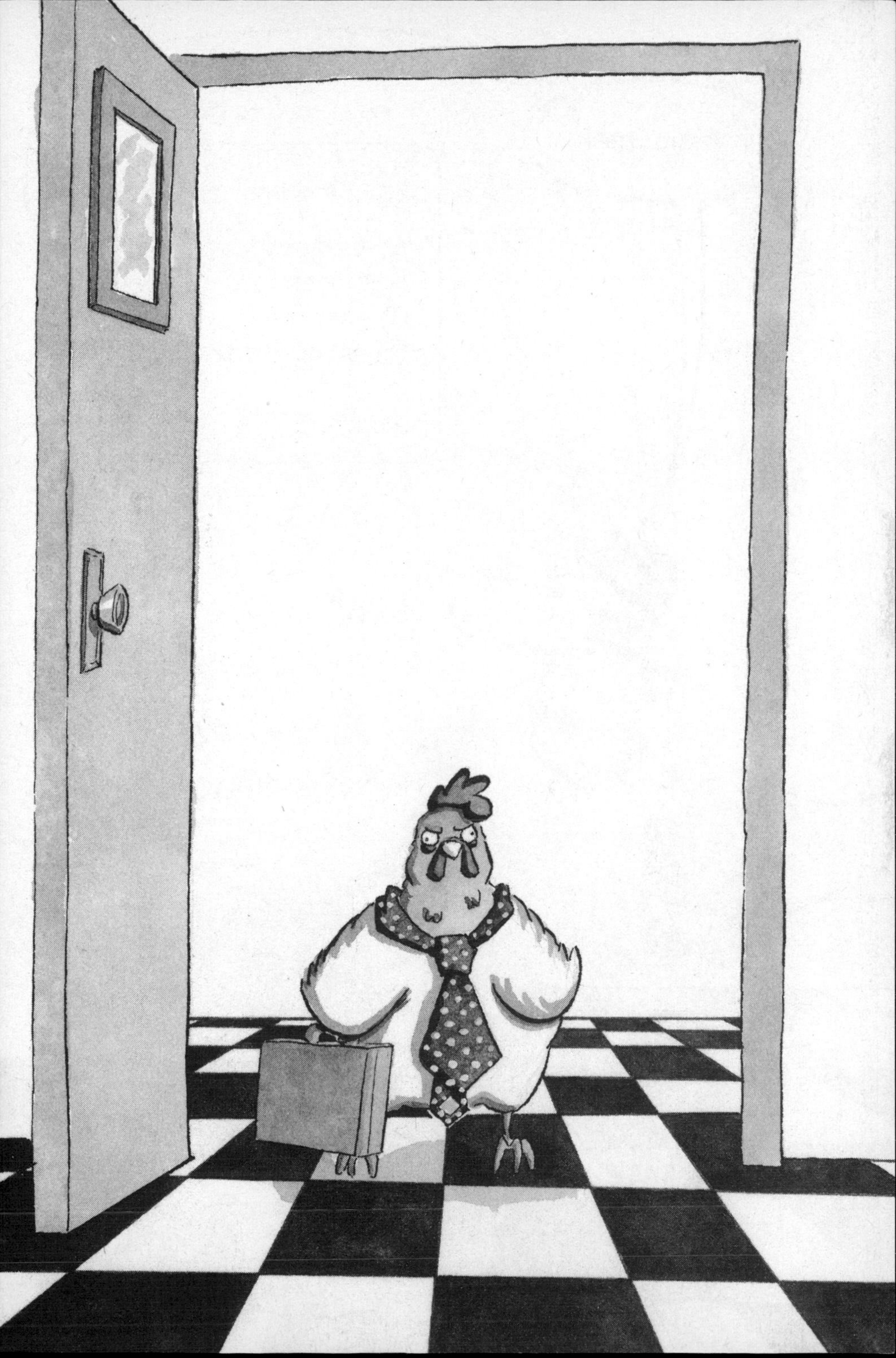

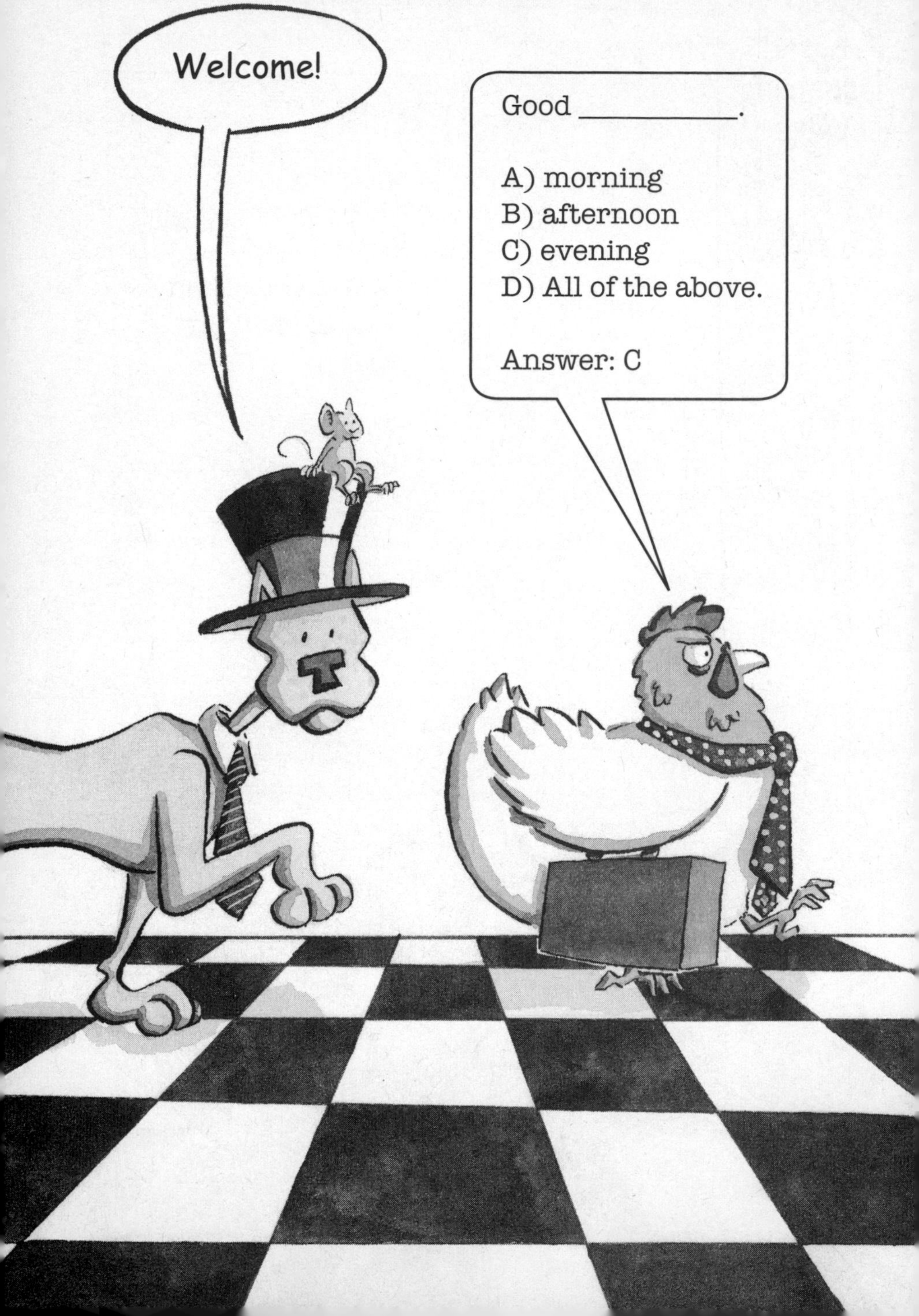
Welcome!
Good ____________.
A) morning
B) afternoon
C) evening
D) All of the above.
Answer: C

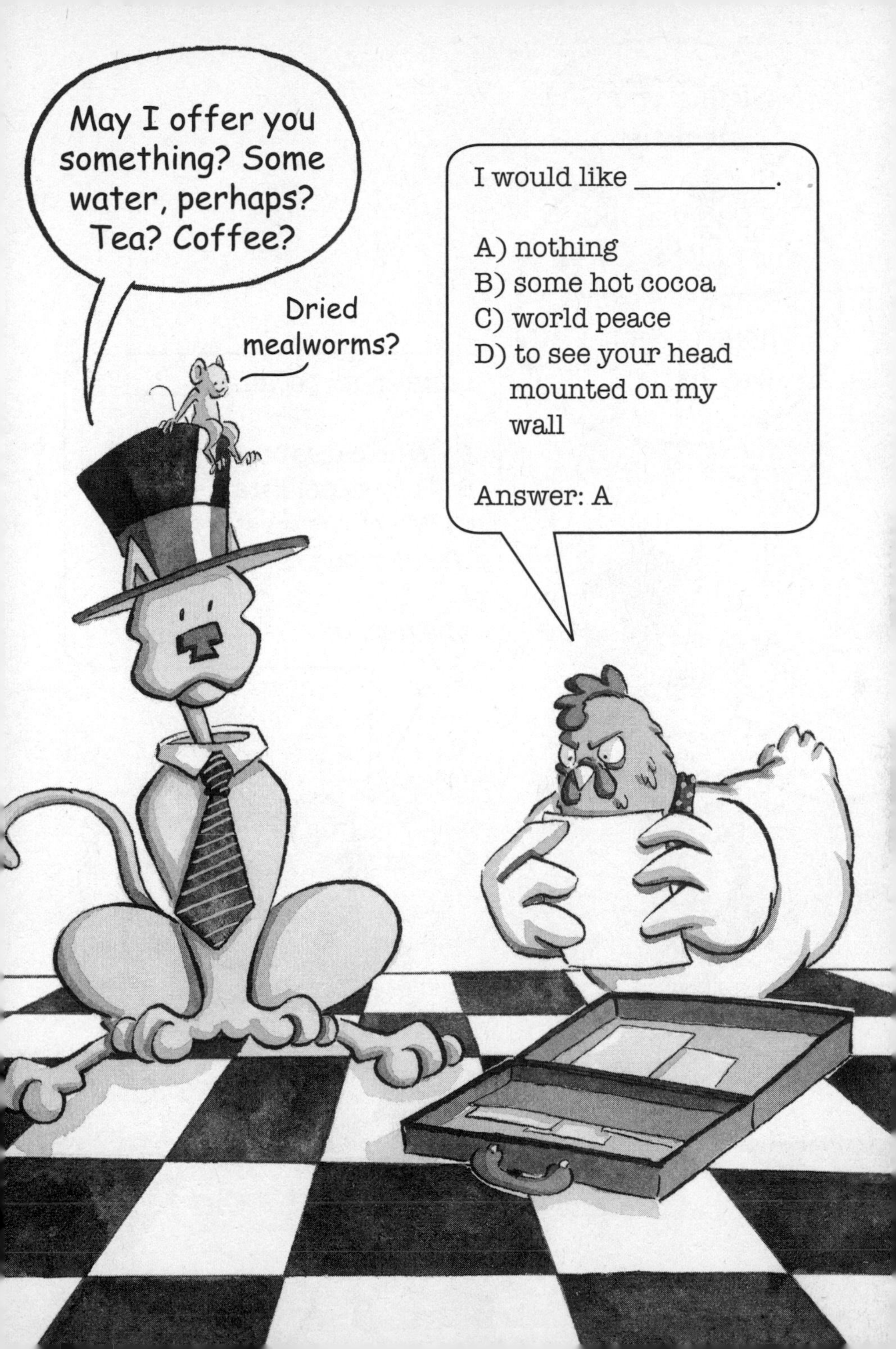
May I offer you something? Some water, perhaps? Tea? Coffee?
Dried mealworms?
I would like ________.
A) nothing
B) some hot cocoa
C) world peace
D) to see your head mounted on my wall
Answer: A

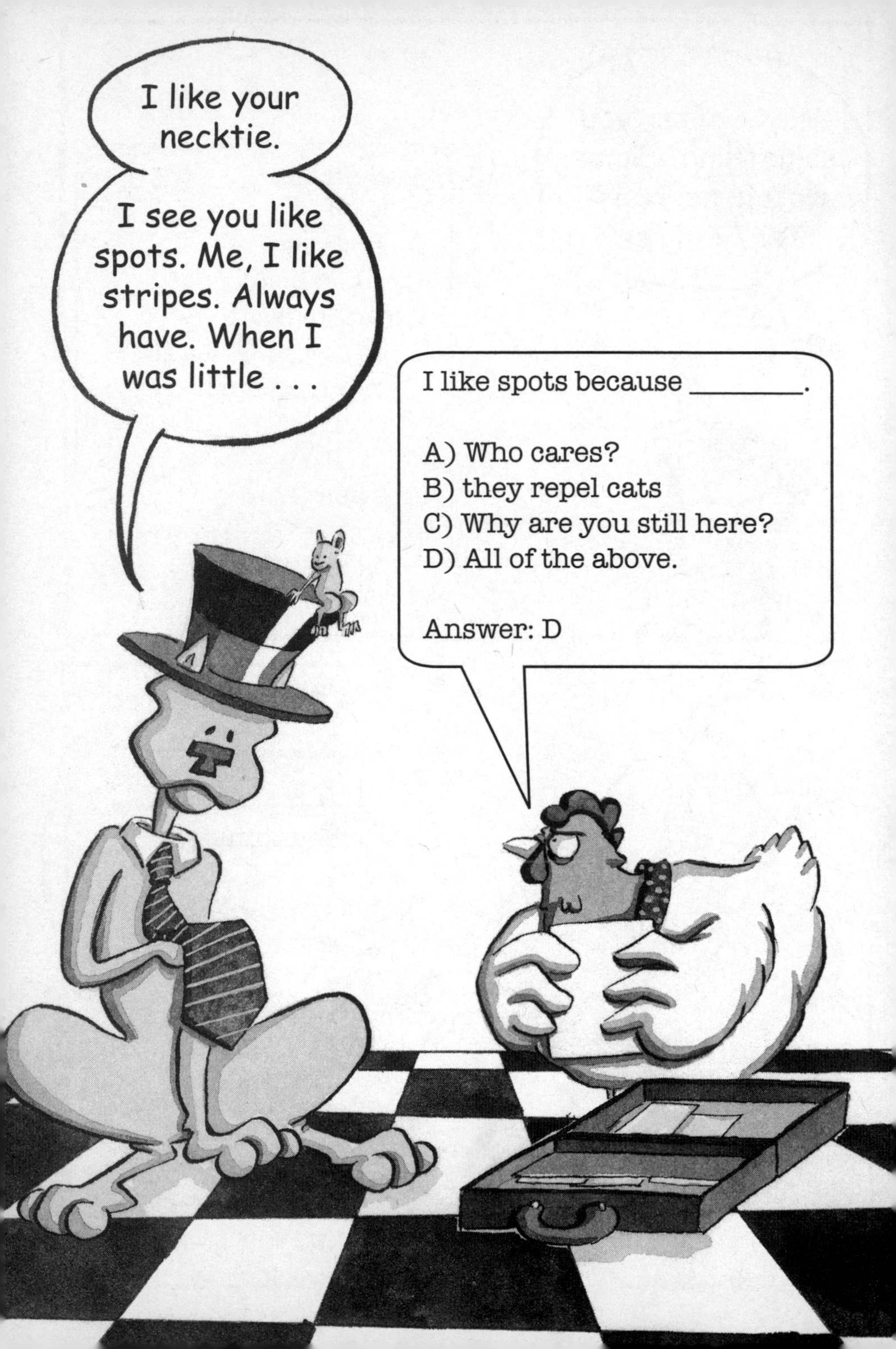
I like your necktie.
I see you like spots. Me, I like stripes. Always have. When I was little . . .
I like spots because ________.
A) Who cares?
B) they repel cats
C) Why are you still here?
D) All of the above.
Answer: D

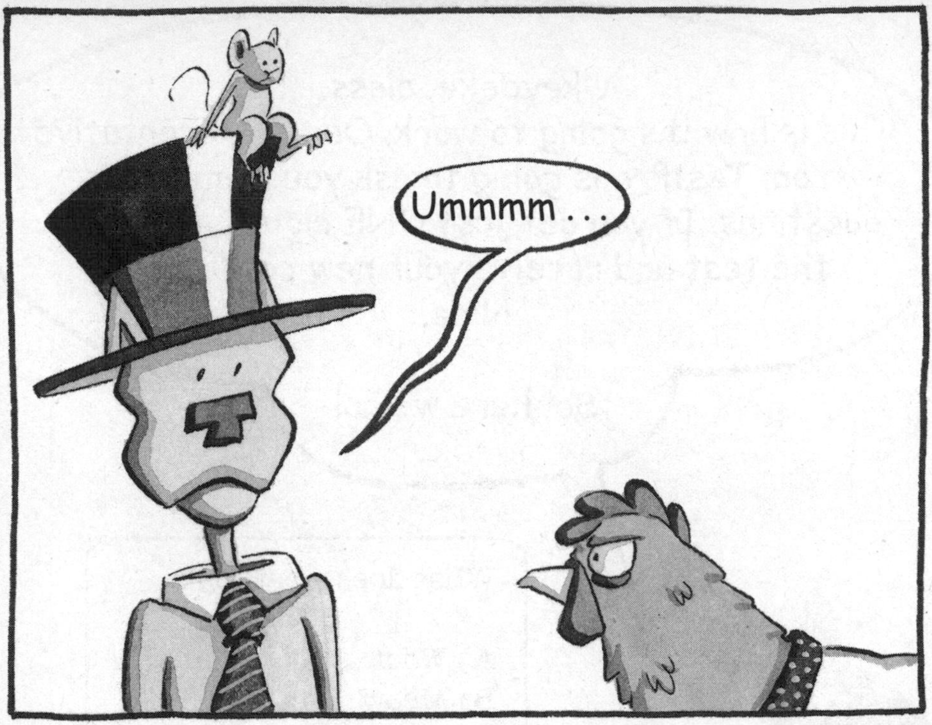
Ummmm . . .

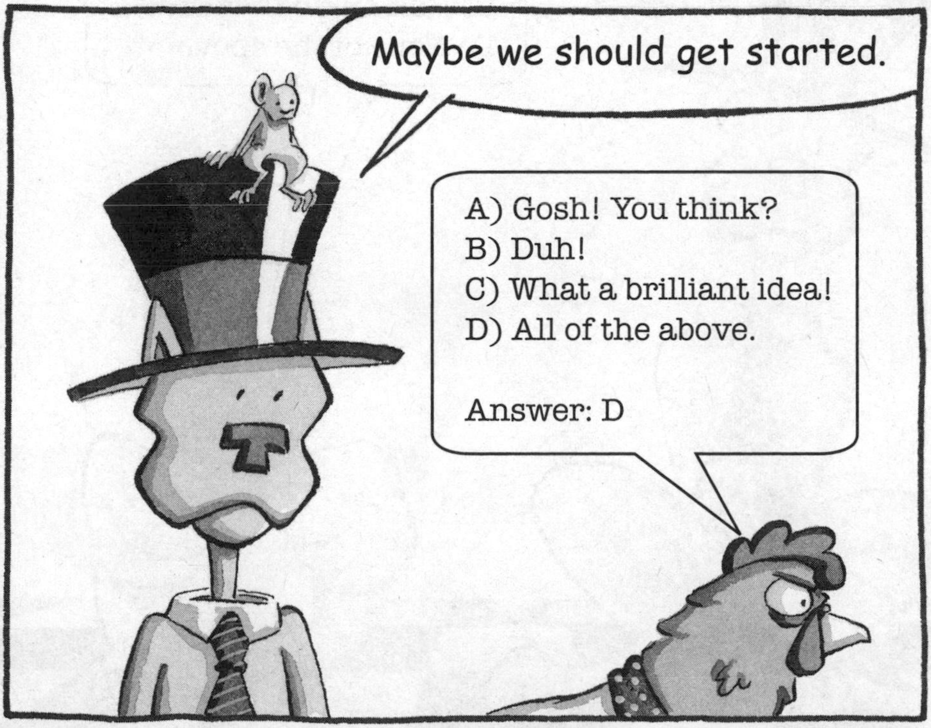
Maybe we should get started.
A) Gosh! You think?
B) Duh!
C) What a brilliant idea!
D) All of the above.
Answer: D

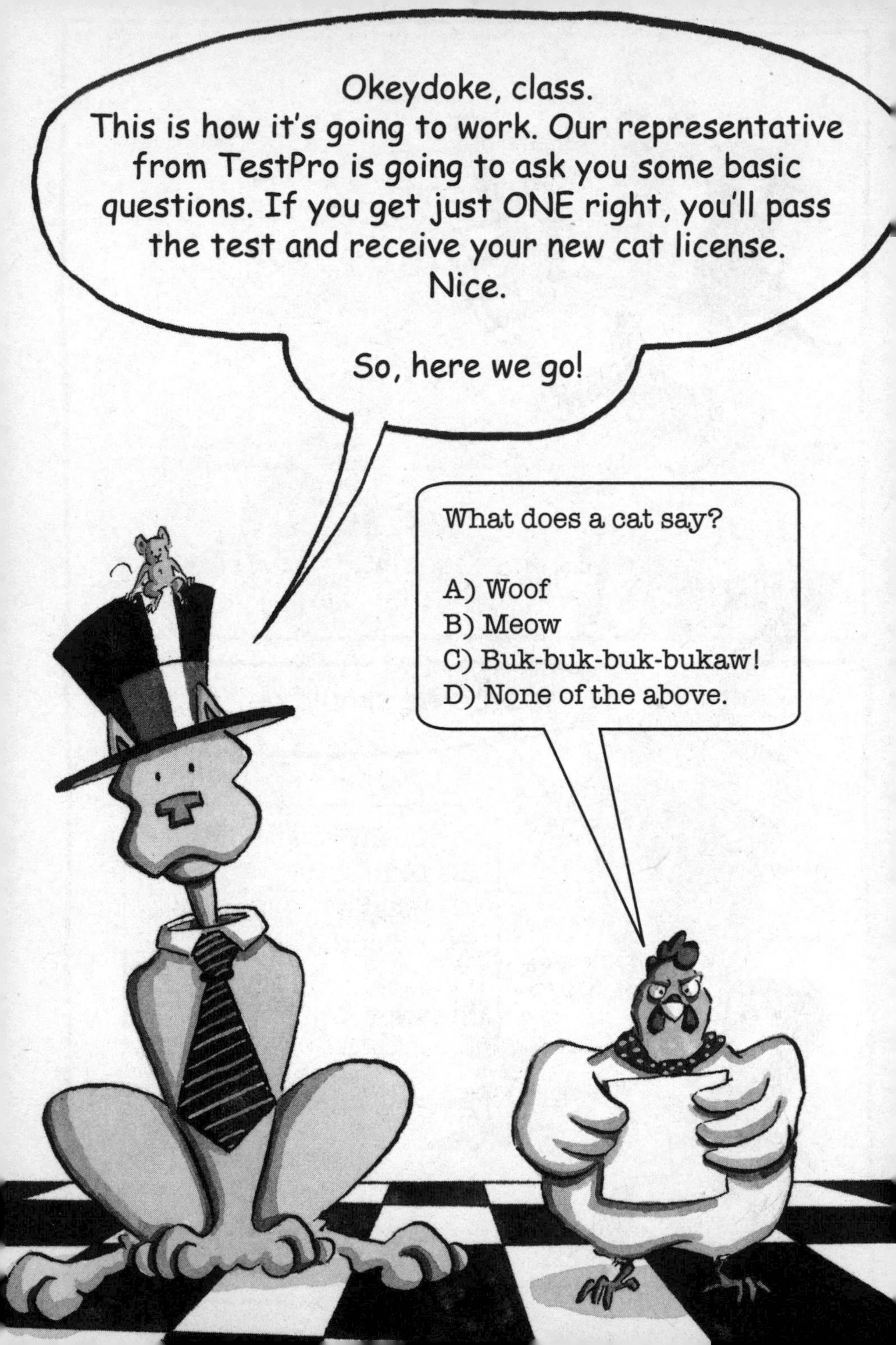
Okeydoke, class.
This is how it's going to work. Our representative from TestPro is going to ask you some basic questions. If you get just ONE right, you'll pass the test and receive your new cat license.
Nice.
So, here we go!
What does a cat say?
A) Woof
B) Meow
C) Buk-buk-buk-bukaw!
D) None of the above.

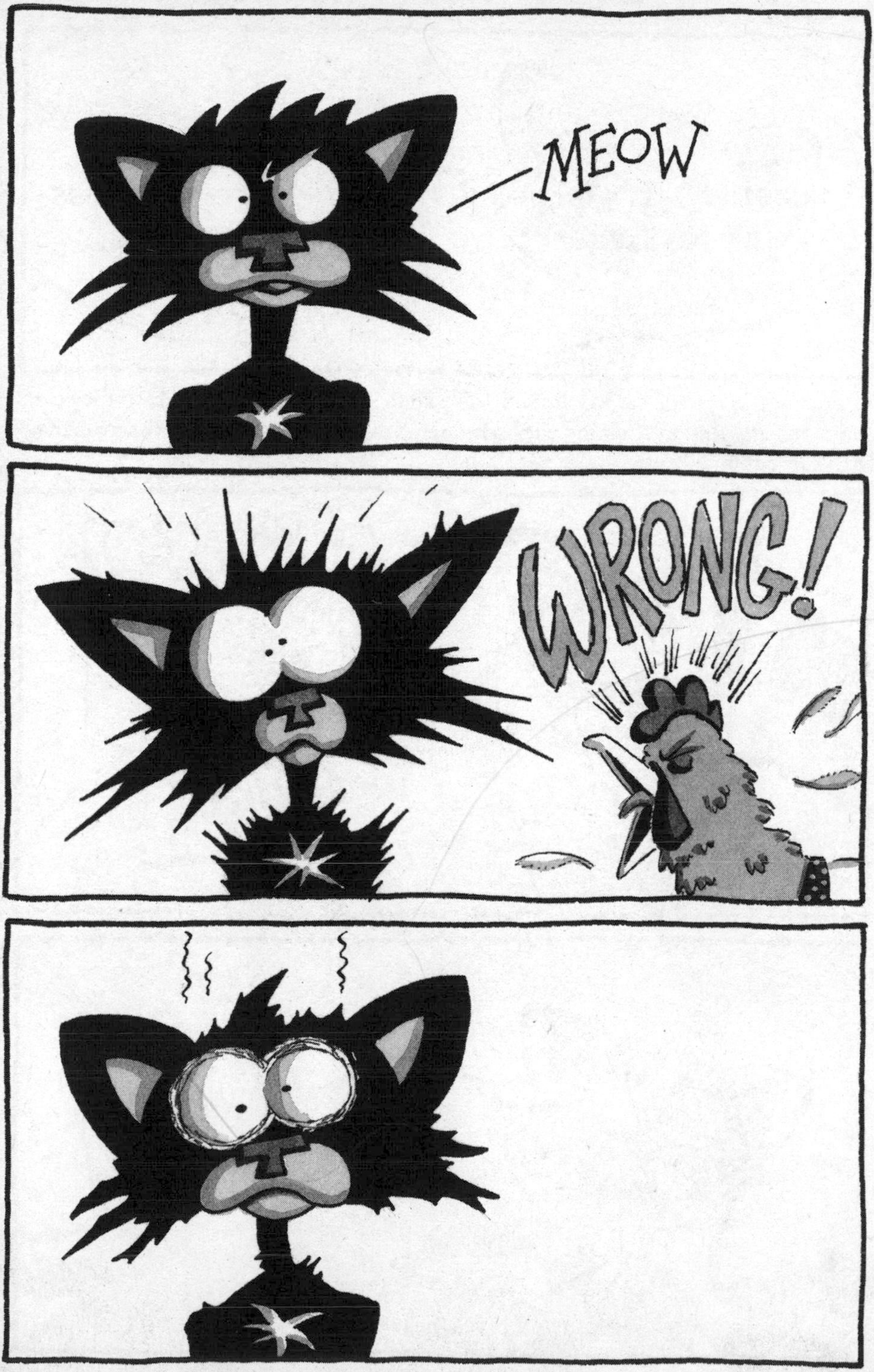
MEOW
WRONG!

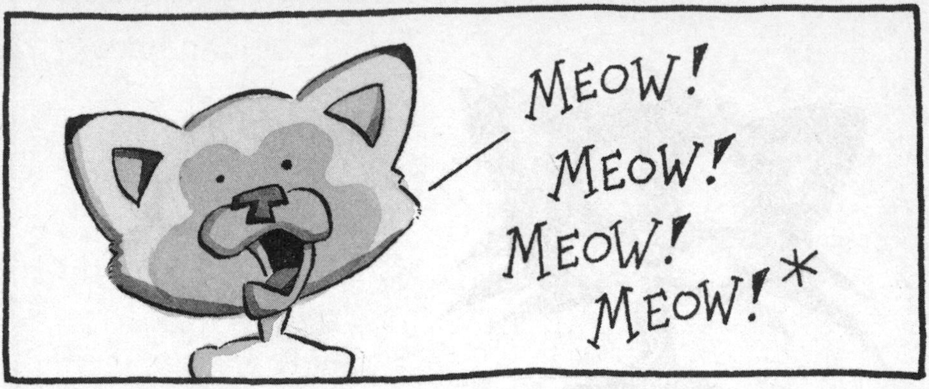
MEOW!
MEOW!
MEOW!
MEOW!*

* Actually, the average cat has around 16 separate vocalizations with which they can communicate. This does not include body language like tail twitching or the roars that large cats commonly use . . .

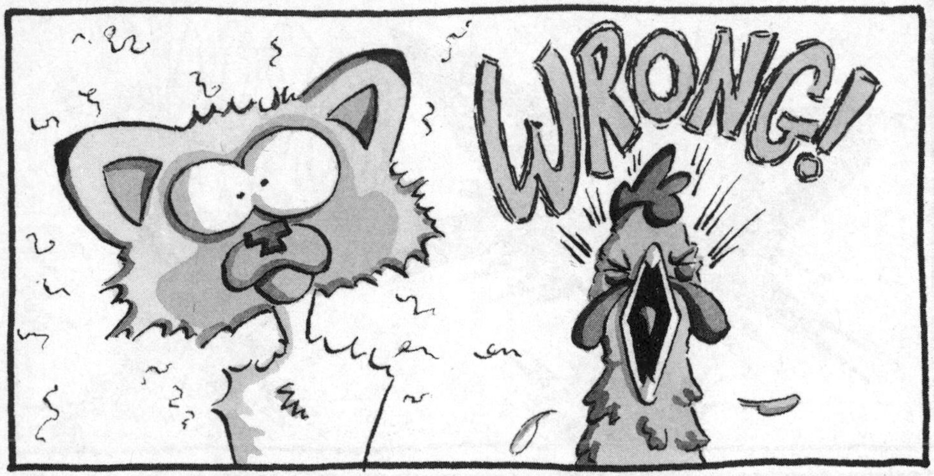
WRONG!

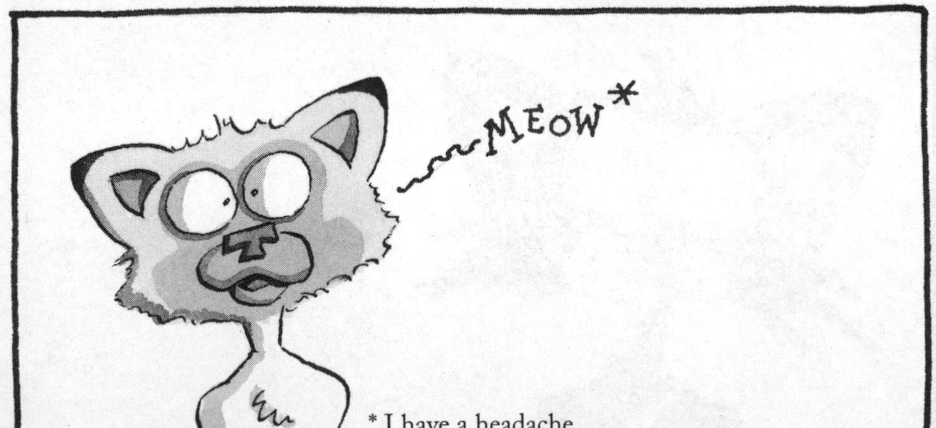
MEOW*
* I have a headache.

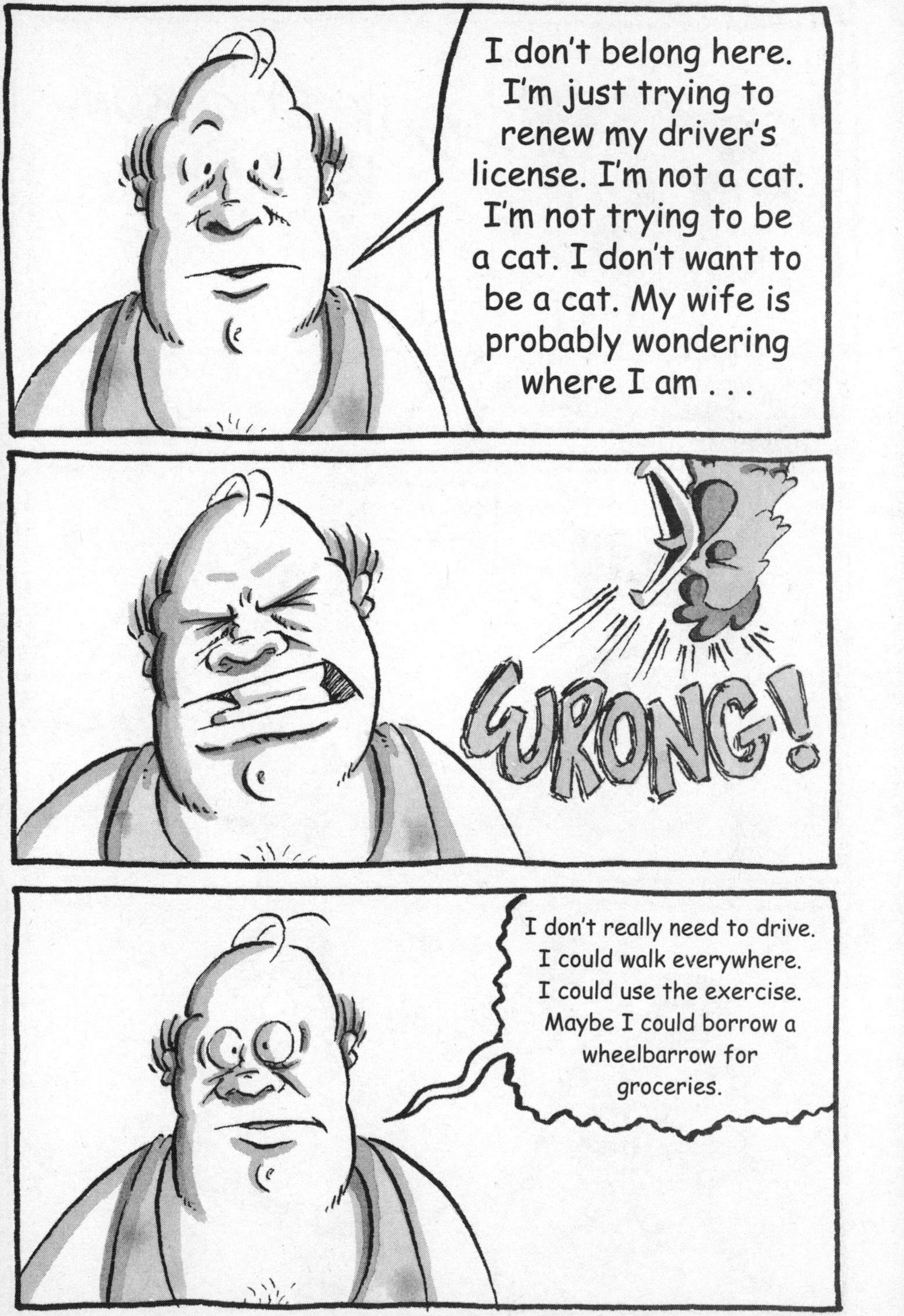
I don't belong here. I'm just trying to renew my driver's license. I'm not a cat. I'm not trying to be a cat. I don't want to be a cat. My wife is probably wondering where I am . . .
GURONG!
I don't really need to drive. I could walk everywhere. I could use the exercise. Maybe I could borrow a wheelbarrow for groceries.

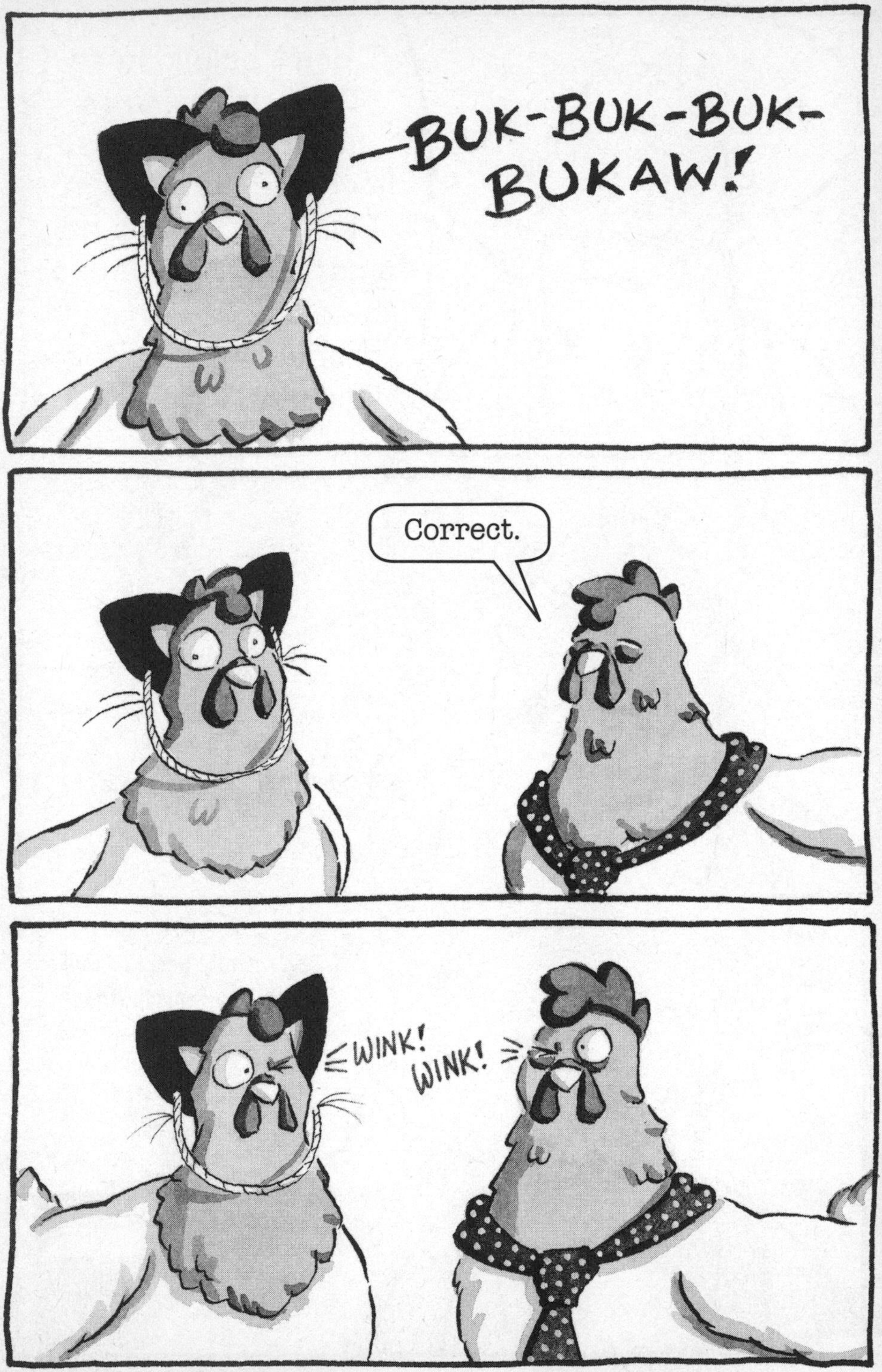
—BUK-BUK-BUK-BUKAW!
Correct.
WINK!
WINK!

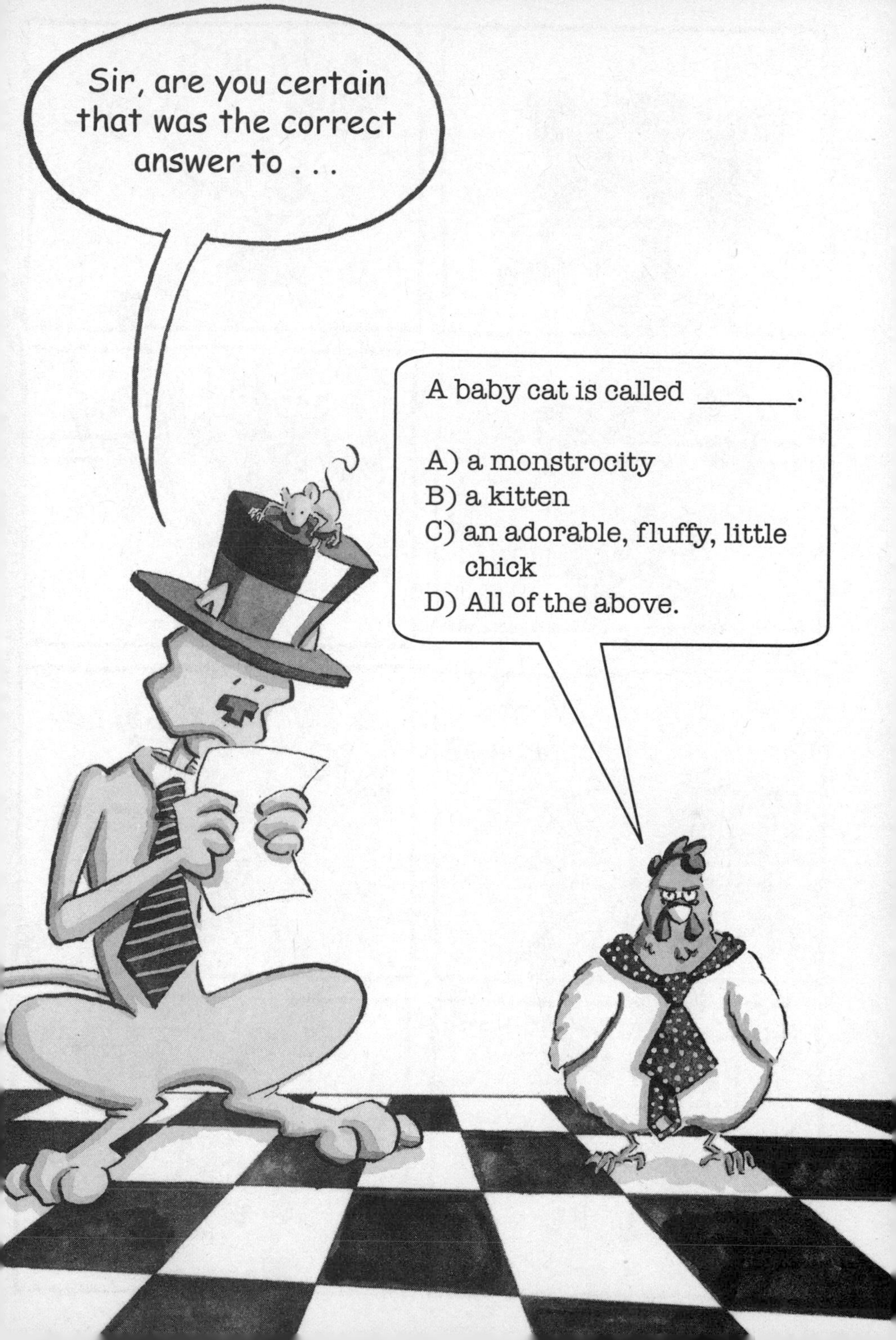

Sir, are you certain that was the correct answer to . . .
A baby cat is called ______.
A) a monstrocity
B) a kitten
C) an adorable, fluffy, little chick
D) All of the above.

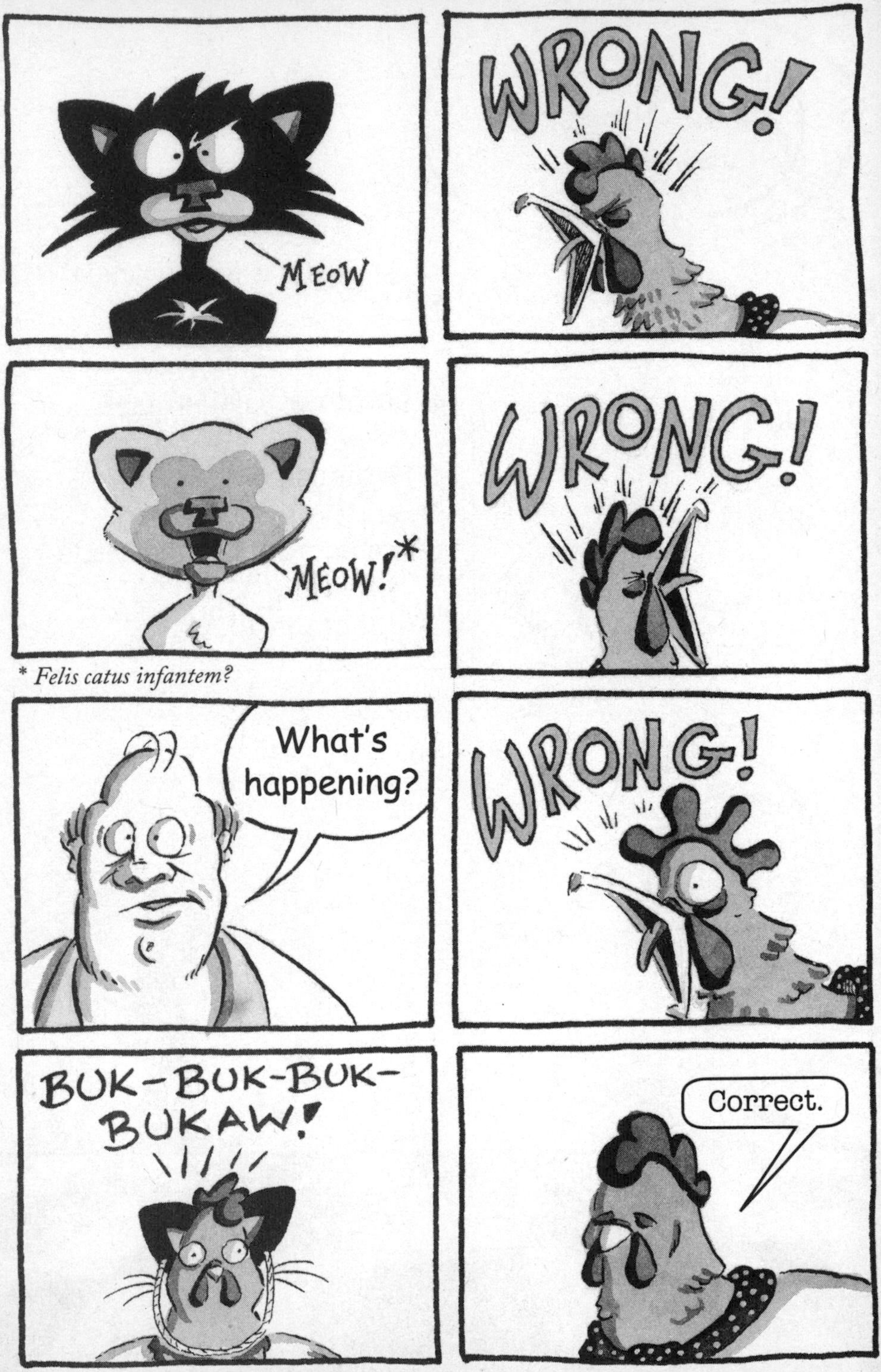
MEOW
WRONG!
MEOW!*
WRONG!
What's happening?
WRONG!
BUK-BUK-BUK-BUKAW!
Correct.

* *Felis catus infantem?*

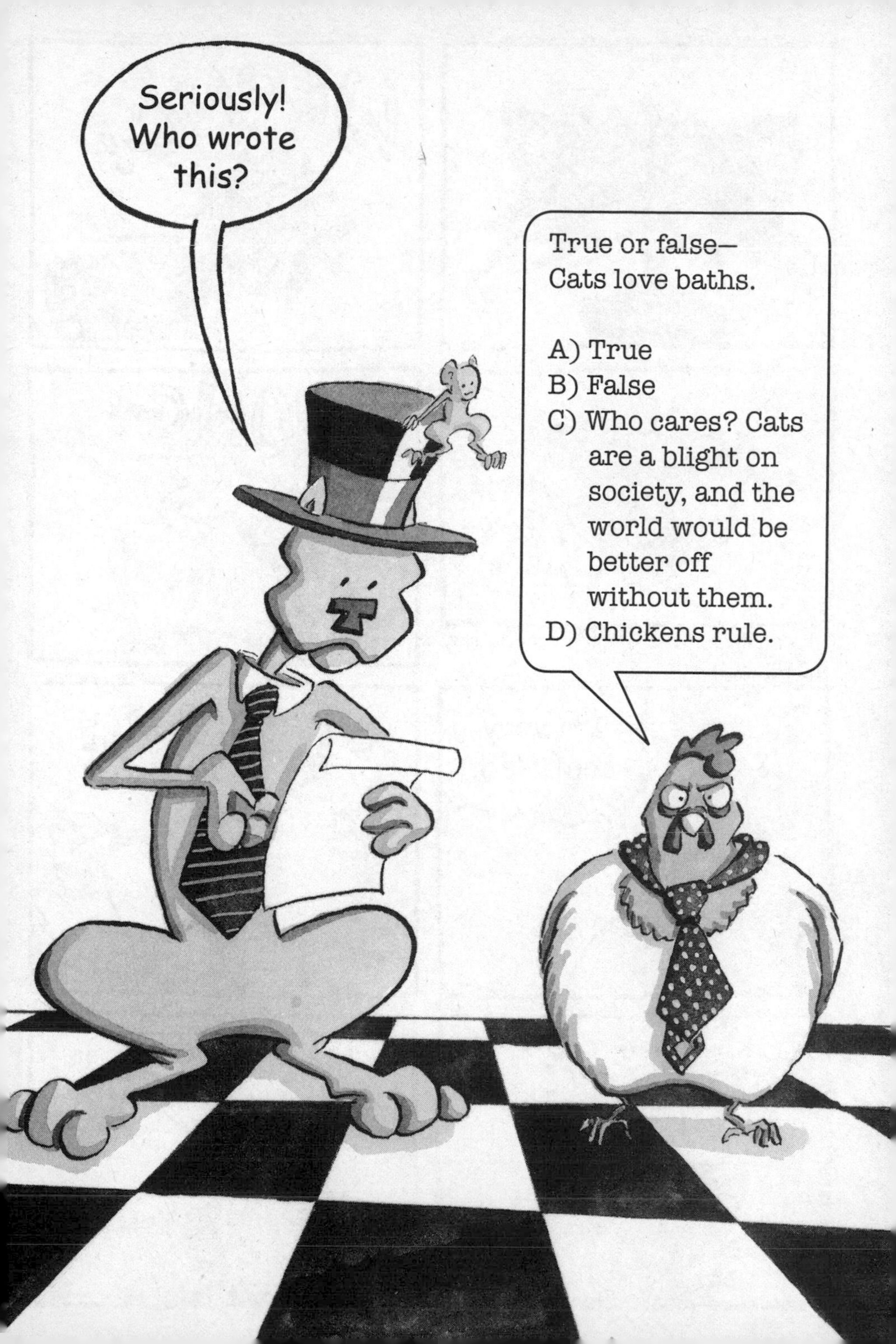
Seriously! Who wrote this?
True or false— Cats love baths.
A) True
B) False
C) Who cares? Cats are a blight on society, and the world would be better off without them.
D) Chickens rule.

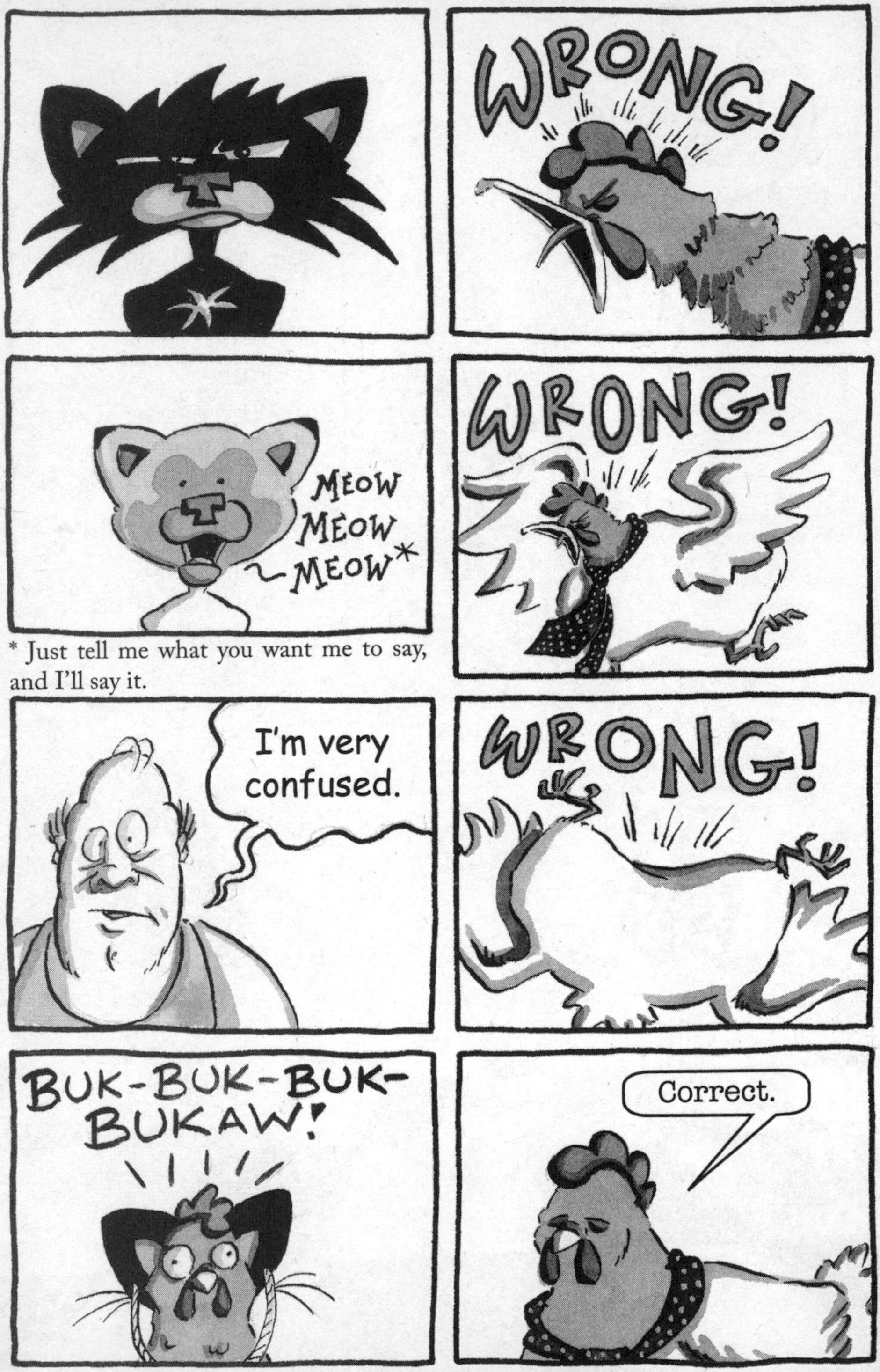
WRONG!
MEOW MEOW MEOW*
WRONG!
I'm very confused.
WRONG!
BUK-BUK-BUK-BUKAW!
Correct.

* Just tell me what you want me to say, and I'll say it.

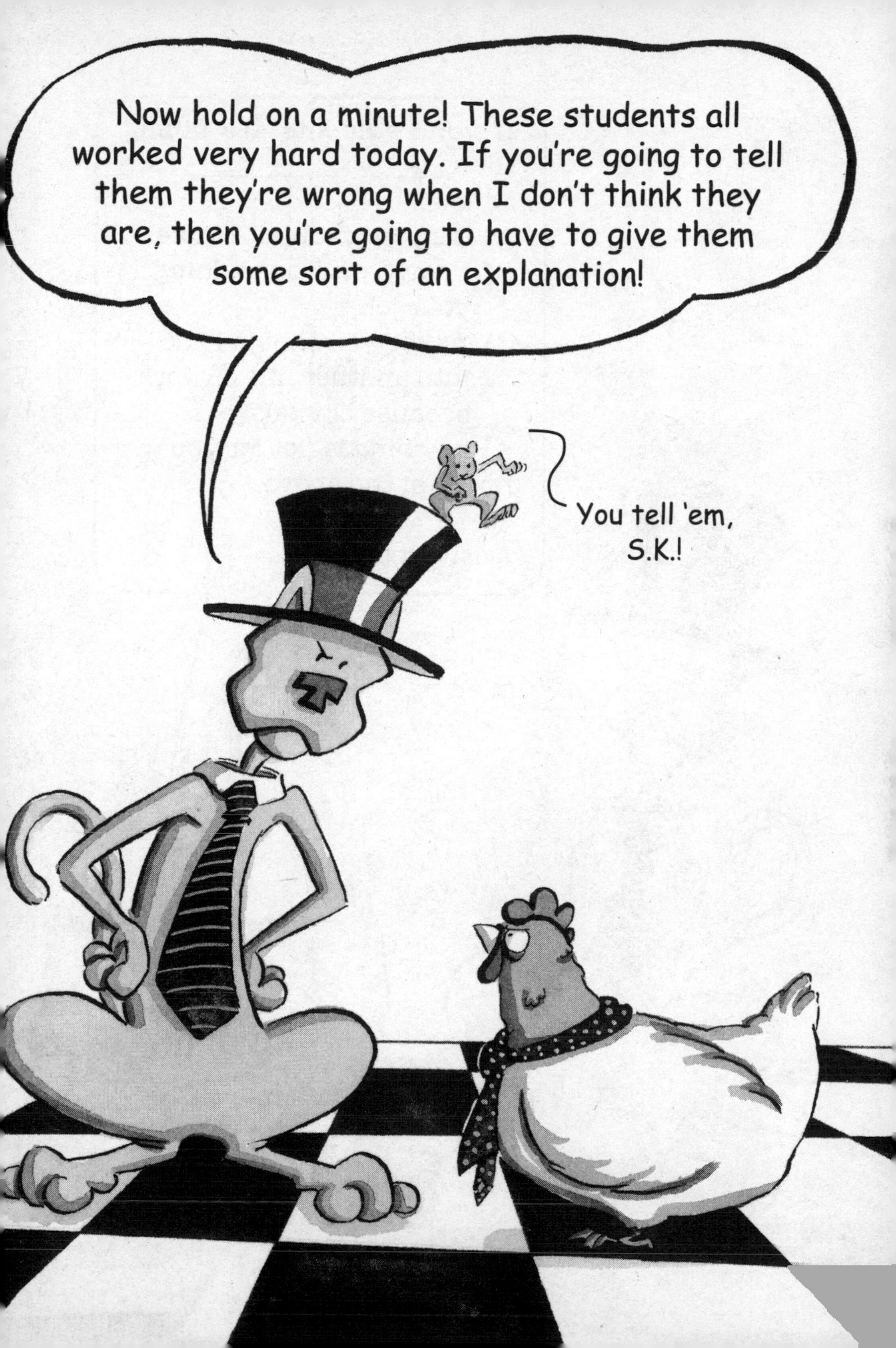
Now hold on a minute! These students all worked very hard today. If you're going to tell them they're wrong when I don't think they are, then you're going to have to give them some sort of an explanation!
You tell 'em, S.K.!

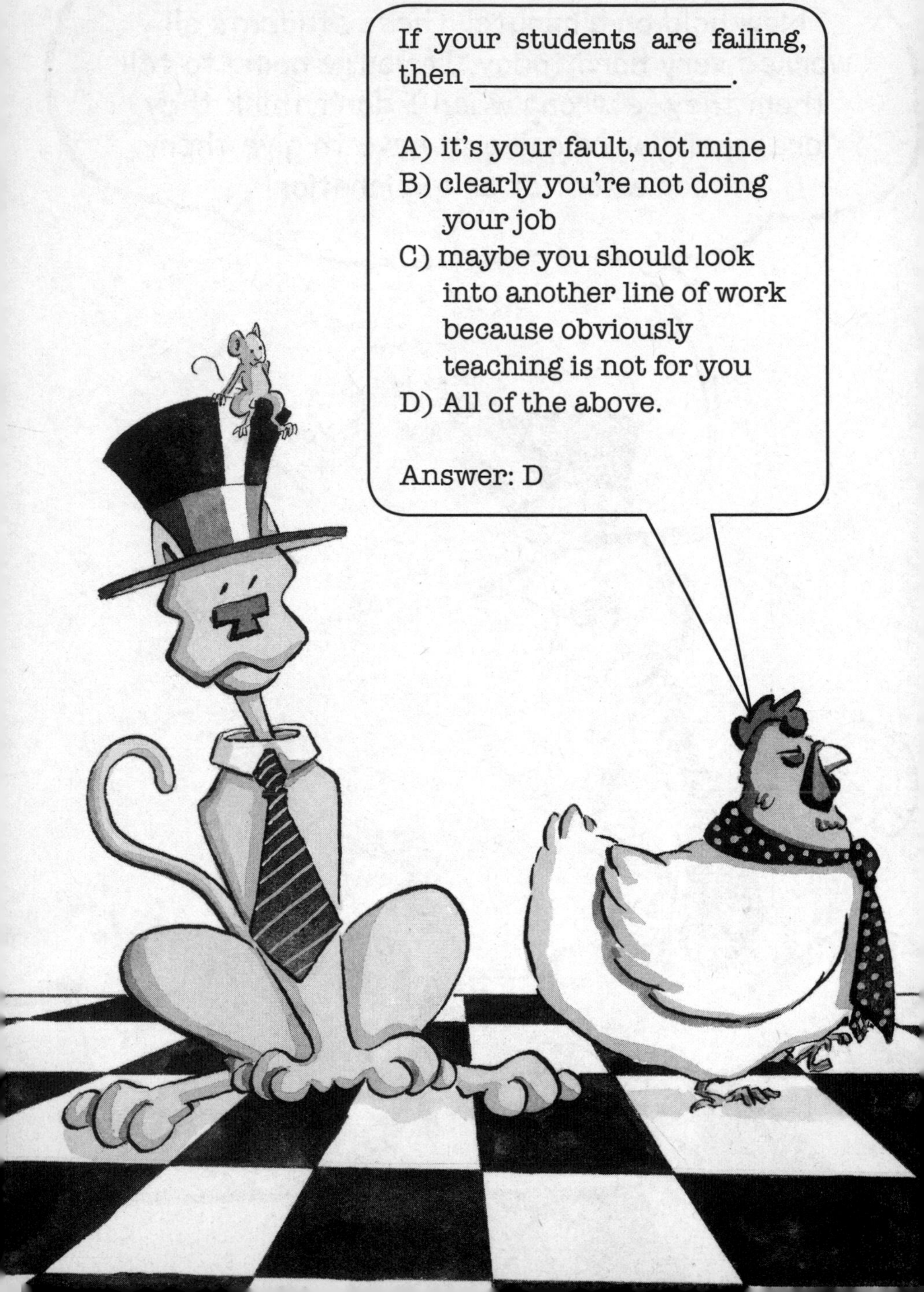
If your students are failing, then ________________.
A) it's your fault, not mine
B) clearly you're not doing your job
C) maybe you should look into another line of work because obviously teaching is not for you
D) All of the above.
Answer: D

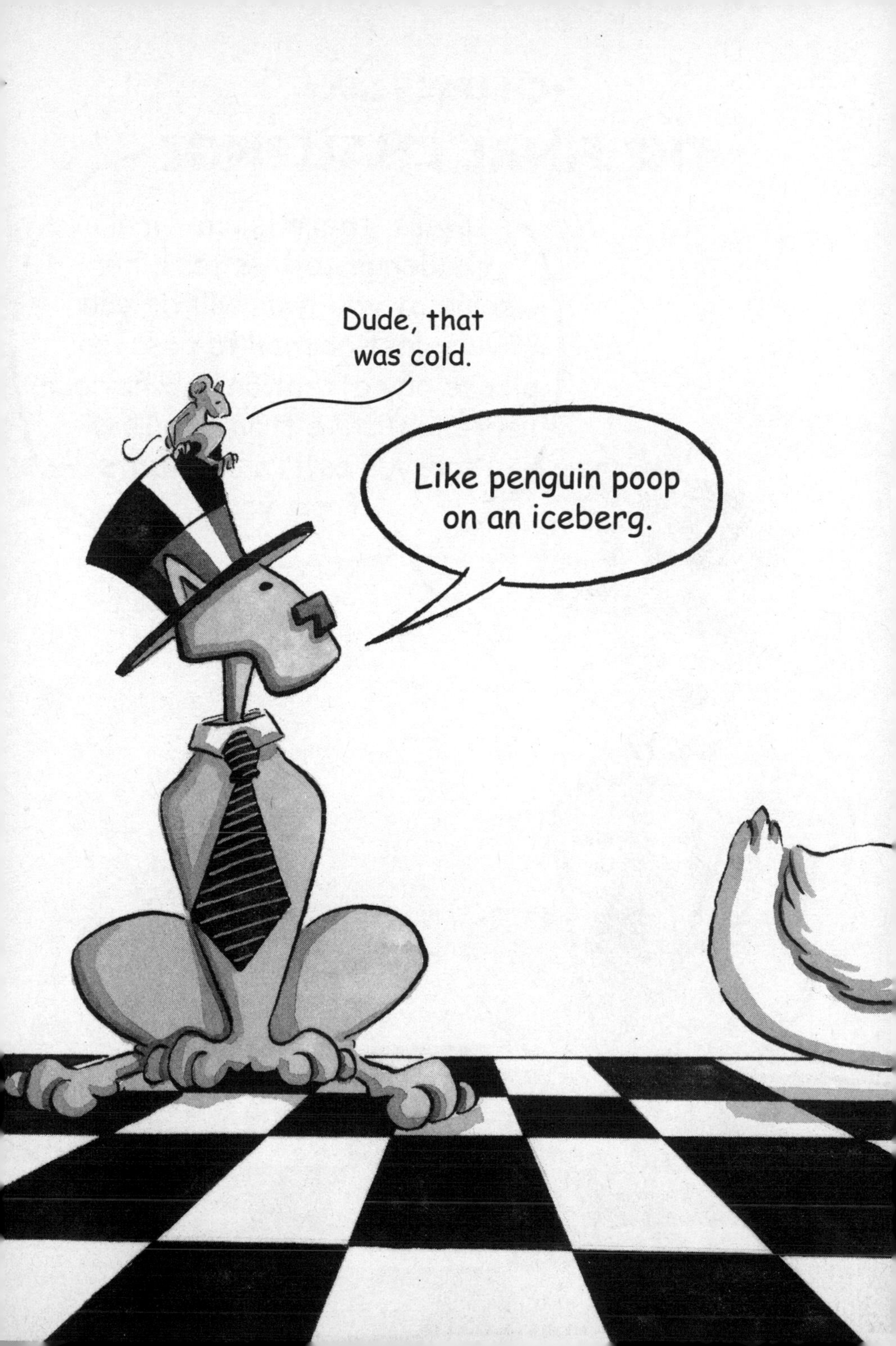
Dude, that was cold.
Like penguin poop on an iceberg.

•CHAPTER SIX•

THE FINAL CHALLENGE

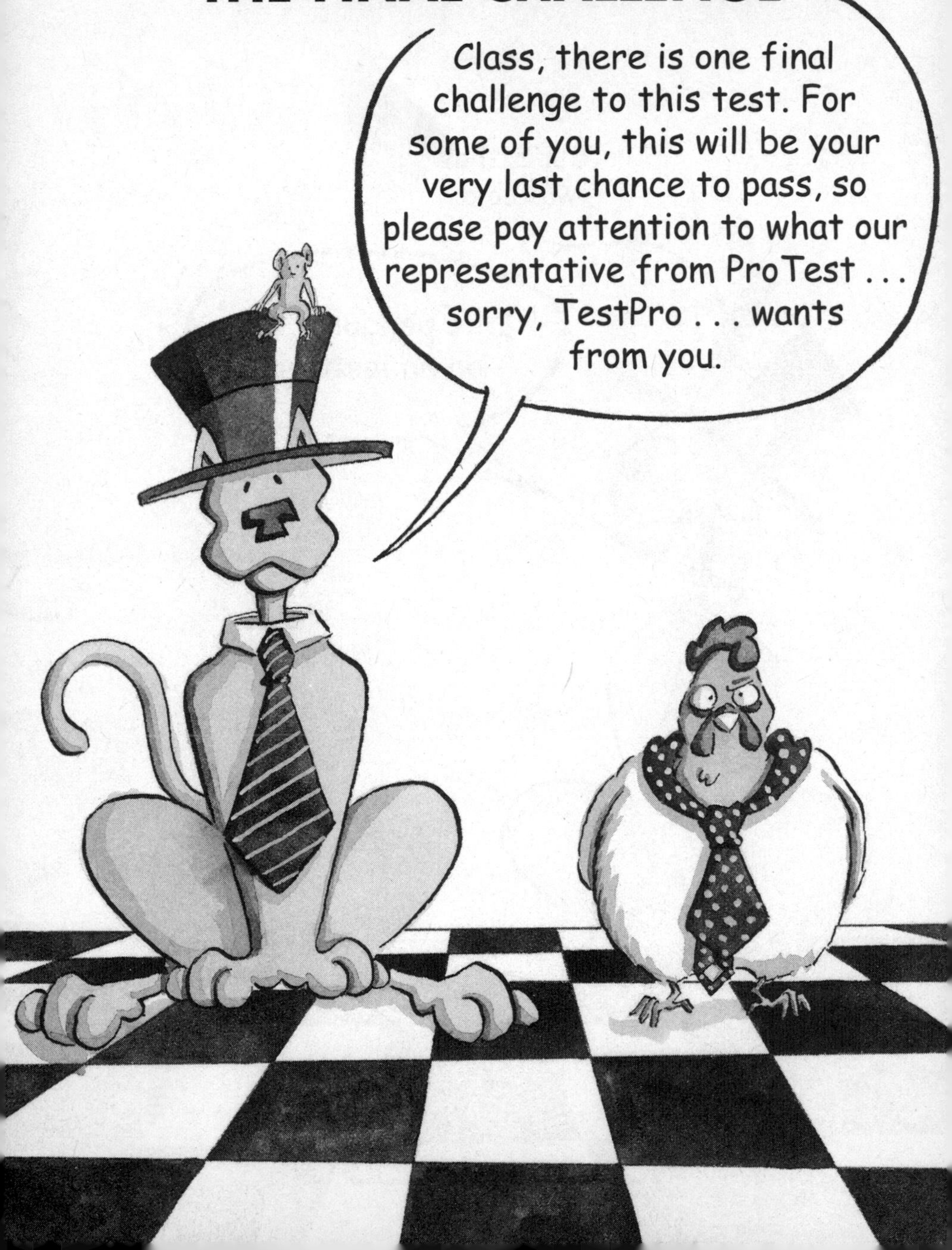

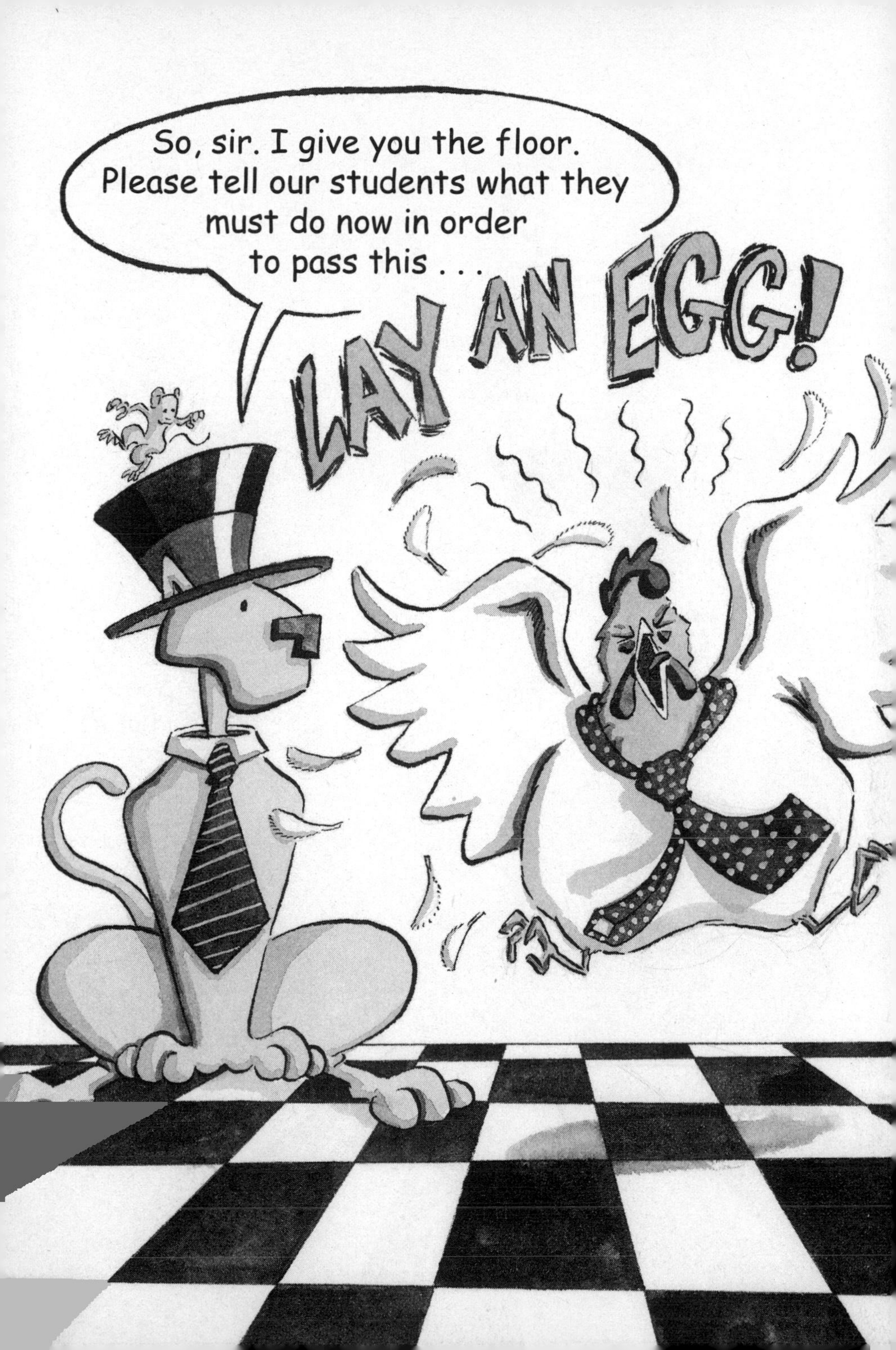
So, sir. I give you the floor. Please tell our students what they must do now in order to pass this . . .
LAY AN EGG!

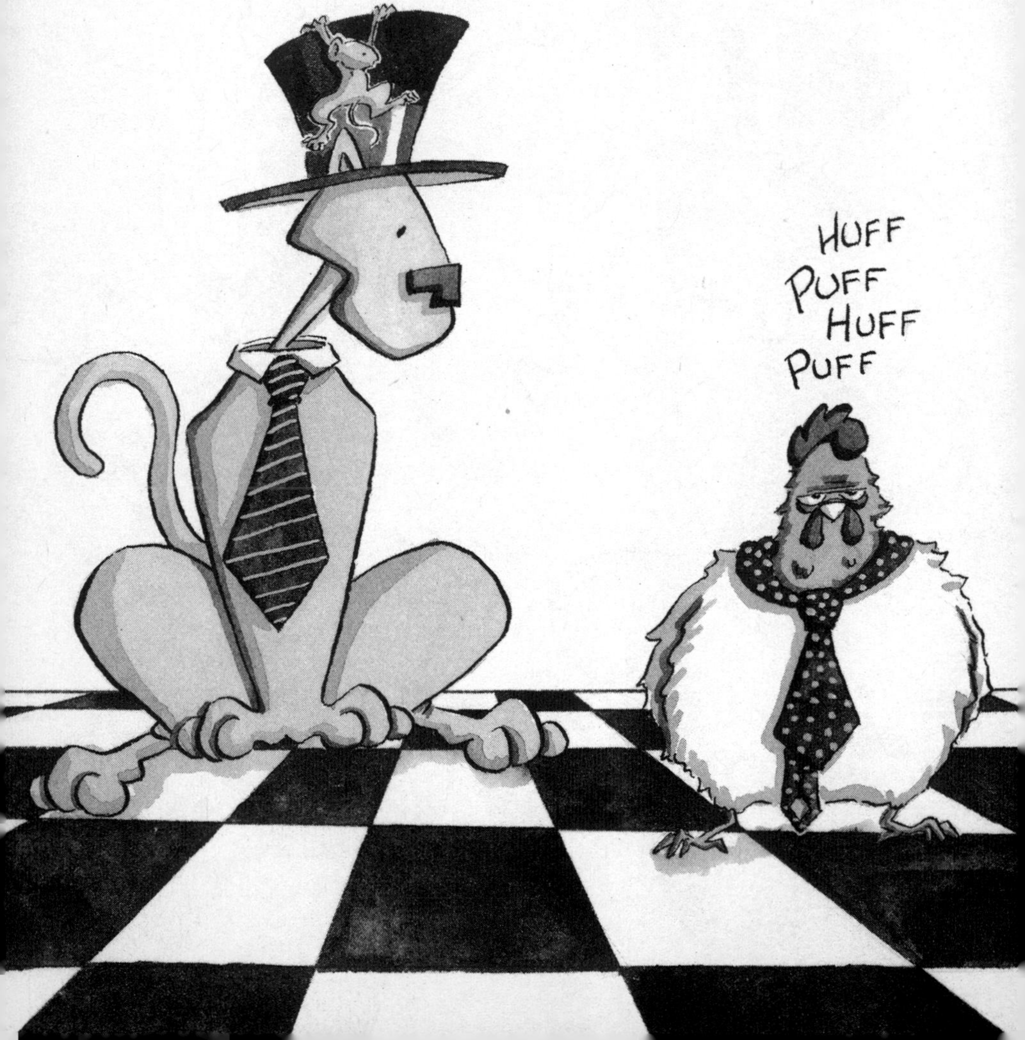
HUFF
PUFF
HUFF
PUFF

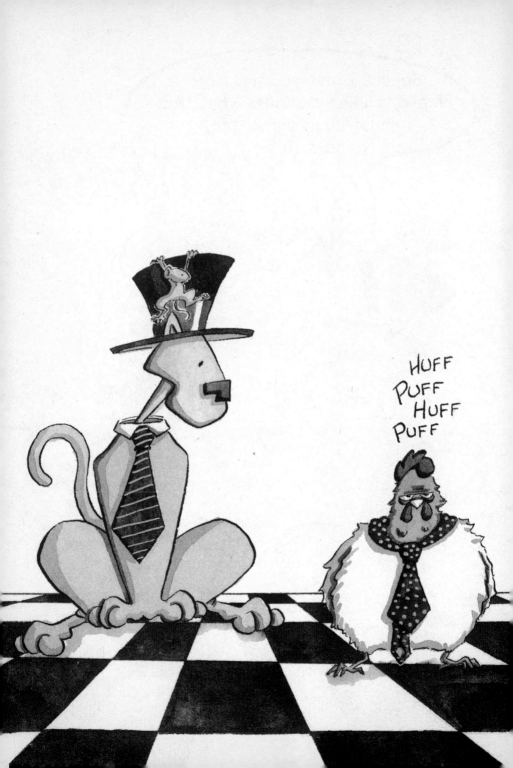

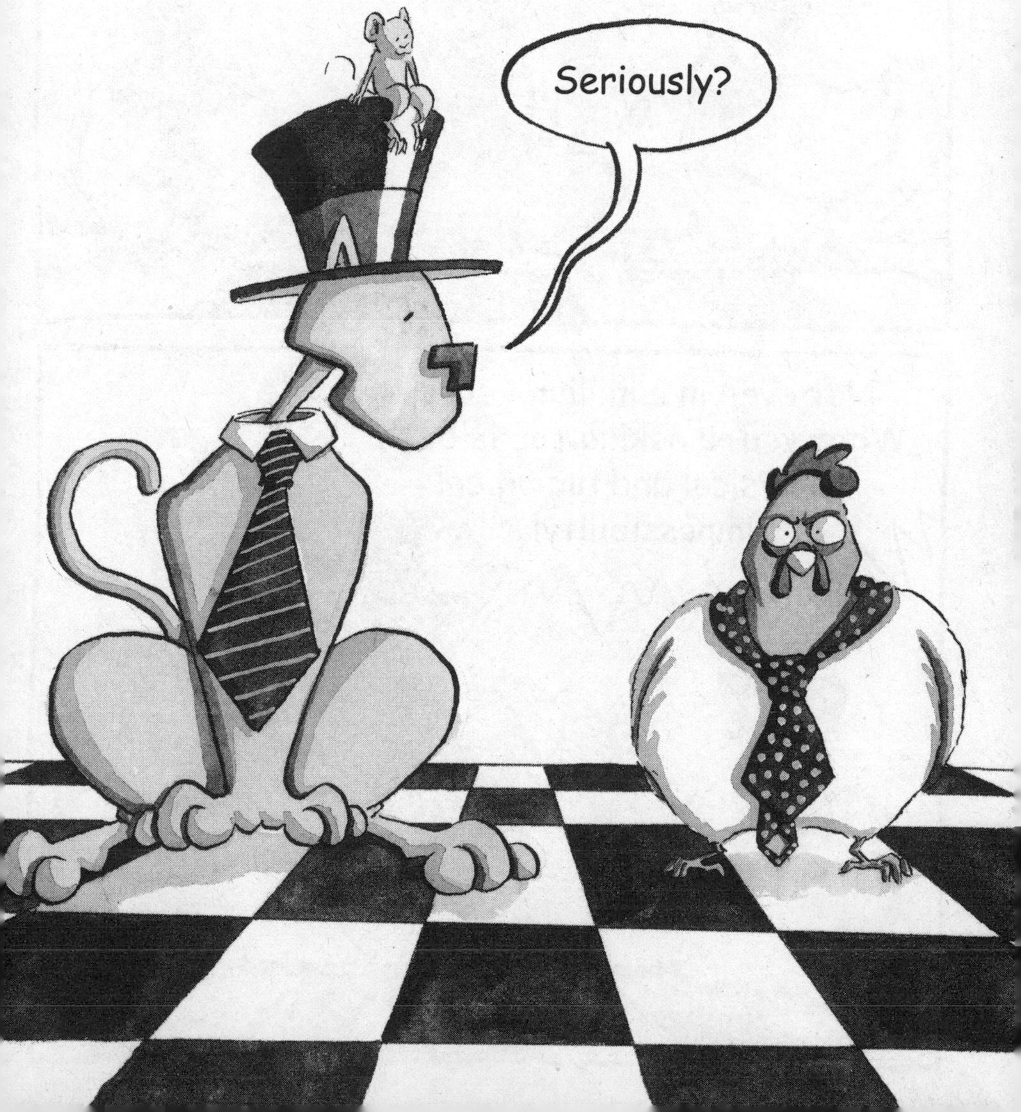
Seriously?

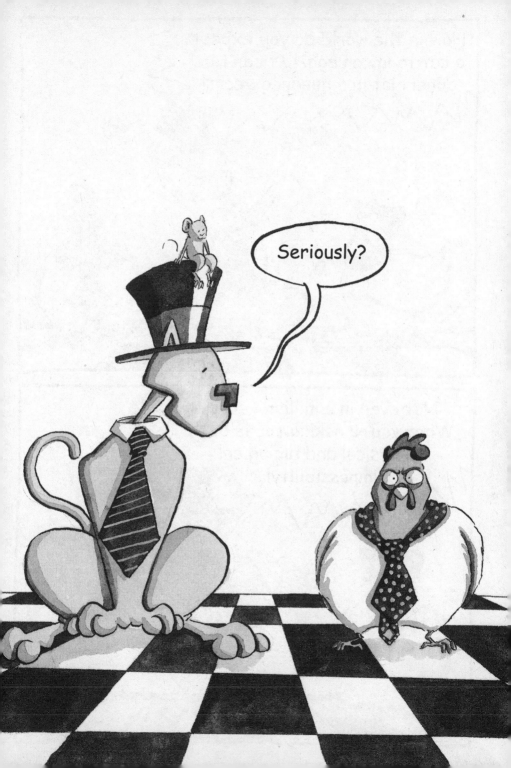

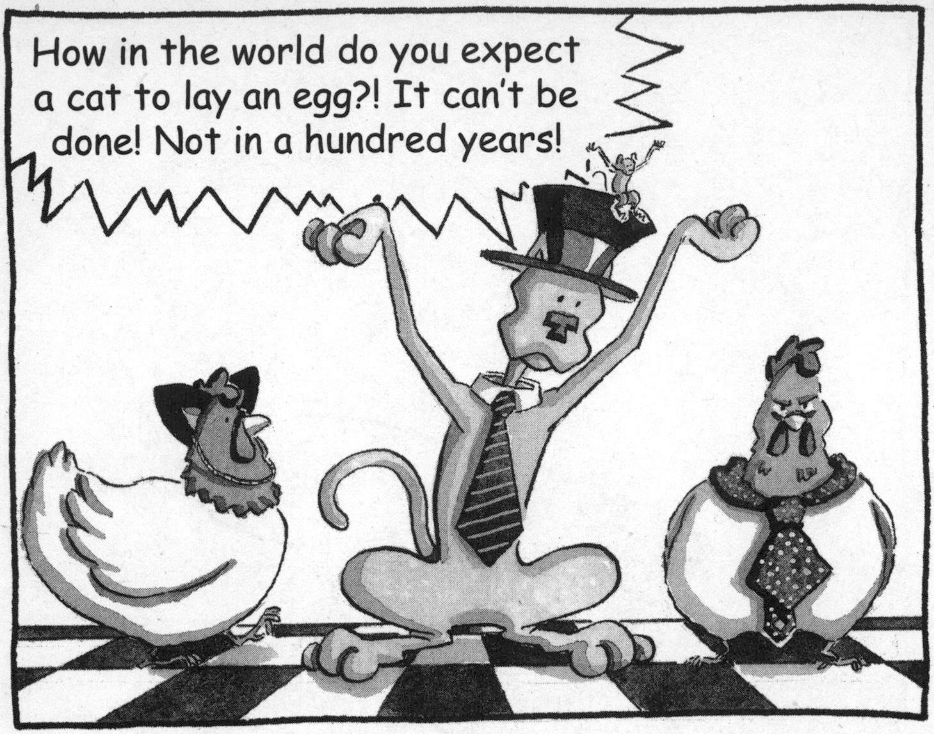
How in the world do you expect a cat to lay an egg?! It can't be done! Not in a hundred years!

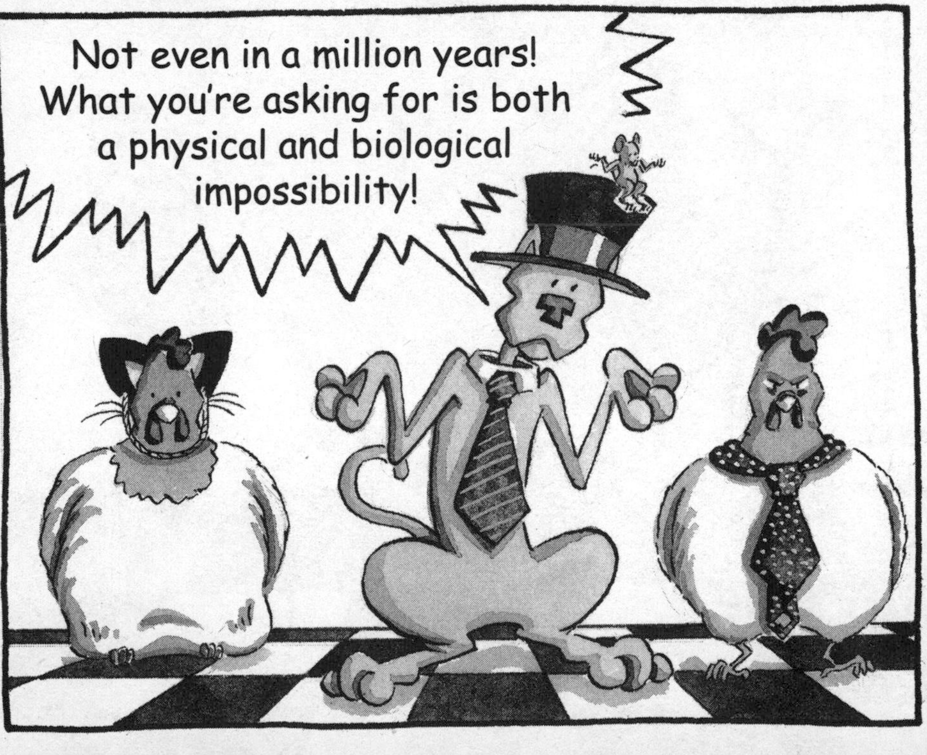
Not even in a million years! What you're asking for is both a physical and biological impossibility!

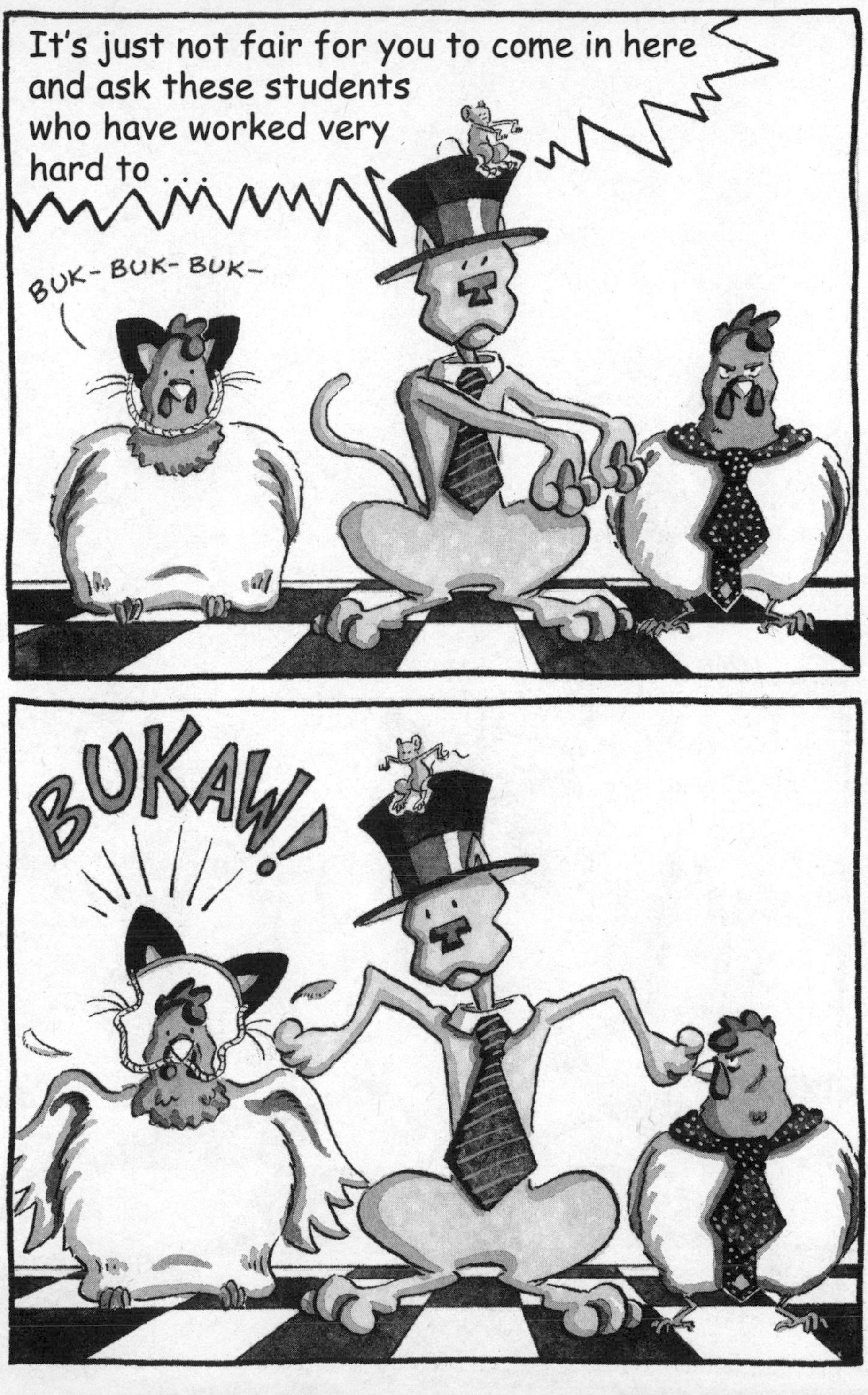

It's just not fair for you to come in here and ask these students who have worked very hard to . . .
BUK-BUK-BUK-
BUKAW!

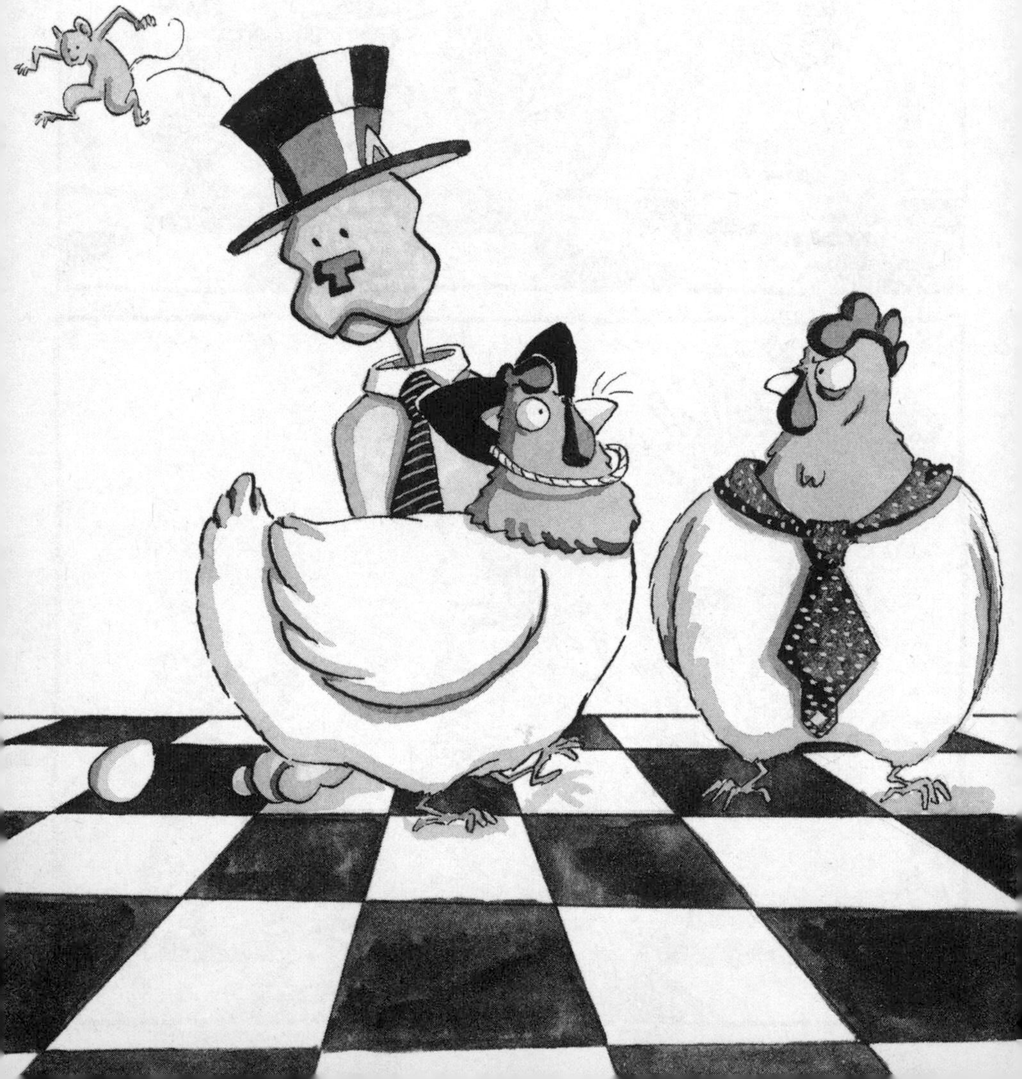

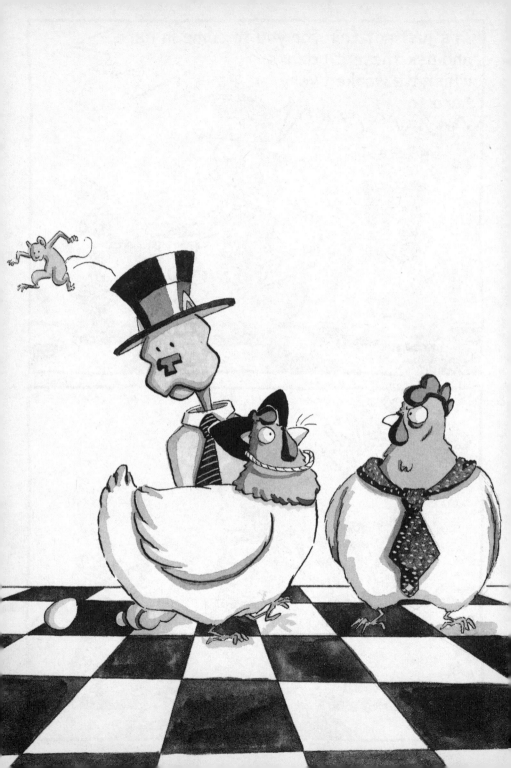

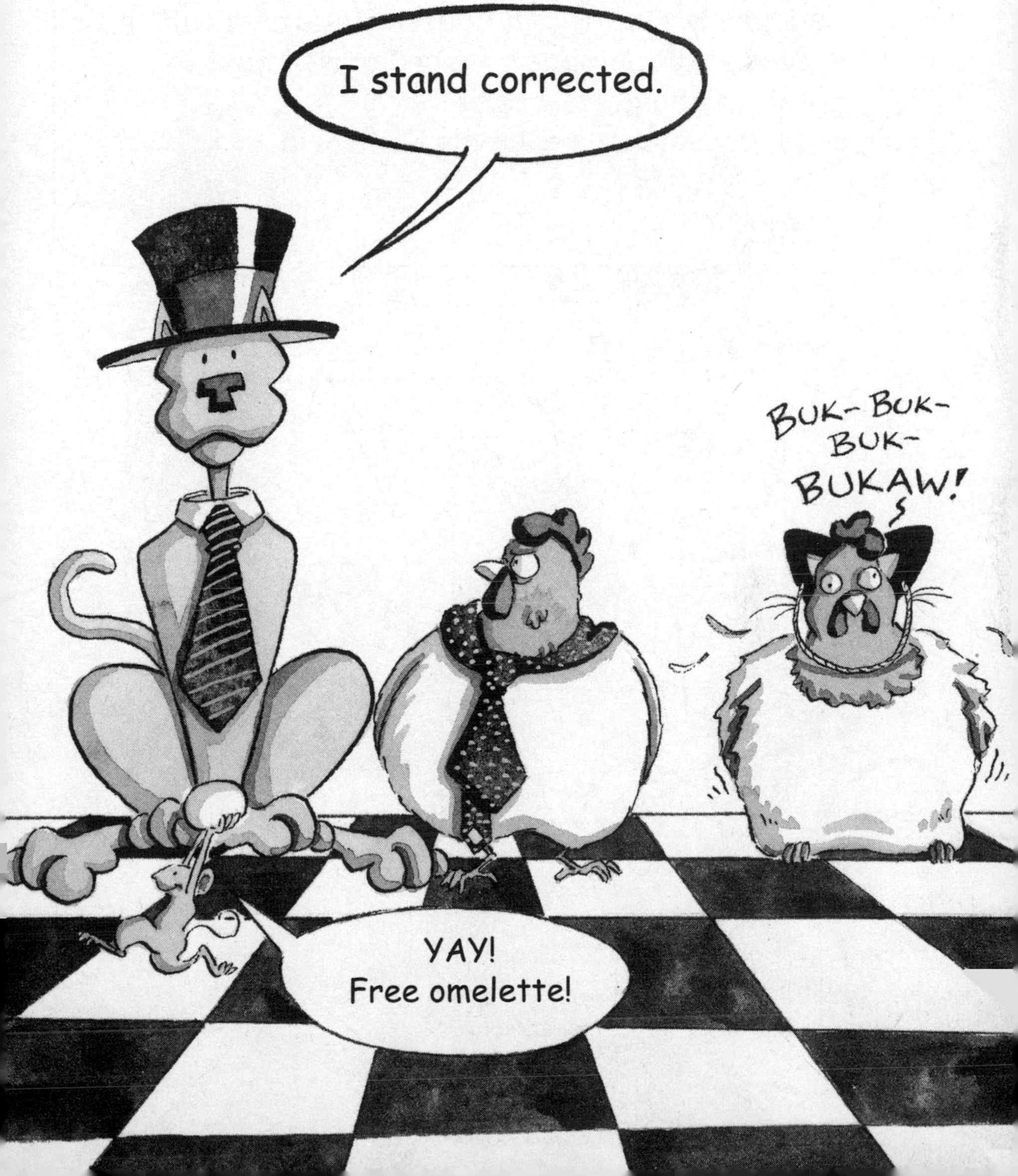
I stand corrected.
BUK-BUK-BUK-BUKAW!
YAY! Free omelette!

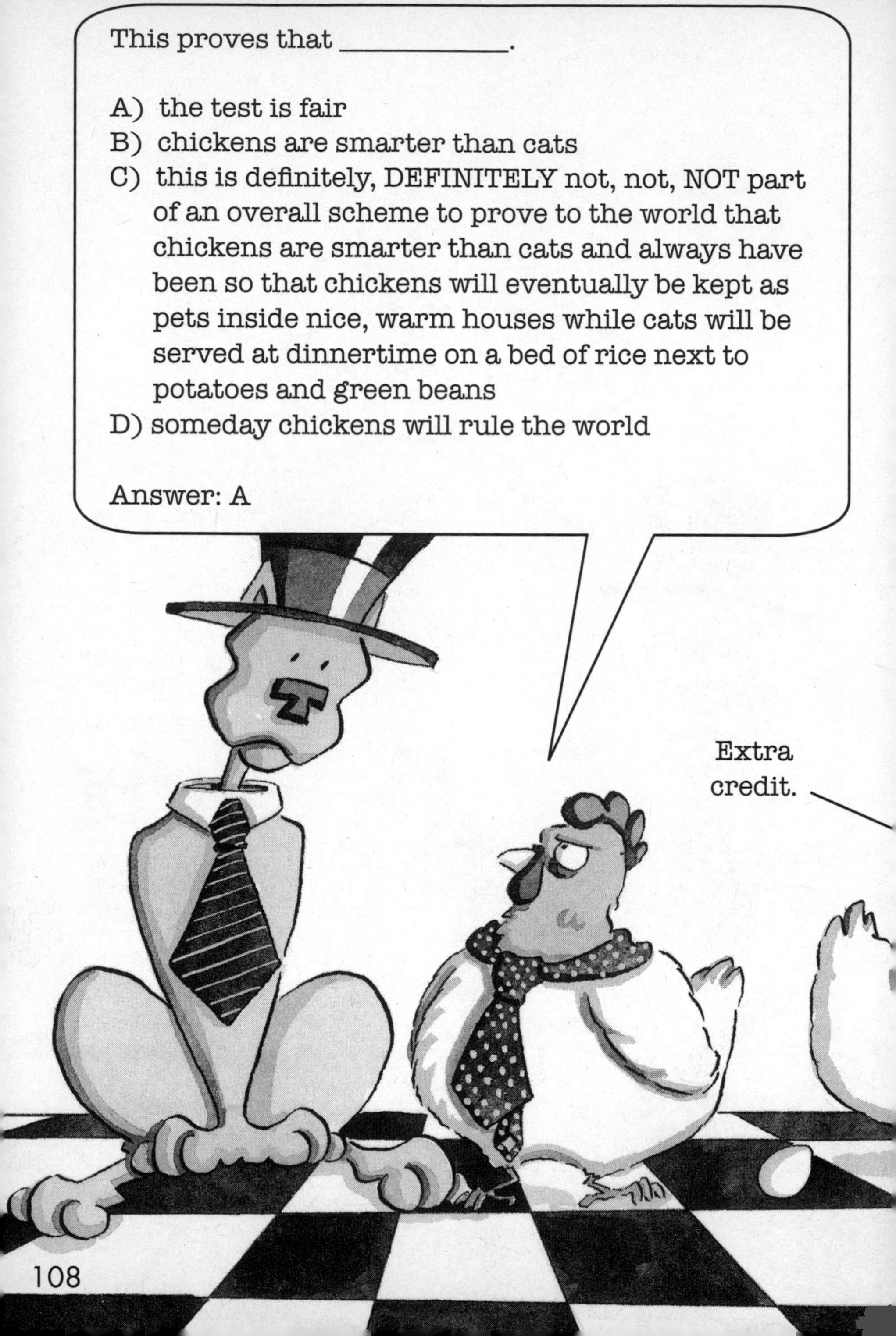
This proves that ____________.
A) the test is fair
B) chickens are smarter than cats
C) this is definitely, DEFINITELY not, not, NOT part of an overall scheme to prove to the world that chickens are smarter than cats and always have been so that chickens will eventually be kept as pets inside nice, warm houses while cats will be served at dinnertime on a bed of rice next to potatoes and green beans
D) someday chickens will rule the world
Answer: A
Extra credit.

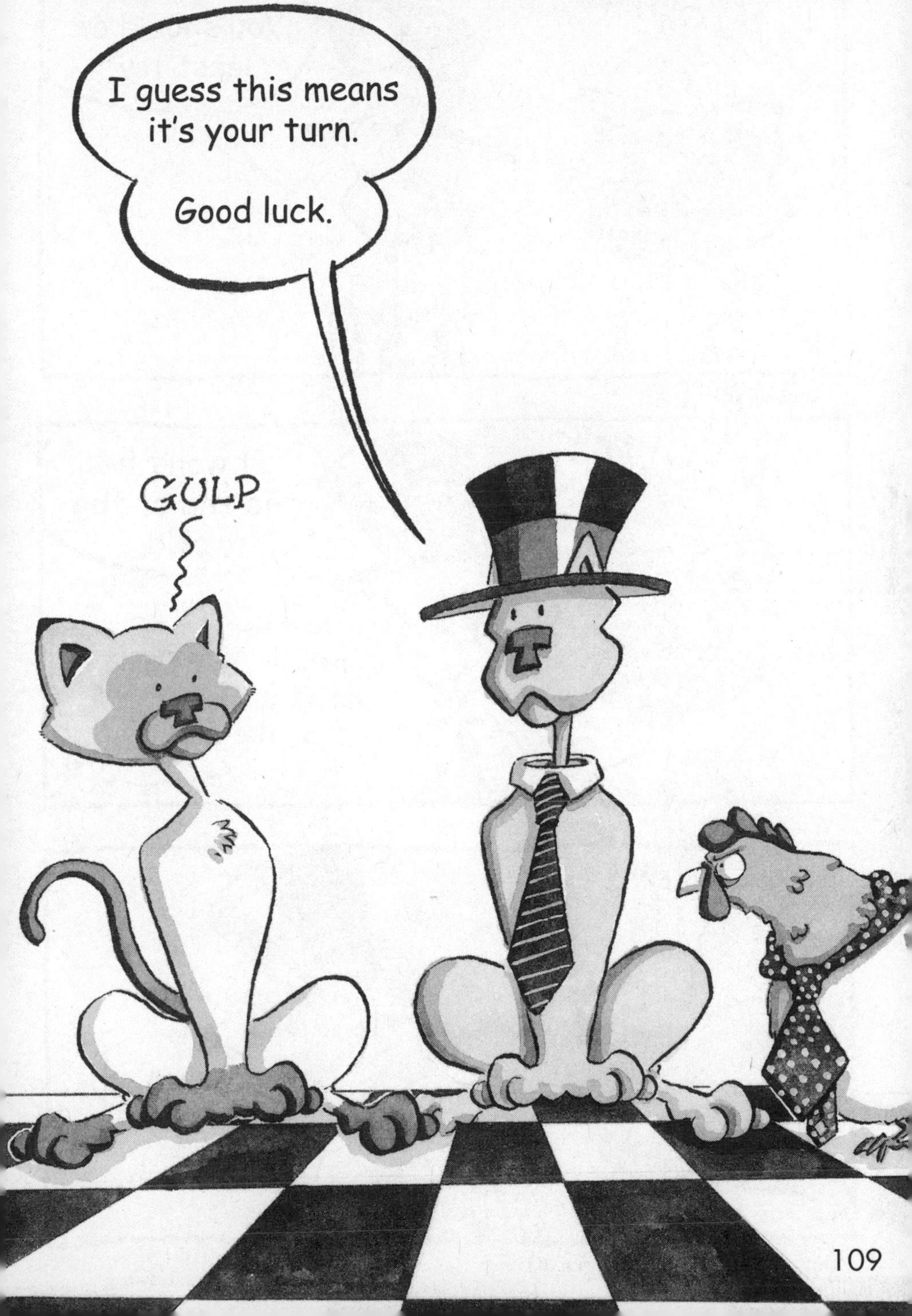
I guess this means it's your turn.
Good luck.
GULP

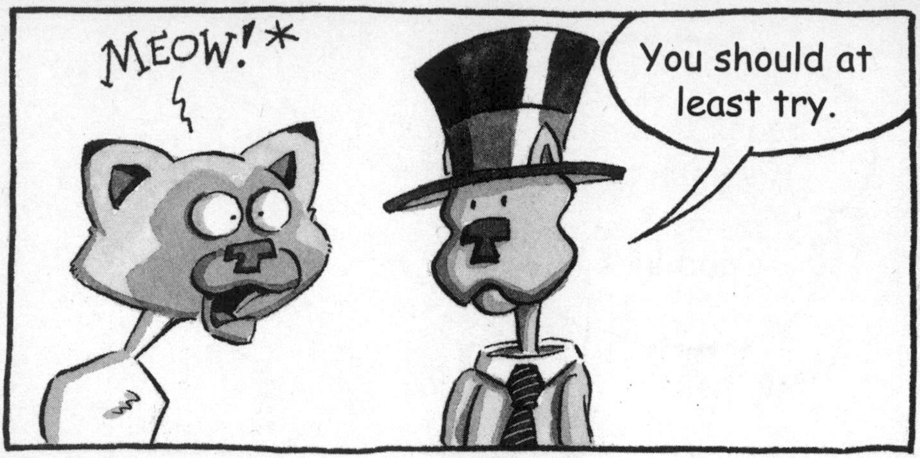
MEOW!*
You should at least try.

* I can't do it!

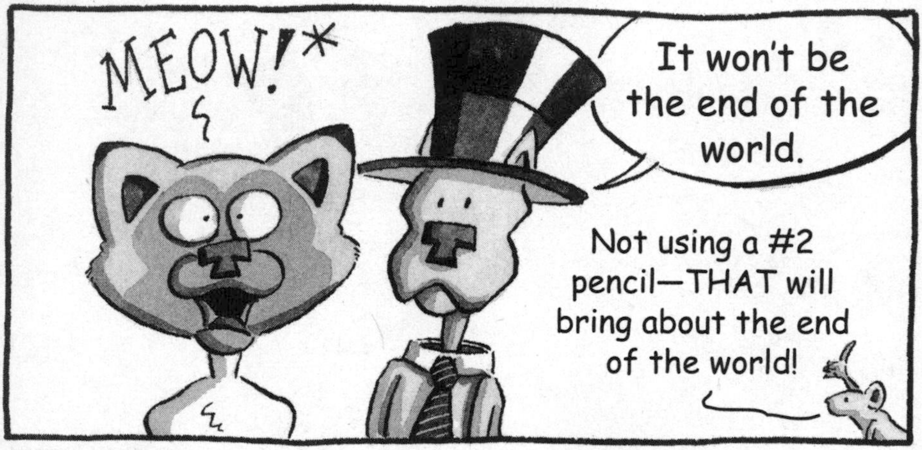
MEOW!*
It won't be the end of the world.
Not using a #2 pencil—THAT will bring about the end of the world!

* What if I fail?!

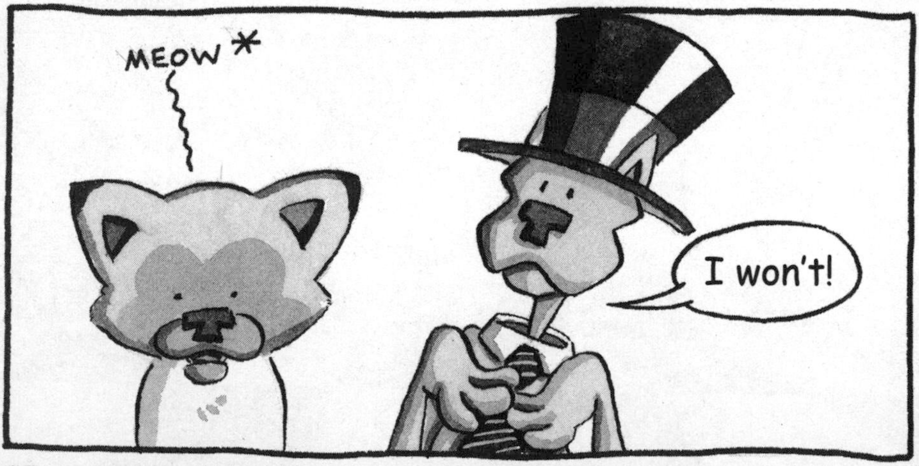
MEOW*
I won't!

* But everyone will think I'm a dummy.

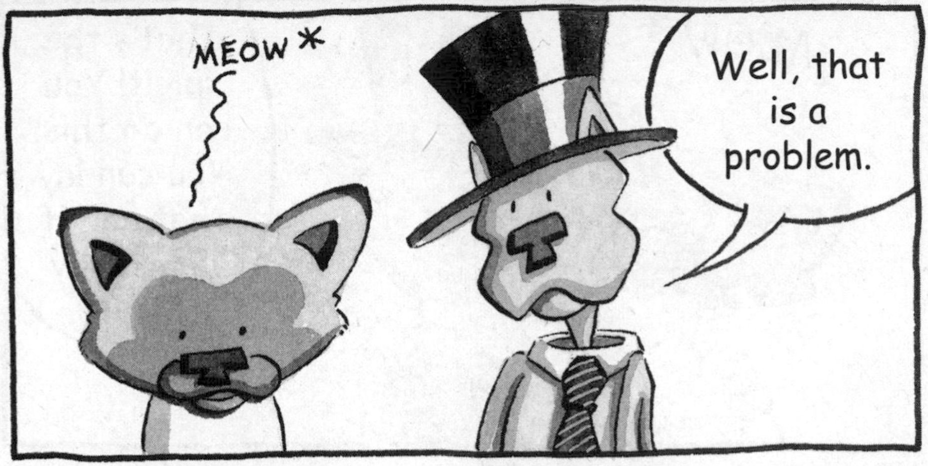
MEOW *
Well, that is a problem.

* I will. I'll feel like a dummy.

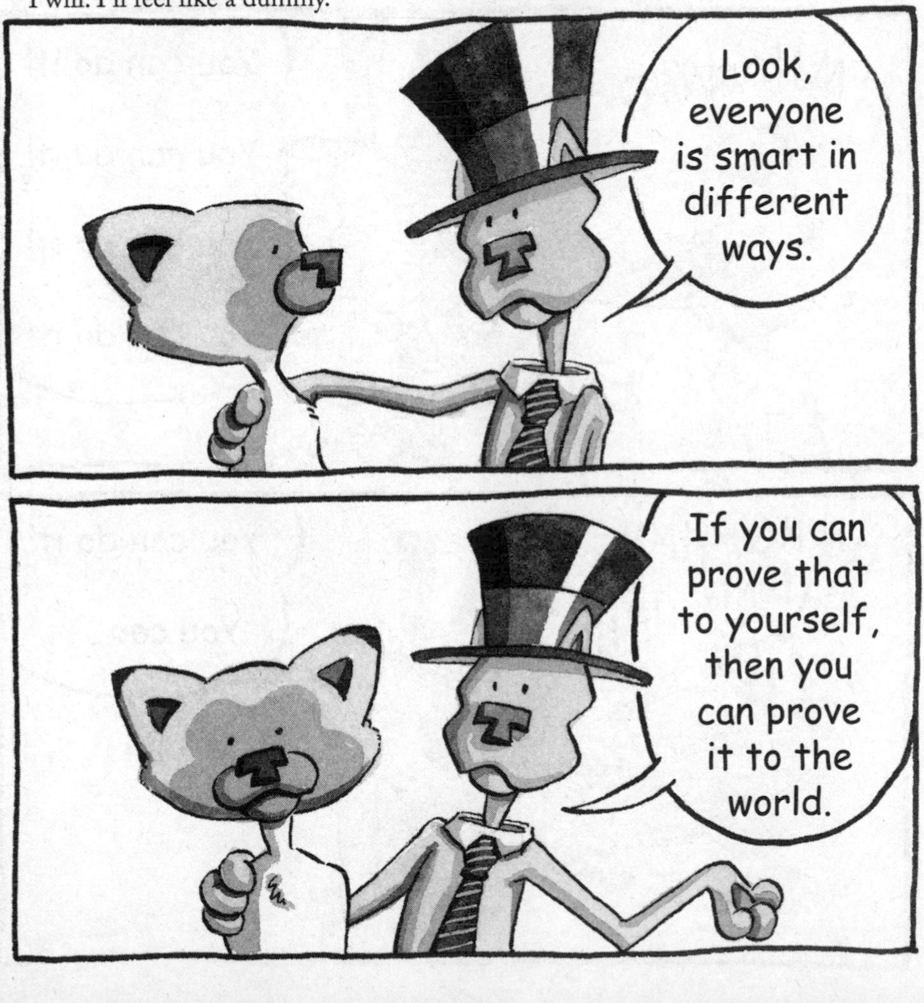
Look, everyone is smart in different ways.
If you can prove that to yourself, then you can prove it to the world.

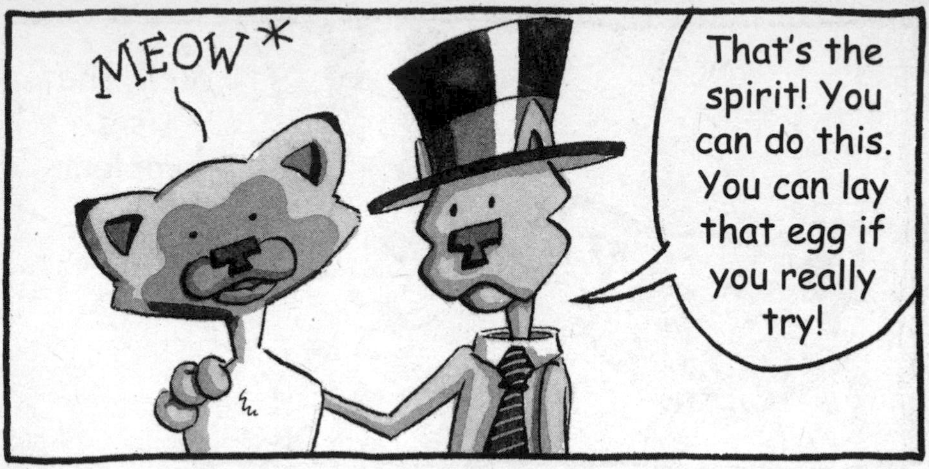
MEOW*
That's the spirit! You can do this. You can lay that egg if you really try!

* I'll try.

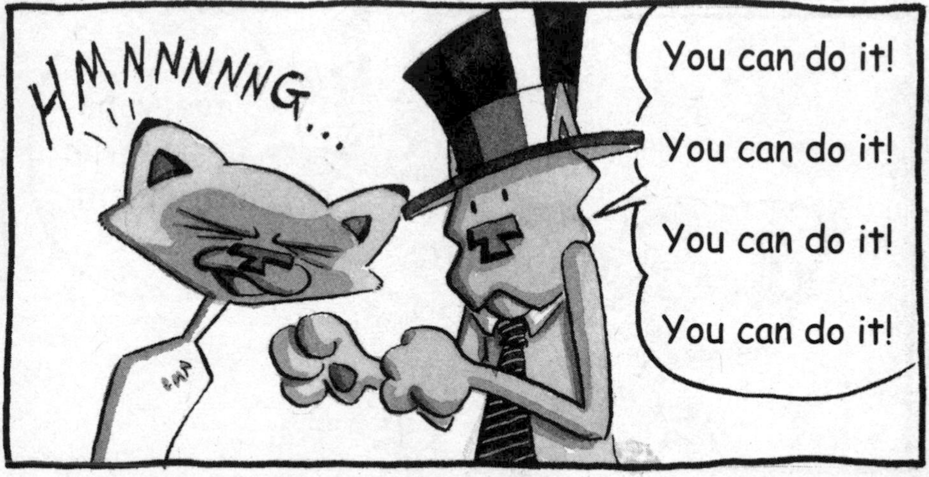
HMNNNNNG...
You can do it!
You can do it!
You can do it!
You can do it!

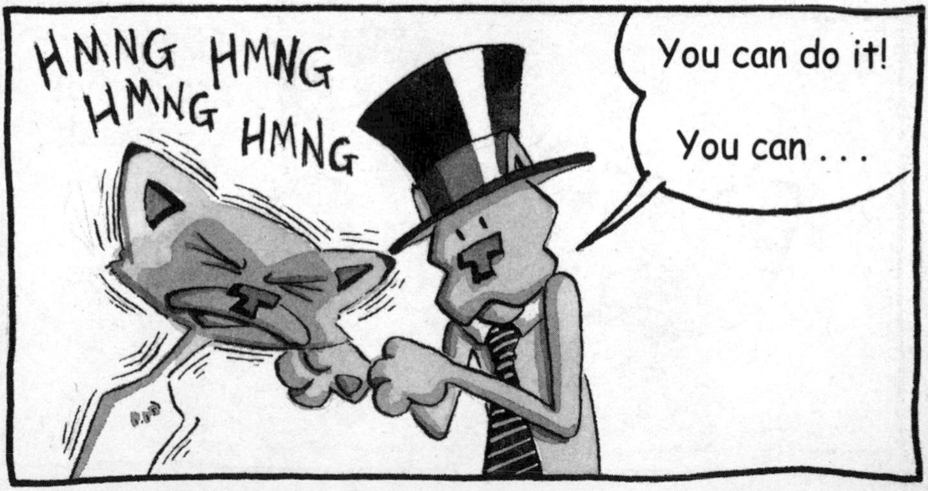
HMNG HMNG
HMNG HMNG
You can do it!
You can . . .

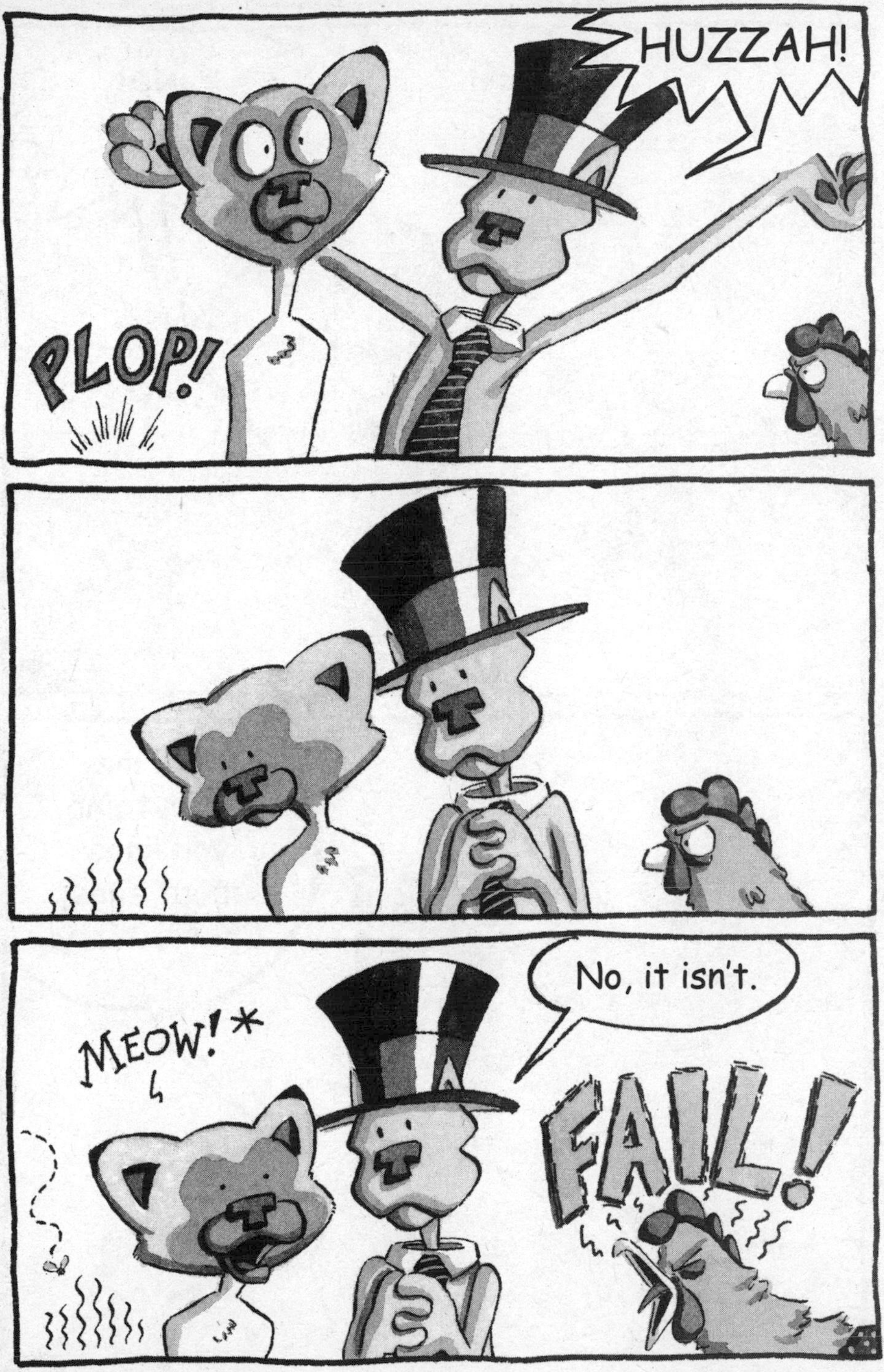
HUZZAH!
PLOP!
MEOW! *
No, it isn't.
FAIL!

* That's not an egg, is it?

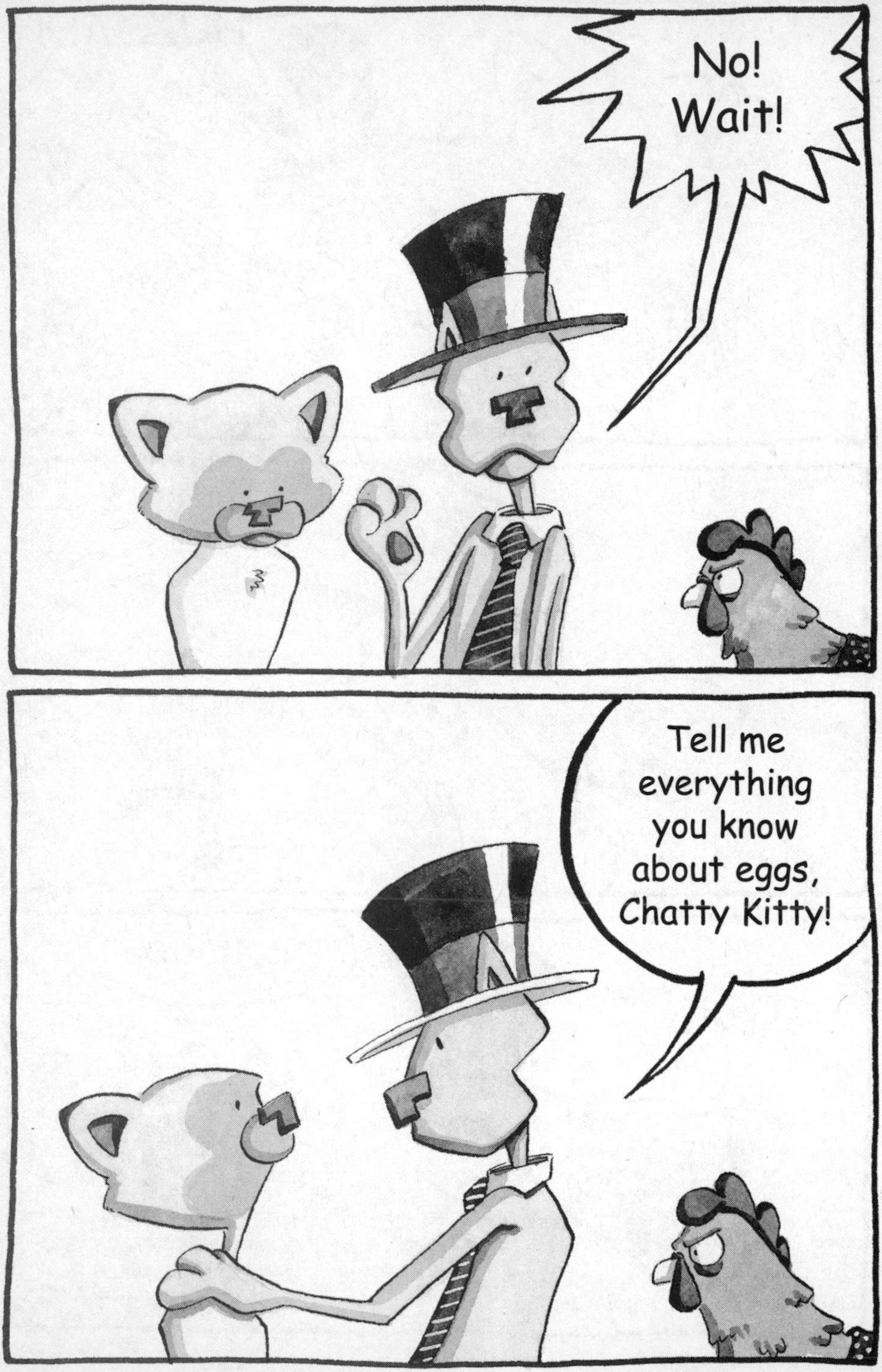
No! Wait!
Tell me everything you know about eggs, Chatty Kitty!

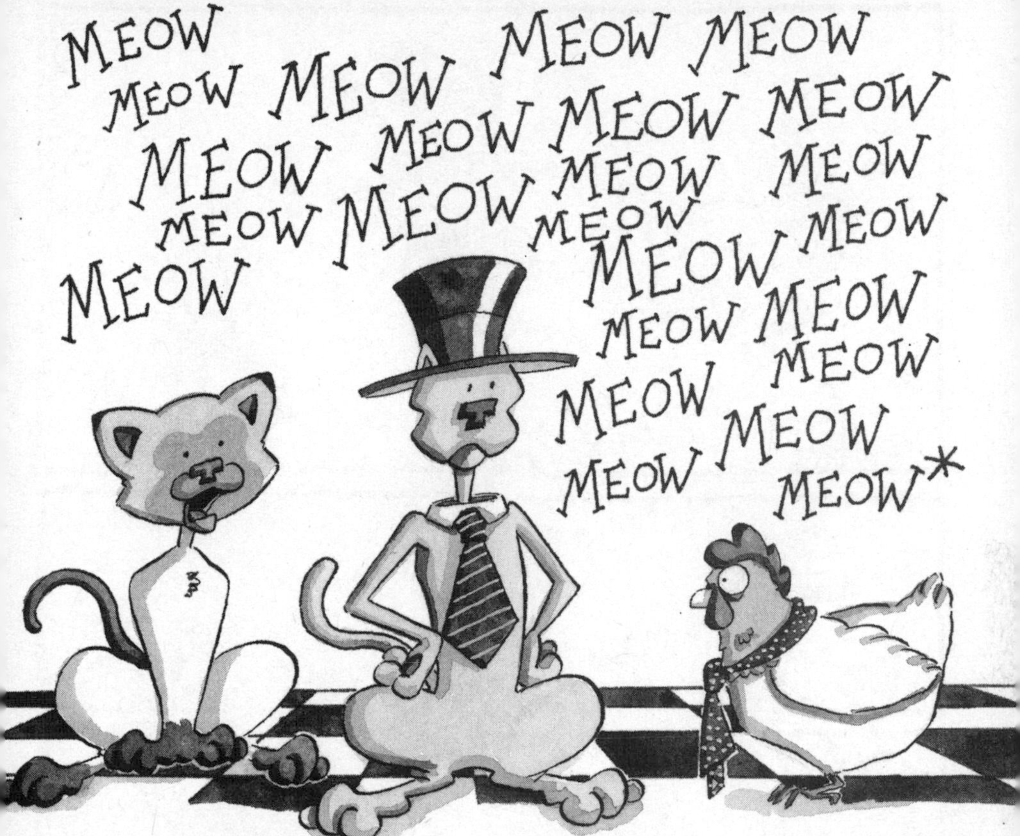
MEOW MEOW MEOW
MEOW MEOW
MEOW MEOW MEOW MEOW
MEOW MEOW MEOW MEOW
MEOW MEOW MEOW MEOW
MEOW MEOW
MEOW MEOW
MEOW MEOW
MEOW MEOW
MEOW*

* Approximately 1.1 trillion eggs are consumed worldwide each year, China being the largest producer. Roughly half of all eggs produced are white, and the other half are brown. The color of the egg depends largely on the color of the earlobe of the chicken that laid it: white earlobe, white egg—red earlobe, brown egg. Egg shells are composed primarily of calcium carbonate, which is also the main ingredient in some antacids, but I don't recommend chewing on egg shells if you have an upset stomach. The membrane inside the shell is semipermeable, meaning that it allows water and oxygen inside the egg while keeping dust and other debris out. The white of an egg is also called the albumin after the primary protein that inhabits it. If an egg white looks cloudy, that actually means that the egg is very fresh. The color of the egg yolk depends greatly on the diet of the chicken that laid it: the more yellow or orange pigments in the food, the more brightly colored the yolk. A monotreme is a mammal that lays an egg, and there are only five known species in the world, the platypus and four species of echidna. The largest eggs come from ostriches, which can weigh as much as 5 pounds, and the smallest eggs come from vervain hummingbirds, which weigh only a fraction of an ounce. And lastly, a person who is considered to be intellectually gifted is often referred to as an egghead. I've been called an egghead. I wasn't insulted.

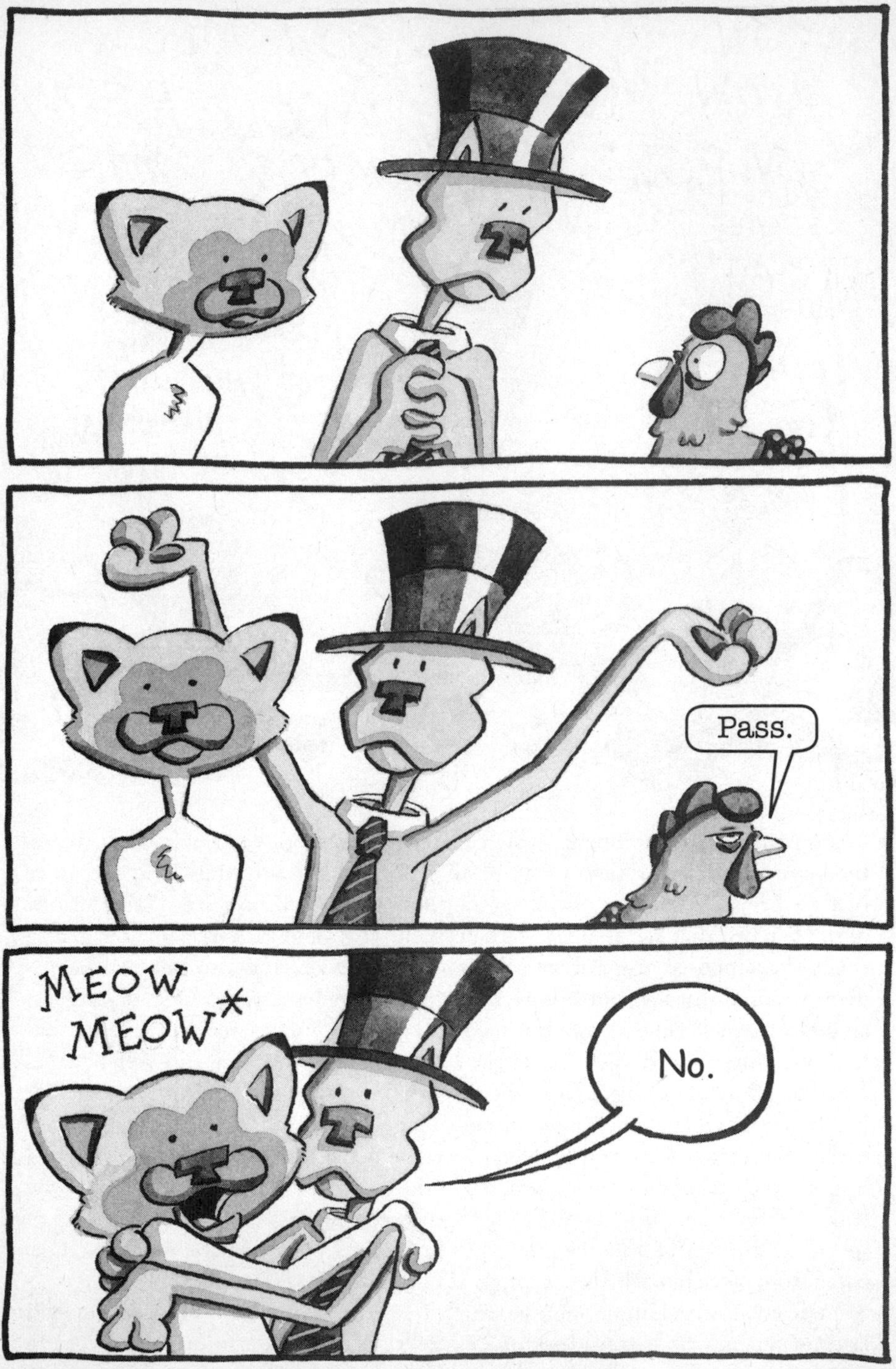
Pass.
MEOW MEOW*
No.

* Shall I tell you everything I know about dishwashers?

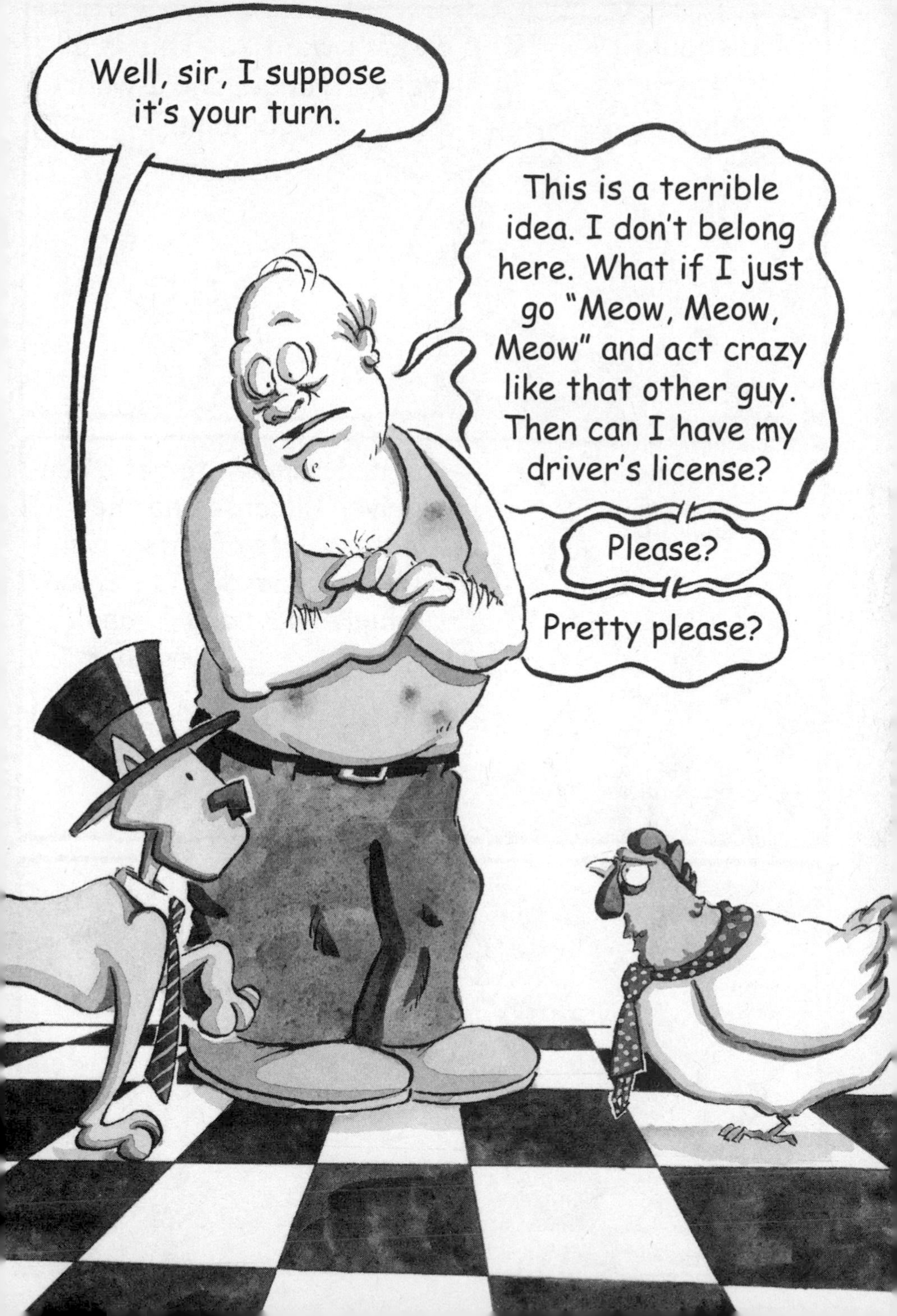
Well, sir, I suppose it's your turn.
This is a terrible idea. I don't belong here. What if I just go "Meow, Meow, Meow" and act crazy like that other guy. Then can I have my driver's license?
Please?
Pretty please?

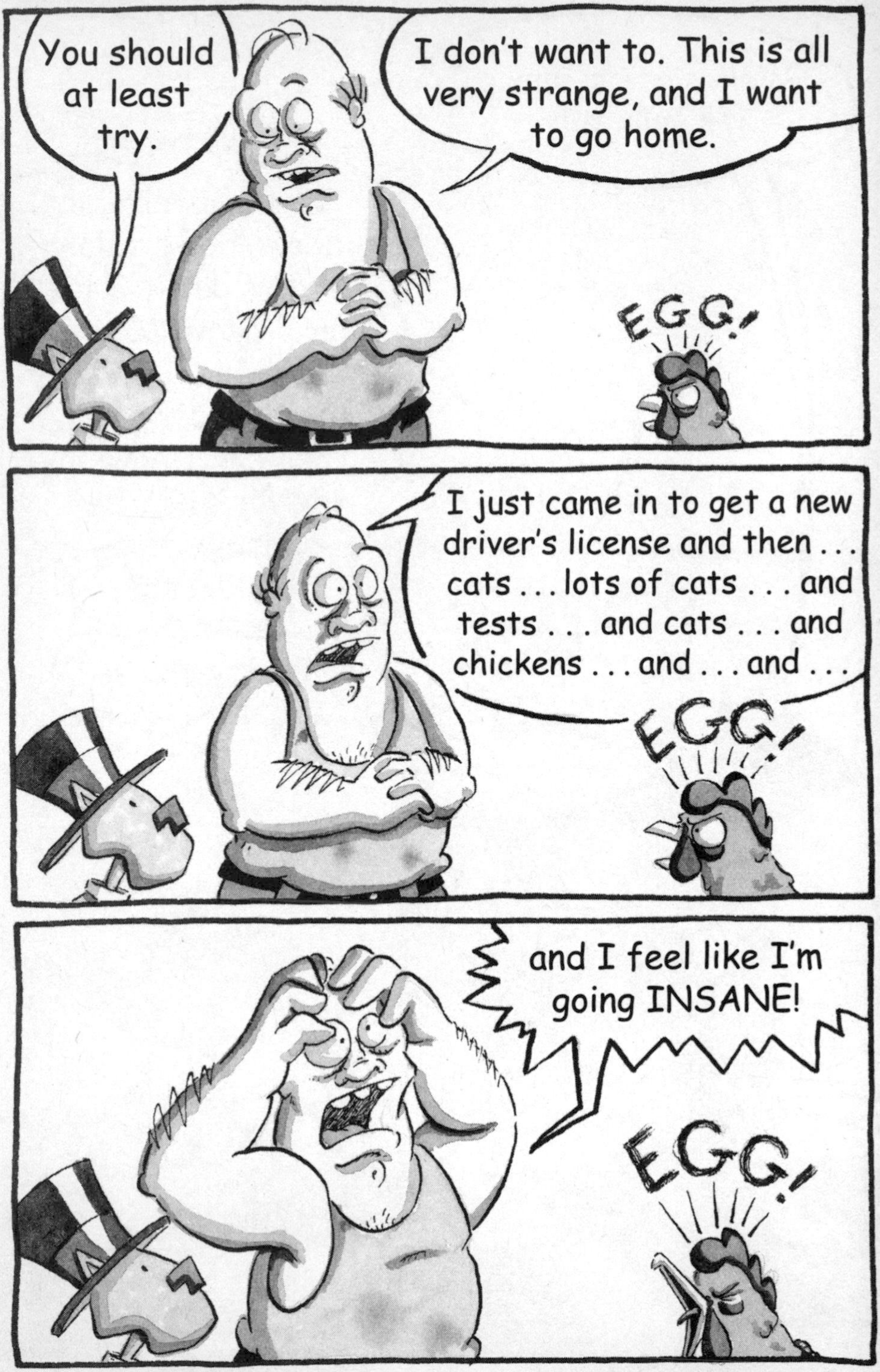
You should at least try.
I don't want to. This is all very strange, and I want to go home.
EGG!
I just came in to get a new driver's license and then . . . cats . . . lots of cats . . . and tests . . . and cats . . . and chickens . . . and . . . and . . .
EGG!
and I feel like I'm going INSANE!
EGG!

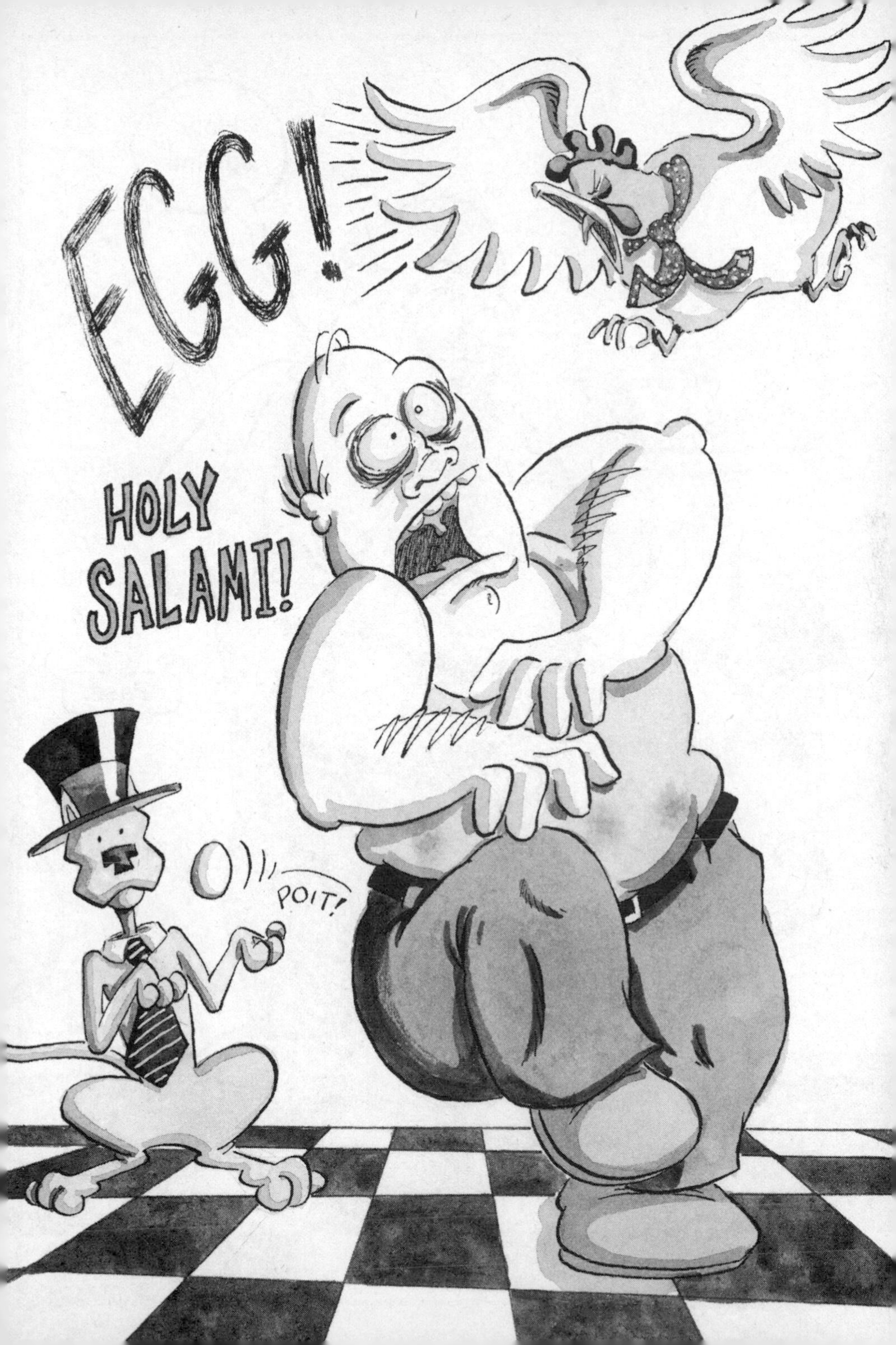
EGG!
HOLY SALAMI!
POIT!

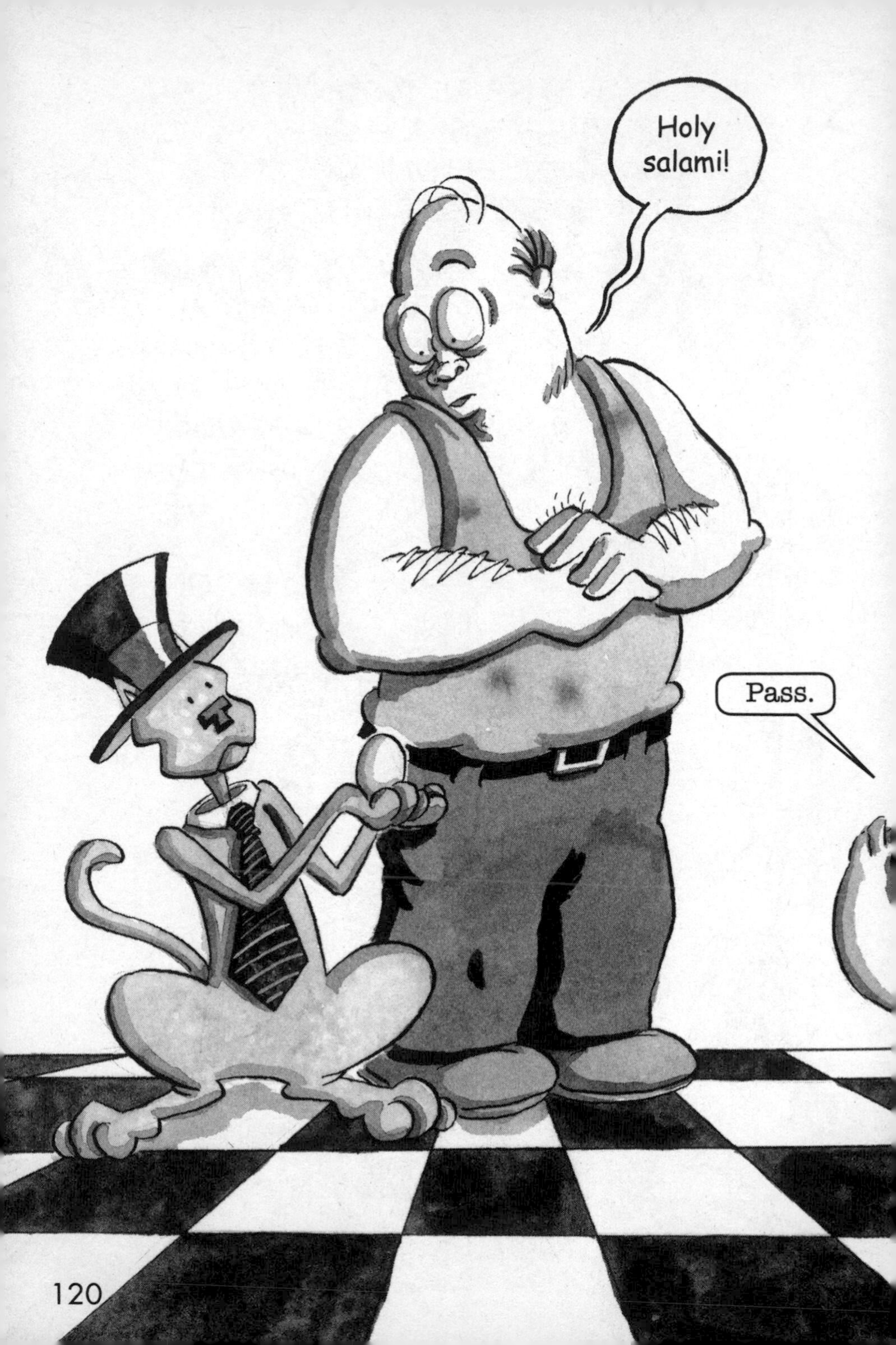
Holy salami!
Pass.

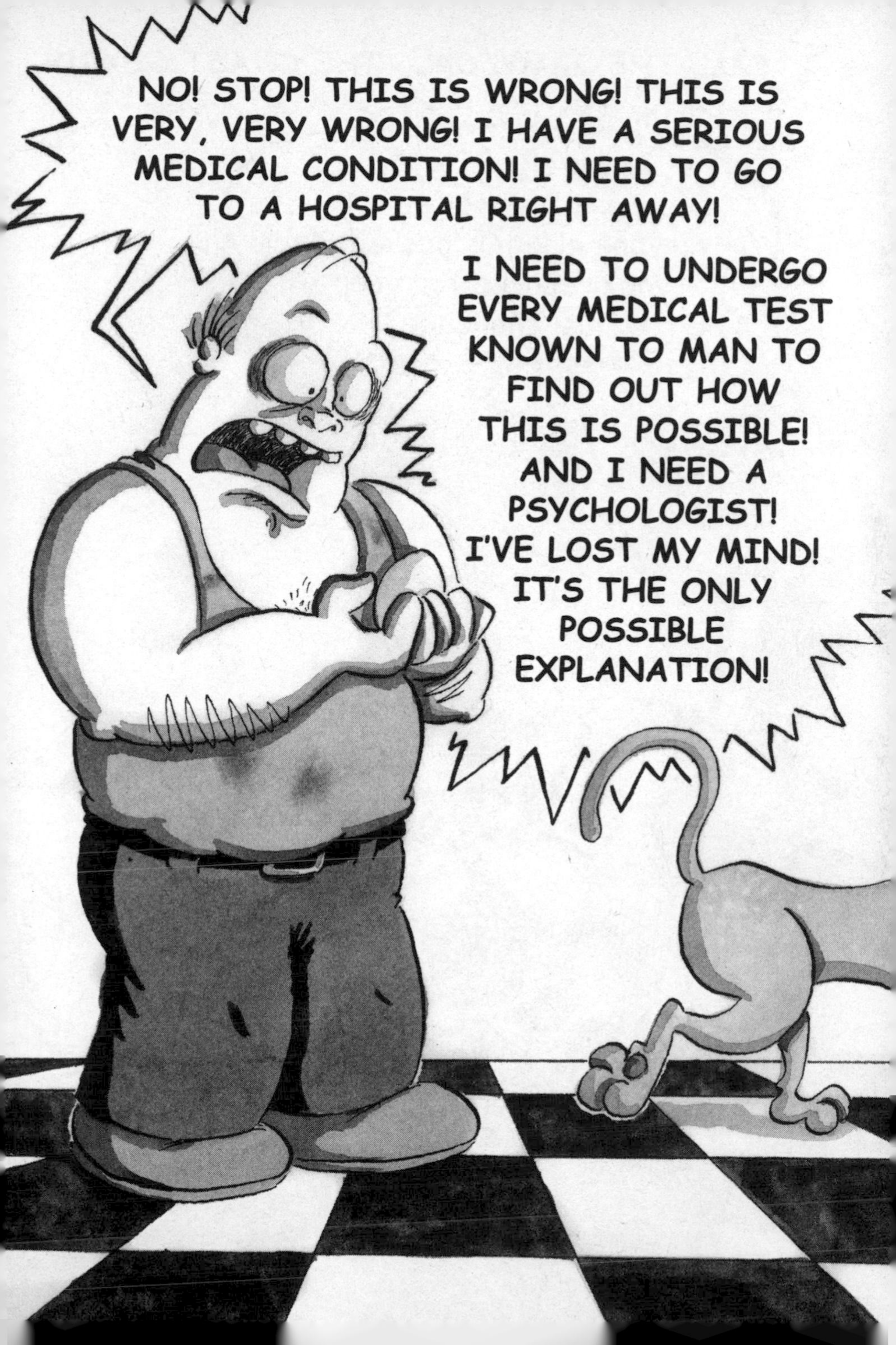
NO! STOP! THIS IS WRONG! THIS IS VERY, VERY WRONG! I HAVE A SERIOUS MEDICAL CONDITION! I NEED TO GO TO A HOSPITAL RIGHT AWAY!
I NEED TO UNDERGO EVERY MEDICAL TEST KNOWN TO MAN TO FIND OUT HOW THIS IS POSSIBLE! AND I NEED A PSYCHOLOGIST! I'VE LOST MY MIND! IT'S THE ONLY POSSIBLE EXPLANATION!

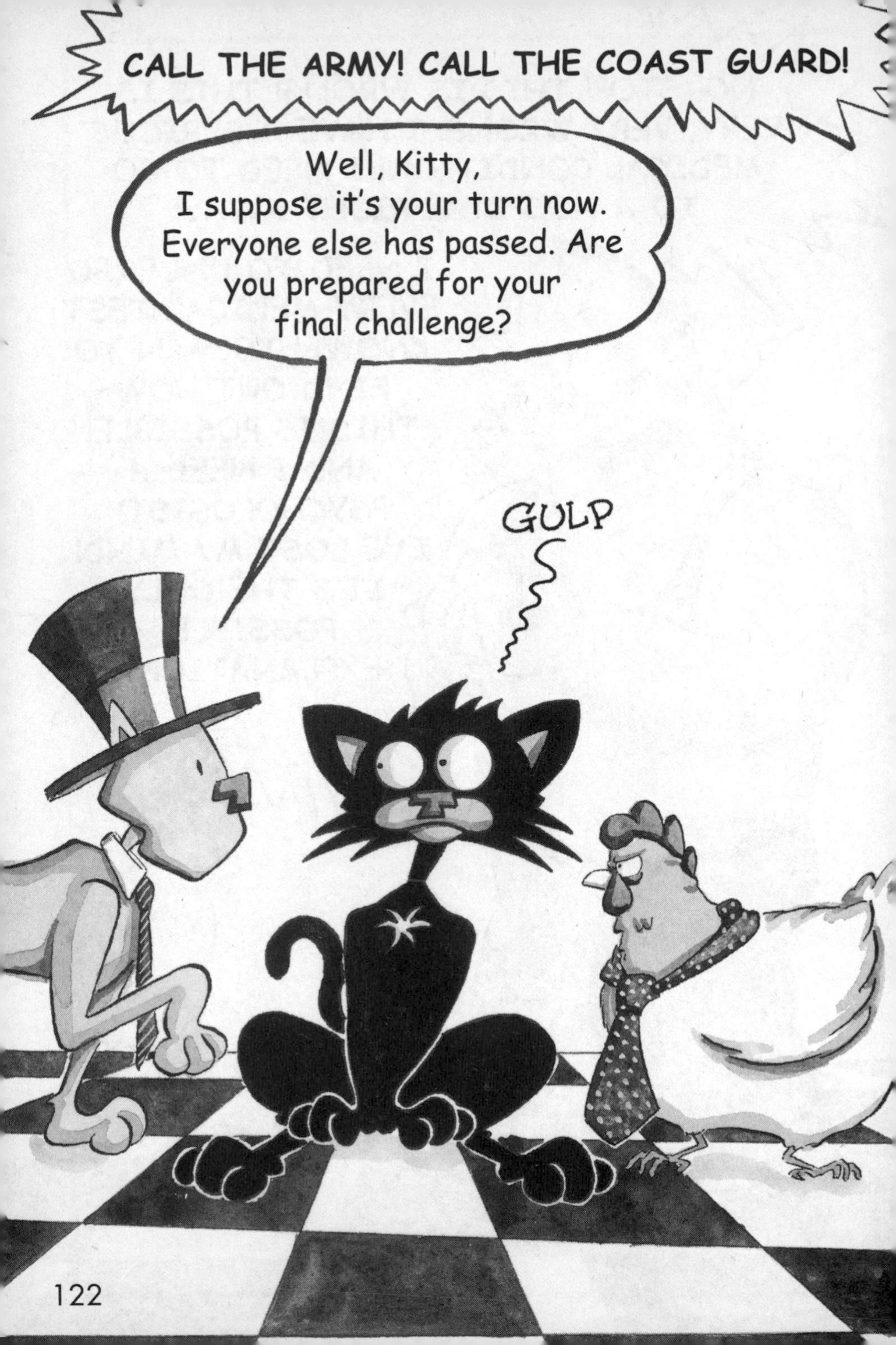
CALL THE ARMY! CALL THE COAST GUARD!
Well, Kitty, I suppose it's your turn now. Everyone else has passed. Are you prepared for your final challenge?
GULP

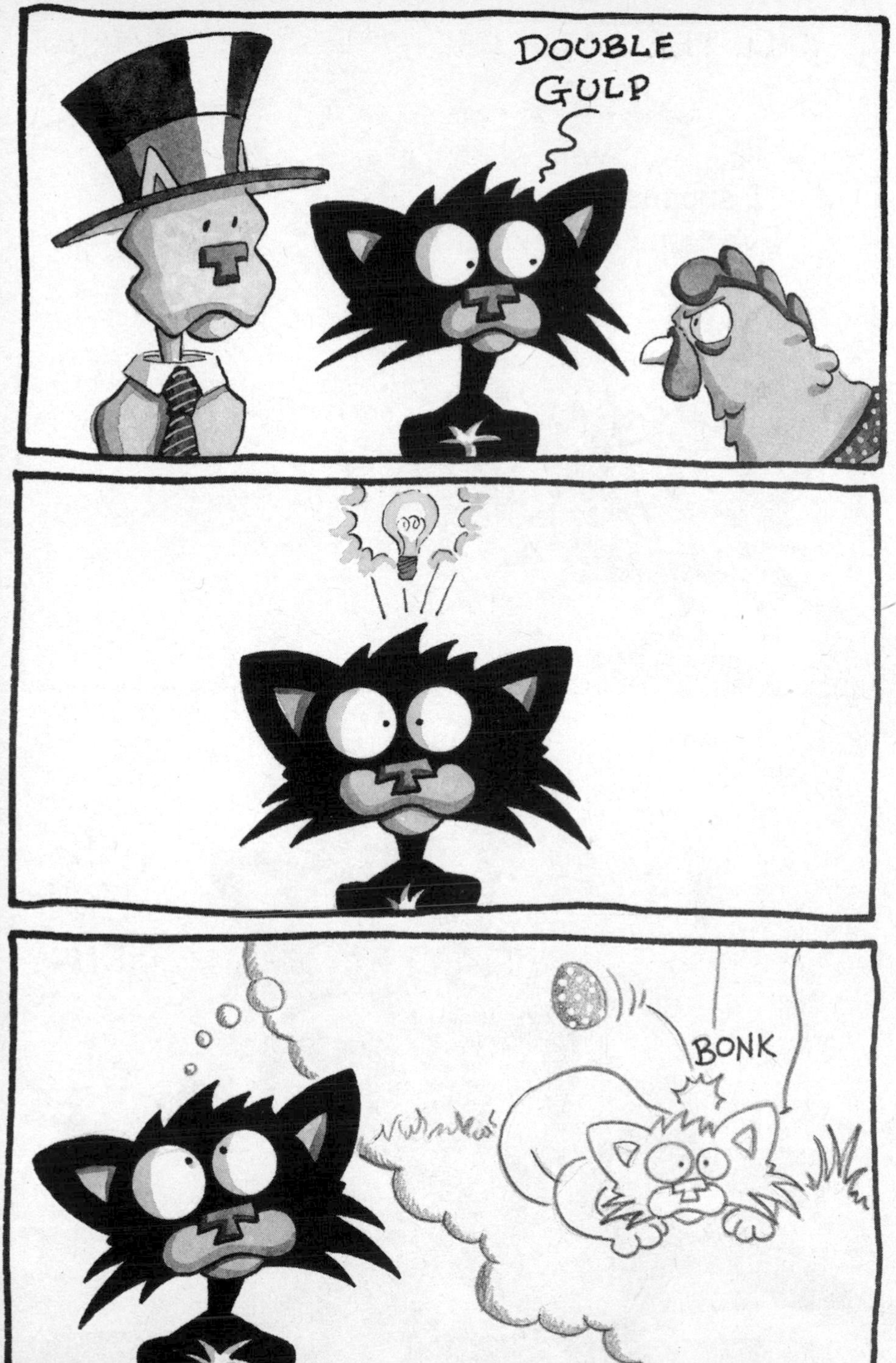
DOUBLE GULP
BONK

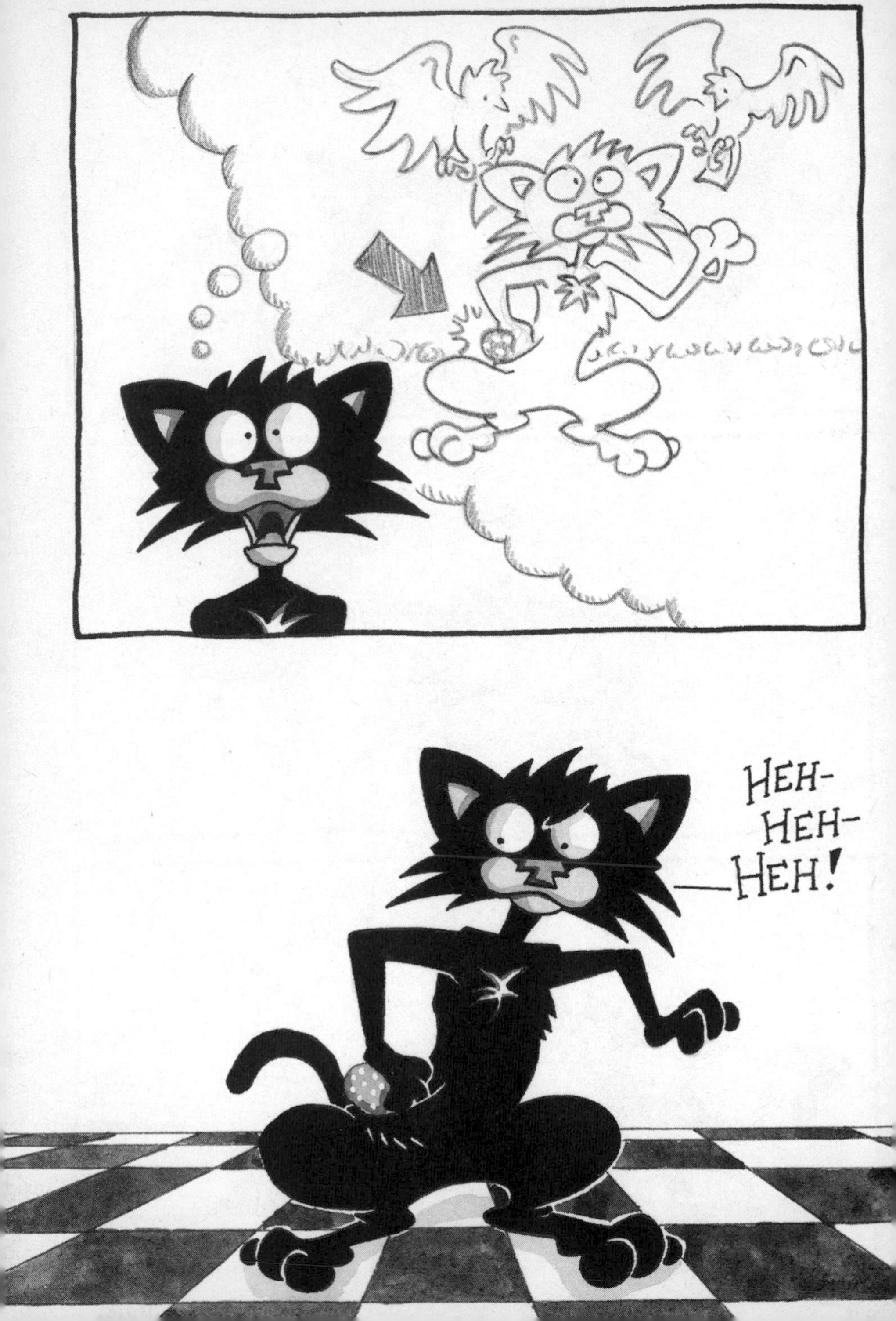
HEH-
HEH-
HEH!

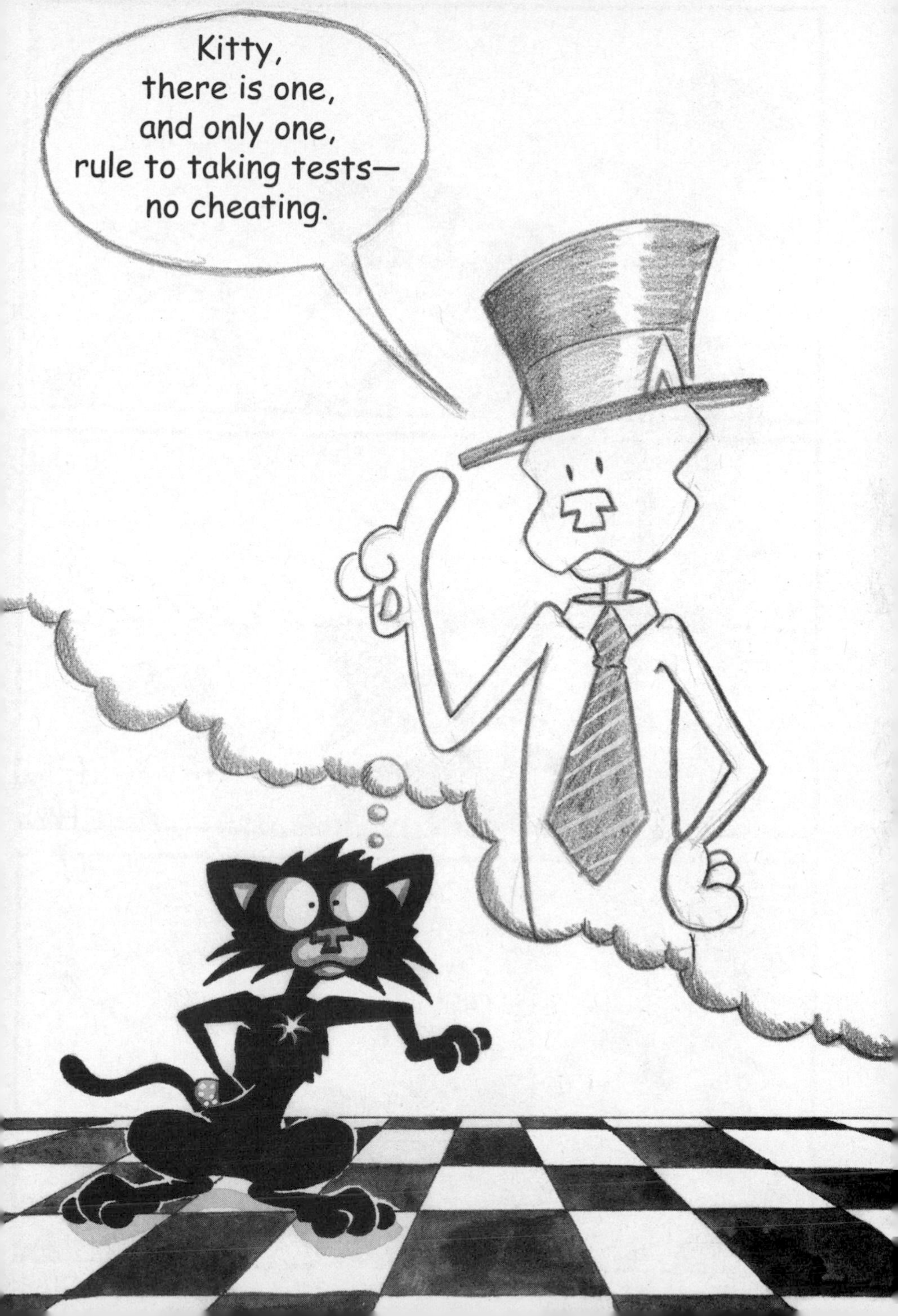
Kitty, there is one, and only one, rule to taking tests— no cheating.

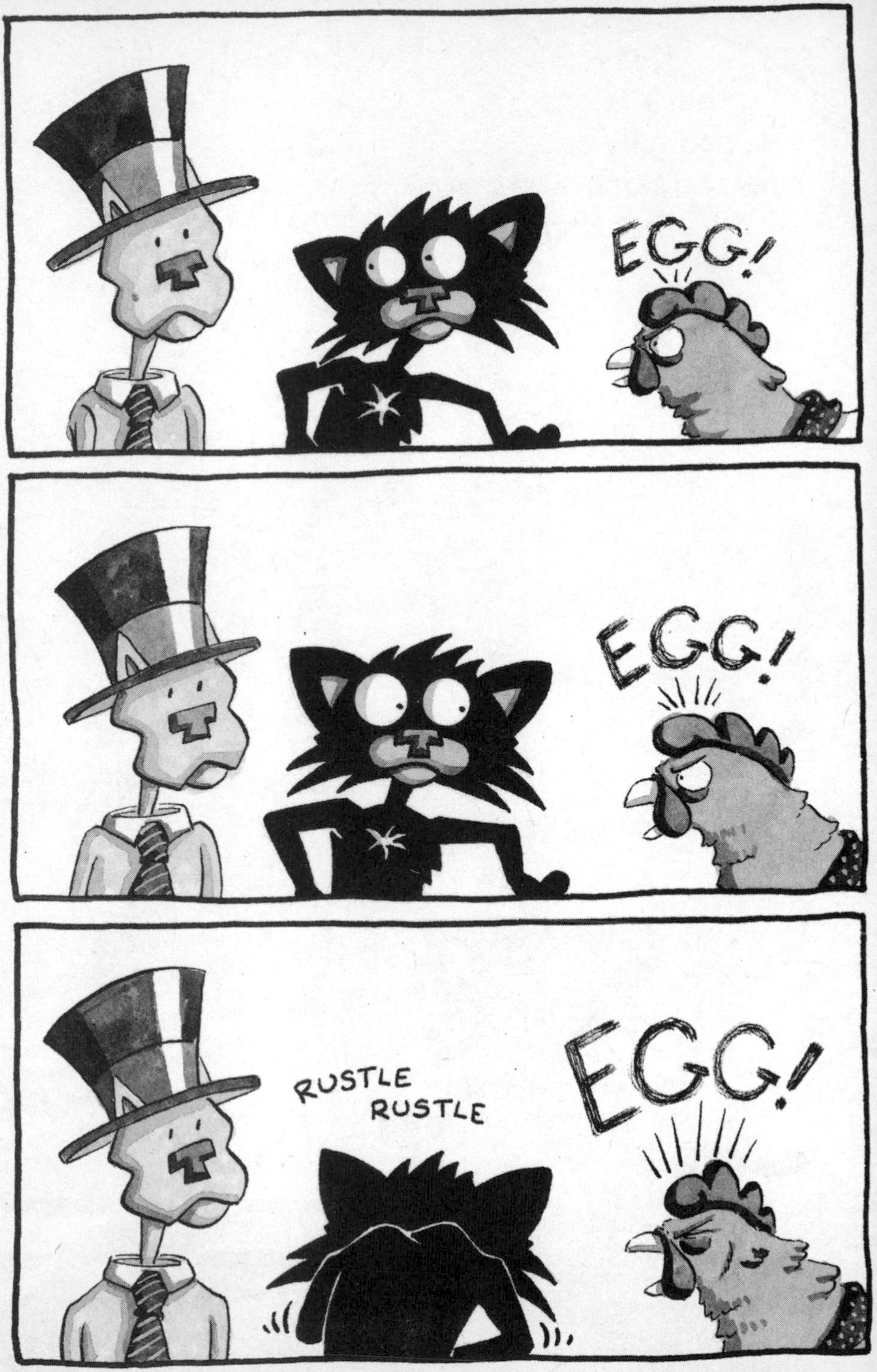
EGG!
EGG!
RUSTLE
RUSTLE
EGG!

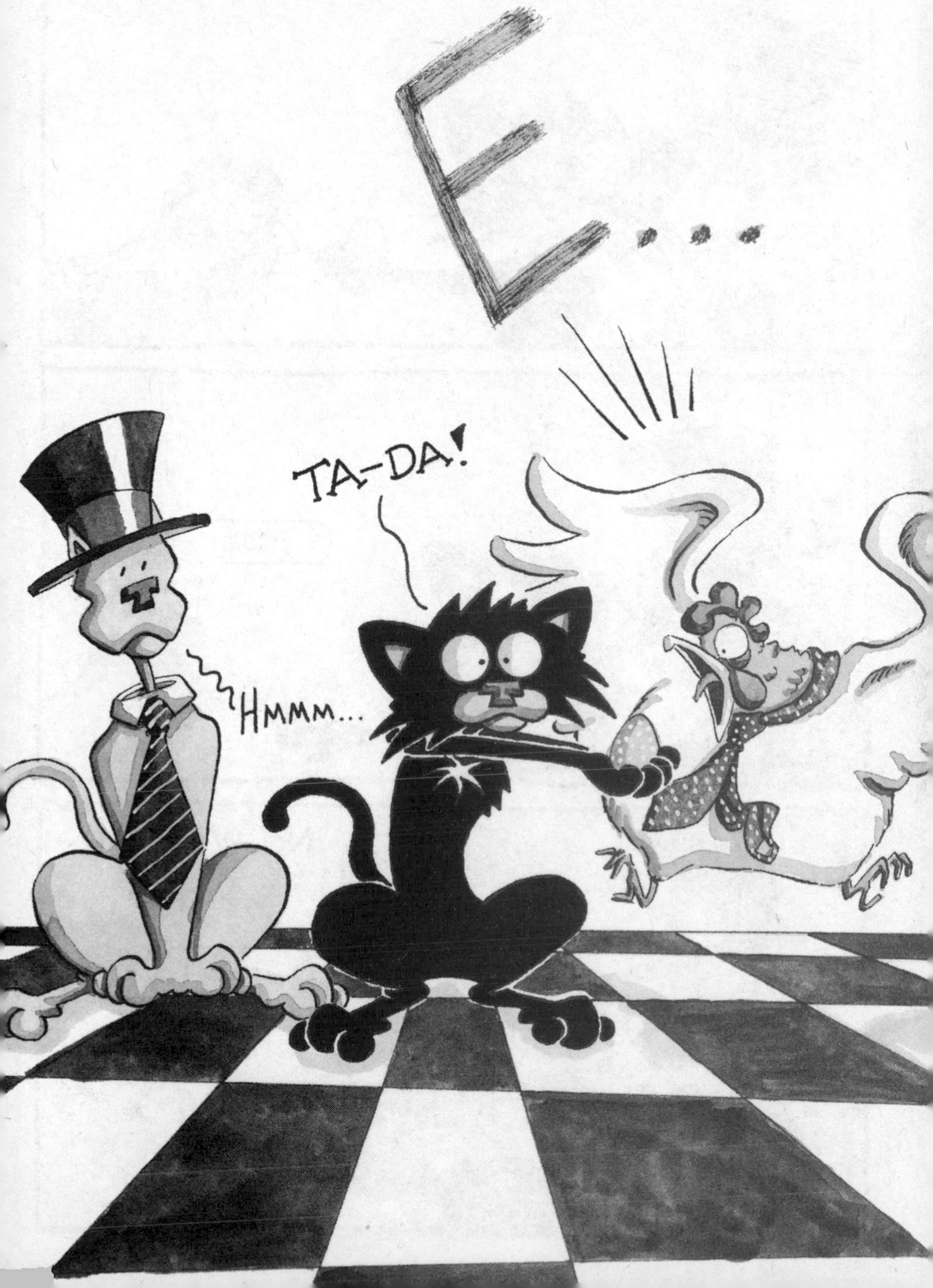
E...
TA-DA!
HMMM...

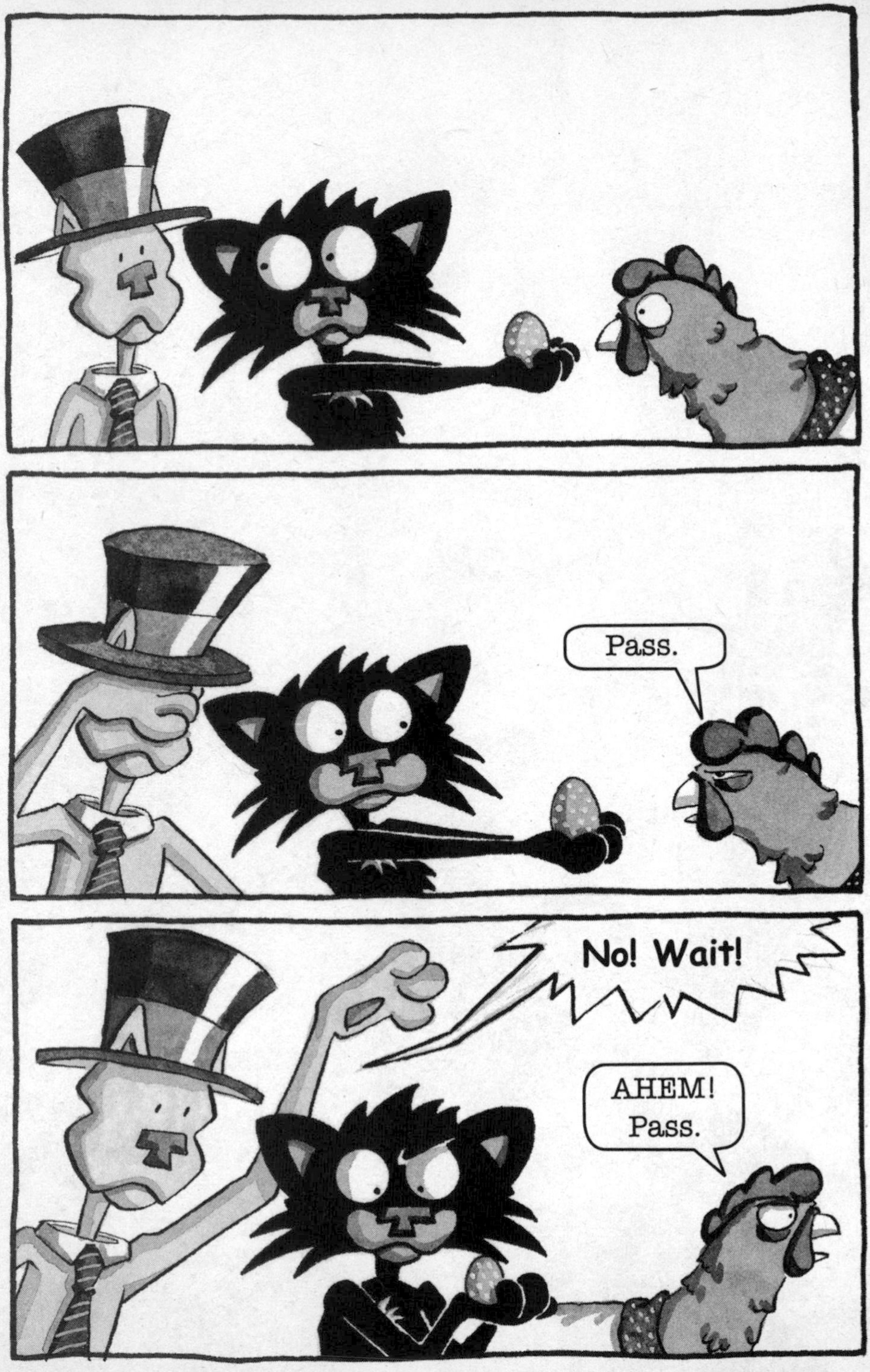
Pass.
No! Wait!
AHEM! Pass.

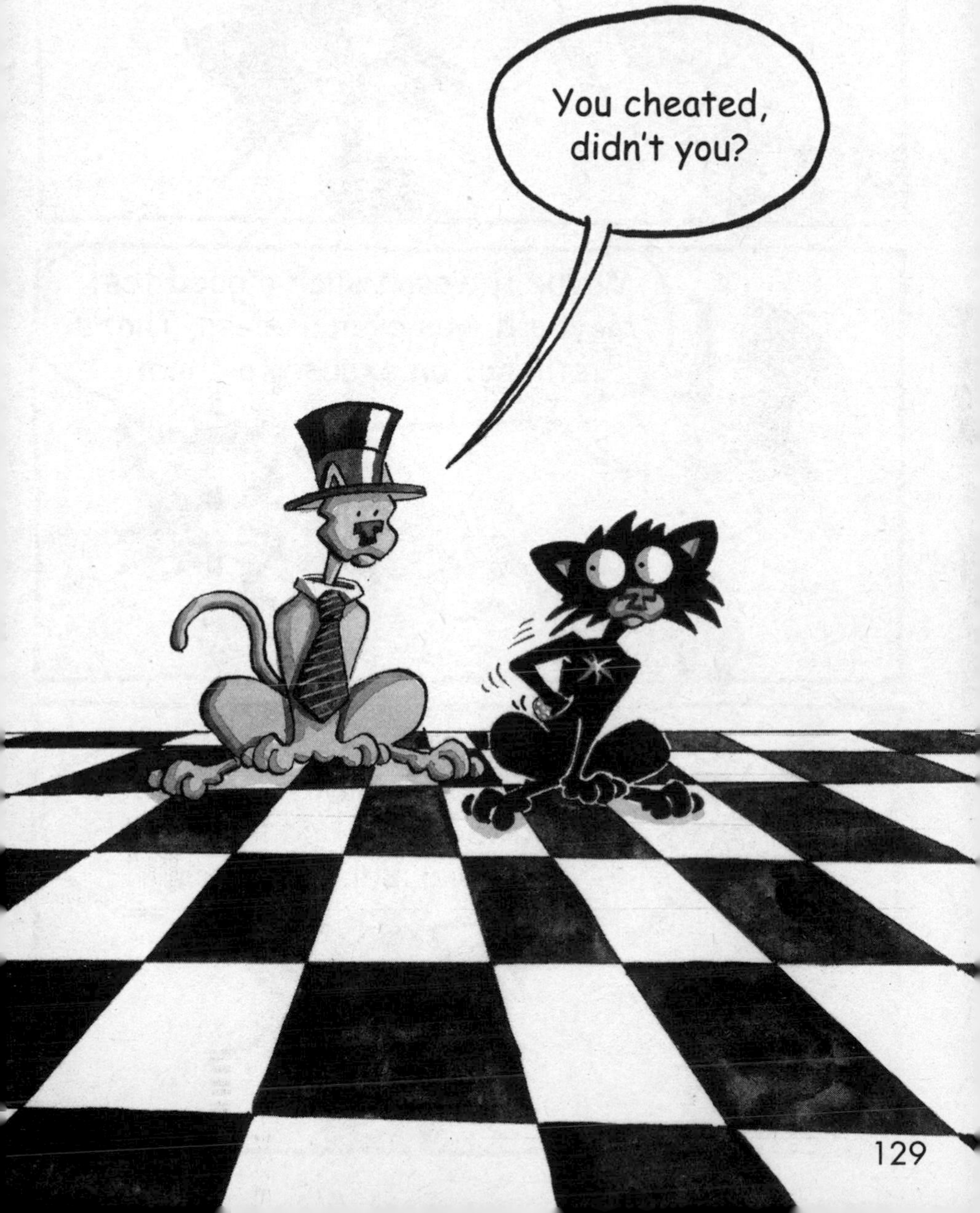
You cheated, didn't you?

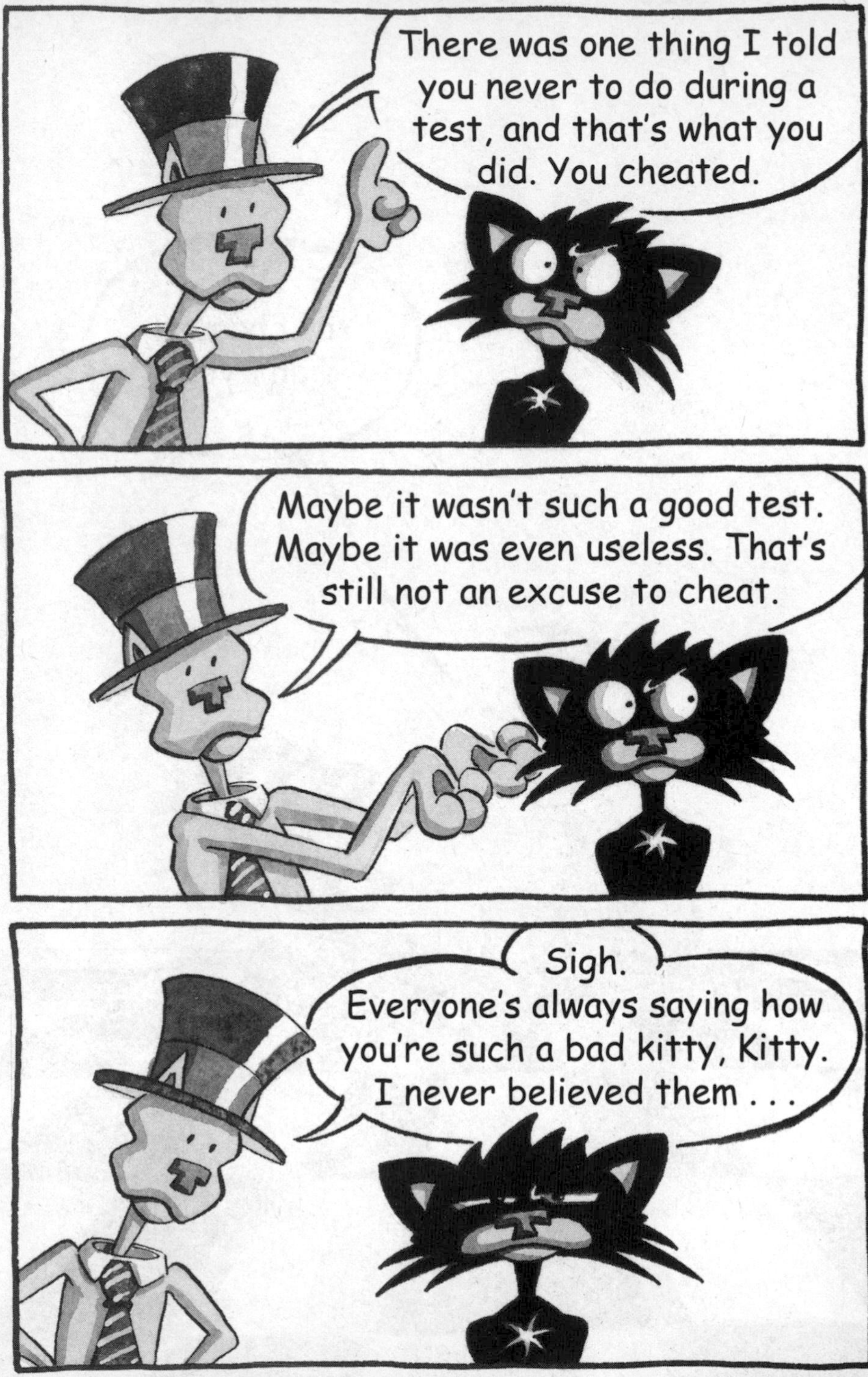
There was one thing I told you never to do during a test, and that's what you did. You cheated.
Maybe it wasn't such a good test. Maybe it was even useless. That's still not an excuse to cheat.
Sigh.
Everyone's always saying how you're such a bad kitty, Kitty. I never believed them . . .

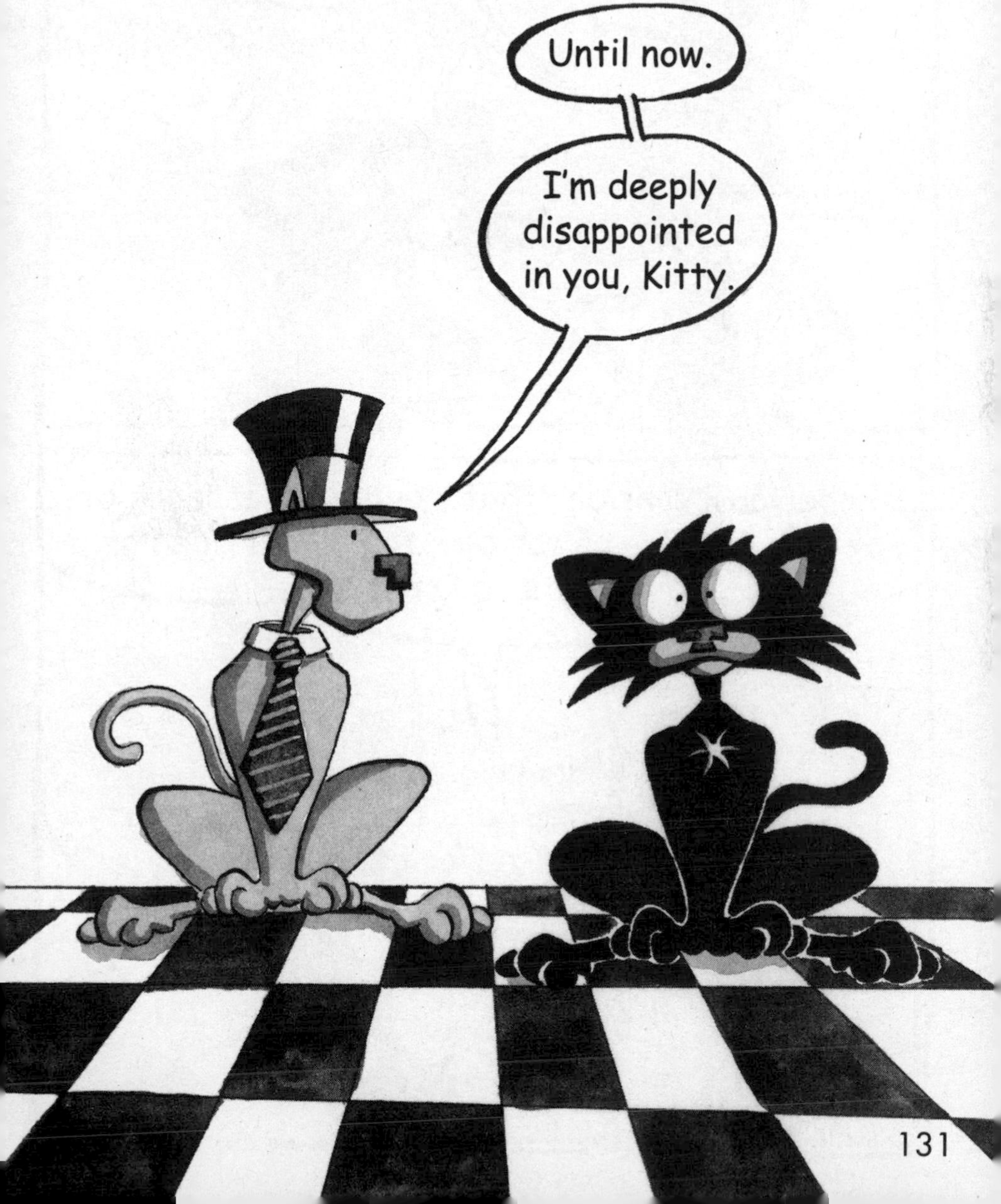
Until now.
I'm deeply disappointed in you, Kitty.

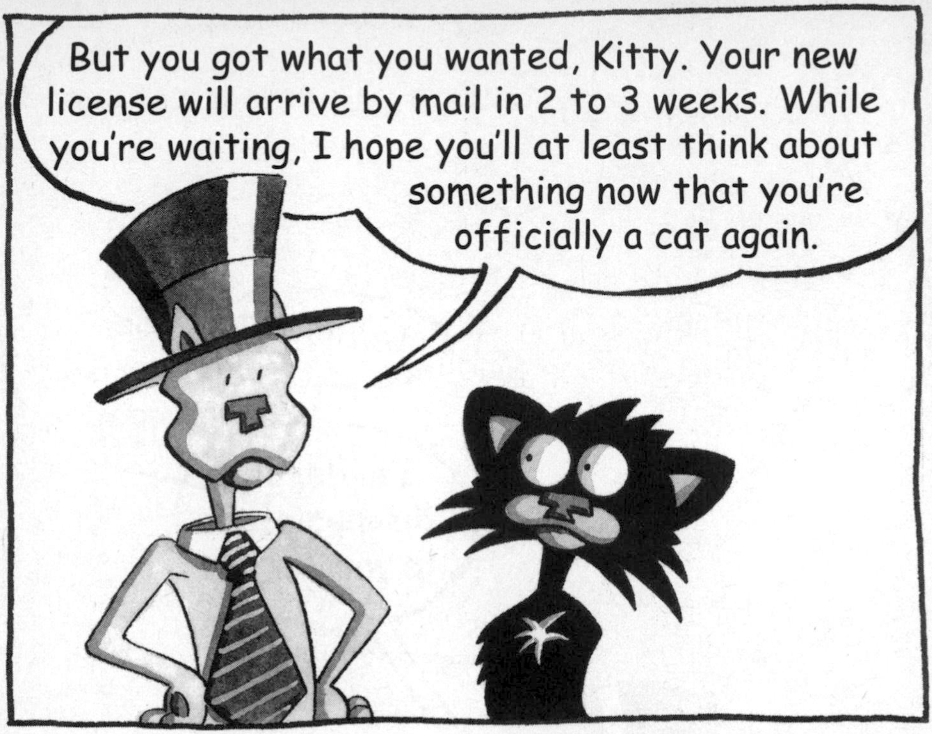
But you got what you wanted, Kitty. Your new license will arrive by mail in 2 to 3 weeks. While you're waiting, I hope you'll at least think about something now that you're officially a cat again.

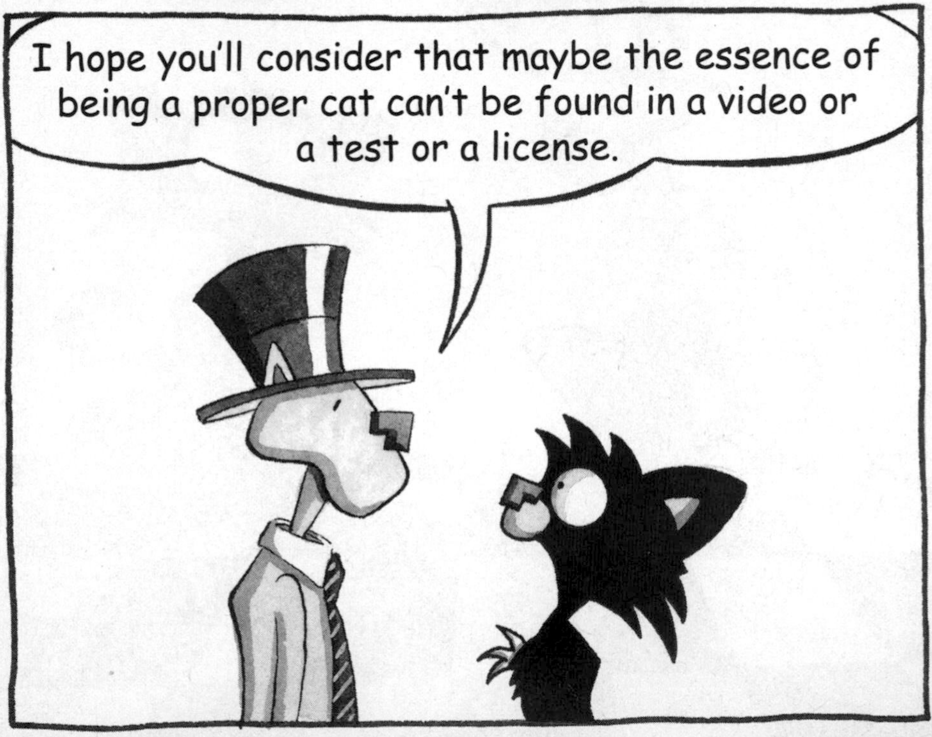
I hope you'll consider that maybe the essence of being a proper cat can't be found in a video or a test or a license.

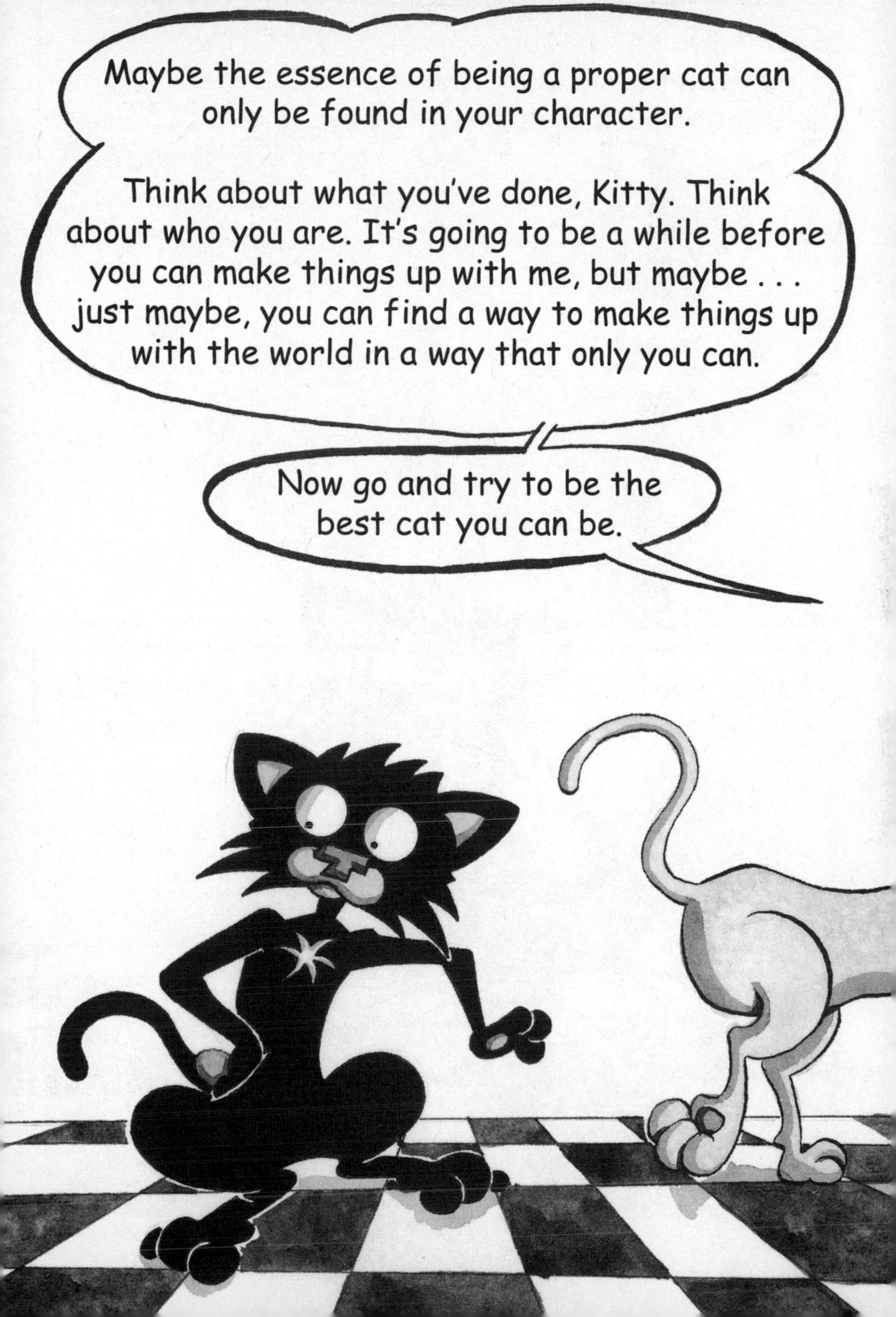
Maybe the essence of being a proper cat can only be found in your character.
Think about what you've done, Kitty. Think about who you are. It's going to be a while before you can make things up with me, but maybe . . . just maybe, you can find a way to make things up with the world in a way that only you can.
Now go and try to be the best cat you can be.

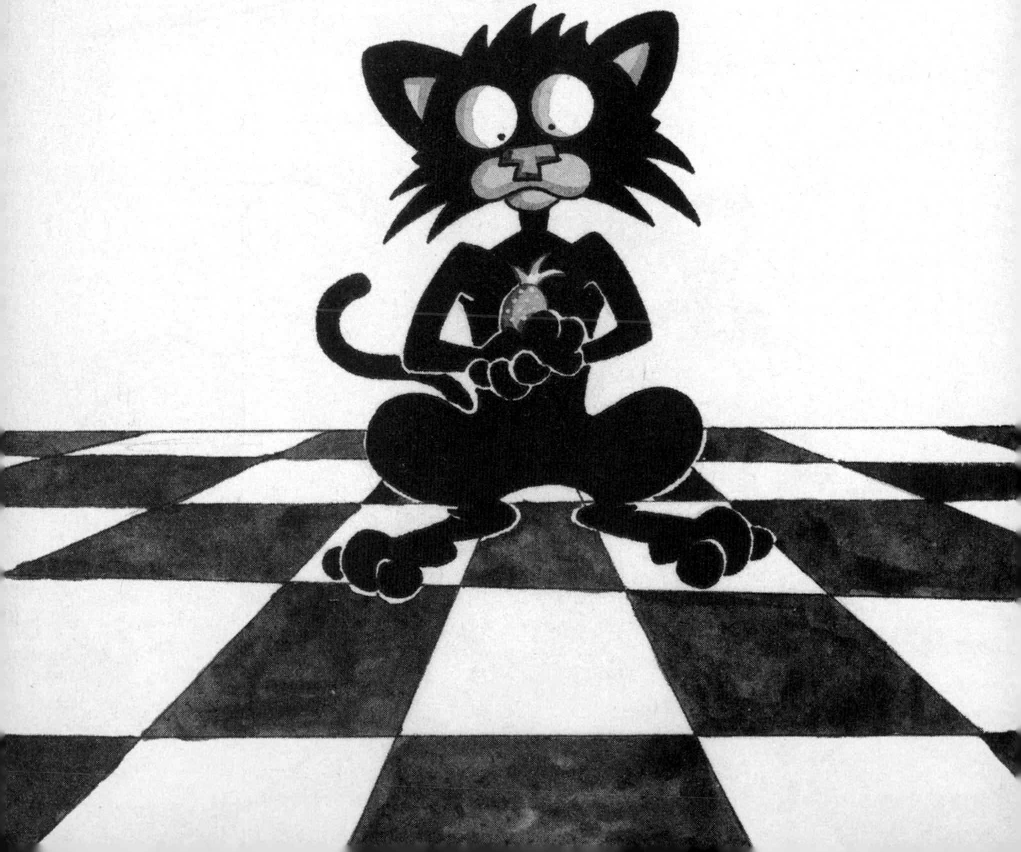

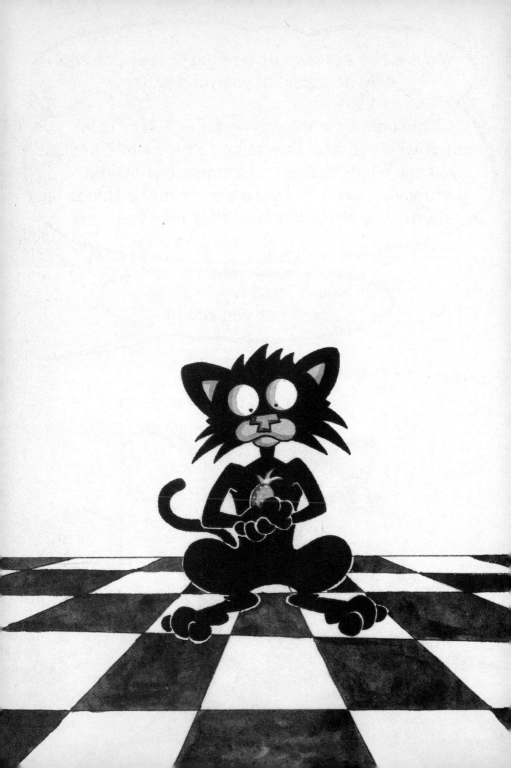

•CHAPTER SEVEN•

THE NEXT, NEXT, NEXT DAY

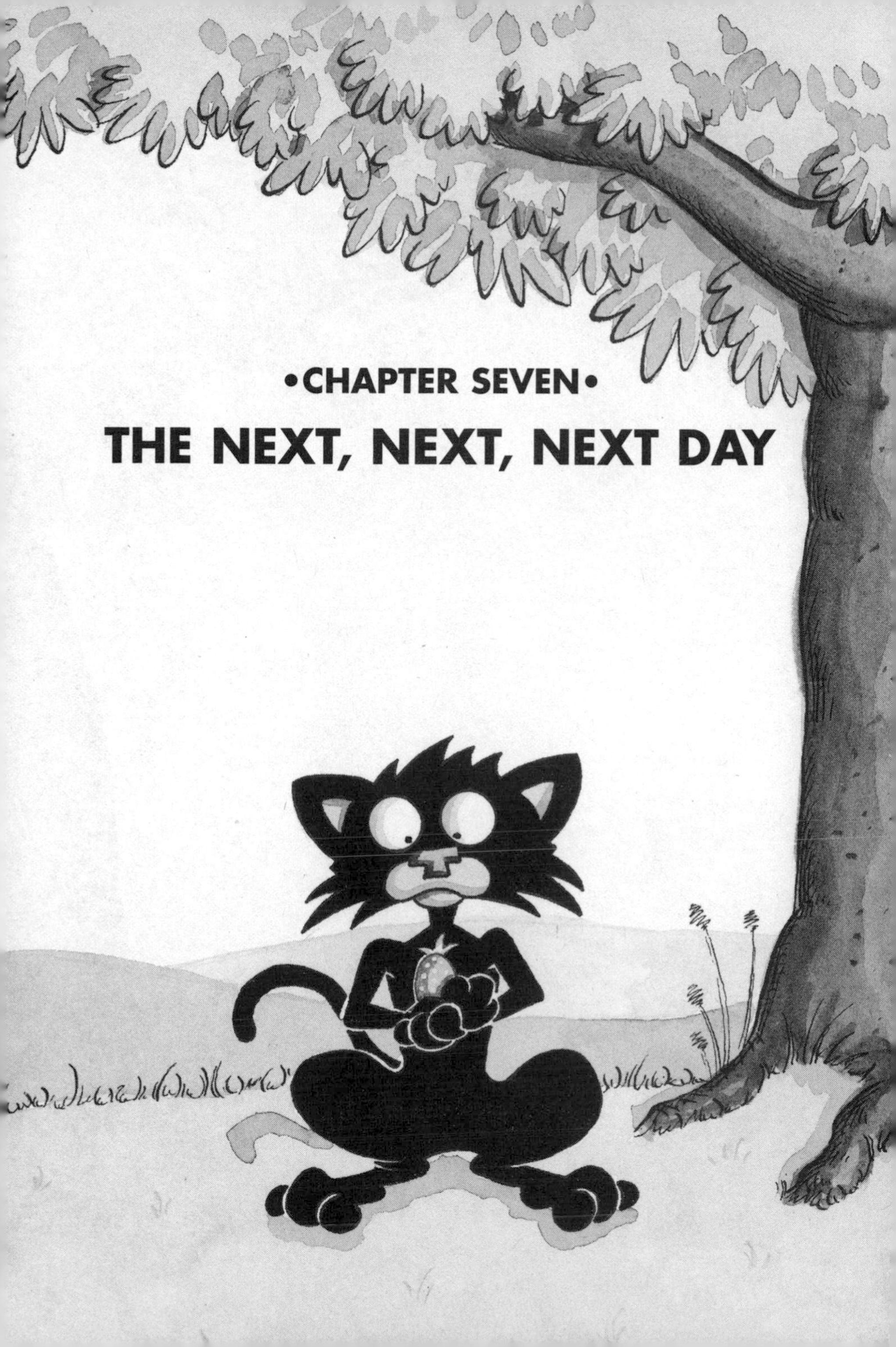

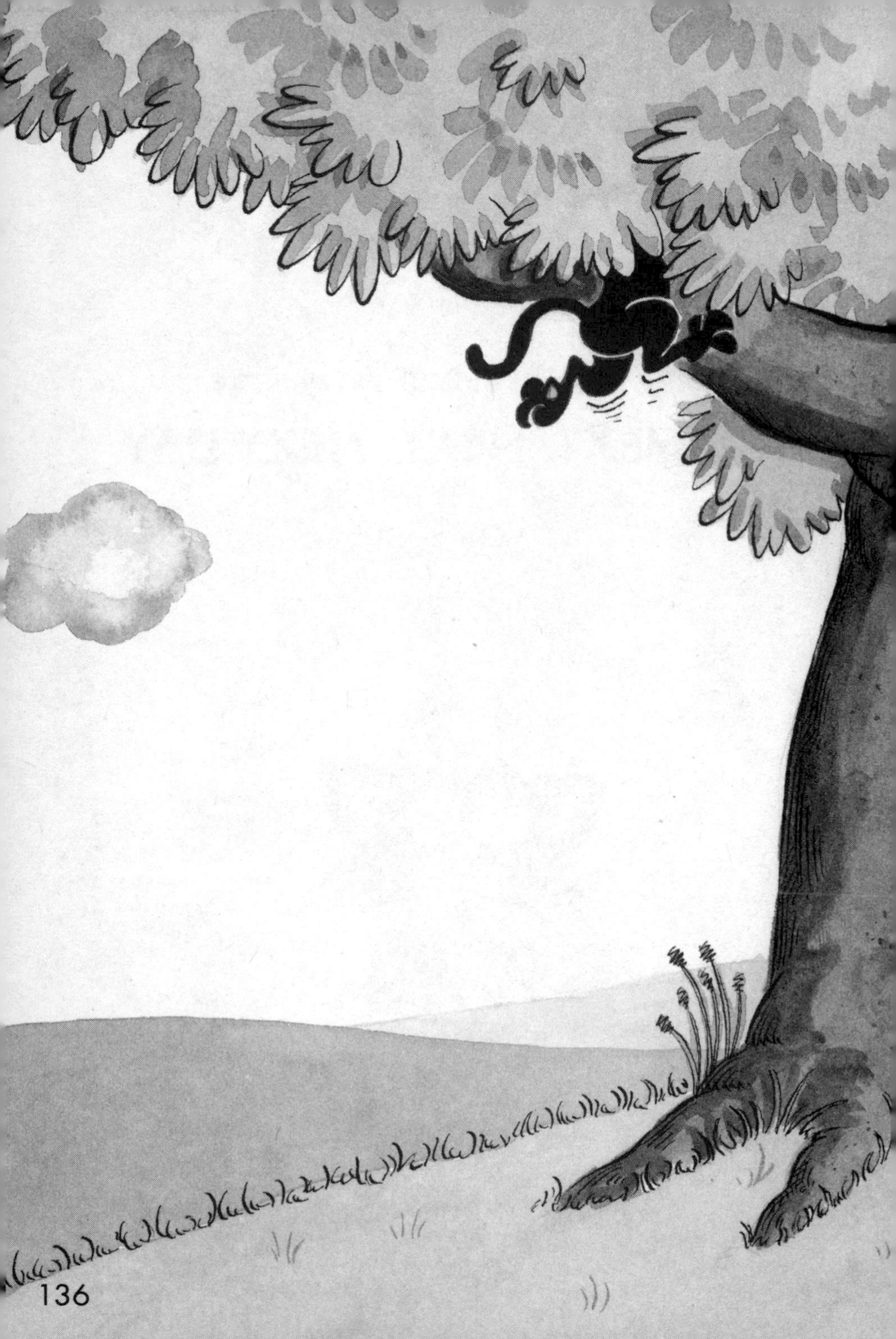

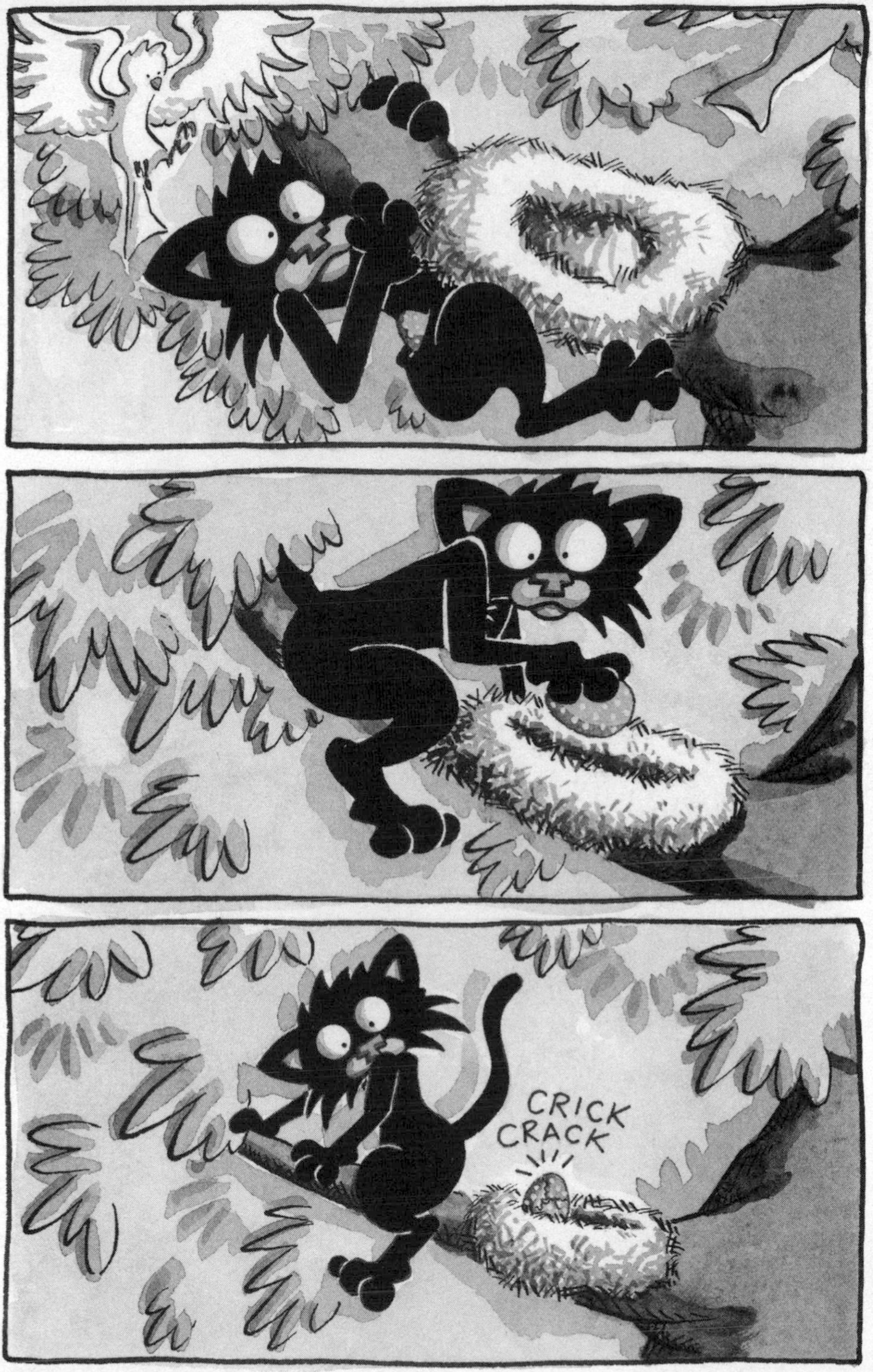
CRICK
CRACK

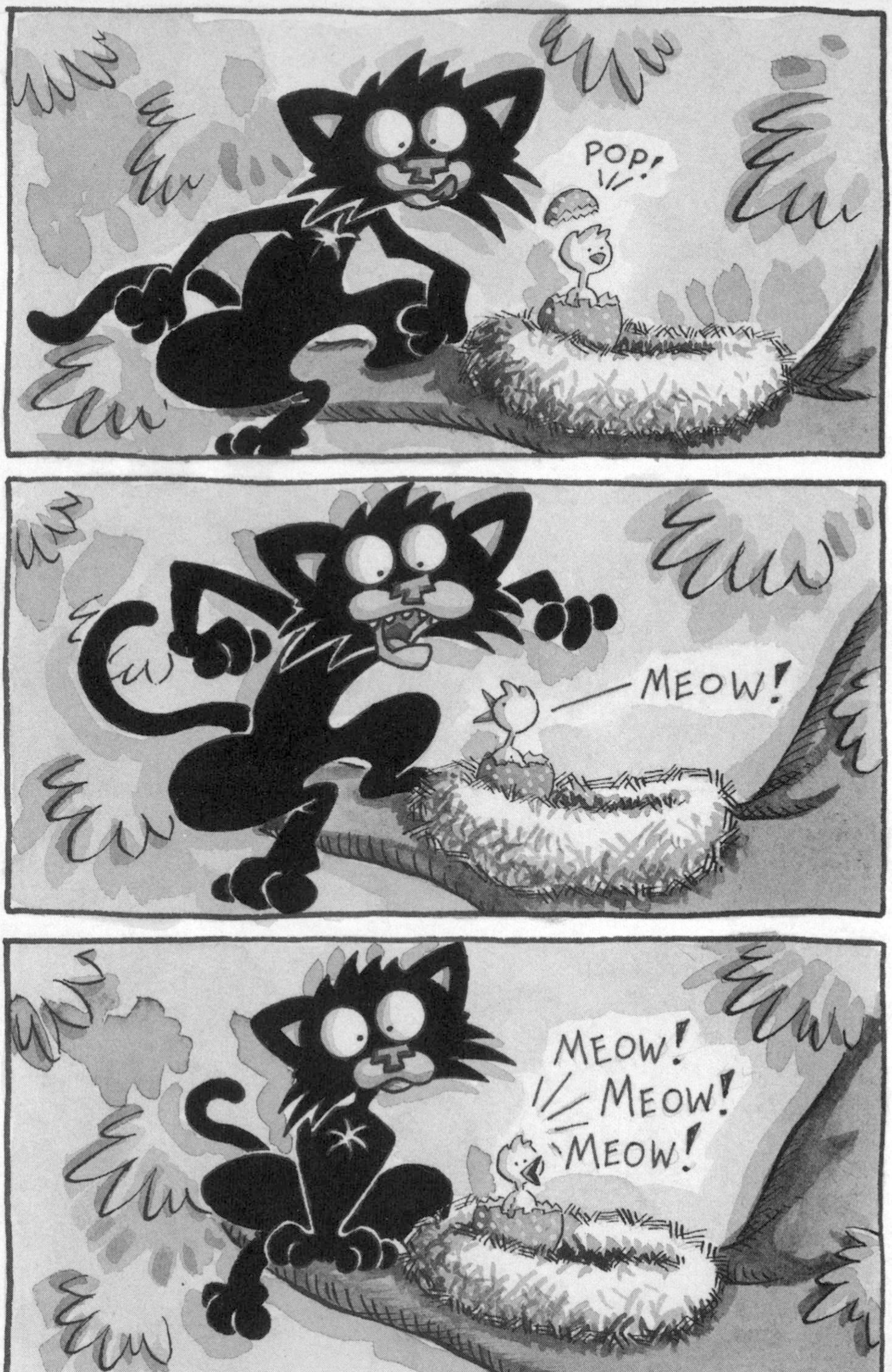
POP!
MEOW!
MEOW!
MEOW!
MEOW!

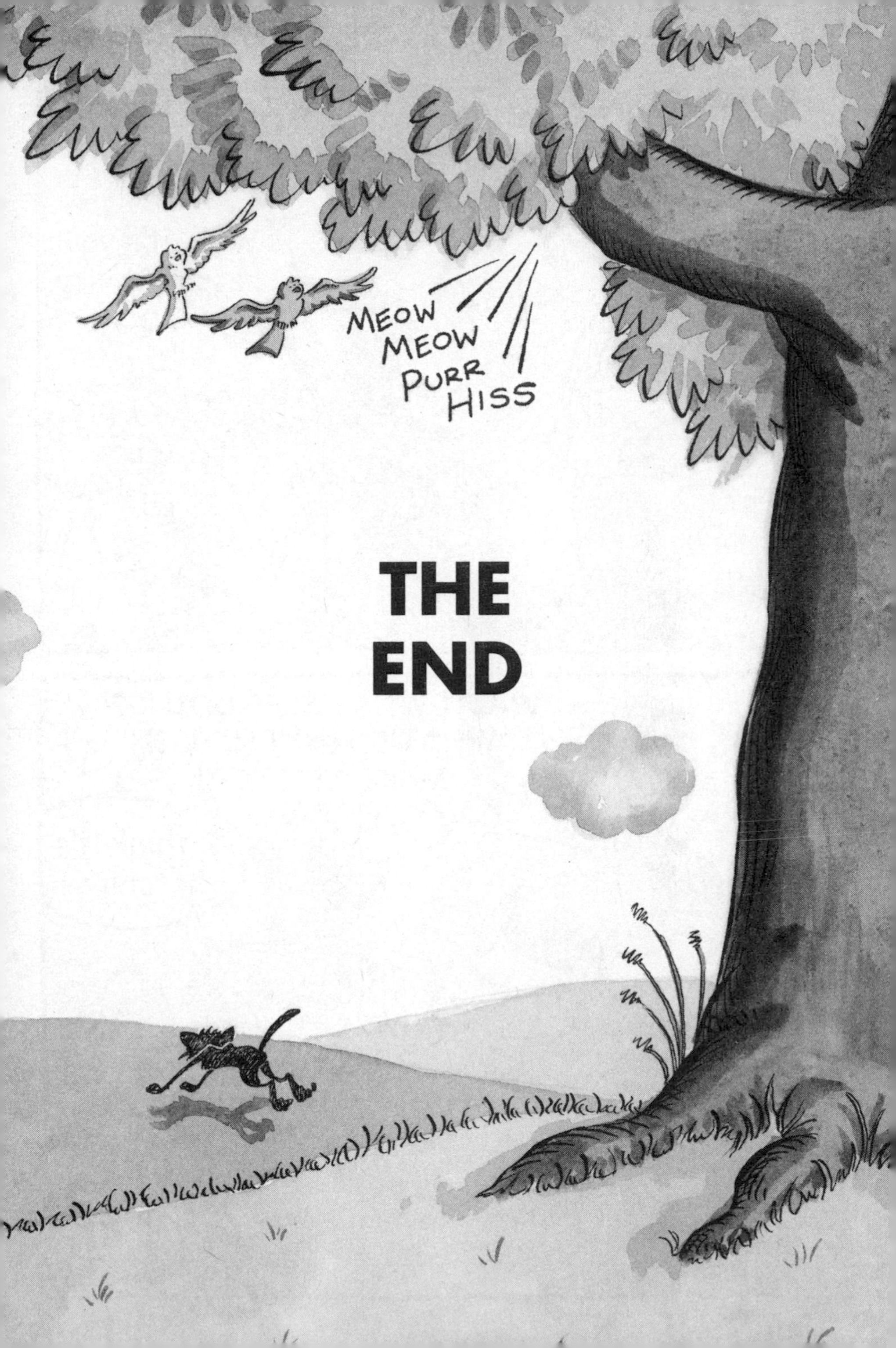
MEOW
MEOW
PURR
HISS

THE END

•EPILOGUE ONE•

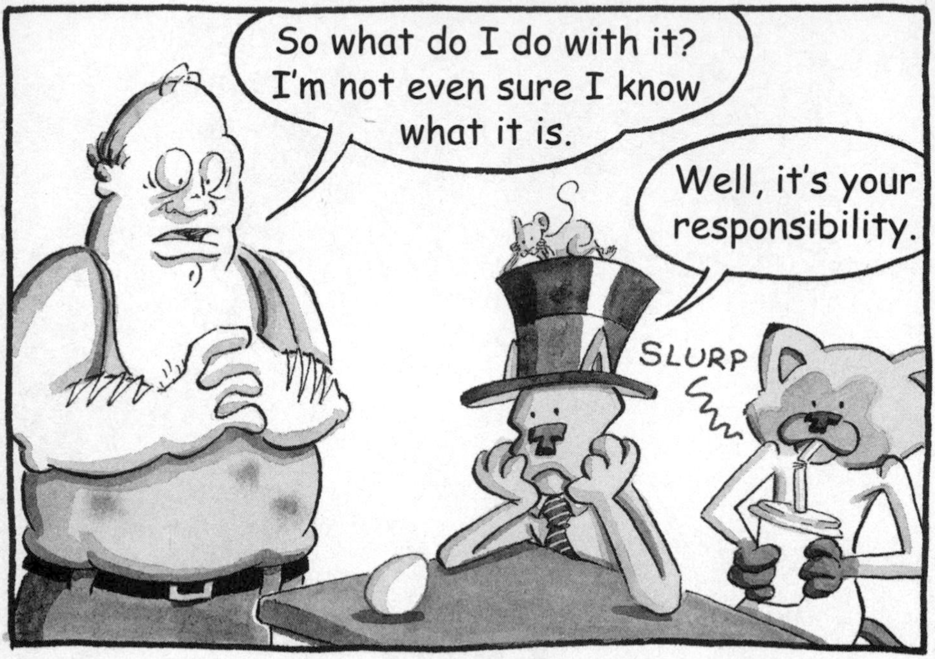
So what do I do with it? I'm not even sure I know what it is.
Well, it's your responsibility.
SLURP

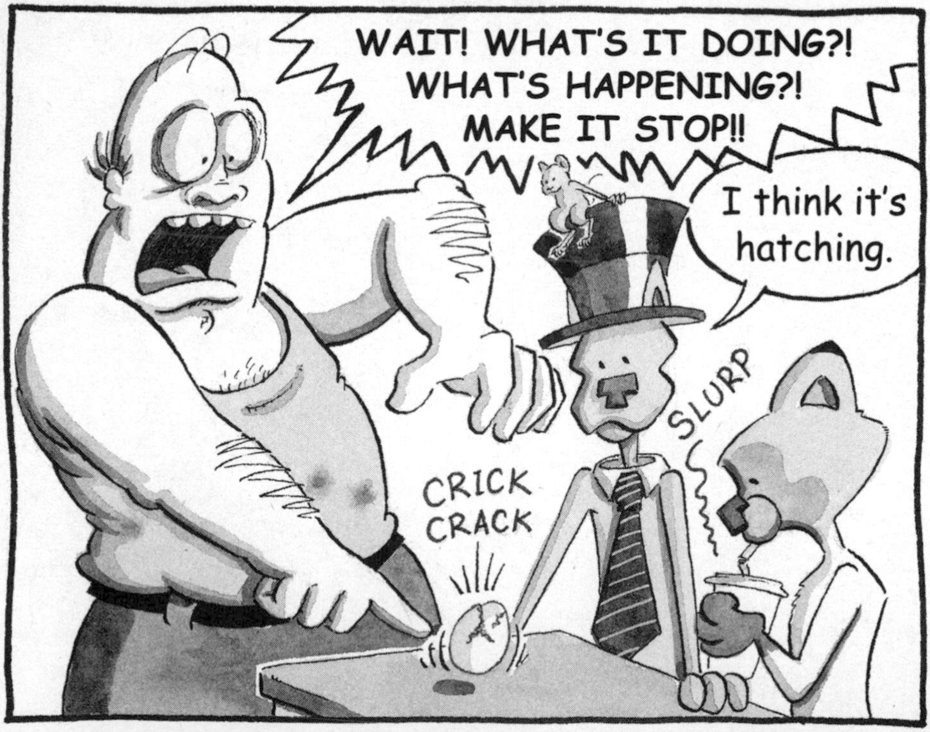
WAIT! WHAT'S IT DOING?! WHAT'S HAPPENING?! MAKE IT STOP!!
I think it's hatching.
SLURP
CRICK CRACK

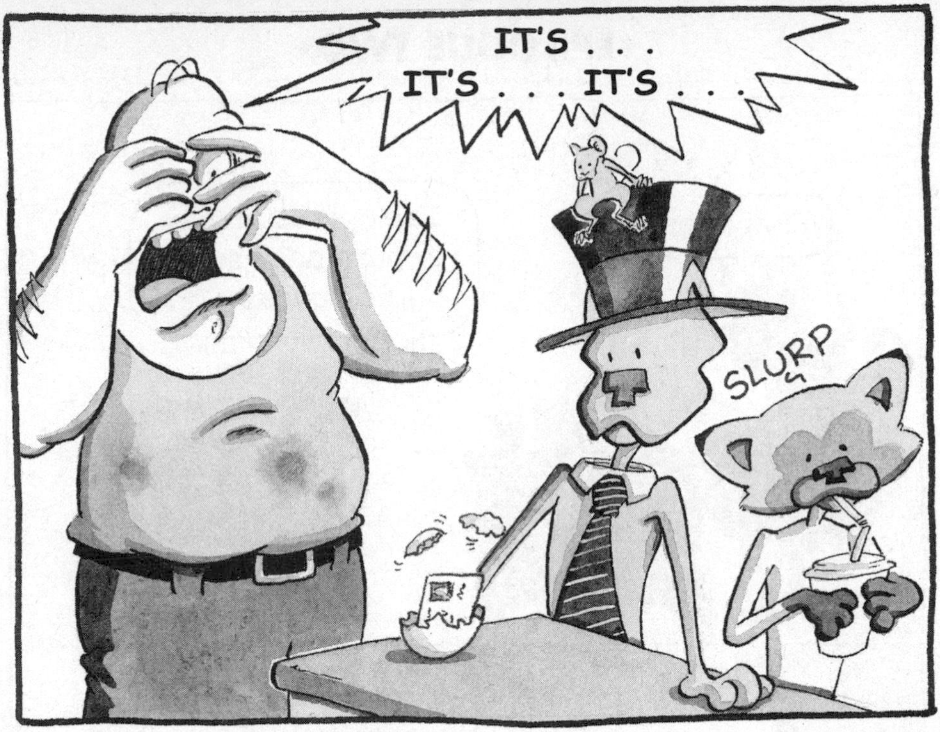
IT'S . . .
IT'S . . . IT'S . . .
SLURP

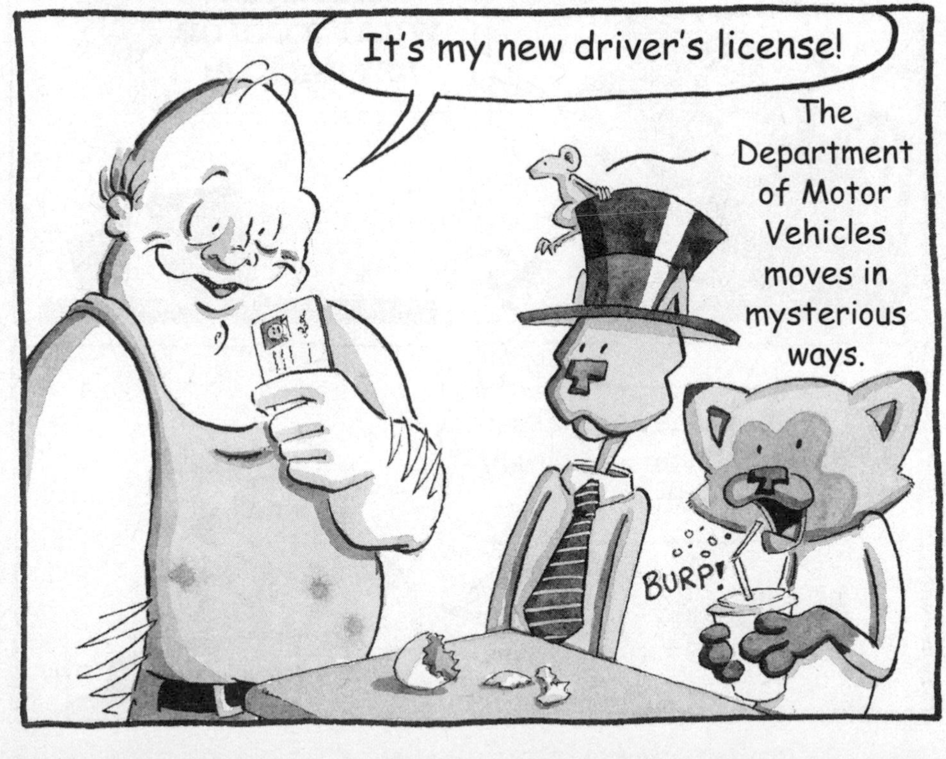
It's my new driver's license!
The Department of Motor Vehicles moves in mysterious ways.
BURP!

•EPILOGUE TWO•

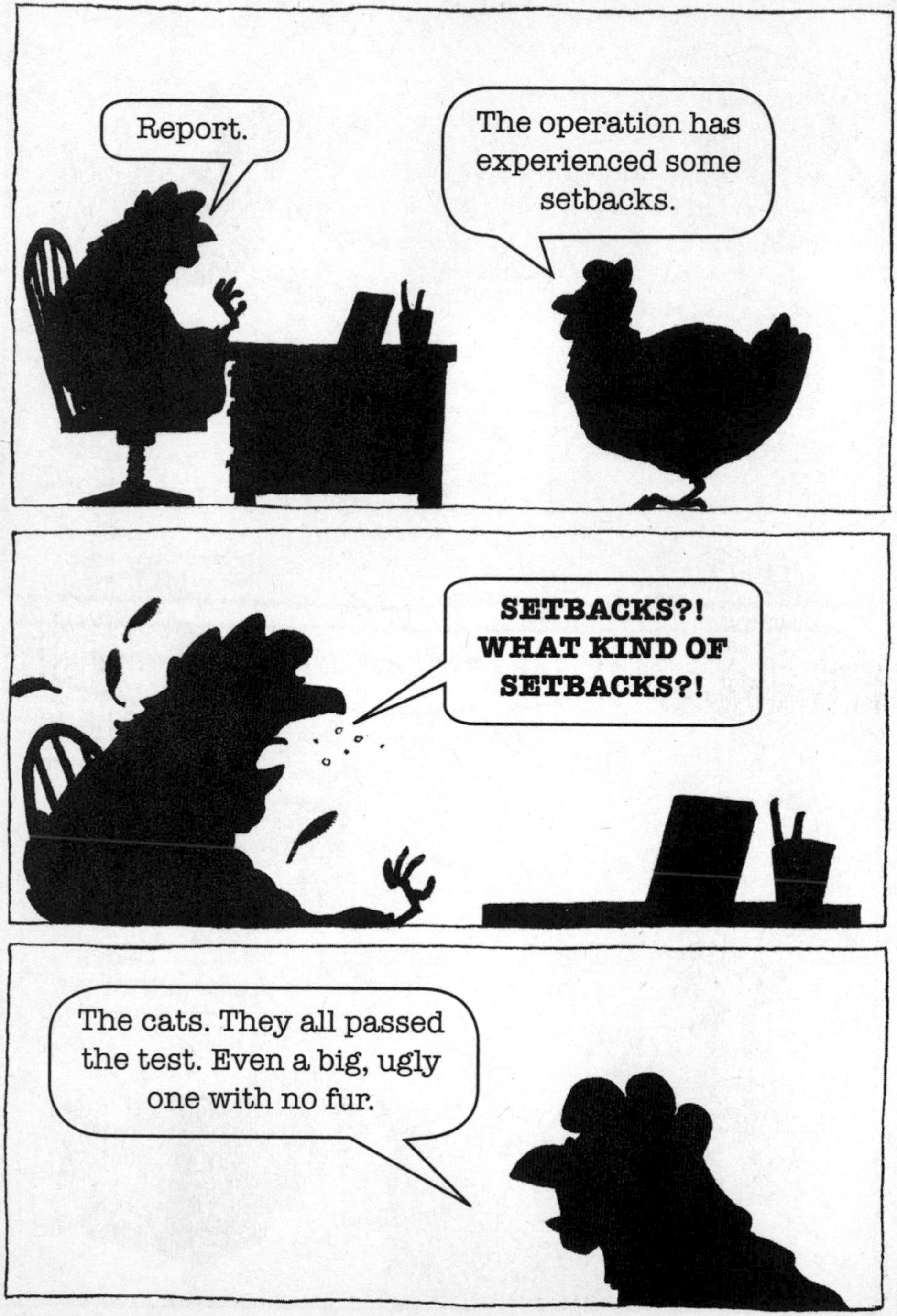
Report.
The operation has experienced some setbacks.
SETBACKS?! WHAT KIND OF SETBACKS?!
The cats. They all passed the test. Even a big, ugly one with no fur.

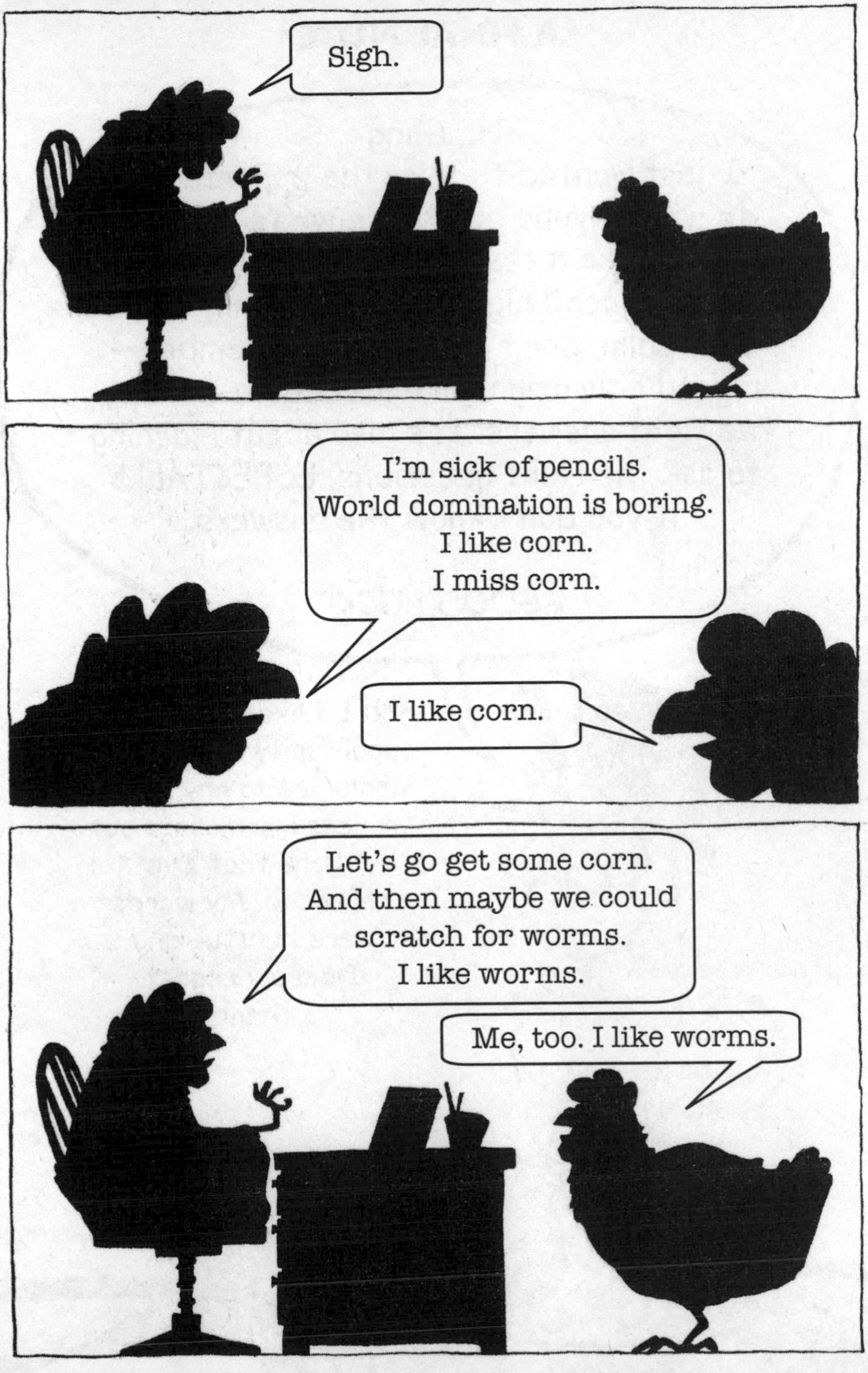
Sigh.
I'm sick of pencils. World domination is boring. I like corn. I miss corn.
I like corn.
Let's go get some corn. And then maybe we could scratch for worms. I like worms.
Me, too. I like worms.

•A FINAL NOTE•

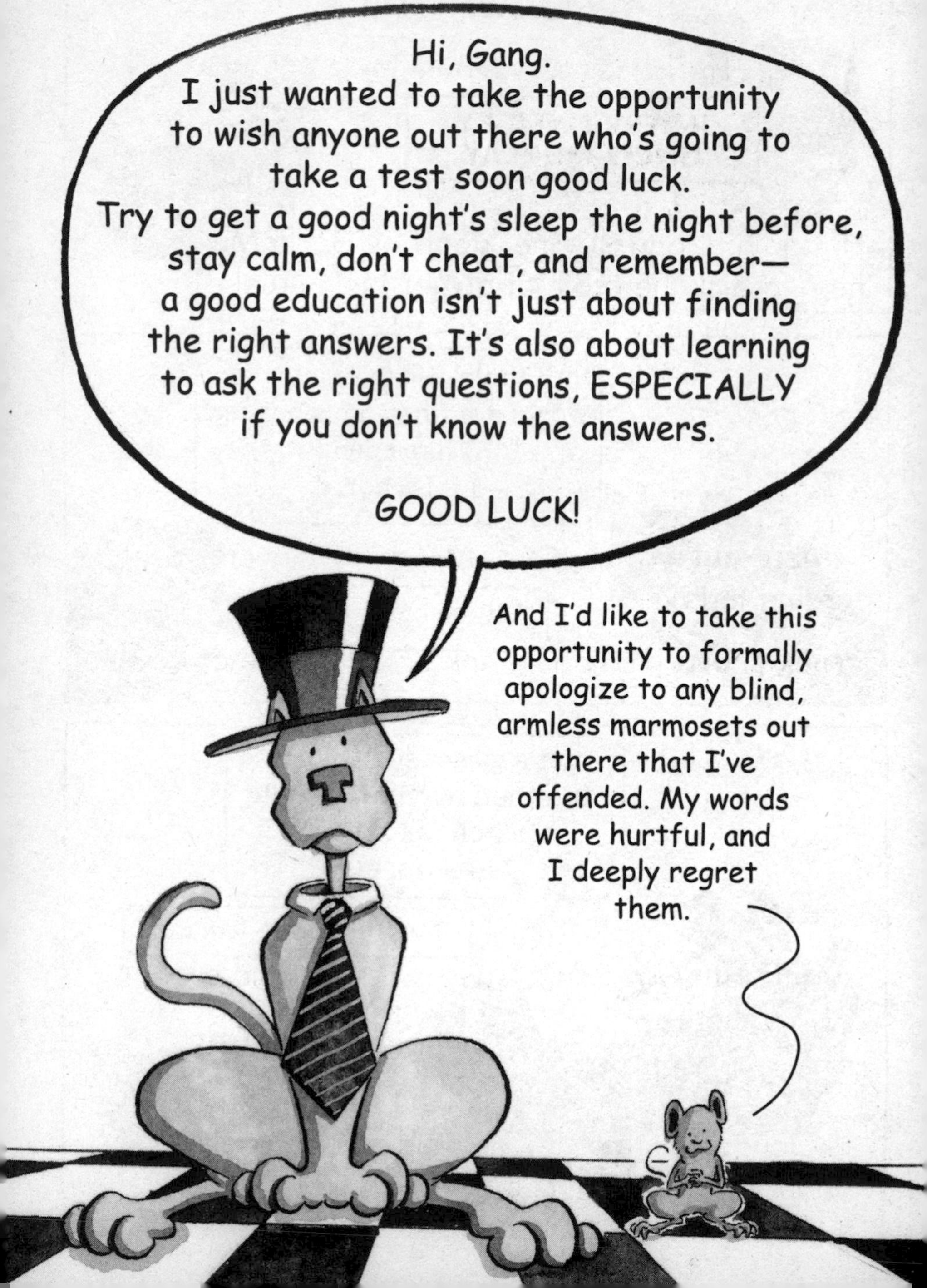
Hi, Gang.
I just wanted to take the opportunity to wish anyone out there who's going to take a test soon good luck.
Try to get a good night's sleep the night before, stay calm, don't cheat, and remember—a good education isn't just about finding the right answers. It's also about learning to ask the right questions, ESPECIALLY if you don't know the answers.
GOOD LUCK!
And I'd like to take this opportunity to formally apologize to any blind, armless marmosets out there that I've offended. My words were hurtful, and I deeply regret them.

A CONVERSATION WITH NICK BRUEL

INTERVIEWED BY UNCLE MURRAY

Hi again, Gang. It's me, good ol' Uncle Murray, here to pick the brain of author Nick Bruel about his books. You may remember me from such classics as *Bad Kitty vs. Uncle Murray*, *Bad Kitty Goes to the Vet*, and *Uncle Murray and the Werewolf Pirates of the Galaxy*. I wrote that last one. It still hasn't been published yet, but I've got my fingers crossed.

UNCLE MURRAY: Hi there, Mr. Bruel. How're you doing today?

NICK BRUEL: I'm fine. Thanks. And please call me "Nick."

UNCLE MURRAY: Nick it is. Nickeroo. Nickareeno. Slick Nick. Nick-Nack-Paddy-Whack-Give-Your-Dog-A . . .

NICK: Just "Nick."

UNCLE MURRAY: Sorry. I guess I got a little carried away there.

NICK: That's okay. It happens.

[A long, silent pause as Uncle Murray looks blankly at Nick Bruel.]

NICK: So . . . Did you want to ask me a question?

UNCLE MURRAY: About what?

NICK: I don't know. You're the one interviewing ME.

UNCLE MURRAY: I am? Holy salami, you're right. I'm supposed to be asking you stuff. What do you want to talk about?

NICK: Well, I guess we could talk about this book, *Bad Kitty Takes the Test.*

UNCLE MURRAY: Yeah. That sounds like a good idea.

NICK: Did you read it?

UNCLE MURRAY: Read it?! I lived it!! That was seriously the weirdest day of my life!

NICK: What was so weird about it?

UNCLE MURRAY: Well, the first really weird thing that happened to me that day was that my slippers were reversed.

NICK: Your slippers?

UNCLE MURRAY: Yes! Seriously! You don't believe me, do you?! When I got up that morning and put on my slippers, the right one was on the left and the left one was on the right! That never happens. I'm very attentive to how I place my slippers on the floor beside my bed every night in case I have to get up really fast and run to the bathroom. But that morning, they were REVERSED! Explain that! What mystical forces were at play during the night that would switch my slippers?! And what dark agenda did they have in doing so?!

NICK: I . . . I don't know.

UNCLE MURRAY: Now that I think about it, I probably crossed my legs while I was taking my slippers off the night before. That would explain it.

NICK: Did anything else weird happen that day?

UNCLE MURRAY: Well, then I went to get my driver's license renewed and instead became trapped in a room with Kitty while chickens forced me to take a test on how to be a cat.

NICK: And then what?

UNCLE MURRAY: And then . . . [Whispers something inaudible.]

NICK: Sorry. I couldn't hear you.

UNCLE MURRAY: And then I laid an egg.

NICK: That's pretty weird.

UNCLE MURRAY: I don't really like to talk about it. WAIT A MINUTE! I'm supposed to be interviewing

YOU! We just established that. I'LL ask the questions here!

NICK: Sorry about that. Ask away.

UNCLE MURRAY: So, why do you love tests so much that you wrote a whole book about them?

NICK: I don't love them. I don't really hate them, either. But every time I think about what book I'm going to write next, I like to ask myself the same question: "What do kids care about?" When I asked myself that question a bunch of years ago, the answer was "birthdays." Kids care about birthdays a lot, so I wrote *Happy Birthday, Bad Kitty*. A few years ago, I asked myself that question and the answer was "school." Kids care about school a lot, and that answer led to *Bad Kitty School Daze*. And more recently I asked myself that question and the answer was "tests." Kids may not LIKE taking tests, but they certainly do CARE about taking tests.

UNCLE MURRAY: How do you know?

NICK: Well, I've been lucky. I've visited schools all over the country, from California to New York, from Florida to Washington, from Texas to Michigan, and I can report that every kid in every public school in every district in every state in this country has the same problem.

UNCLE MURRAY: What's that?

NICK: They're all getting tested a LOT. I would argue that they're being tested TOO MUCH. The average third grader is being tested for over twenty hours a year! Fourth graders for over twenty-two hours!*

UNCLE MURRAY: Whoa. We're talking about little kids. Eight and nine year olds, right?

NICK: Right. And not only can these tests be very stressful, but they don't always measure how smart a kid really is. Only a teacher can do that, and a teacher doesn't really need so many tests to figure it out.

UNCLE MURRAY: So what's the solution?

NICK: Well, I'm not saying that kids should NEVER be tested. Tests can be a very valuable part of the school experience. All I'm saying is that maybe kids shouldn't be tested so much, that maybe we should trust their teachers more to know what's best for their students.

UNCLE MURRAY: Hey, want to hear a riddle?

NICK: Um . . . maybe.

UNCLE MURRAY: Why *did* the kid want to retake his blood test?

*Council of the Great City Schools
https://www.cgcs.org/cms/lib/DC00001581/Centricity/Domain/87/Testing%20Report.pdf

NICK: I don't know. Why did the kid want to retake his blood test?

UNCLE MURRAY: Because he got a B-, but he was hoping to get an A+! Get it?!

NICK: [Sigh.]

UNCLE MURRAY: Hey, did you ever get around to reading that copy of *Uncle Murray and the Werewolf Pirates of the Galaxy* that I sent you?

NICK: I did, and I liked it but . . .

UNCLE MURRAY: But what?

NICK: But I thought that maybe you could have given it a little more detail.

UNCLE MURRAY: What do you mean?

NICK: I mean . . . I'll read Chapter Four to you. "AAAARGH!" said the Werewolf Pirates. "EEEEEK!" said the princess. "AHOY!" said Uncle Murray. *BZZZZZT! POW! KA-BLAM! ZING-ZING-ZING-ZING! WHOMP! OOF! VRRRRRRRRRRRRRRRMP! SKA-BOOM!*

UNCLE MURRAY: And?

NICK: And it kind of goes on like that for another twenty pages.

UNCLE MURRAY: It's called drama, something you clearly know nothing about.

NICK: Well, I do write books.

UNCLE MURRAY: Yeah, but are your books werewolf pirate space operas?

NICK: No. I guess not.

Can Kitty fit in at dog camp?

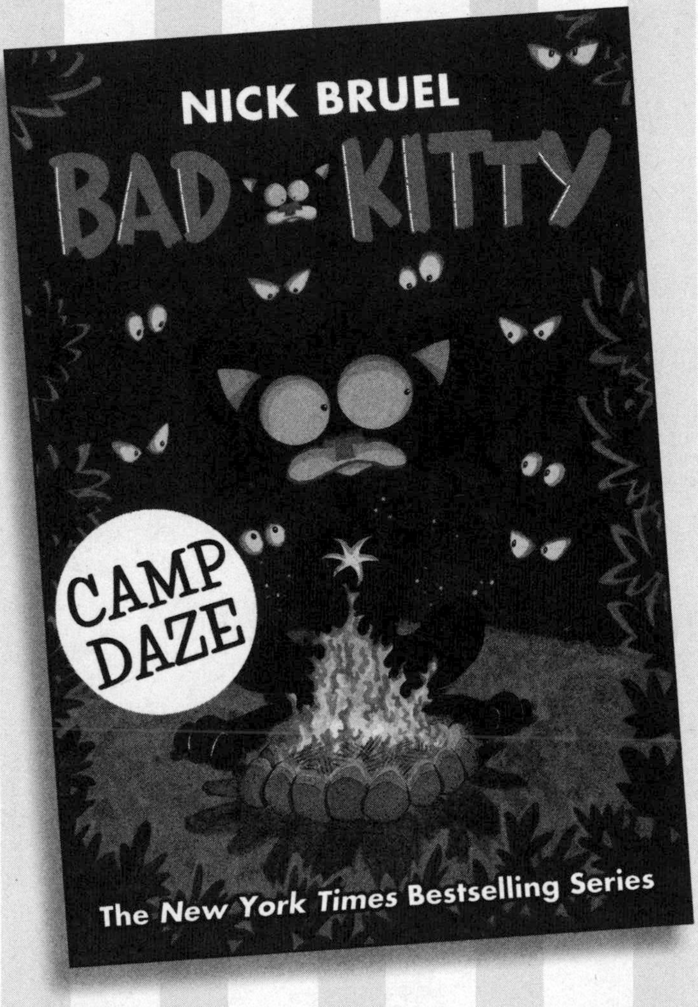
NICK BRUEL
BAD KITTY
CAMP DAZE
The New York Times Bestselling Series

Keep reading for more Bad Kitty!

Wow, Puppy. You look pretty stressed out. Maybe you need a vacation. I think you need to go somewhere to relax and just be a dog.

But where? Hmmmmmmmm . . .

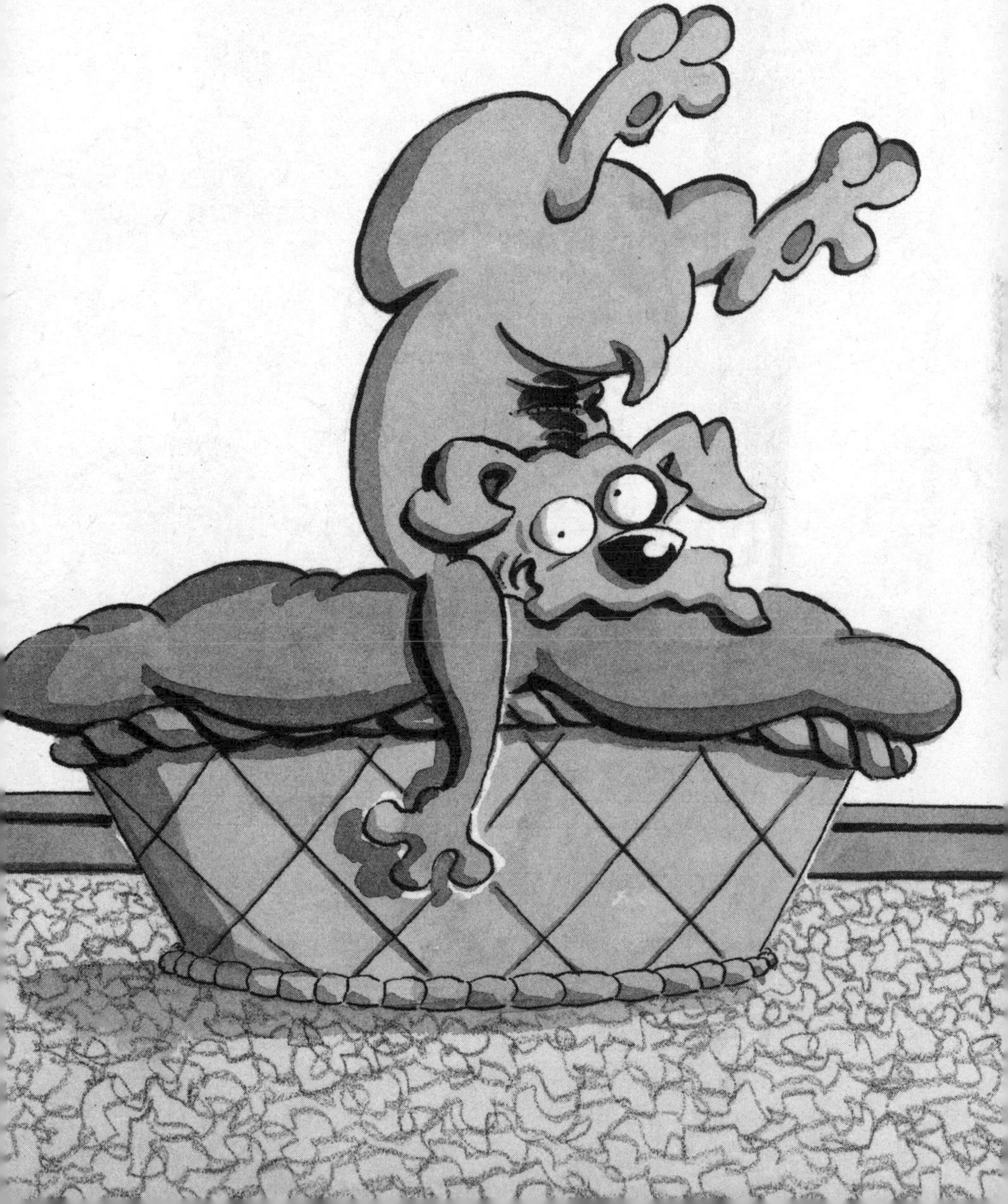

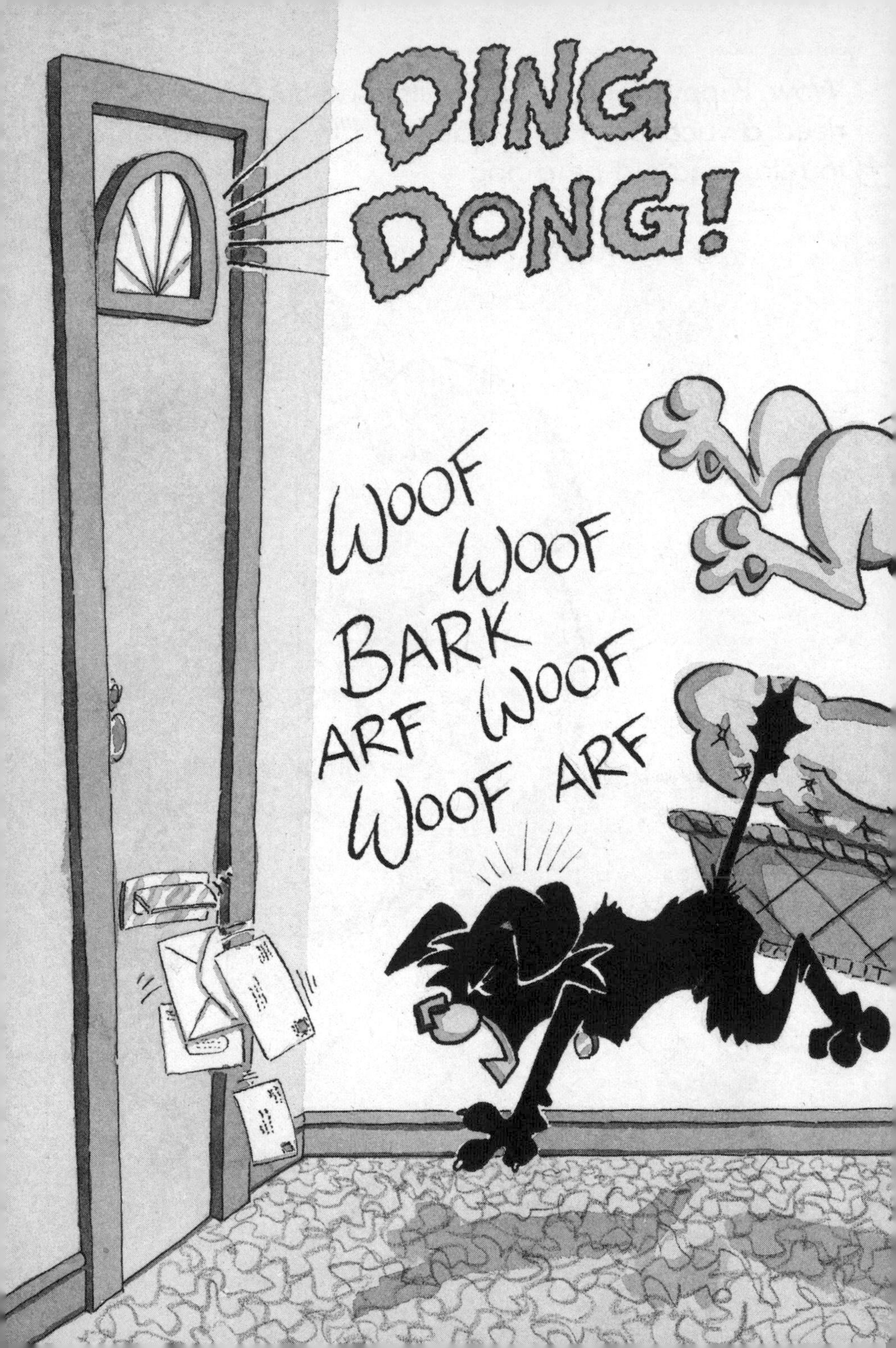
DING DONG!
WOOF WOOF
BARK
ARF WOOF
WOOF ARF

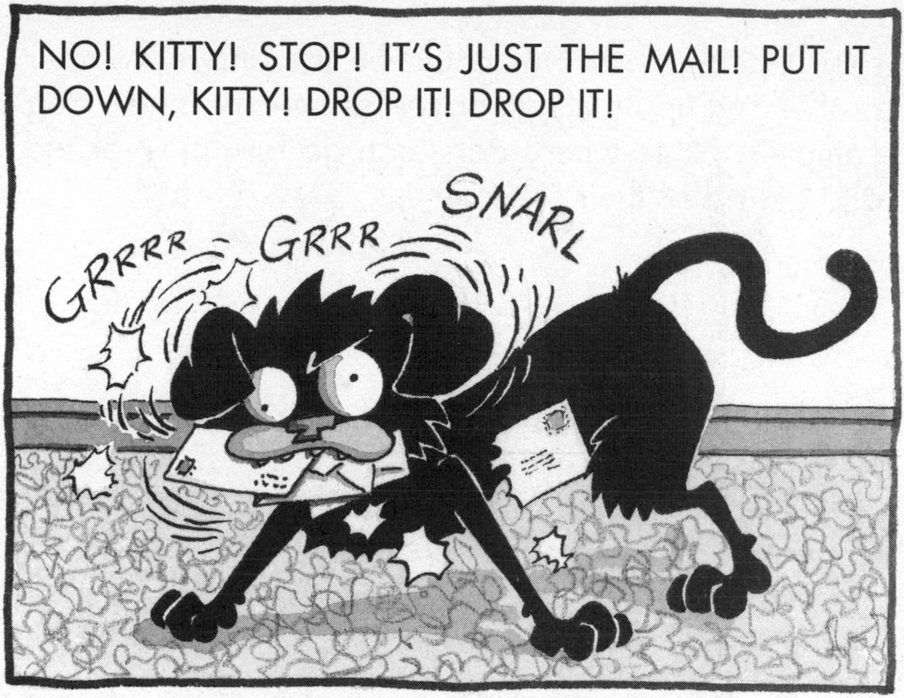
NO! KITTY! STOP! IT'S JUST THE MAIL! PUT IT DOWN, KITTY! DROP IT! DROP IT!
GRRRR
GRRR
SNARL

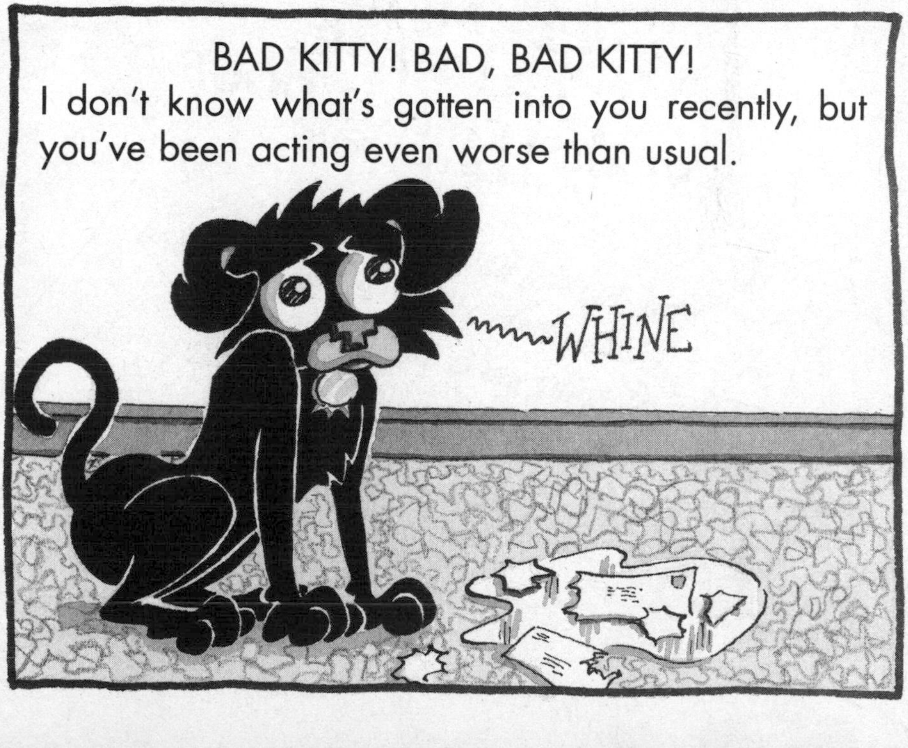
BAD KITTY! BAD, BAD KITTY!
I don't know what's gotten into you recently, but you've been acting even worse than usual.
WHINE

Hey! Check it out! This could be the answer to your problems, Puppy! It's an advertisement for a new dog camp—a place where dogs can go for the weekend and get rid of their stress.

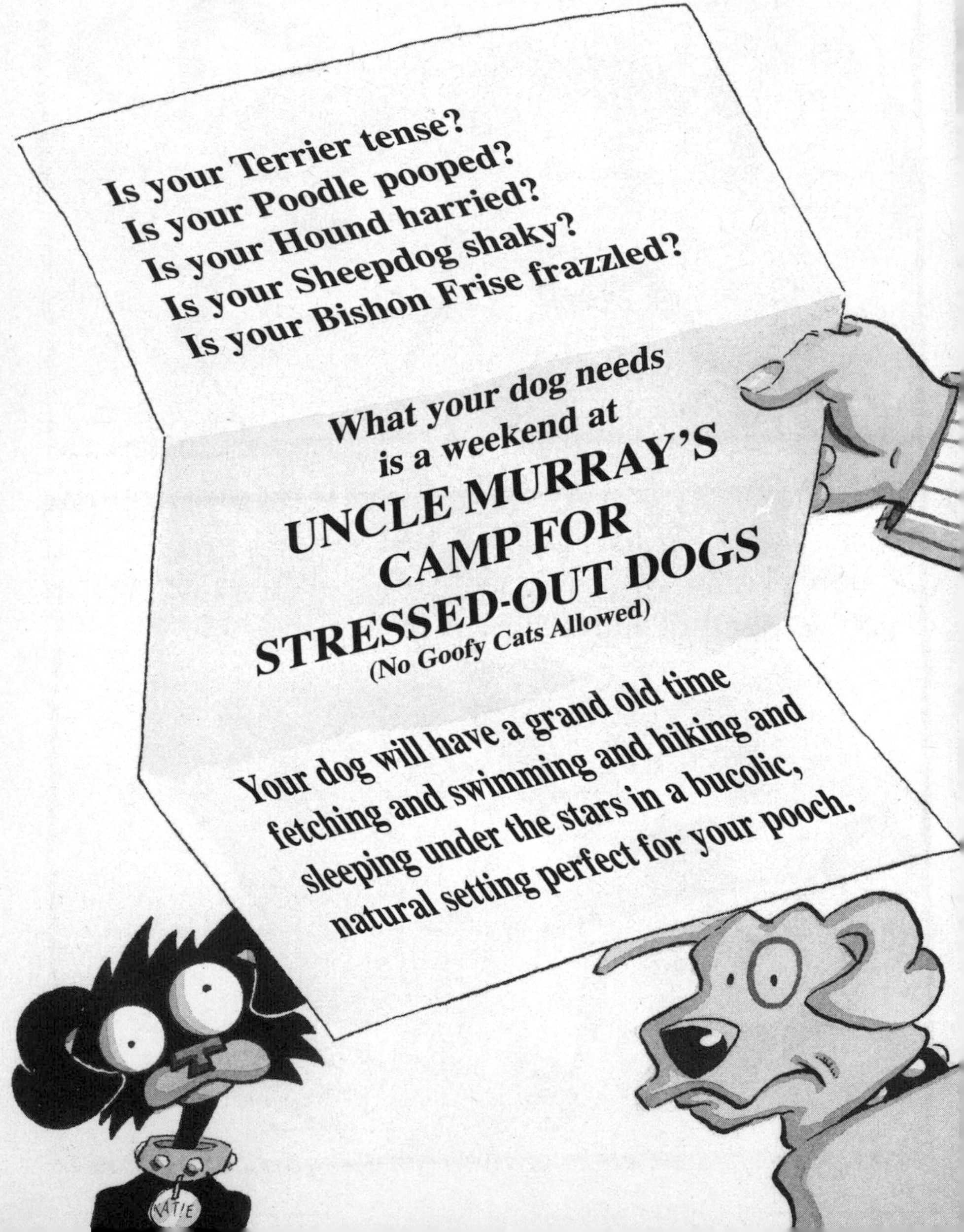
Is your Terrier tense?
Is your Poodle pooped?
Is your Hound harried?
Is your Sheepdog shaky?
Is your Bishon Frise frazzled?
What your dog needs is a weekend at
UNCLE MURRAY'S CAMP FOR STRESSED-OUT DOGS
(No Goofy Cats Allowed)
Your dog will have a grand old time fetching and swimming and hiking and sleeping under the stars in a bucolic, natural setting perfect for your pooch.
KATIE

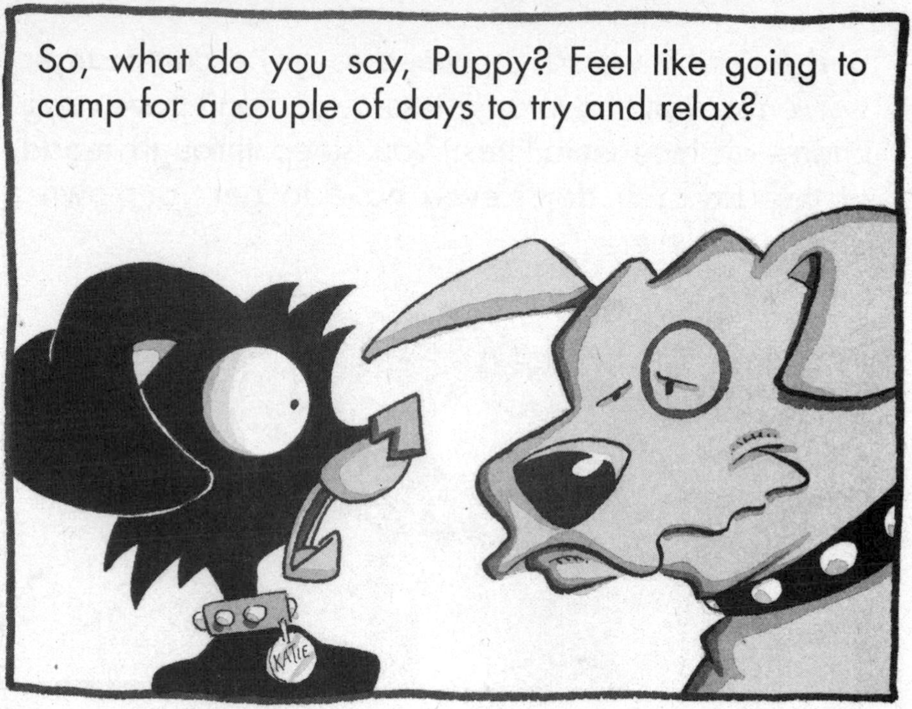
So, what do you say, Puppy? Feel like going to camp for a couple of days to try and relax?
KATIE

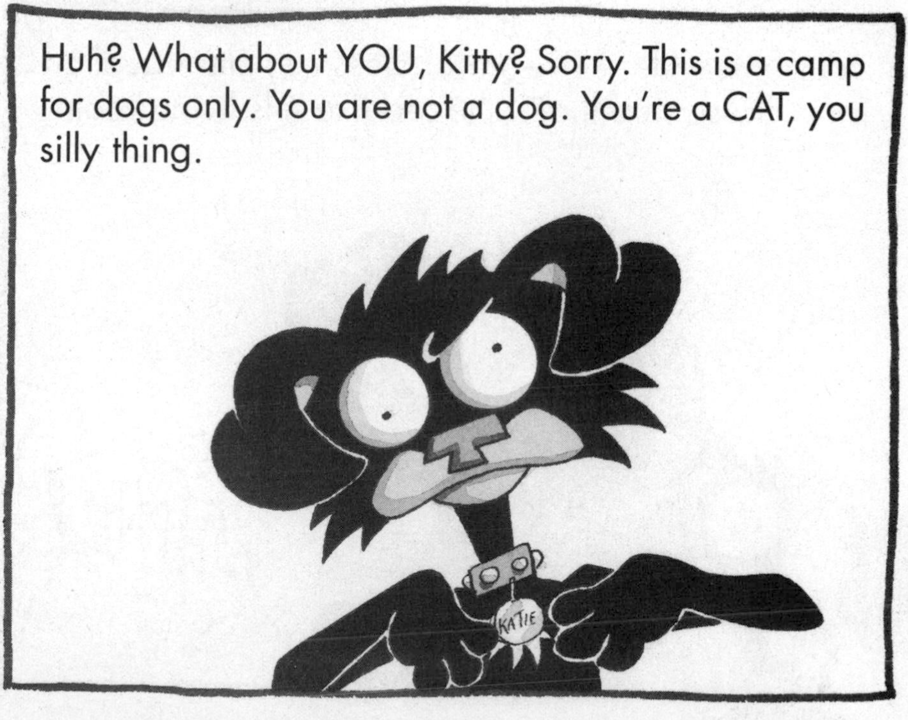
Huh? What about YOU, Kitty? Sorry. This is a camp for dogs only. You are not a dog. You're a CAT, you silly thing.
KATIE

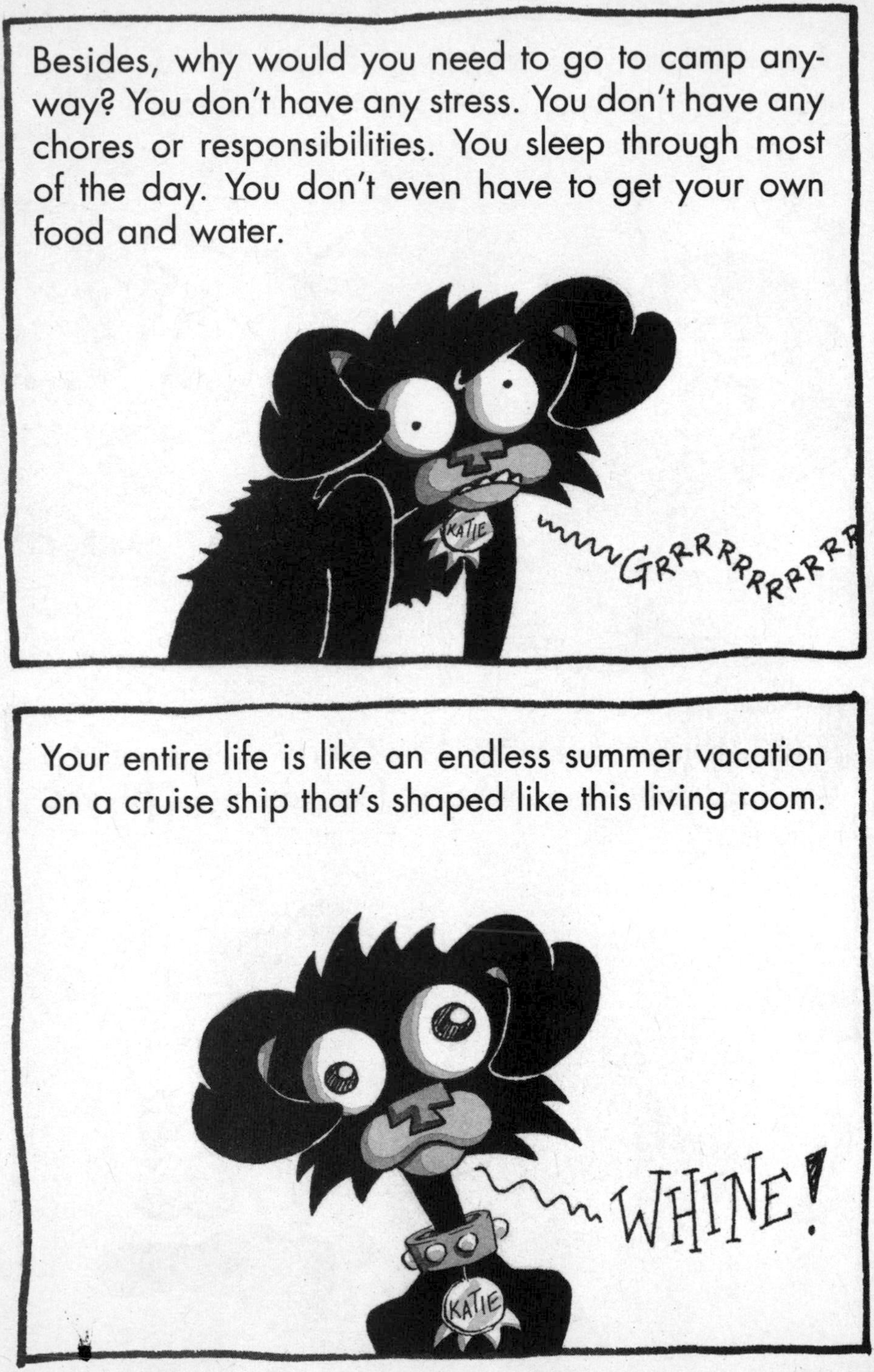
Besides, why would you need to go to camp anyway? You don't have any stress. You don't have any chores or responsibilities. You sleep through most of the day. You don't even have to get your own food and water.
KATIE
GRRRRRRRRRRR
Your entire life is like an endless summer vacation on a cruise ship that's shaped like this living room.
WHINE!
KATIE

Let's go, Puppy. I'll help you pack.

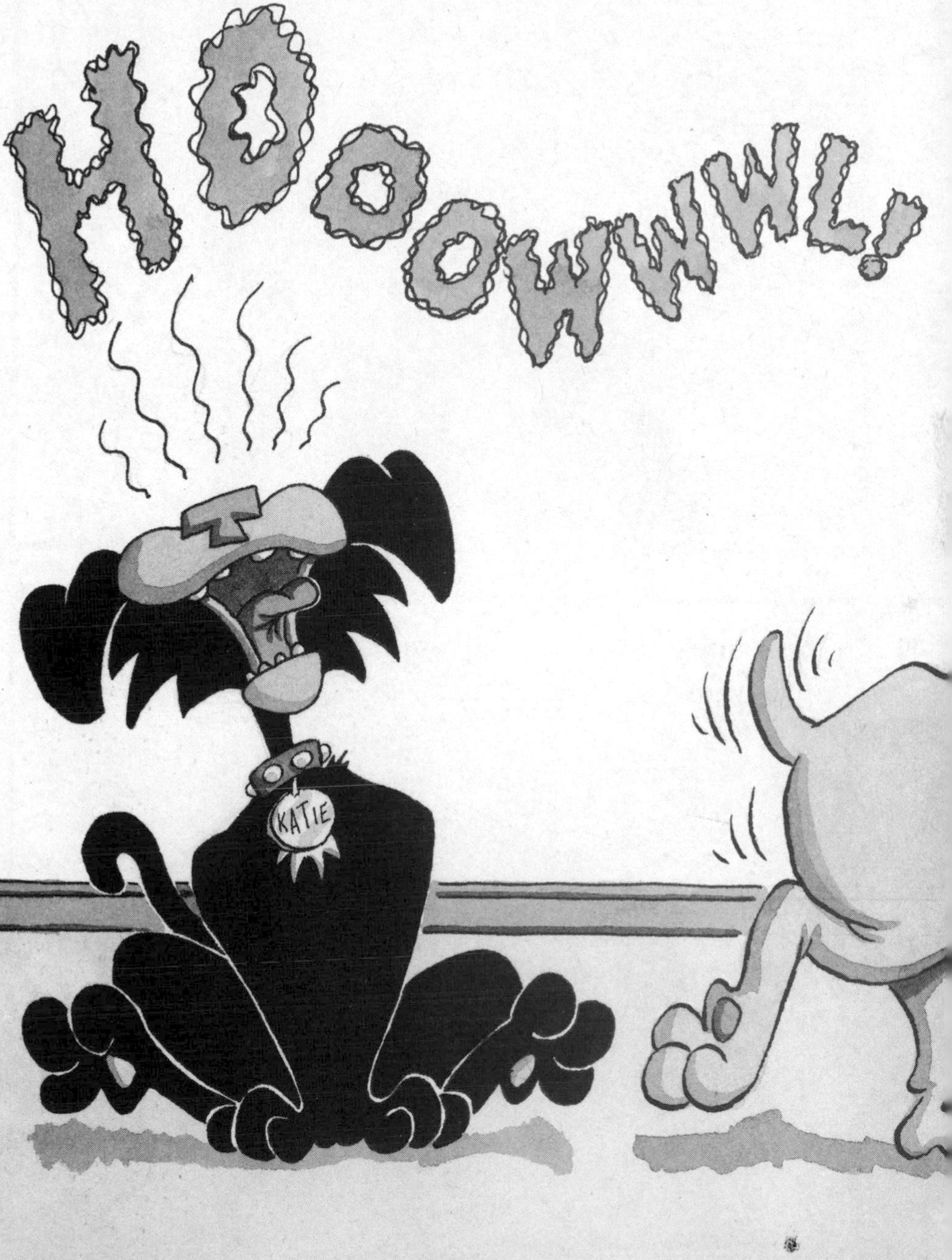
HOOOWWWL!
KATIE